Reviews for
The A

"A robust story of a young lad in the British navy during the Nelson years. A thorough insight and beautiful portrait of those days under wind-blown sails and the creak of wooden hulls. Peter Greene has created a story that shines from every page. An excellent book. He truly nails an insight of eighteenth century sailing ships and their crews."

- ***CLIVE CUSSLER,*** *best-selling author of POSEIDON'S ARROW, RAISE THE TITANIC, THE SEA HUNTERS*

"A heartwarming tale of a boy essentially orphaned in search of his father, SKULL EYE ISLAND never ceases to entertain. Greene's swashbuckling tale of high-seas adventure is pure, uncomplicated fun!"

– ***KIRKUS REVIEWS*** *www.kirkusreview.com*

"Equal parts salt water and page-turning fun, SKULL EYE ISLAND is heir to traditions of Rudyard Kipling and Robert Louis Stephenson. Young adult adventure has a new master, and his name is Peter Greene."

– ***JEFF EDWARDS,*** *award-winning author of THE SEVENTH ANGEL, and SWORD OF SHIVA*
www.navythriller.com

The Adventures of Jonathan Moore Series

Book1: Skull Eye Island
Book 2: Castle of Fire
Book 3: The Paladin Mission (coming soon)
Book 4: The Electra (coming soon)

Praise for
The Adventures of Jonathan Moore
Book 2:
Castle of Fire

"Chock-full of adventurous fun... Greene seamlessly weaves together several dynamic storylines, creating a rich, complex world for readers to enjoy. It's driven by an eclectic, well-drawn cast of characters... Jonathan, Delain, and quirky best friend, Sean Flagon, form a wonderful trio whose escapades will leave readers hooked. A spirited tale of high-seas adventure that will leave readers both young and old anxiously waiting for more!

– ***KIRKUS REVIEWS*** *www.kirkusreview.com*

Book Two

The Adventures of Jonathan Moore

Castle of Fire

by
Peter Greene

illustrations by
Michelle Graham

Cover art and illustrations by
Michelle Graham
www.michellegraham.co.uk

Sven Gillhoolie Publishing
15418 N Castillo Drive
Fountain Hills, Arizona, USA 85268

ISBN-13: 9781480203457

Author's note: This book has been written so it can be easily read aloud. You may notice it contains additional dialogue direction pertaining to who is speaking. This will make reading aloud more enjoyable for all parties. Also, chapters have suggested breaks approximately halfway through marked with * * * * * so you can easily stop and continue the story tomorrow night from a sensible point!

To purchase and learn more about Jonathan Moore adventure books and to join the crew, please visit:

www.ajmbooks.com **or** www.castleoffire.com

Chapters

To my stowaway and true love:

Pammy Delain Sutton Greene

Book Two

The Adventures of Jonathan Moore

Castle of Fire

1
Shadow and Son

In the shadows of the buildings surrounding the London docks at Wapping, a man waited. His hands were both clenched; one holding a blackjack club of hard wood, the other holding nothing but anger and hatred. He peered out to the busy streets at the many gay people rushing toward the waterfront. They were anxious to greet HMS *Danielle* and her victorious crew, the latest heroes of the realm and favorites of the city's papers. In the man's heart was not pride, nor happiness, nor approval of these new darlings of London; there was only the cold burning fire of revenge.

Meanwhile, drawn by a pair of fine bay horses as he traveled in his covered landau carriage toward the River Thames in London, Captain Nathaniel Moore could hear the roaring of ship's guns. At times, he swore he could also hear the cheering of a crowd – or could it be the echo of the horse's hooves as they *clipped-clopped* down the cobblestone street? Certainly the guns were celebratory, not from a battle but a commemoration - the arrival of a *very* important ship.

He adjusted the collar on his uniform then removed the heavy wool blanket about his shoulders. The carriage was cold, usually; however, he had placed more than a few large blankets by the fire in his small apartmentand after an hour or so, carried them into the carriage to aid in keeping warm. This year, 1801, would certainly go down in England's history as the coldest in a century. Staying comfortable was hard enough for a wealthy man such as he, but what of those unfortunates - the people who lived on the streets? Over the past few years, these people had been on his mind, a certain person in particular, and the thought disturbed him greatly. *How could one survive with no suitable shelter? No warmth or proper food? All those frozen nights and wet conditions huddled god knows where* – he thought. *How could they endure, especially the youngest ones? It would be impossible.* However, he knew of one young boy who did survive, and in a strange way, Captain Moore was extremely proud of what that boy had accomplished and was dreadfully sorry for what had befallen them both.

Across from Captain Moore sat Doctor Lane, the surgeon assigned specifically to him by the Admiralty of His Majesty's Navy. Though a great honor to have an esteemed surgeon at his beck and call, Captain Moore considered the Doctor more of a nuisance than a benefit, and as if to prove the point, the Doctor began.

"Captain Moore," said the Doctor, breaking a long silence, "I would strongly advise taking your cane as assistance to your walk and an extra shawl as it can be very damp and chilly on the London docks."

"Can it?" asked Moore sarcastically, as if he, a Navy man his entire life would not know the climate of the London docks. Without hesitation, Doctor Lane continued.

"Why yes, all the salt air and cloud cover, especially at night, traps the cold and fog. It collects, dank and chilly, about the area. It's a wonder more do not become ill who live by the ocean."

Captain Moore chuckled to himself and said "Imagine those whom live *on the water* most of their lives! Yes, Doctor, it is a wonder they don't all take ill. I will follow your advice," and held his cane up for verification of his intent. They lapsed again into silence as the carriage rolled on toward the docks.

Moore had never needed a cane, not in his thirty-nine years of life, until this past summer. As he looked through the frost-covered window of the carriage, watching people rush here and there through the cold streets, he thought about all that had happened. Was it really over three years ago that he had become the sudden and momentary captain of *HMS Helios*? The original captain had been killed early in a clash with a squadron of French ships and Nathaniel was forced to assume command. The battle seemed to last for *days* and Moore, with the crew of the *Helios's* had nearly defeated all the enemy ships - all but the largest one. The infamous French warship *Danielle,* with its seventy-four guns, was too much to handle. The *Helios* had been grievously damaged and was now afire from its scrapes with the other four rival frigates. It was all he could do to save twenty or so of his remaining crew and then surrender.

What followed was three years of captivity in a small French prison just outside of Guéret in central France; his status: *war criminal.* While there, he learned of the untimely passing of his dear wife and the news almost caused the death of him. It was only his desire to return home and be with his son that kept him alive. His only son, who now needed him, drove Nathaniel to escape and spend weeks making his way to the sea, then north along the coast. After many days and nights of sneaking and plodding, Nathaniel *borrowed* a small sailing boat from the shores of Calais and made his way across the English Channel. The waters were not completely calm and there was a wicked wind that swept him eastward, then north, to finally come ashore in Dungeness, England, and thus to freedom.

A few weeks later, he spoke with the captain of *HMS Echo*, a sloop delivering news from the Caribbean Sea. He was told that Captain William Walker of HMS *Poseidon* had taken the French seventy-four gun *Danielle* as a prize and defeated the infamous French Captain Claude Champagne, the very same man who had captured Nathaniel years ago. Though he learned that Walker and his crew had successfully retrieved an enormous treasure, he also learned that the *Poseidon* had been sunk in the process, with many men lost. This shed fear and doubt as to the survival of his son, who was supposedly aboard.

The carriage rambled on and even though it was early

evening, the darkening streets were crowded with excited people, all rushing toward the docks. The cold weather should have kept them away, cozy in their homes with a spot of tea and a warm blanket by the fire. However, here they were, a few thousand Moore surmised, all rushing to the docks. It seemed the word had gotten out that the newly captured *Danielle* was arriving tonight, Christmas Day, and many Londoners wanted to see the heroes for themselves. Nathaniel was also heading for the dock and the *Danielle*, but he cared nothing for the treasure of gold. He went to find his son.

A voice from above, the coachman, called down to Captain Moore and the Doctor: "We 'ave arrived, gen'elmen! London Docks. Pier number four, as ordered!"

Nathaniel turned to the Doctor who looked less than happy to leave the warmth of the carriage to stand in the cold.

"Doctor Lane, no use for us both to freeze. Please, remain here and I will go on by myself. Just a short stretch of the legs."

"By all means," said the Doctor quickly. "Good to exercise the leg."

Nathaniel smiled briefly, collected his cane and hat, then opened the carriage door and stepped into the busy crowd. Closing the door, he took a deep breath of the cool salt air and smiled. Yes, as dangerous as the doctor believed the damp air could be, the docks, the ocean, the ships and all their sights, sounds and smells invigorated him. It was one of his greatest loves, being in His Majesty's Navy and sailing the open sea. The only greater love was his long lost son, Jonathan Moore.

The crowd moved on ahead of Nathaniel and he was happy to allow them to pass. It was still a struggle, the leg not quite behaving as it should. In fact, he had to pause from time to time just to rest. He slowly made his way closer to the docks, passing a few stores with their Christmas wares on display in the windows. Then, after a brief rest, the last of the crowd disappeared around the corner ahead, leaving him alone. He could now only hear the cheers of the crowd in the distance and his own footsteps echoing against the cobblestone.

London Docks, Christmas 1800

As he neared the last corner before the docks, he saw something move in the shadows. Cautiously moving closer, he saw a shape move into the half-light. It was crouched like a beast - but it soon was clear that it was a man, a short one, with his face covered by a scarf and a hood low over his brow. Abruptly, the man rushed at Nathaniel, raising a club over his head as he ran.

"Take this!" The man yelled in a high pitched voice as he brought the club down to smite him.

Startled, Nathaniel reacted with pure fighting instinct. Using his cane as a sword, he quickly warded off the blow. He extended his foot just so as to trip his attacker, who fell crashing to the ground, club flying from his hand to clank harmlessly on the street. Quickly, Nathaniel struck the man across the face with his cane, causing the attacker to cry out in pain. For an instant, Nathaniel could see the man's features: he was young with dark eyes and a stern look above a square chin. He had straight, dark brown hair, gathered in a pony-tail. A welt was rising above his left eye where the cane had struck him. The young man quickly came to his feet and stood, adjusting the scarf and hood to cover his face once again.

"What is all this?" demanded Nathaniel.

"Curse you!" the young man yelled, then turned and ran away.

That was...unexpected! thought Nathaniel. He was slightly flustered, but unhurt. Spending a moment to calm himself with a deep breath, he straightened his uniform and retrieved his hat from the ground. It was now wet and slightly crushed, but a few brushes with his hand made it presentable, at least in the dark. Taking a final look around, he continued on toward the ship.

After a minute or two more, he heard the crowd cheering loudly with many a *huzzah* voiced by the Navy men, lords and ladies that must have been crowding the waterfront. *They are coming ashore! I must hurry, or I will miss them!* Nathaniel thought.

Finally he reached the pier and stood at the entrance of the main berth, holding his breath. Yes, there was a great ship moored there, a seventy-four gunner he recognized very well. The *Danielle* had obviously been repaired and was smartly painted with a gold stripe down the side. *Wasn't the* Poseidon *also gold striped? A fine tribute to her!* thought Nathaniel.

It seemed that the crowd was already thinning; people were returning to their homes, and soon a number of them were moving toward him as they made their way. Some recognized him, mostly Navy men and their families, and this caused Nathaniel to stop and return more than a few salutes. He considered each person as they passed, though; hoping to see if any resembled his son. Searching, searching, searching for a face he could not possibly remember. The last time he had seen Jonathan, his son was barely six years old.

How would he have changed? Nathaniel thought. *What would he be wearing? Maybe I should first locate Walker and ask him where Jonathan might be. Wait! There! A face in the crowd! A boy of eleven or twelve? He is wearing a crewman's garb – black trousers, a heavy wool coat and a tasseled hat. Could it be? Certainly Jonathan would become a ship's hand and a member of the crew. But no, this boy is now hugging and kissing a woman who could only be his mother.*

"Little Paulie Garvey! Oh to hold my boy in my arms again!" the woman shouted.

"Awe, Mum! The men are looking!" the young seaman said, embarrassed.

Nathaniel looked and looked, but there were very few young men in the crew. Some were midshipmen either greeting the ship, or assigned to the *Danielle*. He did finally see one handsome youngster, a midshipman to be sure, standing among his friends at the end of the pier, a solemn look on his face.

Jonathan could not be a midshipman; that would be highly irregular. No, he would be a crew member and dressed as such.

Nathaniel rested on his cane for a moment then

regarded again at the midshipman. He was taller then he originally had supposed, especially compared to the young seaman who stood by his side. *But wait. Isn't that Steward? Next to the midshipman?* Nathaniel thought to himself. *Steward, my crotchety old bosun from the* Troy? *We were marooned together! It seems like a lifetime ago! And next to him, the young Lieutenant Harrison of the* Helios? *I set them both aboard the jolly boat before I surrendered! And there, behind them. That tall Marine Captain looks like ... Gorman. Why the saints be blessed! There is William! William Walker!*

It was then that he caught the eyes of Steward, who briefly smiled and clasped his hands to the midshipman's head. He firmly pointed the boy's gaze directly at Nathaniel.

"My god," Nathaniel called out softly, "Could that midshipman be Jonathan? But how..."

Through the string of festive lanterns lining the pier he gazed in wonder at the young midshipman. The uniform looked new and the boy stood tall and straight. Nathaniel took a few steps toward him, trying to get a better look. *If it is Jonathan, then what a handsome young man he has become,* he thought. A few more steps and their eyes met. In a flash, Nathaniel knew. Memories came flooding back to him like a rush of fire - seeing the boy only seconds after he was born, crying loud and strong; cradling both Jonathan and his mother in his arms as they entered their first home in Hampstead; walking on the beach at the Isle of Wight, searching for shells; and kissing him good-bye as he rode off on the bright August day to his ill-fated command of HMS *Troy*. But most of all he remembered tucking him into his bed and whispering *I love you* as the child drifted off to sleep.

Nathaniel now noticed that all the men next to Jonathan were also watching him approach. There were smiles on their faces.

"Attention!" ordered Captain Walker. The officers and Steward suddenly snapped to, one and all, and gave Captain Nathaniel Moore a smart salute.

After a moment, Steward put his arm around Jonathan and bent slightly to speak in his ear.

Jonathan looked back at his father and with tears of joy welling in his eyes, he started running; running toward him as fast as he could across the short distance, though it seemed to Nathaniel as if it were miles and miles.

Then, Jonathan stopped short. He stared into Nathaniel's eyes, now just a few feet away.

"Jonathan?" said his father. "Jonathan. Oh, just look at you! A-a midshipman? Oh my…my, what have I missed? Can you…? Do you remember me?"

And Jonathan took the last few steps as fast as he could, into the arms of his father.

* * * * * *

"It seems that since we have been away," said Captain William Walker, "the Admiralty has lost all senses if it ever had any. Word is out that you have been promoted to Admiral, my dear Nathaniel."

Nathaniel, still embracing his son Jonathan smiled and nodded. "It has not been approved. I am awaiting confirmation from Whitehall. To be sure, it is an insane world, but somehow, a just one. What a Christmas present you have brought me, William! Oh, Jonathan! What tales we have to tell! When I last saw you, well, you were barely to my hip and now you are almost fully grown."

"It is truly a great Christmas, a better one than I have ever seen!" Jonathan said, hugging his father tightly. "I do remember you Father, clearly as if it were only yesterday. And I have so many questions! First of all, when did -"

"Pardon me, Midshipman Moore," Walker interrupted. "I would suggest holding on to tales and questions until we are all warm by a fire. Shall we return to my home? I am sure Misses Walker and her sister will have a grand feast for us and a few gifts besides! After some ale and dessert, let us all sit down and warmly reminisce. Is that agreeable?"

"As for me," said Koonts, the *Danielle's* purser and trusted friend of the Captain. "I thank you for the invitation, though I must decline. My own wife is waiting for me and though her cooking is only slightly better than Steward's, I am looking forward to her smile."

"Would not 'ave expected that comment from you, Mister Koonts," said Steward.

"He has taken my excuse," said Harrison, not missing a beat. "However, I must decline as well. Please give Misses Walker my apologies. My own family would be quite disappointed if I didn't appear. I met my brother just moments ago and he has rushed home to tell them all I am safe and on the way. Besides, I am sure there will be enough embellishments on the story from Steward and the boys that my color will not be needed."

Gorman, the enigmatic Marine Captain assigned to no ship in particular and also *strongly rumored* to be a spy for His Majesty, declined as well, as did First Lieutenant Langley, with heartfelt apologies, as they both had families. Even Claise, the hand acquired the same day as Jonathan and Sean, said he had a sister who would like to see him.

"Then you are all dismissed," said Walker, "and a very merry Christmas to you all!"

After a quick round of salutes all went on their way. As Walker, Steward and the Moores slowly made their way to the carriage, Jonathan suddenly stopped and turned around.

"Oh my!" he said, scanning the area with his eyes, "Where is Sean?" Almost panic-stricken, he started running back to the *Danielle*, calling his friend's name.

"Who is Sean?" asked Nathaniel.

"Sean Flagon? Well, Nate, that will be a hard one to explain. Let's just say that he and Jonathan are the best of friends. It is almost impossible to separate them."

"Aye," said Steward, "A little daft at times, but by-the-by, a good egg and quite a fine swordsman if I must say so myself. Great tutelage, don't ya know."

"They met aboard the *Poseidon*?" asked Nathaniel.

"No. On the streets of London. Sean Flagon, you will learn, is quite a character, but all of it is right and good. You might as well get used to the fact that you most likely will have *two* sons. They are a matched pair," Walker concluded, laughing heartily.

"We best go after them, then!" laughed Nathaniel.

Jonathan searched frantically about the *Danielle* for Sean, then turned his attention to the nearby docks. There, he caught a glimpse of someone walking ahead, looking down at the street.

"Sean!" he called, "Where are you going? Sean!"

He ran as fast as he could, now and then looking back to make sure his father could still see him. He paused to wave, feeling uncomfortable to be even this short distance away from his father. After receiving a wave in return, he ran on.

"Sean! Stop!" he said, and the boy turned and faced him, tears rolling down his face.

"Sean, what is the matter? Where are you going?" asked Jonathan.

Between sniffles, Sean finally got a few words out.

"That's exactly the problem, Jonny," he blubbered, "I-I don't know where I am going. I'm not sure where my family is and…I thought I would just go back to the streets. Maybe your old alley and box is available."

Jonathan smiled a bit and embraced his friend. After a moment Captain Walker and Nathaniel caught up to them.

"Sean. What a stubborn and silly Irishman you are! I am sure the Captain's invitation included you!"

"By all means, Flagon!" Walker said in a proper and captain-like way. "Are you going to disobey a direct order? Now stop your sniffling, act like a man, and join us for some dinner and a warm bed and bath besides!"

Sean stood straight and stiff, nodding between sniffles as the Captain addressed him firmly.

They resumed their way back to the main street and boarded their carriages. The Moores and Sean joined Doctor Lane in Captain Moore's carriage. Steward accompanied the Captain in his fine coach that had finally arrived. In a line they rode directly to one of the better parts of London and Captain Walker's home.

Jonathan could not help staring at his father and his father also could not keep his eyes off his son. Now and again, they would embrace, even grabbing Sean as well, and after a few seconds they would laugh aloud, seemingly for no reason, but all knew the reason for their great joy.

"This story could have turned out considerably worse, I must say!" said Nathaniel. "To think that after all those years I almost lost you, or you might have even died. I thought of it every day. Death can be cheated, as I know too well, but the luck that I seem to have is quite astounding. I tried as hard as a man could to make my way back to you, Jonathan. It took considerably longer than I would have wished. I am truly sorry."

Jonathan looked into his watering father's eyes and smiled a bit.

"It couldn't be helped, Father. I understand. And I was lucky as well, to make it back to you."

"Aye, luck!" said Sean. "Being Irish, I know about luck. Though it always seems that the smarter and more determined you are - the more luck you have!"

This broke the somber mood and sent the whole carriage laughing once again, even the seemingly humorless Doctor Lane.

"Father," said Jonathan, "How did you escape? How did you make your way back to London?"

"As odd as it sounds, a few French Naval captains that visited me took pity on my situation and delivered mail and the like on my behalf. Some of my friends in the Navy knew of my capture and were able to send money to neutral parties, mostly Swiss bankers. The guards were more poor than honest, so after I collected a small fortune, I paid them to look the other way."

"Dear me!" was all Jonathan could say.

"I think we all will have to tell our tales over dinner," said Captain Moore. "I am curious as to how a boy survives for five years on the streets and why you ran away from your aunt."

Jonathan thought to himself: *where do I start? I barely remember the Boddens, and there is so much to tell!*

"They were not exactly a pleasant couple to be around, Father. They treated me harshly as I remember and they barely fed me. I wasn't allowed to leave the home. At times, I-I even heard them talking about ways to do away with me."

"Dear Lord!" exclaimed the doctor.

"Jonathan," his father said solemnly, "I am so sorry!"

"It's not your fault, sir." Jonathan said quietly.

"Though it is my *responsibility!*" Nathaniel exclaimed, exposing his anger at the Boddens. "I will make them pay for the way they treated you!"

"And I will help you!" exclaimed Sean, caught up in the moment. Again the carriage exploded in laughter, even from Sean.

It was a long ride, though all were comfortable in the carriage, wrapped in blankets. They exchanged a few tales, though all vowed to save the adventurous ones for Captain Walker's table. Doctor Lane took his leave of them as they dropped him at his front door. The carriage rambled on. After a few more minutes they were at the home of the honorable and now famous Captain William Walker.

Amidst manicured shrubbery, flowers and a series of beautiful wrought iron fences, the stately home sat. It was made of red brick, with tall, thin windows and white roman columns. A beautiful stepped walk led them to the front door.

"May I knock the knocker? Just look at it! I'll bet it weighs as much as an eighteen-pound ball!"

The knocker was golden and fashioned as a lion's head. Sean lifted it, having to stand on his toes, and dropped it quickly three times. *Boom-Boom-Boom!* it sounded, causing the boys to jump back in surprise.

"I think you broke the house!" Jonathan laughed.

"It reminded me of the *Poseidon's* guns the first time I fired them!" added Sean.

"Let's all hope that Captain Walker is not angry with us for almost breaking down his door! He does have a temper. Always has," laughed Nathaniel.

"We have witnessed it first hand as well!" said Jonathan and Sean knowingly.

After a moment or two the knob turned and the door slowly opened. Bright light spilled out of the house and onto the stoop as a blast of warm air escaping embraced them. More amazing was that in the doorway before them, was an angel, so it seemed.

The boys looked up and gazed in wonder at the beautiful woman, with golden hair, deep green eyes and high cheekbones. She wore a slender white dress with silver trimming and a white woolen shawl about her shoulders. She smiled at them.

"Welcome, please do come in." she said, with a lyrical voice.

Sean snatched his cap off his head and began bowing.

"Are you an angel?" asked Jonathan, astonished.

"Jonathan!" his father said, shocked and embarrassed by his son's comment. The woman simply blushed and laughed.

"I am Miss Barbara Thompson, young sirs. I am Misses Walker's sister," she replied to the boys, ushering them all inside and closing the door.

"Excuse my son's outburst, Miss Thompson. Though, you truly are a sight for sore eyes, as you have always been."

"Why Captain Moore, thank you so much! You make a girl blush. It is a pleasure to see you again."

Nathaniel took her hand and kissed it. "May I introduce my son, Midshipman Jonathan Moore, and his best friend able seaman Sean Flagon, Esquire, both of HMS

Danielle."

"The famous *Danielle*? Then it is truly an honor and privilege to meet you both," Miss Thompson said.

"I can understand his mistaking you for an angel," said Sean. "Especially since the only faces we are used to seeing look like Steward! Pimply and hairy!"

Just then Steward appeared, dressed and cleaned, however, not any more handsome than he ever was aboard the ship.

"Funny that Mister Harrison is not 'ere, yet the insults never stop!" he blurted out. "Yer coat, Captain. Boys, yers as well."

It was explained by Miss Thompson that Steward attended as butler and all-around servant to Captain Walker when he was ashore. It was a tradition in the Royal Navy.

"I hope he isn't cooking," whispered Sean to Jonathan, whom as usual, told his friend to hush.

"Captain Walker is waiting for you in the study," Miss Thompson said as she led Nathaniel and the boys down a hallway decorated with pictures of battleships and important-looking people. There was a rug running the length of the hallway, and now and again, a table with crystal glass or exotic-looking vases. It was clear to Jonathan that Captain Walker was quite wealthy, most likely from his exploits as a naval captain. At the end of the hallway a door on the right opened to a study, where there, sitting in a tall easy chair by a crackling fire, was Captain Walker. He was already dressed like a gentleman, in a house coat, enjoying a dark colored drink in a fancy rounded glass. All about him were other chairs looking more comfortable than anything Jonathan had ever seen. He wanted to run and jump into one, kick off his shoes and take a warm nap.

"Ah! Nathaniel!" Walker said, not getting up, "I see Barbara has let you in. I heard the door knock - seemed like the whole place was coming down. Must have been Flagon at the knocker."

Jonathan looked at Sean with a surprised expression, both thinking to themselves *how did he know?*

"Misses Walker is in the kitchen supervising the dinner, a pheasant or two as I understand, with sweet potatoes, rice from the orient - how she ever gets it is a wonder, and a ham as well. Ah, good to give up ship's fare!"

"A bath for the boys?" asked Miss Thompson suddenly.

"By all means!" said the Captain, finally rising and walking to a small cabinet. As he spoke he poured another glass full of the dark liquid and handed it to Nathaniel. "Boys, no offense, but we have drawn two large tubs with piping hot water and scrub brushes and soap and even heated towels by the upstairs fireplace. Give your uniforms to Steward and he will freshen them up. Be quick with it, you wouldn't want to miss dinner now, would you?"

"No sir!" said Jonathan and Sean, snapping to attention. They followed Miss Thompson out quickly and disappeared upstairs to a welcomed bath and bubbles.

"It seems, William, that my son is quite well mannered and follows orders. I must thank you for all you have done for him and for me. Honestly, William, I am forever in your debt."

"You were already in my debt before, Nathaniel," Walker said, laughing. "Let us not forget that it was *my* money that got you out of prison."

"True," said Nathaniel. "And I am sure that my accountant has paid you back with interest. Probably at an inflated rate."

"Probably? I am sure of it!" chuckled Walker, "Yet still, let's not forget that time in '89 - that unfortunate instance with Captain Billings aboard the *Fawn*? Wasn't it I that took his wrath instead of you?"

"Ah, yes," Nathaniel said, smiling, "As I remember, it was *your* idea to take the jollyboat ashore and get those strange liquors from the natives, not mine. It was simply my misfortune to follow your advice and be caught. Your choice to insist I was only following your orders was not my doing, though that was the least you could do for me. That could have been my career!"

Walker laughed aloud once again and motioned for Nathaniel to join him by the fire.

"I was a young Lieutenant then," Walker said. "And you were almost one yourself. It was only a matter of time before we both were out from under Billings and on our own ships. Those were the days. All of the adventure -"

"- and none of the responsibility!" they both said together, laughing.

"It is good to see you, Nate. Welcome home!" Walker said and raised his glass.

They sat for a moment, enjoying their drinks and staring into the warm fire. Silently, they both pondered how life had been good, allowing them to continue their adventures. These two friends had led similar lives and had similar success. Knowing each other since their school days they entered the Navy together as midshipmen, first serving aboard HMS *Achilles*. Later, within months of each other, they had obtained their own ship's command. Many of their fellow officers were not so fortunate; having given their lives for the crown, but these two had been lucky and were grateful to be alive. Both had seen their share of wonder and misfortune; had been side by side in battles, faced death and victory, sadness and joy. Theirs was a friendship forged in adventure and service to the crown. They were like brothers, yet closer, bonded by experience and love, a union stronger than blood.

"There are a few questions I would ask you, William," said Nathaniel after a few moments, "before the boys join us for tales and embellishments."

"This one does not need an ounce of embellishment," said Walker, reflecting. "It is quite amazing and unbelievable as any truth that can be told. Sometimes I don't even believe it – and *I was there*."

"I eagerly look forward to the detailed telling;

however, I can not wait to know... how did Jonathan become a midshipman? It is highly irregular, don't you think?"

"For those details, you will have to wait until dinner," Walker said, "but I know what you are asking: did he earn it? Well, I can say, Nate, that neither of us had anywhere near your boy's intelligence, courage, cunning or just plain industry. He *was* the mission, Nate, in more ways than one. Best midshipman I have ever seen. It was a lucky day for you and for England that he was aboard. Flagon, too. Both those boys will go far in the Navy, I would bet my life on it!"

Nathaniel sat, speechless, closing his eyes.

"Now," Walker continued, "it was Steward who found him after questioning the Boddens as you probably know. And I can tell you that Steward scared the living daylights out of them! I wouldn't be surprised if they haven't picked up and left for the colonies by now!"

"Where did he find him?" Nathaniel asked, sipping his warm brandy.

"He found both Jonathan and Sean by Piccadilly. I gave instructions that any seemingly orphaned boy looking to be eleven or twelve was to be brought in off the street and directly to the *Poseidon*. Seems Jonathan was living in an alley and-"

"An alley?" exclaimed Nathaniel.

"Now calm down, Nate, yes, an alley. In a wooden box to be precise. Gallotta, a hand of mine, found him first. Got a kick to the nose and chest for his trouble and Jonathan escaped him. It was Steward that eventually cornered the boy and discovered that he was our prize. His friend, Sean, was found first and said he knew a Jonathan Moore, so, well, we took him as well, just to be sure."

"Not usually proper for a press gang to take youngsters, is it?" Nathaniel asked, knowing the answer.

"Yes, yes, but who would complain? Their parents? We were sure we could bend the rules a bit. Nate, you will surely not believe what happened on this mission. And your boy was the one behind it all. And wait until he tells you about Champagne."

Nathaniel was shocked into silence. Jonathan met Champagne? How could that be? What twisted plot could have brought those two face-to-face?

"Then it is time we eat and get all the answers!"

2

Dragons in the Admiralty

Roasted pheasant with plum sauce. Sweet potatoes with sugar and cinnamon. Fresh rolls with cream butter and dates. Thick gravy with white wine sauce. Curried rice and peaches. Beef Wellington and mashed potatoes. And as if there was not enough, a ham that had been boiled in honey.

At first Jonathan could not believe all the food was real. It seemed he had died and went to heaven. Both boys tried as hard as possible to use their best manners, but in the end, they were actually slurping so loud, Captain Moore had to remind them that they were not in the cockpit of the *Danielle* and that there were ladies present.

But what if it all went away? thought Jonathan. *There is too much to eat at once. I had better find a way to save some, just in case!*

For dessert: flaked-crust cherry pie that was unbelievably scrumptious, with coffee besides and a scoop of delicious vanilla iced cream. Pear tarts with sugar glaze. Plum pudding. Chocolate éclairs. After eating many quickly, Sean did all he could not to belch, however, Jonathan was not so lucky in restraining himself. Just the same, it was all excused.

"Misses Walker," said Jonathan in an official tone after eating his third éclair, "coming from a street person such as myself, from one not having the luxury of ever eating indoors as far as I can remember, or even having food close to this magnitude, I must say that this is the best meal I have ever had, bar none."

"I agree, Misses Walker," added Sean. "If I never eat again, it will be because nothing can come close to such fare. Remarkable!"

Misses Walker blushed and looked to her husband. "Where ever did you find these boys, William? I would like to keep them both around me, for when I am feeling blue!"

"My dearest, if we could find a few more like these on the streets of London, Bonaparte would be shaking in his boots! Not only are they gracious, but they can fight as well," answered Walker. "I can't agree with them more. Truly a most enjoyable dinner. Can we leave the dishes to Steward and retire to the study? I think a few tales are in order. If we keep the gore and violence out of the telling, maybe the ladies would enjoy the story?"

Miss Thompson giggled and addressed her brother-in law: "William, don't leave out all the excitement! We are grown women of the modern world! We can stand a little bit of detail!"

"Then off we go," Walker said, and after a few whispered instructions to Steward, he led his guests to the study. All chose comfortable chairs and pulled them close to the fire. Walker added a few logs and poured another drink for Nathaniel. Jonathan settled by his father on a large sofa and held his hand. Sean rather sleepily took up the last cushion next to his friend, leaning heavily on the padded arm. The clock in the corner rang nine times as if to say "Time to tell tales!"

"Now, where to begin?" asked Walker as all had finally settled in. "There is more than one story here and some start before others! Nathaniel, I think since you have the longer story, maybe you should begin?"

Nathaniel Moore told the story of his assignment to HMS *Troy*, a thirty six gun frigate, and saying good-bye to his small family. As he recounted his disastrous journey from England to the prisons in France, he noticed that with every hardship, with every battle or delay, Jonathan was shaken and seemed concerned as if the tale was happening at that precise moment.

"No need to worry, Jonathan!" his father said. "I made it back in one piece as you can plainly see!"

"Sorry, sir!" he said, relaxing a bit. "It was a good story, though scary at times."

Then Captain Walker told of the procurement of the treasure map from the spy, Frasier, and the *Poseidon's* race across the Atlantic in pursuit of the *Danielle.* Misses Walker was truly amazed by the bomb making abilities of Sean and when she turned to address him for details, all noticed that the boy was already fast asleep on the couch.

Walker finished his part of the tale by explaining, in minute detail, the final battle that ended with his taking possession of the French seventy-four *Danielle.* At times he even used glasses and books as ships and islands to replay the scene on a low table he had moved to the middle of the room. Whenever Nathaniel would grab a glass to suggest a different course of action, Walker would somewhat playfully slap his hands away, retrieve the ship and announce that it was he, not Nathaniel who was present at the battle. This made the women laugh and giggle at the men and their toys.

"How ever did you retrieve the treasure?" asked Miss Thompson."

"Ah, said Walker, "this is Jonathan's part of the story."

"I went ashore with Gorman and two marines," he began. "We followed Frasier's treasure map that in short order, led us to a heart-shaped beach. The map explained that *'On the heart-shaped beach, look south with a yellow sun and see the skull and the prize',* but there was no skull! Just a low reef, or so it seemed. When the yellow *morning* sun arose, the tide went out and the reef was actually an island - shaped like a skull!"

He continued telling the tale, those not knowing the outcome sitting in disbelief, however, smiling and clapping all the same, especially at the point of finding the treasure. When he told of Champagne's appearance and his idea to sink them in their tiny boat, Jonathan was proud at first, then seemed disturbed when he told of the sharks and Champagne's demise.

"I had to turn my head. I couldn't watch," he said. His

father reached around him and patted his shoulder.

"Jonathan, life is hard and war is even more difficult. You did what you had to do - to save your friends. And since it was Champagne who captured me, I have to say thank you for evening the score in such a dramatic way. England owes you her gratitude."

Steward entered and refreshed drinks and the like. At this break in the conversation, the ladies retired to *perform some secret maneuvers and plans of their own* as they explained. After a brief silence and a few pokes at the fire, the conversation continued.

"Now that it is just the *officers,*" said Nathaniel, "I must ask Jonathan about his days on the streets."

"It was hard at first," he said after a long pause. His eyes seemed to darken as he remembered those times. He certainly did not want to hurt his father with the sadness that surrounded those days. But after a bit of encouragement, he launched into his tale.

"If Sean were awake he could tell you there were long stretches of days where we ate nothing at first. But we teamed up and found odd jobs where food was the pay. After a while, we had almost steady work at a variety of places, and though we only ate once a day, we did sufficiently well, considering."

Jonathan told of the harsh winters he suffered through and the meanness of the bullies and men on the streets, but never in a way to solicit pity or guilt, just stating the facts as they were. Nathaniel listened through clenched teeth and fists, suffering the tale and blaming himself for all that had happened. In the end, he found that he could only wonder at his son's cheery attitude and refined manners, certainly better than could be expected from one who had lived a short life filled with adversity. *What character he has,* thought Nathaniel, and he was proud of his son.

"I must say," Jonathan continued, "After all that, I am certainly the most fortunate boy alive! Not only to have my father by my side, but to have such a great extended family as the Walkers and my relations from the *Danielle*. Even crotchety old Steward has been like a mother to me. Harrison, like my older brother, and of course, Sean. He is an inspiration and a model of bravery, though now," he continued, looking at his friend, "he seems less attentive - yet still happy as a kitten!"

As if on cue, the clock now struck twelve. They had been telling their tales for three hours straight and it was now time for bed. As they rose, quite unexpectedly, the door knocker boomed three times. Walker looked at them all in wonder.

"Pardon me," he said and exited toward the front door. When he opened it, he was shocked to see Gorman standing there in the cold night. He held a small package, wrapped in plain brown paper.

"I'm dreadfully sorry to disturb you at such a late hour, Captain Walker. But I have both good and bad news and believed it best to deliver it in person."

"Please come in, Captain. A cup of coffee?"

Gorman refused politely as Walker closed the door. Captain Moore and Jonathan made their way to them as well.

"Gorman!" said Moore. "What a pleasant surprise. I never did thank you enough for your part in all this."

"Don't mention it," said Gorman, tipping his hat, then removing it. "Truly a privilege to assist in anyway, Captain. Is there a place we can talk, gentlemen?"

Walker led them to the study, where Sean was still asleep on the couch; the ladies had gone upstairs to fix beds for all the guests. It had been decided that the Moore's and Sean were to stay here for the night. Steward had already bedded the horses from the carriage in the stable and wrapped them with warm blankets.

All sat once again save Gorman, who stood by the fire and took a pear tart that somehow had remained on the serving dish.

"Again, Captains, so sorry for the inconvenience," Gorman said. "Here is a small gift for young Flagon. Can you please have him open it tomorrow morning?"

"Of course," said Walker. He took the gift and set it on a table by the cabinet. "You mentioned good and bad news, Captain Gorman," Walker continued, "Please clarify."

"Why, yes sir," Gorman said. "The good news first. You are invited to a meeting tomorrow at one in the afternoon precisely -"

Walker exploded.

"By the gods and saints! I have just gotten back!"

This outburst caused Gorman and Jonathan to bolt upright and stiff, standing at attention. Sean even awoke and quickly stood, rigid, staring straight ahead. Nathaniel could only chuckle.

"I am sorry, sir," added Gorman before Walker exploded again.

"We have been ashore less than seven hours and I can't be left alone! I need time to relax! I am not going to meet with anyone tomorrow or the next day, I can assure you! Not even to meet with the King himself!"

Gorman seemed to choke a bit, then took a breath and said "Then I will ask that you tell him yourself, sir."

"Tell whom?" yelled Walker.

"The King," said Gorman. "It is His Majesty King George himself who has requested your presence."

All were dumbfounded. They stood in silence for what seemed to be minutes, now and again looking at each other in unvoiced astonishment.

"T-the King?" asked Jonathan.

"Holy…" said Sean.

"Yes," said Gorman smiling. "I could send word that you are ill, Captain, but I am not sure that will be acceptable."

Walker finally regained his senses and nodded his head firmly.

"Well. Of course. I will be there promptly. Please tell His Majesty that I am grateful and honored as well."

"Yes, sir," Gorman said, adding, "It is at Windsor

Castle and it is not just you, sir. He wishes to see Lieutenants Langley and Harrison and midshipman Moore and his father. Flagon as well. I do believe you are all to be decorated."

"Decorated?" asked Sean.

"Like a tree for Christmas?" asked Jonathan.

"No, no," said Captain Moore. "He will most likely grant a few gifts and - oh Lord. This could be a *knighthood* for you, William!"

Walker now was truly shocked into silence. He thought of what an honor to be made a Knight of the Realm, Sir William Walker. But he quickly shook this off.

"It would be the death of me! I'd lose my command. I'd have to join parliament! Let's not hope it comes to that. I just want the *Danielle* and an open sea!"

They all reflected for a moment about what they each would like their futures to hold, and it was odd that though unsaid, they all knew they wanted the same thing. To be at sea once again.

"There is more, I am afraid. The bad news. Before our lunch, Captain Walker is to be before the Admiralty. For review… and a court's marshal."

"What?" This time it was Nathaniel who exploded. "Of all the ridiculous -!"

"What is a court's marshal?" asked Jonathan.

Gorman explained that it is a trial of sorts, with Admirals as the judges. In any matter where a ship is lost, a reason must be given. A decision must be made to either punish the captain, or dismiss the matter.

"I am sure it will be dismissed, sir!" Jonathan said. "We will stand with you and -"

"You never want to go before the Admiralty, Jonathan," his father said. "It is always a roll of the dice. Logic and reason have no place there. I have seen the most preposterous judgments handed down. I will attend, of course."

With that, Gorman bid them all goodnight, as he had not yet been home to his wife this evening. He wished them a merry Christmas and good luck for tomorrow. All watched as the Marine left, and each silently pondered Gorman's true role in the military. A spy? Most assuredly, but to what extent? He had obviously been to see the King already, or at least his aides. He remained a mystery.

After a brief discussion, it was decided that nothing could be done about anything until the next day. All were exhausted and needed rest.

After changing into night clothes, Jonathan and Sean were escorted to a small room on the upper floor, where a window offered a grand view of the city. Miss Thompson had them tucked in tight and added another log to the small fireplace in the corner. Within minutes, Sean was fast asleep, snoring away, a smile on his face. Miss Thompson sat by his bed and stroked his hair from his face. *What a charming boy!* she thought. *It would be a proud mother who could claim him as her own. I only wish that someday, I may have one such as this.* She bent over and placed a kiss ever so gently upon his forehead. She could not be sure, but it seemed that in the flickering light of the fire, Sean's little smile grew just a bit.

She then moved to Jonathan, fluffed his pillow and smiled. He was still awake, but sleepy to be sure.

"A long day, Jonathan? A long few years?" she asked.

"Yes, ma'am. And I thank you for your kindness," he said. After a moment, he asked "Can you believe we are to see the King? How should I behave? I-I don't know how to bow properly or salute a King. Does one salute a King? What will I wear?"

Miss Thompson smiled and shook her head.

"I have never had an audience with the King," she said, "however, I am sure you will be briefed as to how to behave. Your father has seen him and will instruct you, I am sure of it. As for what to wear, I have to say that your midshipman's uniform looks quite striking on you. I will have your blouse and trousers washed and pressed in the morning. Steward will fix your coat and hat. Now please go to bed, Mister Moore."

"Again I thank you, Miss Thompson," Jonathan said through a yawn.

As she rose to leave, Jonathan had one more question.

"Did you know my mother?" he asked in almost a whisper.

Miss Thompson was shocked, but then recovered quickly. Of course Jonathan would want to know about his mother, but probably felt cautious asking his father. She sat back down next to his bed and held his hand lightly.

"I knew her, yes. We met a few times before your parent's wedding and once after, at a ball. She was a beautiful and kind woman, Jonathan. Your father was very much in love with her and they made a charming couple. Everyone who knew her was fond of her. She was a wonderful and caring mother."

"I know that. I can only just remember her face, just a little," the boy said. "She was kind to me, as you are."

"And she would be proud to see you now, Jonathan. As proud as we all are of you. You have become quite a charming and accomplished young man. Your father told me how it was the hope of being reunited with you that kept him alive through all his trials. Did you also know that he was alive, waiting for you to be found?"

But there was no answer. Jonathan had finally fallen asleep.

Miss Thompson smiled and fluffed his pillow once again. As she was just about finished, her hand brushed against something under his pillow - an object covered in cloth. She removed it slowly to discover that it was a napkin from the table. Upon unwrapping, she found an untouched dinner roll and a slice of ham. Further unfolding revealed a plum tart and a few other bits of food.

She then rose and went to Sean's bed. Under his pillow she found a wrapped pheasant's leg, two rolls, three slices of ham and a half eaten chocolate éclair. Concerned, she took all the food and turned to leave the room.

A figure stood in the doorway, and at first she was startled, almost crying out, but then recognized Nathaniel Moore, smiling.

"Thank you for tucking them in. I needed a few words with William," he said softly.

"But of course," she whispered. "How long have you been eavesdropping?"

"Eavesdropping?" Nathaniel said, smiling warmly. "Well, I have been accused of a great many things, Miss Thompson, but I have never been accused of eavesdropping. However, if you must know, I heard your whole conversation with Jonathan."

Barbara held out the food she had taken from beneath their pillows. Nathaniel looked at it quizzically.

"Did you not get enough to eat at dinner, my dear?" he asked.

"Really, Captain Moore!" she said, pushing him into the hallway and closing the door. "I found these under the boy's pillows."

Nathaniel looked at the food again and slowly nodded.

"It appears the lessons of the street die hard," he said. "I am afraid they do not yet trust that they will never return to their hard life of near starvation. This must make them feel better, more secure. At least that is my best guess."

"The poor dears!" said Miss Thompson. "But we can't allow them to have meat under their pillows! Whatever should we do?"

Nathaniel took the rolls and tarts from her and set them back under the boy's pillows. He kissed them each goodnight and returned to the hallway.

"Miss Thompson, I thank you again for your kindness. I wonder if he ever will be, well…whole again, though…he seems to be just about fine."

"If there is anything I can do to help, Captain Moore, please do not hesitate to ask," she said.

"Please, Miss Thompson. Call me Nathaniel if you could find it agreeable."

Barbara Thompson smiled, blushed, and looked into his eyes.

"I do find it agreeable," she said.

* * * * * *

December twenty-sixth arrived at the Walker home to much buzzing and excitement. Though not the traditional day to open gifts, it would have to do for the Walkers, Moores, a Flagon and a Thompson. Breakfast was served quite late due to the sleeping-in of the guests, however, once all were present, the meal became more of a brunch. There were eggs, bacon, ham, biscuits and freshly squeezed orange juice and even butter milk. The devouring took less than twenty-minutes, though hours to prepare.

Eventually, after being invited to the formal living room by Misses Walker and Miss Thompson, the boys opened the large double doors and there saw a massive Christmas tree decorated with small gifts, candies and treats and colorful, shiny trinkets. Petite candles here and there on the tree's boughs glittered happily.

"We added a few touches here and a few gifts there," said Misses Walker proudly. "And some early morning shopping bolstered the gifts!"

"Look Sean!" Jonathan said. "Have you ever seen anything more beautiful in your life?"

"No, Jonny Boy! Not even those fancy fishes I saw in the seas of the Caribbean!"

As the adults took their places in chairs about the tree, the boys sat on the comfortable rug that covered the floor, right by all the presents. There were not too many by most standards, but to Sean and Jonathan, it was a cornucopia of gifts. Captain Walker himself passed out the brightly-wrapped presents and made everyone open each package one at a time for all to see and admire.

Jonathan received mostly clothes from Miss Thompson and Misses Walker, as he really had none except for his uniform. The thick wool socks and extra pair of shoes he especially liked. He did receive a small cooking stove from none other than Steward, who instructed him on its safe usage and finer points. Jonathan actually hugged the man, slightly causing Steward to become speechless for a moment. Captain Walker gave Jonathan a map of the world and a matching case to fit it inside. Jonathan was enamored with the map and he and Sean vowed to memorize every country, city and feature before the New Year. His father gave Jonathan a thick, wool navy coat and pocket watch that looked to be made of gold.

"Your mother gave it to me when I became a captain. May it serve you well, if you ever return to sea."

Sean received clothing from the ladies as well, and from Steward, a small fighting knife that he could wear in a simple leather sheath tied to his leg. Though the women thought it a bit dangerous for a young boy, Steward assured them that Sean was probably the best swordsman on the *Danielle,* maybe with the exception of himself, and that this innocent, little *letter opener*, as he called it, would pose no trouble for Sean. Sean thanked Steward heartily as he strapped the knife to his ankle.

"I was not sure as to your desires, Sean," said Captain Moore, "however, I was able to get something wrapped with the help of Miss Thompson. Not a true present, per say, but something I think you will find agreeable."

He handed Sean a small box, no bigger than a deck of playing cards. As Sean opened it, he wondered what it could be. There was thin paper inside that also needed to be unwound. Finally, Sean held up a simple silver key on a silver chain, both tarnished with age and use. He looked at Captain Moore with a questioning face.

"The key to my apartment at Charring Cross," said Nathaniel. "I would be most honored if you would consider yourself one of the Moores, at least until you find somewhere else you would like to live."

Sean reacted slowly, considering all this and what was being offered. He had been without a family for almost as long as Jonathan and there was no telling where they were now. He had left them because it was clear that they could not afford to raise all their children in the city. On their farm in Ireland, when times were good, he remembered each child doing work and providing food for the table. But once the Flagons had moved to the city, there was nothing to do but beg. And that barely provided enough for Sean alone, much less an entire family. So he ran off one summer day and figured his family was better off with one less mouth to feed.

Now, a real home, *probably a very nice one at that,* he thought, was being offered. And he would be with Jonathan, like brothers.

"I-I don't know how to thank you, Captain Moore," he managed to say.

Jonathan just smiled and nodded to his father. "We are inseparable, Sean. So it only makes sense!"

"Well, Jonny," Sean said, "the last time we were separated, I had to blow up a ship to get you to come for me! Let's hope that isn't the case with your father's house!"

The room exploded in laughter once again.

"Flagon!" bellowed the Captain, "Your mentor, Captain Gorman dropped this off last night for you. He asked that you open it this morning. Don't disappoint him now."

Sean was surprised and opened the package quickly. He held it up for all to see.

"A book! With a sword on the cover!" said Sean as he leafed through the pages. At first he smiled, however, after a few moments of looking at the contents of the book, disappointment slowly settled upon his face.

"What is it, Sean?" asked Miss Thompson.

"It's the Legend of King Arthur, dearie," added Misses Walker.

"Oh!" Jonathan said. "Sean never has had the opportunity to learn to read!"

They all looked to each other, wondering why Gorman would send the boy a book if he was illiterate. Gorman was not mean spirited, so there had to be a reason.

It was Jonathan who eventually provided an explanation.

"Sean, I remember your wish to become a Royal Marine someday and I am sure that Gorman is telling you that to accomplish that, you must learn to read."

Everyone nodded, believing that was certainly the meaning behind the gift. Sean pondered it for a moment, then smiled.

"Even if that is not the reason, I could learn to read, couldn't I?"

"I will teach you at first," replied Miss Thompson, "and I am sure Jonathan will help you when you are aboard your next ship."

"Of course I will!" said Jonathan.

"That is *if* you are aboard another ship," added Captain Moore.

The announcement caused the entire room to lapse into silence. Jonathan was not sure he understood.

"I-I beg your pardon, Father?" he said.

"We can discuss it later Jonathan, however, at this point, I have been without you for over five years. I am very reluctant to let you go just yet."

Jonathan was stunned. He couldn't imagine not being on a ship ever again. Even if his father meant that it was only for a little while - but how long? *Then again*, Jonathan thought, *I have only just come back and I have not seen my father for over five years. I want to be with him forever and ever. But I love the sea. I am now a midshipman! What else could I ever be?*

After a moment more of silence, Captain Walker stood up and reminded them all that they had a busy day ahead. First was the appointment at the Admiralty, then an audience with the King.

"So let us prepare for both the bad and the good, gentlemen. We must look ship-shape and be at our best," said Captain Walker.

* * * * * *

Jonathan walked with his father, his best friend and Captain Walker across the large mall before the great building of The Admiralty.

"This is Whitehall, boys," said Nathaniel.

Two domes rose from the top of the four-story stone building with a great parapet between. The windows were tall and thin, and for such an immense building, the entrance seemed insignificant and common.

With some trepidation, they all walked inside.

"Boys," said Walker, "Within these walls is the largest collection of bloated, un-feeling, stern and politically wretched men ever collected into a single body. The Admirals in Whitehall govern all the doings of the Royal Navy and only the King himself can change their decisions. They decide who is to receive punishment and who to receive favor. They decide on which ship a new or re-assigned captain is to receive and on what duty he is to perform."

"These are not trivial men, boys," Nathaniel said in a whisper. "They rule their world with an iron glove and will not take any insolence from a Captain much less a young midshipman and a seaman. You two are to wait outside the chamber and speak only when spoken to, do you understand?"

"Yes sir," the boys said in unison, now second guessing their decision to come along and support Captain Walker. It seemed like facing the admirals was as dangerous as a battle at sea.

"Father," said Jonathan softly, "Aren't you now going to be an Admiral too? Can't you help Captain Walker and keep the other Admirals in line?"

"Yes, I may become an Admiral," his father said, "though unfortunately, I am not one yet and when confirmed, I will be a very *lowly* admiral at that. I will be some help, as I am in favor with many here, but still, things can and do go horribly wrong here quicker than a storm can brew in Hades and blow twice as hard."

They walked on through the dark stone halls, their

footsteps echoing loudly and soon descended a flight of stairs. At times they passed other naval officers, some who acknowledged them, other who rushed past, heads down. Eventually, as they walked another long hallway, they stopped at a slightly open area, where two benches sat on either side of a large double door.

Gorman appeared from a side passage and he solemnly opened the doors for them. Captain Moore walked in first, followed by Walker. Gorman paused and addressed the boys.

"Jonathan and Sean," Gorman said. "Please wait on the benches here and for God's sake, be quiet!"

The boys nodded their heads as if to say 'yes' and immediately took a seat on the hard, stone bench.

They could hear voices from within and some chairs being moved about. Both listened intently, trying to follow the discussion. After a while, they could hear the goings on as if they were actually sitting in the room itself.

"Now on this twenty-sixth day of December, in the year eighteen-hundred, I, Admiral John Barrow open this board of inquiry concerning Captain William Walker, formerly of the lost *HMS Poseidon* and as of now, unassigned to any ship in His Majesty's Navy."

Jonathan and Sean listened closely as another Admiral who called himself Worthing, read an account of the battle between HMS *Poseidon* and the French seventy-four, *Danielle*. Jonathan was amazed at the detail about the battle, which could have only come from Captain Walker himself. It not only took into consideration the maneuvers in the ocean, but the position of both ships at any given time during the battle, of the wind, and who had the advantage.

"Now to read your words directly, Captain Walker," said Worthing, "'And upon a final confrontation, *Poseidon* afire and damaged in fore and aft masts, taking on water, was maneuvered straight alongside the *Danielle* and after a brief misaimed fire from the enemy deck guns, I instructed a carpenter's crew to cut the main mast and pull it down as to land upon the *Danielle*. I then called for attack and all hands boarded the enemy via the mast-bridge or other means. We were victorious, took the *Danielle* after much fighting and set about salvaging anything we could from the sinking *Poseidon*.'"

"That is correct," said Walker.

"And the *Poseidon* was un-salvageable?" asked Admiral Barrow.

"Yes, sir, Admiral," answered Walker.

"Though in various reports from your officers, more than one mentions that you ordered them to ignore the flames and prepare for boarding the enemy. Could it be that your desire for a larger ship and a larger prize payment clouded your judgment?"

Walker was shocked that the Admiral could say such a thing. The *Poseidon* was a proud ship and a fast one as well. No captain in his right mind would ever want to lose such a graceful and valuable ship as the *Poseidon*.

"Begging your pardon sir, no," replied Captain Walker, somewhat angry at the suggestion. "My judgment was not clouded. It was clear to me that if we tended to the fires on the *Poseidon*, we would be sunk and many men lost, the mission a failure. I had to have a sea-worthy ship. I took the *Danielle* for the good of my men and the mission, which as you know, was of the utmost importance and highly successful."

"Indeed," said Admiral Barrow. "I know of the headlines in the papers and the adventure you had. Not many are as lucky as you, able to traipse around the world, taking prize ships and the like. You have done quite well for yourself, Walker. Living high off the hog -"

"I am not sure what that has to do with anything, Admiral -" Walker added in his defense.

"- however, the loss of a vessel of His Majesty's Navy," continued Barrow, "is a serious issue. We must look at all angles and possibilities. I am sure something could have been done to save both ships."

"Not likely, sir," said Walker, still fuming slightly.

At this, the boys could hear Barrow taking a large breath, like a dragon pulling in massive amounts of air to light the fire that was sure to burn out of its mouth in hot torrents of flame.

"What did you say, Walker?!" exploded Barrow. "Are you questioning my perception of the situation? How dare you! I would think you would realize that I hold your future in my hands! Of all the gall!"

The next voice the boys heard, after the fire had subsided, was the calm voice of Captain Moore.

"Now, Admiral Barrow, Captain Walker meant no disrespect. He was just relaying the fact that he was there, in the heat of the battle, and was privy to a unique perception of the encounter as it did unfold. As I am sure the Admiral well knows, there is no view of combat quite like the front row."

"Coming from a man who has lost two ships," said Barrow, "you would know."

There was a silence. The boys could hear another dragon sucking in air, enough to light an even bigger flame than the first.

"Why Barrow, you *bloated toady*! How *dare* you suggest there was any inappropriate action taken in my commands of the *Troy* and the *Helios*. If I were any lesser of a man I would fly across this desk and teach you a lesson in battle strategy! You pompous mule! You wretched bilge rat! You moronic -"

"Is that your father?" asked Sean, now feeling that the door that separated the two dragons within was not quite strong enough to protect them.

"I believe it is!" said Jonathan. "And I thought Captain Walker had a temper!"

"Sit down, Moore!" exploded Barrow. "Know your place as I do mine. I will say what I want when I want! I am head of this review board, not you! You are cooking your friend's goose now and as well as scuttling your own promotion to Admiral! Henceforth, you *both* are unassigned! No ships! The *Danielle* will undergo repairs and be renamed and will be assigned to the next Captain in line. As for you both, you will remain landside and we will inform you of your next duties shortly."

"Unbelievable!" exploded Captain Moore. "This will not stand, I tell you!"

"Nathaniel, please..." said Walker. He sounded defeated and embarrassed. His friend, trying to help, had caused more harm than good.

"William," said Nathaniel angrily, "they had their minds made up before we came in this room! They have decided to rename the ship and that takes some time and doing!"

Barrow chuckled a bit. "And what if we did? I know you are the darling of the press, Moore, and that Walker is a new hero of the crown! But you are still, both, servants of this board and will treat it with respect and deference. Wait until the rest of the Admiralty hears about this!"

"And the King," came a voice softly, but firm and clear.

"Who is that?" asked Jonathan from the other side of the door.

"Sounds like Captain Gorman to me!" said Sean. By this time both boys were sitting upright and shaking perceptively.

"Pardon me," said Worthing, "Who are you to speak, Gorman? We know your status as a sneak and a spy, and how you are tied up in this mess."

"Being a sneak is essential to being a very effective spy, Admiral Worthing, and I am both sneaky *and* effective. And if by *'this mess'* you mean the successful recovery of the Spanish treasure, then I am glad to be part of it. I also am a conduit to the King, who requires me to report directly to him after each of my missions, including this one. I am sure he would be shocked to hear of this outcome, in fact, he has asked me to inform him of the board's decision and recommendations. Gentlemen?"

With that, Gorman stood and motioned Walker and Moore to the door.

"You are not dismissed!" yelled Barrow, shocked.

"However," said Gorman, "You may be. To His Majesty's Palace, Captain Moore? Captain Walker? The King awaits us!"

With that, the three strode out of the chamber, leaving the bloated Admirals to decide if, indeed, they were truly on their way to the King.

"Send a guard to follow them," ordered Barrow. Worthing, now visibly nervous and pale, silently but quickly walked out.

The carriage clopped along the Bath Road on the way to Windsor Castle. The men inside were both laughing and nervous at the same time. The Admirals had reacted to their mission in an unbelievable way. Walker was being punished for losing the *Poseidon,* receiving no credit for successfully capturing the much larger *Danielle* or for retrieving the treasure worth close to a million British pounds. Nathaniel Moore was being held up at Captain and not to receive his promotion to Admiral. It could not have gone any worse.

"Gorman," Captain Moore said, "I believe you slightly stretched the truth about your duty to the King?"

"How so, Captain?" Gorman asked.

"Do you indeed report to him all the details of your missions, their outcomes and the results of board reviews?"

Gorman looked out the window and stared at the passing park. Most of the trees had lost their leaves, the flowers had all wilted from the cold winter nights. A cool drizzle was beginning to fall. It was not quite cold enough for snow, nor warm enough for a stroll. *Typical London weather,* he thought.

"I *have* met the King on a few occasions," Gorman said, smiling, "though my field reports are usually given to his aides. I certainly don't report the outcomes of the Admiralty board's decisions. Ha-ha! Though the bloated Admirals don't know that." He then motioned with his hand pointing to the rear of the carriage. "When their little spy who is clumsily following us -"

All looked out the window to see a carriage following close behind them. Inside was clearly Worthing and another, a young officer. They turned their heads when they noticed they had been discovered.

"-sees us turn onto the Long Walk leading to the Castle, they will quickly reverse the decision. If not, I have enough dirt on them both to change the outcome. Oh, it is a great thing to be in the cat bird's seat, as the Americans say."

The carriage moved on and within moments they had reached the Long Walk leading to Windsor Palace. As they turned onto the path, Jonathan and Sean were stunned into silence. The road led directly onward in a straight line for what seemed like a mile, flanked by a field of unblemished snow on either side continuing for a hundred feet. There, it was bordered by enormous trees planted in straight lines creating a wall that announced the beginning of the forest.

"Will ya look at that!" said Sean as he turned his eyes forward.

Ahead of them upon the top of a low rise was the most incredible castle. Wide and high it stood, with great white stones for its strong walls reaching up over four stories; parapets sitting atop the structure like a King's crown. Tall, arched windows accented the façade and a great iron fence and gate surrounded the structure. It was watched over by Royal Guards standing just past the gate next to a great, dark wooden door.

Surprisingly, there was a small crowd waiting there by the gate. *It must be for the King,* thought Jonathan. *Maybe he will greet us at the door so people can get a good look at him.*

Windsor Castle

But as they opened the door to leave the carriage, the small group started to cheer. Some called out to them, others waved. *Huzzah! Huzzah!* came the call from the few Navy men within the crowd.

"This is for us?" asked Jonathan.

"Do not let it go to your head, son," his father warned. "Keep your mind sharp and wits sharper. An audience with the King is also serious business and it would be best if you and Sean would address him as *Your Majesty*, if you must speak at all."

"Aye, sir," the boys said, observing the crowd.

Suddenly, Jonathan met eyes with a young man in the gathering. He caught his gaze due to the fact that unlike the other smiling and cheering faces, this one was scowling and had part of his face covered by a hood and scarf. Their eyes met for a moment longer and then - he was gone. He had either moved behind someone else in the crowd, or had hastily run away.

3
Audience With George

They entered the palace, removing their hats and remaining as silent as they could. A doorman escorted them inside and as they were expected and prompt, they were directed down a long hallway to a sitting room. Though it seemed that some of the castle was undergoing repairs, they still marveled at the fancy wall paper and luxurious furniture as they waited for their audience. Shortly, they were greeted by a servant, though a very important one.

"Good day, Captains, young sirs," he said. "I am the King's personal secretary, Army Colonel Herbert Taylor. His Majesty will receive you in a moment. Please make yourselves comfortable and excuse the condition of the receiving room. We are renovating. Do you require anything?"

Captain Gorman spoke for the group and said everything and everyone was perfectly alright. They required nothing at the moment.

After Taylor left them, the boys practiced their bows, had their jackets brushed by Walker, Gorman and Captain Moore repeatedly, and were told to stand up straighter than was humanly possible. Shortly, Harrison and Langley appeared and the tale of the Admiralty was told. Both agreed that this was a shocking development, that something was behind it and that it certainly would not stand.

"We will make sure that something is done," said Captain Moore.

The boys then asked about Harrison's Christmas meal and his family.

"There was much eating and some drinking as well. I

do like a proper ale and a goose when I can get one! It seems that you boys also had enough to suit you?"

They each agreed and described each present and each dessert in minute detail. Jonathan wanted to mention to Harrison that his father was not going to allow him back on a ship, but this was not the best place to have that conversation. It still weighed on his mind and he was not sure how to change his father's decision. For now he would let that concern rest.

Shortly Colonel Taylor returned to lead them into a large room, with wooden paneling, a high ceiling and laced grayish curtains that haphazardly covered the windows. A few chairs had been covered with what looked to be bed sheets, all signs of the renovation. The chairs were set facing a raised platform, much like a smaller version of the poop deck of the *Danielle,* and on it was a great chair. To each side were two servants, dressed in frilly red and gold jackets. They stared ahead, unmoving.

There, wearing a white wig was a tall stately-looking man in a red coat much like Captain Gorman's, yet longer and trimmed in bright gold. His forehead was high, his eyes wide and expressive. His nose was slightly large, but not ugly by any means and his lips small yet rosy. He looked up from a plate of fruit and cheese and wiped his chin daintily with a white napkin.

"Spe-len-did! Spe-len-did!" he said, voice booming as he pronounced the word 'splendid', as if it had three syllables.

"Your Majesty," Colonel Taylor said. "May I present to you the heroes of HMS *Danielle.* First, Captain William Walker."

Walker walked ahead a bit, but stopped at a considerable distance away from the King and bowed slightly, extending one leg forward. Jonathan and Sean watched, knowing that they would need to perform the same bow. And even though they had practiced for at least an hour this morning, *well, it is the King of England!* they thought. *We had better bow as well as we can!*

Next, Captain Gorman was introduced, then Jonathan's father, then Harrison and Langley. Finally Colonel Taylor said:

"May I present to his Royal Highness, Midshipman Jonathan Moore, instrumental in the retrieval of the treasure and in the dispatching of the French Captain."

Jonathan walked up to where the others had stopped, well short of the throne and bowed as pretty as you please. He looked the King right in the eye and said, for some unfathomable reason:

"Nice to meet you, your highness."

The room was shocked into silence. Even Sean knew one was not supposed to address the King until he specifically asked a question of you. Jonathan quickly realized that he had made a mistake and bowed again as if to say *may I start over?* He was terribly embarrassed and was now shaking all over. Jonathan kept his gaze to the ground and waited a moment.

"Ha ha!" said the King, laughing. "Spe-len-did, this one is! And it is a pleasure to meet you as well Jonathan Moore. And who is that behind you?"

Jonathan assumed the King was asking him a question, so he responded.

"This, Your Majesty, is able seaman Sean Flagon. He is my best friend and actually made a bomb while he was captive aboard the *Danielle* and used it to great effect to slow the ship so we in the *Poseidon* could catch up. Come on, Sean!" Jonathan said, waving his friend up to the imaginary line. Sean quickly rushed up, made a hasty bow, then remained stooped as he retreated back where he had started. He felt safer just a little bit away from the King.

"Very well then!" said the King. "I have heard some details, mostly about the fact that you found the treasure and brought it home! However, no one told me of the bomb! That is quite good! And I assume, Captain Walker, that the battle was ferocious, was it not?"

"Yes it was, Your Majesty," answered Walker. The room lapsed into silence.

"Is there anyone who can give me the details? I do so love a good accounting of my ships!"

"But of course, Your Majesty," answered Walker, who then, very briefly, told the King the finer points, turn for turn, of the battle and the final minutes of the *Poseidon* as they abandoned ship and took the *Danielle.*

"Ah, well Captain Walker, sometimes you have to spend a ship or two to win the war. A fine trade in any case. I understand the *Danielle* is quite a ship, is she not?"

"She is a most sea-worthy lady and a fine fighter," Walker said. "I wish I could continue commanding her myself. Alas, this is not to be as I have been informed just this morning by the Admiralty. I am to remain without a ship for the foreseeable future."

The King furrowed his brow and looked sideways at the Captain. He did not seem pleased. Of course, Walker was using this discussion to his advantage and was springing a trap on Barrow and Worthing.

"Without a ship? My best fighting Captain? Moore, you are privy to the workings of the Admiralty. Explain this."

"By all means, Your Highness," responded Captain Moore. "It seems that some in the Admiralty believe that Captain Walker somehow made an error losing the *Poseidon*. They believe he could have somehow beaten the *Danielle*, retained his ship and also retrieved the treasure."

The King held his discontent clearly on his face. He started shaking his head.

"I am no man of the sea, but I know poppycock when I hear it. What is your opinion, Captain Moore?"

"It is my opinion, having faced the *Danielle* and her escorts, that she is overpowering when compared to the *Poseidon*. Even with half her guns, the *Danielle* is a tough match. Captain Walker fared better than any other against her. He deserves our -"

"By all means!" bellowed the King. "Which imbecile made this determination?"

"That would be two imbeciles, your highness,"

answered Captain Moore. "Admiral Barrow and Admiral Worthing."

Gorman was visibly shaking with laughter, a squeak popped out as he was trying to conceal his joy. The plan had worked better than he could imagine. All soon looked at him, even the King.

"Pardon me, your majesty," Gorman said, trying to regain his composure, "I - ahem -" He coughed a few times. "I seem to have got a tickle in my throat. Ever so sorry."

He was handed a small glass of water from one of the servants and the King continued.

"Herbert, I want to see those Admirals tomorrow morning! I will have them replaced immediately!" commanded the King, looking at Captain Moore directly. "Now, where should we send them?"

"If I may suggest, your highness," said Gorman, interrupting, "Australia is in need of assistance. All those criminals there. Quite an unpleasant position, but someone has to do it."

The King thought for a moment, then smiled. "I do like the idea of that. Yes, Australia it is. Now on to other business. I have also heard there was an interesting development in the actual procurement of the treasure?"

"If Your Majesty would permit," suggested Walker, "Midshipman Moore could inform you of the final minutes of his confrontation with the French Captain Champagne?"

The King was visibly excited and turned to face Jonathan.

Jonathan's heart raced for a moment. He was now to address the King directly for the second time. *It is almost now a conversation!* He said to himself. *This is an important moment. I had better perform well. A deep breath should help.*

So he drew in air and began somewhat nervously. As he noticed the King listening and enjoying the tale, he relaxed and effortlessly told of the search for the skull, the finding of the treasure and the unfortunate appearance of Champagne.

"I suggested in a secret sort of way, that Captain Gorman here should deliver the treasure to Champagne right away! Which he did by -"

"Wait a minute!" said the King. "I think I know! You tossed the heavy chest into Champagne's boat...and it sunk!"

"His Majesty is correct!" laughed Jonathan, happily.

"Spe-len-did!" said the King. "Ingenious idea young man! Then what happened?"

Sean, now with his guard down and feeling more at ease, jumped right in and took up the tale. The other men, seeing that the King was enjoying the young boys, allowed them to continue and even smiled a bit as they told the tale.

"The sharks did the rest, Your Majesty," said Sean, inching his way closer. "Chewed them right up. Jonathan turned away, but I had to watch. Fascinating and horrible at the same time. 'Couldn't have happened to a nicer man' I said at the time!" Sean then laughed aloud and shortly the King and the rest were all laughing together.

"I do love a successful mission, don't we all? Well, well, well. I am proud of you. All of you. England is grateful for your service. I am of a mind to reward your loyalty and dedication. Captain Moore, you are being considered for promotion, I understand, so I am not sure what else you would want, hum?"

"Your Majesty," said Nathaniel Moore, "just to serve you in the Royal Navy, in any capacity, is reward enough. If I could do so forever, I would be a happy man."

The King smiled and then simply said "I cannot control all the fates of time. But I can... *persuade*... some at Whitehall. So be it. You are to be my personal adjunct to the Admiralty and can choose any assignment you desire. Herbert, make sure this is communicated to all the proper channels."

"Yes, Your Majesty," Herbert said as he jotted notes on a ledger book he carried in his hand. Captain Moore was shocked at the King's generosity and hated to bring up the point that he had effectively been turned down for a position as Admiral just this morning. He glanced at Walker, who motioned with a nod for him to bring up the subject. Luckily, Gorman was attentive as usual and spoke first.

"As adjunct, Your Majesty, it is customary for the rank of your servant to be an Admiral. That would require a promotion for the modest Captain Moore."

"Now I believe," said the King, surprised, "that you were already up for promotion, Captain Moore. It was in all the papers. You were to become Admiral rank. What is the issue?"

"It is the imbeciles, Your Majesty," said Gorman, "Barrow and Worthing seem to have forgotten the service Captain Moore has rendered to the crown. Sinking several frigates and damaging a third-rate man of war is not accomplishment enough for them, I assume. They have, quite frankly, halted the promotion as of this morning."

"What in the name of heaven is going on in that building? I will address this at the earliest opportunity!" shouted the King. "Do they not know there is a war on?"

"Pardon them," Gorman said, "They are only imbeciles."

"Colonel Herbert, take a note!" said the King, flustered and more so angry. "Now, I will remedy that situation shortly. Walker, what can I do for you?" asked the King. "It has been suggested that a knighthood is in order and I couldn't agree more. How do you hold with that?"

"Whatever pleases Your Majesty, I am but a humble servant," said Walker, politely bowing.

Jonathan knew what Walker really wanted and thought that it must be told to the King.

"Your Majesty?" Jonathan called out.

"Jonathan! Please know your place!" his father said quickly.

But the King held up his hand for silence. He looked at Jonathan and smiled.

"I have a feeling that the younger Moore is not aware of the proper protocol when discussing state matters with the King of England. There are some finer points of order he is unfamiliar with. Speaking his mind."

"I am so sorry Your Majesty," his father said, bowing. "He has been away for a long time, lost actually. Please accept my apologies -"

"Nonsense!" said the King. "It is refreshing to hear the bare truth from time to time. Midshipman, what is it that Captain Walker really wants, eh?" The King smiled in a humorously evil way.

Jonathan smiled as well. "Your Majesty, I know all the desires of everyone in this room, except for Captain Gorman, who is secretive and mysterious and therefore hard to peg. But I do know that Captain Walker wishes to have a fast ship, cruise for battle and win prizes! I hear he earns a small amount for each French ship he captures and he is good enough to share it with the crew! His wife told me he has gotten *more* than most captains. That is how he has obtained such a beautiful home! You actually must go and see it!"

"I will take that as an invitation!" claimed the King, smiling at Jonathan the whole time. "Captain Walker has mentioned a desire to stay in command of the *Danielle* so we will make him a knight of the realm *and* give him command of his favorite ship. Herbert, take a note and express my orders at the Admiralty. Captain Moore, as my adjunct, we will have him accountable to you directly."

"Yes, Your Majesty, it will be my pleasure," said Captain Moore.

"There is always room for a few more of Boney's ships at the bottom of the sea, or to be added to our fine fleet via capture. That, I assume, is your specialty Captain Walker?"

The room, again, was stunned. Less than an hour ago, the Admiralty had taken Walker's entire future away, his prospects for command were in great doubt. Now it had all been turned around utterly and completely. Gorman continued to disguise his laughter as a cough and received another glass of water.

"It is my specialty, your Highness," smiled Walker, "and I will execute your order with the utmost seriousness and dispatch."

"Now, Mister Langley," continued Jonathan. "The men love him and respect him, and you should have seen him when we attacked the *Danielle*! I am told he was out in front, slicing through enemies left and right. He led the way! He is an excellent swordsman and taught me more than a few tricks. I honestly believe he lets Captain Walker win when they fence, though both are excellent and I would fear having to face them – even if just for fun! Mister Langley should have his own ship, of course."

"Jonathan!" shouted Langley, unable to stop himself. Yes, that is what he desired, his own command, *but there are rules,* thought Langley, *and an order to these things. One can't just jump the ladder, as they say, and get a ship out of turn!*

"A nice fast forty-four would suit him fine," added Jonathan. "Everyone in the Navy knows those are the most desirable. And he would need to be promoted to Captain, of course."

"Make it so, Colonel Taylor," said the King, "unless *Captain* Langley objects?"

Langley just shook his head vigorously and bowed.

"What of your friend Sean?" asked the King, now directing his gaze at the young Irishman.

"Sean?" said Jonathan, thinking. *He is contented with just a bed to sleep in and a few good friends. And now that he will be living at my father's house, my house, what more could he possibly want?* He looked at Sean for an idea, but his friend just smiled and shrugged his shoulders as if to say *I don't know, I don't need a thing!*

And then it hit Jonathan like a bolt of lightning.

"He wants to be a Royal Marine, like Captain Gorman! The beautiful red coat will go well with his hair, don't you think?""

"Yes, yes it would! Is that what you desire, bomb-maker?" asked the King.

Sean reflected for an instant. "I don't believe, your

highness, that I could ever be a marine quite like Captain Gorman," Sean said. "He is handy with sword and pistol, and a great leader of men. But I would gladly attempt it!"

"Captain Gorman, is this possible?" asked the King.

"He will need to pass his exam and he will need a sponsor, your majesty," said Gorman, smiling as if he was setting a trap for someone. "That will be difficult, with no true connections to those in power -"

"I will sponsor him!" said three voices at the same time. Captain Moore, Langley and Harrison had all volunteered at once.

"Spe-len-did!" laughed the King. "I will let you men fight it out to see who will be the boy's sponsor. We must be sure the right people are informed. Gorman, can you arrange his exam for us?"

"With pleasure, Your Majesty!" said Gorman with a bow.

"And what of Captain Gorman? Is there anything he desires?"

Jonathan tried but could not think of a single thing. Gorman was a mystery, and though he felt he could trust him, and considered himself a friend, he really knew nothing about him. What could he possibly want?

"I, your majesty, enjoy the free life. Please assign me to any duty as long as it involves the downfall of Napoleon," said Gorman graciously.

"I know a little of your exploits, Captain Gorman," said the King, "and am told sometimes it is better to not know what you are up to or your whereabouts. Let us leave your gift for later. You may request it whenever it is needed."

"Very gracious, your majesty," said Gorman, bowing again.

"Spe-len-did!" said the King. "What of Lieutenant Harrison? He has newly been promoted, is this correct?"

"Mister Harrison?" asked Jonathan. "Yes. And he is the easiest of them all! I know his true love!"

"Jonathan?" squawked Harrison, "Whatever do you

mean?"

The King looked shocked and frowned. "I am not sure even a King can help a young man with the girl of his fancy, but is it advice you seek? Hum?"

"Oh no, Your Majesty," laughed Jonathan. "She is not a girl! Harrison's love is the Periwinkle! He knows her lines, her sails and her history!"

"The Periwinkle?" asked the King. "What is that?"

"He means HMS *Paladin*, your majesty. A graceful sloop, sometimes used as a packet," said Captain Walker.

"Oh! The *Paladin!* I know her!" said the King. "I have actually been aboard. She is fast and there is not a ship more beautiful in the navy of any country. However, I believe such a coveted command is hard to get. Lieutenant Sutton, whom I met at last year's ball, was assigned to her. And that just recently, as I recall. This may be hard to accomplish even for me, you know. A King can't take away a favor from one to give to another."

"I understand completely, Your Majesty," said Harrison, "I am greatly satisfied serving with Captain Walker. I have much to learn before assuming command of a ship, whichever one I receive."

The King was deep in thought and shook his head a bit. "I will have to discuss this and give it some further consideration, however, I'd advise you, Mister Harrison, to learn what will serve you well and learn it quickly. I will not forget your accomplishments. Now, all we have left is Jonathan. Young man, what is it that is your true desire?"

Jonathan realized that he knew the aims and dreams of almost every one of his friends, but not himself. He had found his father; he had food, clothing, a place to live and friendship. The only other thing Jonathan wanted was to return to the sea, though his father had said that was not to happen. How could he choose between the sea and his father's wishes?

Looking up, Jonathan noticed that everyone was watching at him intently, and his father, seemingly reading his mind, was staring most keenly.

"I-I really…have all I need, Your Majesty. I have been without my father for five years…and that is my desire, to be with him. And to sail…" Jonathan's voice trailed off as he considered the disagreement with his father.

The King noticed the tension between the two Moores and after a moment, had figured out the issue. He smiled and said quietly:

"Then you as well, Jonathan, have a favor to use when and if you ever need one. Mind your father well. I am sure that your future will be bright. Fate allows those who aspire to achieve, isn't that right, Captain?"

Captain Moore realized that the King was suggesting a course of action. The message was not lost as Nathaniel had come to appreciate the fact that Jonathan was a talented young man and was needed in the Navy. However, he was also his son, his only family, and he was missed by his father. *Couldn't he stay in London for a short time to make up for all the years of being apart?* Nathaniel thought. *Then again, the King* is *the King.*

"Yes, your highness," he said. "Fate will allow."

* * * * * *

It was only a matter of hours for the city of London to hear of the knighting of Captain William Walker, now, of course, formally addressed as Captain *Sir* William Walker. Within a day, all the London newspapers had numerous accounts, some even factual, about the mission to Skull Eye Island, the subsequent audience with King George, and all the gifts that had been bestowed upon the victorious crew. Equally interesting to some, was the fact that Captain Moore was now reunited with his son, Jonathan, and they were living happily in his small apartment on Charring Cross Road.

Also reported in the papers was the sudden transfer of Admirals Worthing and Barrow to assist in the governing of the penal colony on the island-continent of Australia. The articles explained the horrible conditions of the island

and the almost hellish climate and exotic diseases running rampant throughout the land. By all accounts, Australia was a most inhospitable place.

The next several weeks Jonathan and Sean spent with Captain Moore, when he was available, and when not, with Mister Harrison. The three boys spent many days eating together, visiting the vast Royal Naval Libraries and even fit some fencing into their busy schedule. In fact, there seemed to be almost as much fencing as there was eating.

One afternoon, in the early spring, Miss Thompson appeared at the Moore home and took the boys into the small study in the back of the receiving room.

"It is time for your reading lessons, Sean," she announced, causing Sean to run enthusiastically for his copy of "The Legend of King Arthur". However, upon his return, Miss Thompson produced a small board and chalk, and proceeded to drill Sean on the letters of the alphabet, their sounds and how they formed a few simple words.

"Miss Thompson, begging your pardon," said Sean after trying to sound out the letters c-a-t into a word, "Shouldn't that be spelled k-a-t, as the 'c' sometimes has a soft sound as in...*ceiling*?"

"You are about to find, Mister Flagon," she said "that the English language is more of an art form than a science, am I right Jonathan?"

"Indeed, Miss Thompson. Wait until you study the formation of vowels together, as in 'i' and 'e'. It is simply chaos that someone with too much time has decided to create a conflicting structure around. Impossible, but you will overcome it."

"After all," Sean said optimistically, "I can speak it more or less! How hard will it be to read?"

As Miss Thompson continued teaching her lessons over the next few weeks, it seemed that Sean progressed nicely. He was soon reading simple sentences from the other books she brought over, mostly nursery rhymes and the like, but they gave Sean confidence. Jonathan also joined in the lessons as well. Though he had found a few books to read while he lived on the streets, it was still a welcomed refresher for him. Each night, as they were sent to bed, they read the books that had been given to them by candlelight, until they fell fast asleep.

Toward the middle of January, Captain Walker was sitting in his study when an envoy from the Admiralty delivered a message - his new assignment. Walker retreated to the fireside, added a log, poked about the ambers, and opened the letter. With a warm drink by his side, he began reading.

To the honorable Captain Sir William Walker:

This is to inform you of your immediate assignment by His Royal Majesty to perform a specific favor to the King. You are forthwith instructed to contact Governor Dowdeswell of the Bahamas and obtain information as to the activities of French and American privateers and other criminals about the Caribbean Sea. After exploration of the area and capture or destruction of any illegals encountered, please return for further orders after a period of four months.

Please depart at your earliest convenience. Your new ship assignment is HMS Doggard, *formerly known as the French seventy-four* Danielle, *as it has been renamed.*

Sincerely,

Admiral John Barrow, London, Sunday, January 11, 1801

Walker read the note again to be sure of its contents. The mission itself was a peach, an easy assignment usually welcome by some captains. Normally, Walker would scoff at such a simple errand, however, with the loss of Langley to his own command, and more than likely Jonathan and a few others, it would be a chore to take a new vessel out to sea. A simple task of cruising the warm and pleasant waters of the Caribbean looking for a few left over scraggly pirates would suit him just fine. The chance of some prize money for the capture of a pirate ship or two was also a welcome event.

It was the other item in the letter that upset him greatly. According to the orders, the *Danielle* had been renamed the *Doggard.*

"What in all the blue blazes is the meaning of that name?!" he yelled aloud. "The *Doggard*? By all the saints! The most preposterous title for a ship I have ever heard! What were they thinking?"

And as he re-read the letter it became obvious. The order was surely the last action and insult, from Admiral Barrow. It was the Admiral's way of punishing him for having him sent to Australia. And Barrow himself had signed it.

"Well," said Walker to himself as he sipped his brandy, "If that is all the old goat can do as his last action of his post at the Admiralty, then good riddance to him. I will take it up with Nathaniel when the time is proper. But now, I have work to do. Misses Walker!" he called, "I am off once again! Come have a listen!"

As Walker spoke with his wife, a light afternoon snow began to fall outside, adding a delicate layer to the already present coat of white that covered the city. Not far away, Jonathan, Sean and Captain Moore accompanied Miss Thompson to Piccadilly Circus, to explore the streets and shop at the many stores. The apartment on Charring Cross, according to Miss Thompson, needed some 'cozying' and a female touch was surely needed. They searched for new furniture, some rugs and even a few choice meats and cheeses for the cupboard. The gentlemen, secretly bored beyond all belief, but keeping smiles on their faces, waited outside a butcher shop while Miss Thompson engaged the proprietor. They had been at it all day, and though mostly at the direction of the lady for all purchases, Jonathan had himself picked out a small silver-chained necklace with a delicate silver dolphin hanging as a locket. In one of the eyes was set a small blue crystal.

"Jonny, it is beautiful!" said Sean, with a perplexed look on his face. "But, well…it is a little…*girlish*, isn't it?"

"Sean, you ninny," Jonathan said. "It is not for me. It is for Miss Delain Dowdeswell, if ever I should see her again."

"Ah. That is all well and good then," Sean said. "Steward stopped by this morning and mentioned that the *Dani* is assigned to the Caribbean again, so I am sure we will see all the Ladies Dowdeswell in our travels. Captain Walker will not want to split up the three musketeers, meaning us and Mister Harrison. Ha-ha! We do make him look good!"

"True!" said Jonathan. "Either finding treasure or obtaining a new ship for his needs, we *are* quite valuable to him."

Jonathan then stopped short when he saw the look on his father's face. He was not necessarily displeased, but worried. The few times they discussed the topic of returning to sea, his father soundly disapproved. Nathaniel was quite set against his son leaving just yet. Jonathan had now come to the realization that Mister Harrison, Sean, Steward and Captain Walker might take the *Danielle* on an adventure without him. That would break his heart, as would his leaving his dear father behind. *No matter what may happen*, he thought, *I am lost again.*

Miss Thompson now exited the butcher shop, carrying a few small packages. "There are more inside, Nathaniel," she said, "Only a few dozen."

"We will see about the future, gentlemen," said Captain Moore, "but for now, let us concern ourselves with the gathering of these packages Miss Thompson has chosen and load them in the carriage. I am sure it will take only three or four trips!"

"Captain Moore!" Barbara said, surprised, "Are you *suggesting* that I have purchased too much?"

"No," Nathaniel said, "I am not *suggesting*. I am stating a fact!"

They all laughed and began loading packages as the carriage arrived. It was only a few moments before Nathaniel noticed that Jonathan was missing.

"Jonathan?" he called calmly, but soon, after looking about and not seeing his son, a fear came over him. His heart raced. "Jonathan!" he called loudly, and turned his head frantically searching.

Sean and Miss Thompson abruptly stopped their loading, to immediately see the concern on Captain Moore's face. They began looking about as well.

Did he run off? Upset with me? thought Nathaniel, *or did someone take him? Some past adversary?*

After a frantic moment or two, Sean reached up and tugged the Captain's sleeve. He pointed to the entrance of an alley, where they all saw Jonathan, his back turned to them, addressing a small boy. The boy had a dirty face and was dressed in rags. He stared intently at Jonathan. They could not hear what was being said, however, the boy was listening keenly and nodding his head. Jonathan reached in his pocket and handed the boy more than a few small, paper-wrapped items, then all of the spending money his father had given him. It may have totaled only a dozen or so shillings, but on the streets, that was literally a fortune. The boy looked at his prize, nodding again as Jonathan spoke. Jonathan put his hands on the boy's shoulders, then hugged him tightly.

"Dear, dear, dear," said Miss Thompson, "Sean, does he know that boy?"

But there was no answer. Sean had also run off, to another shivering, homeless boy standing on a corner nearby. He, like Jonathan, handed over the hidden food he had stored in his wool coat and then his shillings.

* * * * * *

February the sixth came overcast, with a drizzling rain in the very early morning and a slight chill. However, as the sun rose from behind the clouds at a bit past eight the brisk air was bearable. If one stood and faced the sun, the warmth that promised spring was certainly felt. The once snowy streets where now clear and even the dampness of the alleys and fields was slowly drying.

Inside the apartment on Charring Cross, Jonathan awoke as the day lightened and made his way downstairs to the small kitchen. His father was already there, silently reading a paper and sipping tea with a spot of cream in it. Jonathan quietly filled his tea egg with aromatic black tea and placed it in his chosen cup. From a pot on the stove he added almost boiling water and let it steep for two minutes. On the table was a wicker basket filled with small cakes, surely from Miss Thompson and most likely delivered late last night. She seemed to be, well, *about quite often*, Jonathan noticed, and doting on the men with all the care and concern of a wife and a mother. As far as Jonathan was concerned, that was perfectly welcome. Though he missed his mother dearly and had for all the years he lived on the streets, now he was beginning to accept her passing, as much as one could expect. Possibly the appearance of Miss Thompson lent a gentle hand. Besides her great beauty, she was kind, tender and actually, quite fun. *The house could use a little laughter*, Jonathan thought, *and Miss Thompson brings that in abundance*. She didn't even mind the teasing the 'boys' dealt out and could come back with a clever remark that was jarring and unexpected. Sean, Jonathan and Captain Moore eagerly looked forward to her visits and outings.

As Jonathan sipped his tea, he occasionally looked at his father and sometimes even took in a breath as if he was about to say something. Then he would stop, second guess himself and exhale. After repeating this two or three times, his father took notice, and after the fourth or fifth inhale and exhale, he finally put down his paper and stared at the boy.

"Jonathan? You have something to say?" his father asked softly, knowing the subject that was about to be addressed.

"Why, yes," Jonathan said, "though I do not want to interrupt your reading."

"Well," his father said, smiling easily, "it has been interrupted now, so let us have at it."

Jonathan took another deep breath and stared into his father's eyes. He wanted so much to stand at attention, to stare out the window as he did in Captain Walker's cabin so many times before. The staring allowed him to think and speak clearly. But now, looking into his father's eyes, which became dark with sadness each time he asked to sail with the *Danielle*, made it difficult to express his thoughts. He knew his father would miss him. Once again, his father's eyes were now dimming once again.

"Of course, the *Danielle* sails this afternoon, as you know, and I wish to discuss my sailing along with her. I recognize we hold different opinions on the matter, however...I just can't seem to let it go."

"I understand that, Jonathan. The sea is a strong lure for you, as it is for me as well," said his father, softly. "It is within our blood to sail, as it was in my father's and his father before him. And some day you will return. But as I have said, I have only been with you for five weeks and I am not ready to part with you. Not yet."

"Nor do I want to part with you," Jonathan said. "I wish we could sail away together, on our own adventures - silly I know, but it is a dream I have." Jonathan was now seeing a ship in his mind with his father at the helm, himself in the tops, scouting for French frigates.

"I think it will be a long time before I am ready to command a ship, Jonathan. And even then, having you aboard would not be fair, would it?" his father said. "I could only favor you above others and discipline would be hard to maintain, of course – though, it is a nice sentiment, my son."

Jonathan became quiet for a few moments. He felt that staying home while his friends sailed off would be unbearable, and missing his father just as horrid. *Torn again*, he thought.

"I only know no matter what I do, I am between the devil and the deep blue sea," he mumbled. "And I don't even know what that means. I had heard the men say it on occasion aboard the *Poseidon*."

His father chuckled a bit and reached out to hold his son's hand. "It is a comment about a difficult task aboard a ship. The planking of the side of the ship that meets the water is called a *devil*, and it needs much caulking with pitch to keep the water out; a difficult task, especially considering that one is suspended over the side as the ship is moving through the waves, becoming soaking wet just inches above the sea. It is a bad place to be - between the devil and the deep blue sea."

Jonathan nodded. "Yes, and that is where I am – between staying with you and…"

Just then, Sean appeared from upstairs, scratching himself everywhere imaginable, yawning, stretching and finally asking: "I assume that is a basket from Miss Thompson, bless her every way to Sunday! And a bit of tea? *Spa-len-did! Spa-len-did!*" he said, pronouncing the word much as the King had done just a few weeks ago.

After breakfast was completed, Jonathan assisted Sean in his packing and preparation. With a heavy heart he warned Sean of the dangers and requirements of the mission.

"Make sure, Sean Flagon, that you stay close to Hudson, Hicks and Harrison. They will teach you well. And mind Steward! He is a cantankerous old fish-wife to be sure, but he means well, and -"

"Aye, aye, Jonny Boy," Sean said quickly. "I will remember it all. It's not my first trip, don't ya know? I'll be fine. And you behave for yer Da and Miss Thompson. Stay out of trouble, now."

In the early afternoon, the boys, Captain Moore and of course Miss Thompson, boarded the carriage and began the short journey to the London docks. Sean was in his seamen's garb and wool coat, Jonathan and his father in their uniforms, and Miss Thompson was dressed smartly in a warm coat, woolen grey and long, almost to the ground.

Jonathan tried to smile, but only a small tear came to his eye. "Sean?" asked Jonathan meekly. "Would you grant me a special favor?"

"Surely, Jonny boy," Sean said, still digging through his sack, checking to make sure he had everything.

"Would you give this to Miss Dowdeswell with my apologies and my best wishes? Tell her I hope to see her again soon?"

He held in his hand a small, delicately-wrapped package with a golden bow about it. Sean looked up and his eyes widened.

"Is that the dolphin? Of course I will give it to her. I – I'm sorry, Jonny."

Jonathan gave the package to his friend, then turned to look out the window. As Miss Thompson faced Nathaniel, she could see the indecision on his face. He quickly looked out the window as well. All rode the rest of the way in silence.

4
The Nemesis

The new docks of London at Wapping, rarely held warships, but on this day, HMS *Doggard*, of course known to all as the *Danielle*, was moored front and center off Reardon Path. A crowd of a few dozen were always in attendance to marvel at the ship, as it had become a tourist attraction of sorts. As the carriage slowed, Jonathan looked out and noticed not only the *Danielle*, but another ship.

"The *Trident*," he announced flatly, and all turned to see the great ship, though it was slightly dwarfed by the much larger *Danielle*. At a recent party held by Captain Walker, for the purpose of celebrating the sailing of the crew on their next assignment, they had been informed by none other than Mister Langley himself that he had been assigned as Captain of the *Trident*. He had also received his orders to join a small squadron of ships off the French coast. Maybe they would see each other, many had said, and all laughed knowing that the ocean was so vast, the chances were slim.

The carriage came to an abrupt stop at the wharf and slowly they all exited, with Nathaniel assisting Miss Thompson. From their position on the street, they could look almost directly across the way to the deck of the *Danielle* and see the crew busying themselves. Some regulars were not there, as Mister Langley had *stolen a few*, as Captain Walker happily pointed out to all who would listen, namely the well-seasoned Gallotta, Smalls and Jenkins. However, Jonathan did see Steward and Harrison, and Watt, ever present at the wheel. Of course, squeaky-voiced Koonts was aboard with his giant book, collecting information, writing names and watching all that came on and went off the ship. At least Garvey was still there, and Smith and Jones, so Sean would have a few good friends about his own age to keep him company.

HMS Danielle *and* HMS Trident *at Wapping*

"Off I go, Jonny Boy!" Sean said, and for the first time, he finally took in the weight of what was happening. He had been with Jonathan since they were young boys, six years old, through the hardships on the streets of London and the trials of their lives at sea. They had seen morning suns rising above the waves, expanse of sails spread to catch the breeze, roaring guns, sword fights, storms, death and treasure - yet always together.

"Oh my, Jonny," Sean said with a tear as he hugged his best friend tightly. "I-I will miss you."

Jonathan fought to hold back his tears.

"You are my brother," he said to Sean, still holding him, "and we will sail together again, someday. God's speed, Sean Flagon."

Many present on the dock and aboard the *Danielle* saw the boys embrace. The crew of the ship watched in sadness as all were aware that Midshipman Moore, their good luck charm, would not be traveling with them.

As Moore watched this scene, he saw Captain William Walker watching as well. William stood stone faced, yet staring at his friend, as if to say: *You must let him go. Do not withhold from him his rightful destiny upon the sea. I will do all in my power to return him safely.*

If those words were actually in Walker's mind, it mattered not. They were now in Nathaniel's. He witnessed the sobbing of both boys and also heard the sniffles of Miss Thompson. *I remember being a newly promoted midshipman,* he thought. *To be at sea, I would have run away with my shipmates, even against the wishes of my father.* He did not love his family any less, yet the lure of the ocean was strong in the Moores, like the pull of the moon that caused the tides; it could not be stopped. He knew in his heart that Jonathan was a Moore, just like the generations before who took to the waves. Yes, he wanted to be with his son, however…

"Jonathan," his father said. "I see your heart is breaking and mine aches as well. I love you, but I can not hurt you. I will go back with the driver and return with your gear. Go. Before I change my mind."

Jonathan slowly let go of Sean and turned to face Captain Moore. He felt no joy with this news, for immediately, his longing for the sea was replaced with a growing sadness of separation.

"I will make you proud and I will return as fast as I can," he said, embracing his father. After a long moment, Miss Thompson bent to kiss Jonathan, then turned away to the carriage.

"Jonathan," Nathaniel said, now holding the boy squarely by the shoulders, "inform Captain Walker that I, as the King's personal adjunct, have assigned Midshipmen Jonathan Moore to HMS *Danielle*, until further notice."

Nathaniel watched as Jonathan and Sean ran up the gang plank to greet Koontz. As the boys turned to wave good-bye, another midshipman, slightly taller and heavier than Jonathan also walked up the plank. His eyes were on Captain Moore.

Sean reached the deck first and heard a soft *meow* just loud enough to startle him.

"Stewie!" he called and ran on to greet his favorite ship's cat. The great mouser, Stewie was adopted by Sean during his captivity aboard the *Danielle,* before her capture by the British. There were many cats aboard and they were prized by the crew, for the most part, because they kept the rats and mice in check. Stewie was certainly a favorite as he looked remarkably like Steward, with his whitish beard and scruffy look.

"Did ya miss me?" said Sean as he scooped up his pet.

Jonathan waved one last time to his father and stood at the top of the gangway, laughing at Sean.

As Nathaniel ducked his head into the carriage, the other midshipman moved quickly behind Jonathan, unseen. With a dipped shoulder, he pushed Jonathan hard, causing him to stumble, strike the side of the plank, drop his belongings on deck, and fall dozens of feet directly toward the cold water below. As Jonathan fell, he looked upwards and caught a dizzying glimpse of a turning face and then a pony-tail moving away fast.

Was I pushed? he thought.

Jonathan hit the water hard and the icy waves covered him immediately. His wool coat and uniform suddenly weighed many times more than when dry and he struggled to recover to the surface. After much thrashing, his head reached air once again. He gulped a large breath. Looking to his right he saw the *Danielle* bobbing closer to him, now pushing his body toward the side of the pier. *I will be crushed,* he thought.

"Help! Overboard at the plank!" he yelled.

Sean, recognized the voice and called for others to assist as he ran to the plank and tossed a rope over the side. Jonathan grasped the line immediately. It would only be seconds before he would be crushed.

With the help of Koonts and several others, Sean began pulling Jonathan out of the water. They worked fast and strained mightily. Jonathan suddenly was lurched upwards from the water, and due to the crew's speed and strength, almost flew over the gangplank. Crew members immediately stripped him of wet clothes, wrapped him in a dry blanket or two, and comforted him as he shook from the cold. Claise, who was nearby, went to retrieve a hot cup of coffee.

Jonathan accepted the drink gratefully and repeatedly said *'No problem, I am fine'* and *'not sure what happened. I must need to regain my sea legs'.*

Harrison appeared on the gangway and observed Jonathan, hair still wet, being babied by the crew. With a puzzled look on his face, he approached the scene.

"Well, Mister Moore," Harrison said, "did you forget to bathe this morning and decided a swim would do?"

The crew laughed briefly, but the revelry was cut short as Captain Walker appeared, flanked by two unknown lieutenants. Jonathan looked up as the others stood at attention, then scrambled to his feet and saluted the best he could, as he was still wrapped in blankets.

The Captain exploded.

"By all the sirens and harpies, what is going on here?!" he yelled. "This is not a circus or a bath house! Moore? What is the meaning of this?"

Jonathan cleared his throat and tried to speak, but nothing came out. He had forgotten what a temper Captain Walker possessed, and after all the peaceful and serene days he had spent with him at his home, Jonathan was surprised by how loud and angry the *Captain-at-sea* could be. It was Koonts that spoke first.

"Begging, your pardon, Captain," he said in his high, squeaky voice, "it seems Mister Moore had a misstep and ended up taking a plunge off the gangway. We retrieved him, no harm at all."

"A misstep?" said Walker. "Is that the case, Mister Moore?"

Jonathan thought about what he had seen as he fell, just a blurry face and a ponytail - however, there were many ponytails aboard the *Danielle*, in fact, there were probably more bobbed heads aboard than not. *And the push?* he thought. *Could it have been an accident? Maybe someone with a crate or sack of flour? Turning sharply? Not even knowing what they had bumped into? That is the most likely scenario.*

"It does seem so, sir." Jonathan answered. "I believe I bumped into something, or someone, and over I went. An accident, I am sure."

The face of Captain Walker scrunched a trifle and he looked at Jonathan quizzically. His temper seemed to be building.

"Very well, then," the Captain said, holding back an obvious outburst. "Please be more careful, Mister Moore. This is a fighting ship of His Majesty's Navy and we conduct ourselves with professionalism and grace at all times. And Mister Koonts?"

"Yes, sir?" Koonts said, now expecting the outburst to be aimed at him.

"Make sure the deck and gang plank are clear of obstruction!" bellowed the Captain. "By all the saints and sinners, having officers tripping over debris and disorderly loading of supplies? I want this corrected *now!* Mister Harrison? Get Mister Moore to the doctor and get him some dry clothes! When you are finished, I want to see you both in my cabin! And Claise! Blast it! That coffee smells wonderful! Get me a pot immediately and for God's sake, teach Steward the proper procedure needed to make a decent brew!"

"Yes, sir!" Claise replied. The Captain spun on his heels and marched away aft to his cabin.

As the crowd dispersed, Claise leaned over to Jonathan and said: "Nice to see you again, Mister Moore."

Later, in the Captain's cabin, Jonathan stood at rigid attention with Harrison by his side, staring out the rear window. Indeed, the room had been repaired completely after the *Danielle* was won in battle. It now contained a little more comfort than the cabin of the *Poseidon* and Walker easily fit a larger table, two comfortable chairs, two sets of drawers instead of one, a handsome cabinet that held a sextant and mapping devices, and even four lanterns hanging in the rafters of a slightly higher ceiling.

Walker was sitting in one of the comfortable chairs that he had pulled up to his table. Still standing were the two lieutenants Jonathan had seen on deck. As ordered, there was a steaming pot of coffee on the table, along with a few pastries, a cup of milk and a plate of cheesed and toasted anchovies. Walker sipped the coffee silently as he considered the assorted maps and papers on his desk. Finally he looked up.

"Mister Harrison? I think you know the two senior lieutenants assigned? Jonathan, this is Lieutenant Holtz, my second in command, and Lieutenant Blake."

Both men nodded to Jonathan. Holtz was almost as tall as Captain Walker and had a surprised look on his face. Jonathan waited for him to speak, as if he were about to ask a question, or seek clarification on what he had just heard, however, as the moment lasted, Jonathan realized that was not the case. Holtz just looked that way, probably all the time. He had a dark complexion and his beard looked like it had been growing for more than a day or two. His hair was dark and short, his eyes permanently squinted, the color indiscernible.

Blake was shorter and his pale, round face seemed disinterested, as if he had better things to do than attend to the Captain. He looked out the window and glanced about the cabin, as if in his own world. Not once did he look anyone in the eye.

"Mister Moore," Walker said without looking up from his meal, "you are to report to the deck and assist Mister Koonts in logging ship's stores and crew until your father delivers your things. Once they arrive, stow everything away in the cockpit, clean your uniform and dry it, and introduce yourself to the other two midshipmen aboard. You will be joined on this cruise by Wayne Spears and Timothy Lane. You are dismissed."

"Yes, sir!" Jonathan said, and spun on his heels, leaving the cabin as fast as he could.

Captain Moore and his carriage reappeared at the dock at just past four as the sun was beginning to set. With him was a servant who carried a large foot locker and a few extra boxes. Nathaniel walked steadily up to the *Danielle,* then up the plank and instructed the servant to set the locker and supplies down on deck and return to the carriage.

"Good see you, Captain!" said Koontz, loudly, as if to warn the surrounding crew to stand at attention. All snapped straight as Nathaniel tipped his hat ever so slightly. Within a few moments, Captain Walker appeared with his two new lieutenants in tow, along with Mister Harrison. Steward was also present, looking as grumpy and frumpy as ever.

"Return to your duties, men," boomed Walker, then turned to address his friend. "It is a pleasure and honor to see you Nate."

"Thank you, William," said Captain Moore softly. "I will only be a minute; don't want to delay your departure. If I could have a word with Midshipman Moore, I would be most grateful."

"Steward?" called the Captain. "Please send for the midshipman, on the double."

"Aye sir," Steward said, "and I assume ya mean Jonathan, as Cap'n Moore probably couldn't give a care fer any of the other midshipmen, as they ain't related whatsoever."

"I have noticed the new placard on the ship, William. HMS *Doggard*? I believe a parting gift from Admiral Barrow?"

"Yes," said Walker with a grimace, "my only solace is in the fact that within a few months, the good Admiral Barrow will be eaten alive by mosquitoes."

"And you will be sailing the beautiful waters of the Caribbean again," said Nathaniel quickly, changing the subject. "Certainly your mission is a peach, but with so many Spanish and French settlements in the islands the chance of a prize should be relatively high, don't you agree?"

"One can always hope," said Walker, smiling once again. "And there may be a few pirates as well, however, one look at the *Dog*- er, I mean…" he paused, "I mean the *Danielle* and her seventy-four guns will have most of them running."

"And what of Gorman? Is he aboard for this adventure?"

"It is too tame a duty for him I am afraid," said Walker chuckling. "He is off the Cape Verde Islands to do a little checking on the Portuguese and the Spanish at Santiago. He is to take the *Paladin* there within the month."

With that, Jonathan appeared and stood at attention. Even though this important Captain was his father, ship's protocol demanded formal manners and actions.

Captain Walker and the others said their good-byes and smartly left Nathaniel and Jonathan alone.

"Jonathan? Why are you wearing seaman's garb?" his father asked, matter-of-factly.

"I had an accident, sir, a silly one actually. I … I fell off the gangplank into the water. Just clumsy, Father, having to get reacquainted with the ship, that's all. I was very excited!"

His father was astounded. "What? My lord! Jonathan, you could have been killed!"

There was an uncomfortable pause. Then his father relaxed a bit and smiled.

"Well, be careful Jonathan, and mind Captain Walker and Steward. Watch out for Sean. Remember, sometimes, not all dangers are flying the French tricolor!"

"I am not sure what you mean, exactly, father."

The Captain looked grave for a moment and sat on a crate nearby, the better to look Jonathan in the eye.

"It might be nothing, Jonathan, but the night you arrived in London aboard the *Danielle,* I was attacked on my way to the dock."

"Father!" exclaimed Jonathan, "Were you hurt?"

"No, no I wasn't. A young man appeared out of the shadows and tried to club me on the head, clumsy as he was. He ran off before I could get a good look at him, though with a quick glance, he resembled an old adversary of mine. We were midshipmen together for a while and were in competition for ship assignments. We both became Captains at about the same time, but I believe I got the better ships and assignments. As usual, many men blame their misfortune on others, before looking at themselves. He may still hold a grudge."

"Where is he now?" asked Jonathan.

"He is assigned a sixth rate, a brig, the twenty-four gun *HMS Simplex*. He is currently escorting merchant vessels and the like. Not a plum assignment by any means," Captain Moore said.

"What is his name?" inquired Jonathan.

"Spears," his father said, "Captain Derrick Spears. I believe he has a son about your age."

This froze Jonathan to the bone. He remembered that Captain Walker asked him to introduce himself to the two new midshipmen, Lane … and Spears. *Should I mention this to my father?* he thought. *Another reason to keep me ashore?*

"There are a few extra supplies in your locker," his father said finally, standing up and adjusting his hat. "Look for them when you have a moment." Nathaniel took a second to stare at his son intently. "I will miss you."

"And I, you!" Jonathan said sadly.

With that, the two Moores, father and son, smartly saluted each other.

* * * * * *

Upon assembling the crew for inspection, Lieutenants Holtz, Blake and Harrison took their positions on the poop next to Midshipmen Moore, Lane and Spears, all dressed and in a line, facing the bow and the crew. Jonathan tried to look to his side, to see the other midshipmen, though it was difficult. He could barely make out their shapes, let alone their faces.

All of the men present were arranged on deck and many in the tops, ready to set sail. The marines were lined up along both sides at the rail and they stood at attention. Shortly, Captain Walker appeared from his cabin and stood in front of the deck, with Koontz and Watt joining immediately. He took a deep breath before addressing the men as a group.

"I welcome all the old *Danis* and the new," Walker said, booming his voice so it could carry and be heard by all. "I am a fair captain and I play by the book. I also share the riches we may accumulate and I share that by the book as well. Do your duties as best as you can, and if you can't… do them even better!"

This caused a small wave of laughter throughout the crew. "Respect your officers, for they lead you, and respect your new brothers, for they will save your life."

This solemn note was accepted by the crew as they looked at faces familiar and new, and realized that for better or worse, they were a family with a mission to perform.

"Lastly," said Walker. "It has come to my attention that some of you have been referring to our ship as HMS *Doggard,* as it is set on the placard affixed to the stern. I will remind you that the most grievous offense aboard this ship, one that will be met with the most serious and painful lashing, will be set aside for those who refer to this *beautiful* lady by that infernal name! Her name is the *Danielle*. From the moment we cast off, all will refer to her at all times by that name. Am I understood?"

"Yes, sir!" and "the *Danielle*!" came the response from well over three hundred voices, many fully understanding and agreeing with the order.

"Then add sail and cast off!" said Walker.

The crew ran to their stations quickly and a modest amount of sail was let down on all three masts as the mooring lines were released. Slowly and gracefully, the ship caught the wind and left the dock, magically transforming from the dreaded *Doggard,* into the dashing HMS *Danielle*.

Jonathan left the main deck, and dragging his small locker that had been left by the gangway in a neat stack with his other items, soon reached the cockpit, the room where he would stay with the other midshipmen. The room was a small, dark and crowded place on the orlop deck, just below the two gun decks. It was aft, right behind the mizzen mast, the rear most of the three tall masts of the *Danielle*. The rest of the crew, the seamen and able seamen, all were berthed on the orlop, yet all in front, or before, the mizzen mast. Some men actually stayed on the gun decks in hammocks, not the most coveted place, actually quite dangerous. In a storm, a loose gun could destroy many things in its way and kill a man in an instant.

Jonathan slowly opened the small door to the cockpit. No one was there. Lifting his locker, he entered alone.

The room was certainly not as spacious as the Captain's quarters, nor even close to the bunk room the Lieutenants shared. It was just large enough to fit three bunks, one atop the others, and have a small area by the door. Each corner had a wooden chest standing, one labeled 'Lane' and the other 'Spears'. Jonathan put his much smaller locker in the remaining corner. It would be strange not having Sean and Claise as roommates, living in the *closet*, as they had called their past quarters aboard the now lost HMS *Poseidon*.

A knock came to the door. Jonathan opened it, expecting to see his new roommates; however, he was pleasantly surprised to see Sean.

"Well, well, well, if it isn't our little sardine!" Sean said referring to Jonathan's mishap at the gangway.

"Come in, Sean!" Jonathan said excitedly. "A bit bigger than the *closet*, but still a closet, don't you think?"

Sean looked around and nodded.

"A bit quieter than where I will be," he said. "I am now in with the rest of the crew, in a hammock in the orlop before the mast. It will be lively, I am told, and I won't lack for company. There are almost three hundred men aboard, Jonathan, can you believe it? With three lieutenants including Mister Harrison and a few other officers as well. And there are twice the marines we had aboard the *Poseidon*."

"Not to mention the midshipmen, of course," Jonathan said, smiling.

At that moment, the door to the cockpit opened and as if on cue, two midshipmen entered. With four boys in the room, it was crowded to be sure and Sean tried to wiggle his way out into the hall, but the taller of the two new midshipmen stood in his way.

"Pardon me, sir" Sean said, reaching for where his hat would be if he had one, to tip it in a salute of sorts.

The taller midshipman glared at Sean.

"And just what do you think you are doing in these quarters, seaman?" he said angrily, gritting his teeth into a tight smile that looked anything but welcoming.

Sean did not answer right away. He maneuvered himself to the door and stared at all three of the midshipmen. It was clear that the taller of the two was slightly larger than Jonathan, the other was shorter, but stockier. He was, actually, a bit plump.

"He was visiting me," Jonathan said. "He is my guest."

The taller one turned to Jonathan and looked at him for a moment, sizing him up. As he spun his head, a brownish-blonde ponytail was visible.

Interesting, thought Jonathan.

The tall midshipman then looked to Sean with a slightly less angry smile appearing on his face.

"Friends? Well that is cozy, isn't it, Lane?"

"Yes it is, Spears," Lane said.

Jonathan now knew who was who. Spears, possibly the man who had attacked his father, had a pony-tail. *It is all still circumstantial,* thought Jonathan. *However, I better keep an eye on him.*

"I am Midshipman Jonathan Moore," Jonathan said, extending his hand to Lane, who took it heartily, and then to Spears who did not.

"I know who you are," Spears said. "I've seen your name in the papers. A hero, right Lane?"

Lane just nodded, not sure if he should smile, frown, or do nothing. So he just stood still.

"Jonathan has even met the King -" Sean began.

"Did I ask you a question, carious swab? Then why are you speaking?" yelled Spears. "You may not have heard, but a crewman doesn't speak to an officer unless spoken to! Don't you understand? Or are you stupid?"

"Hold on, there, Spears," Jonathan said. "Sean is a valuable member of the crew and has special favor with the Captain -"

However, as Jonathan spoke, Spears pushed Sean hard, causing him to stumble backwards out the door and slam against the wall across from the cockpit door.

"Get out of here and don't return unless I invite you!" Spears yelled.

Jonathan had reached the boiling point.

"Spears!" he yelled.

"What, Moore? I have a right mind to report this man to the Captain for punishment! He didn't even salute when I entered the room!" With that he stepped into the hall and gave Sean another push, this time knocking him to the ground.

Jonathan moved quickly to the hall, ready to defend his friend.

"A gnat couldn't have flapped a wing it was so crowded in there," argued Jonathan. "He tried to salute. He did tip his cap. And..."

"And what, Moore?" Spears said, now turning to face Jonathan directly. "Do you think I care about your opinion? You're a new midshipman and I have been one for the past two years, so mind your place!"

Jonathan looked Spears in the eye. He spoke slowly and calmly.

"You have no rank above me and certainly no manners either. If you should ever touch seaman Flagon again, I will learn of it. And I will have you on the deck so fast you will think you are a fish out of water."

Spears held Jonathan's gaze, then slowly chuckled.

"Moore, I seriously doubt that *you*–" Spears said, now pushing Jonathan backwards with his open hands on every other word, "- can *do* anything *about it!*"

Surely this Spears character delighted in pushing people around, especially ones that he had either the rank or size advantage over. Jonathan had seen his type before: a bully. They seemed to be everywhere, not smart enough to get through life using their wits, so they used violence. While living on the streets of London, Jonathan saw many and he mostly avoided them, however, from time to time he had to face them, try to use his head and sometimes also his fists to make the best of it.

"You had better watch yourself," said Spears with a

little laugh, "Or *you* will be the *fish* out of water!"

Jonathan looked quickly at Sean, who was now getting up off the floor, but not all the way. Sean was on all fours like a low table, and not moving, positioned directly behind Spears, just staying put. And that gave Jonathan an idea.

He relaxed his stance, as if to signal to Spears that he had given up, and then, after a moment, he exploded with amazing speed and shoved Spears quite harshly, causing him to stumble backwards, then clumsily trip over Sean. The thud of Spears' head hitting the deck sounded like a cannon ball being dropped to the planks.

"I warned you that I would put you on the deck!" yelled Jonathan, angrily. He immediately leaped over Sean and landed on Spears. They began tussling. A few blows were landed. Suddenly, a voice boomed loud and clear. It was Lieutenant Holtz.

"By all the Gods!" yelled Holtz, his normally quizzical face still on. "What in the world is going on here?"

Jonathan and Spears immediately stopped fighting and stood at attention. Behind Holtz, Mister Harrison appeared.

"Jonathan? Spears?" asked Harrison. "Are you fighting? And in front of a seaman? Truly unbelievable!"

"We must advise the Captain!" Holtz said.

Harrison looked to Jonathan, knowing that the Captain would not be pleased and Jonathan would certainly not fare well. Though he was the Captains favorite, Walker was always firm, but fair. He would punish both Jonathan and Spears.

"Yes, we must," said Harrison. He had no choice.

Of course, the Captain called Spears, Lane and Jonathan into his cabin. Even Steward, who brought in cheesed anchovies and some soft bread, was surprised upon hearing of the altercation. All the Lieutenants and Koonts were present, all was shocked into silence.

Walker was sitting on his new comfy chair, like a king

on a throne, however, he began inhaling a great amount of air. The old dragon was back. He paused, then, exploded.

"What in the world of men happened? Moore, somehow you manage to fall off the gangway, then less than an hour to sea, you engage in a shoving match with Midshipmen Spears! There will be no more buffoonery or there will be hell to pay! Moore, explain why you were seen striking Midshipman Spears!"

Standing at attention, shaking like a leaf but still staring out the window, Jonathan told the Captain exactly what had happened. However, when the Captain asked Spears for his version, it was quite different.

"Sir, I believed seaman Flagon could use some instruction on etiquette," Spears said calmly and respectfully. "I believed he did not know the cockpit was for officers only. I politely asked him to leave. That is when Moore struck me."

"That is a lie!" Jonathan called.

"How dare you call me a liar!" cried Spears.

"Captain, he pushed Sean to the ground more than once, then attacked *me!*"

"Silence!" boomed Walker. The Captain sensed this situation was not as it seemed. He didn't know Wayne Spears at all and barely knew his father, a sort-of malcontent; a captain in the lower echelon of names in the Admiralty. He did, however, know Jonathan Moore, and starting a school-room tumble was not in his character. Walker remembered how Jonathan had turned an ugly situation with a past shipmate, Gallotta, into a fast friendship. Even the common seamen considered Jonathan a true gentleman. *No matter,* he decided, *I can't show favoritism.*

"I have heard your part of the story, Midshipman Moore! I find the whole issue extremely unbelievable and distasteful! Lane, you were there, what did you see?"

Lane paused for a moment, then, looking at Spears, said "It is just as Midshipman Spears has explained it, sir."

Jonathan was shocked. It was clear to him that Lane

was lying for Spears.

Walker now sat silently, glaring at the three midshipmen before him. He grumbled for a few moments, then stood so quickly that all three youngsters jumped back. He drew in another unbelievable amount of air. This explosion was so grand, that all the crew that had happened to come near the stern to *unofficially* listen, jumped at least a full foot in the air.

"This will not stand!" Walker boomed. "Schoolyard tussles aboard His Majesty's ship? I will know all that goes on aboard my ship, as I know all the men and their temperaments! It is my world here, gentlemen, and I use the word *gentlemen* lightly! Lieutenant Blake?" boomed Walker.

"Yes sir!" Blake said, snapping to attention, afraid the wrath of Captain Walker would now be aimed at him.

"Midshipmen Moore and Spears must learn to work together," bellowed the Captain, thinking for a moment or two. "Have them get pitch and brushes and check the delve on both sides of the ship, on the double!"

"Yes, sir!" called Blake, and he immediately ran out of the room to both carry out the captain's order and escape any collateral fire that the dragon was expending.

"Midshipmen, dismissed!" Walker stated forcefully, and all three turned and ran out of the cabin as fast as they could.

"If I may, Captain?" said Koonts.

Much calmer, now that the requisite blasts had been loosed, Walker turned to Koonts, his anger completely subsided.

"I would think we should ask Sean Flagon for his side of the story, yes?"

"To what purpose, Mister Koonts?" asked the Captain. "He would agree with Jonathan, of course."

"Yes, sir," said Koonts.

"I certainly know what is going on here," the Captain continued.

5

Between the Devil and the Deep Blue Sea

After a full day at sea, the men were back in their habit, cleaning decks with holystones and water, polishing everything metal, painting everything wooden and tightening every rope and sail to give the *Danielle* more speed. She was moving at a smart eight knots, headed due west toward the Caribbean Sea and the Bahamas.

The food, made now by Claise, was certainly better fare than Steward had prepared nightly for the crew during the last mission. All consumed it gratefully.

"I had found some special spices in an old shop near my sister's house in the east end," Claise said to Garvey as he scooped a bowlful of sweet curried beef and potato for the youngster, "and I spent all my pay on them. They should serve us well."

Garvey thanked him and walked carefully to an unusually silent table on deck and sat with a group of unusually silent men who were intently concentrating on the tastes within their bowls. They were all coming to the conclusion that Claise was a master, and a master on a large scale. All his meals were wonderful.

"Quite the change from Stewards slop" said Smith as he gulped down a spoonful.

"Better than my mums, I tell ya," added Jones.

Other men could smell wafting aroma as they worked in the sails and rigging, awaiting their turn at the table. Even Steward had to agree, as he peeked into the pot.

"Ah, Claise," Steward said as he sniffed the simmering stew, "It do smell like fare from one o' those finer shops in London. Ya will have ta give me the recipe so I can duplicate it myself!"

Just then, Mister Harrison happened by and said "You might also want to give him your head and hands, Claise. Steward needs more than a recipe to make a good meal!"

The crew within earshot erupted in hearty laughter.

Jonathan heard the laughter, but had no idea as to what humor had caused it. He could see nothing of the happenings on the deck, as he was suspended over the side, on a plank held by a rope harness. By his side, he had a bucket of black, tar-like pitch, thick and hot. It, too, was secured with rope to the plank he sat upon. He also had a length of wood, like a broom handle, with a thick gathering of stiff animal hair tied to the end. He dipped this brush into the pail of pitch for the hundredth time and splattered it on the side of the *Danielle*, spreading it between two adjoining side planks. After he finished all he could reach from his sitting position, Jonathan would call upwards to one of the deck hands, who would adjust the harness holding the plank. At times this would move him a few more feet toward the stern or upwards, and at other times, to his dismay, he would be moved closer to the swirling water below. Jonathan would then start applying pitch to the next section of the ship.

At the face of this, it would seem that the job of applying pitch to the delve was not altogether too harsh a punishment. However, the *Danielle* was at top speed and the constant spray of ice-cold water dousing Jonathan's legs was slowly numbing them. There was also the sticky pitch that seemed to get everywhere: in hair, on face and all over clothing.

I am between the delve and the deep blue sea, as my father had said. The only happiness I have, said Jonathan to himself, *is found in the knowledge that Midshipman Spears is suffering the same discomfort as I. A petty thought, yes, but still comforting.*

Eventually, Jonathan finished for the day, (it would take at least two more to complete the entire port side) and retired to his bunk. Lane was there and nodded coldly, then got up to leave. It was now getting dark and Spears would return soon. It gave Jonathan only a few moments to change from his wet and tar-stained seaman's garb and put on his uniform. First, however, he opened his locker and took out his belongings.

Inside there was a supply of wool socks, nightshirts, an extra pair of shoes and a warm woolen hat, much like the one Steward had tossed overboard so many months ago.

"New life!" Steward had said then. And at that time, it seemed exciting and wonderful. Now, his life was tainted by his troubles.

His mood changed for the better as he found a small paper-wrapped box within his locker, with an elegantly written note attached. It read *"To assist you in finding your way home to us"* and was signed by Miss Barbara Thompson. Inside, was a small compass, made of the finest metals and seemingly coated, in part, with gold. It was an amazing treasure and Jonathan gazed in wonder at its beauty. He then placed it in the pocket of his uniform coat that was hanging on a peg by his bunk.

Another wrapped package was quite larger, at least two feet in length, and this had a more heavy script on its note that read: *"This was my own piece. It took me around the world and back again, through adversity and hell itself. Please employ it along with all your wit and industry to come back to your small family. We will miss you. God's speed, my son."* This note was signed by his father.

Jonathan removed the plain brown wrapping paper to discover a wooden box with a simple silver latch in the center. He opened the box and gazed upon a wonderfully crafted telescope, the wood stained in dark cherry and rings of gold around the eye piece and the lens. He expanded the instrument to its full length. The movement was smooth and yet tight and heavy. It was obviously well made and would be a prized possession. *I must protect this from wandering hands,* Jonathan thought.

He smiled broadly at the gifts, but what made him

even more delighted was the fact that both notes, one from his father and one from Miss Thompson, used the words 'us' and 'we' instead of 'me' and "I". *Could it be,* he thought, *that my father and Miss Thompson do fancy each other?*

The journey from London to the Bahaman Islands was routine and as much as could be expected was expected and dealt with. Leaks were plugged, as Jonathan and Spears had completed their punishment and caulked all the delve almost completely. Anything metal was polished daily, everything wooden painted, and life aboard the *Danielle* was actually calm, yet busy. Meals came and went, watches were completed and marines drilled and practiced shooting and sword play. Luckily for Jonathan, he was able to eat meals with Sean and avoid Spears and Lane at all times except two. One was while sleeping, and it was known by all of Jonathan's close friends that he literally slept with one eye open. The other time he could not avoid Spears was during his lessons with either Koonts, Harrison or on the rare occasion, Mister Watt. In these sessions, Spears was well behaved and showed no aggression toward Jonathan at all.

Before his going to bed, Jonathan made a habit of collecting Steward and together, they would visit Sean in the orlop. They would appear and greet all, most of the crew still saluting Jonathan out of respect. They would then settle in as Sean attempted to read from King Arthur. Jonathan would hold pages while he lay next to Sean, so he could also follow along. It was slow going at first, as the legend was no nursery rhyme.

"It befell in the days of…Uther the Dragon..."

"Uther *Pen*dragon," corrected Steward, calmly and caringly, as he picked fleas and untangled mats of hair off Stewie.

"Uther *Pen*dragon," Sean continued, "when he was king of all England, and so….re-gend-ed?" asked Sean.

"Reigned," said Steward. "It means to rule, like a King

is supposed to do, yes?"

"It is spelled strangely," said Sean.

"I told you it was chaos," added Jonathan.

"Keep reading, young Flagon," said Steward, a little more forcibly than before.

"When he was king of all England, and so reigned, that there was a mighty duke in. . . Cornwall - Hey, I have been to Cornwall! Remember that little boy we met on the streets that had the lute with no strings. Jonathan?"

"For the love of the saints," Steward angrily, "read the blessed book and concentrate!"

"That there was a mighty duke in Cornwall," Sean continued, "that held war against him long time."

Each night another few pages fell and it was not long before Sean was reading well enough for others to listen. At times, he had a crowd of ten or more enjoying his reading of the tale.

On about the eleventh day at sea, Mister Harrison appeared on deck and found Jonathan at his post, on the bow, looking straight ahead as the *Danielle* sailed westward with the wind and sun at her back.

"Good morning Jonathan!" Harrison said with a smile. "Have you seen anything of interest?"

"Not at all Mister Harrison," Jonathan replied, "Just sea, sky and an occasional cloud. There is a darkening ahead, a possible storm I would guess. I have sent word to Mister Watt, at the wheel."

"Spa-len-did! Spa-len-did!" said Harrison in his best imitation of the King. "We do have something special planned for today, gun practice! Are you game, Jonathan?"

Jonathan smiled and took in a deep breath. The guns were loud and dangerous, but they certainly broke the monotony of tasks and duties. One could only take so much polishing and sanding.

"I will look forward to it with great anticipation, Mister Harrison!" answered Jonathan happily. "When are we to begin?"

"Toward sundown, I hear," Harrison said. "And I am here to tell you that you have been assigned the management of the upper deck and Spears the lower deck."

"Oh," said Jonathan, visibly concerned at the news that Spears would be anywhere near him.

"Jonathan," said Harrison, "I am not your older brother, yet, I do believe you and I are close friends, is this true?"

"Of course," Jonathan answered. "We have been through a lifetime together it seems and I am ever so grateful for all you have done for me."

"Then let me do you another good turn, if I can. Tell me about Spears. What really happened in the cockpit?"

Jonathan thought for a minute about that day and the fight with Spears. He had discussed the events with Sean, but neither could decide how to correct the Captain's perception. It was most unpleasant and the idea that Captain Walker was angry with Jonathan was eating at him constantly.

"It is exactly as I stated to the Captain, Harrison. Spears started pushing Sean, then me, and one thing led to another - but Spears was doing all the leading, until the end. You know me well and you know that I would never start a fight at all, much less start one over something silly."

"This is true, Jonathan," said Mister Harrison, smiling a bit, "and that is what is most perplexing. I can't say I know exactly what the Captain feels, but he also knows you and he knows that Spears comes from a somewhat shady background."

"The plot thickens, Thomas," said Jonathan. "My father mentioned to me that he was attacked at the dock, the night we returned from Skull Eye Island. He thought that his attacker resembled an old adversary, a Captain Derrick Spears."

"Well," Harrison said, looking about to make sure he was not over heard. "Midshipman Spears is indeed the son of Captain Derrick Spears, now in the Admiralty at the assignment desk. Previously, he commanded a sixth rate, a brigantine, the twenty-four gun *Simplex*. The thing is, Jonathan, a captain of his age should have had a much, well, *larger* ship before taking an office job. I am sure he blames your father for his lack of promotion."

"But why? My father mentioned that they were not friends, but…"

"I am not sure I should tell you this, however, Captain Spears has told some, and I have heard it myself, that his misfortune is the result of your father getting all the plum assignments and maneuvering his way to put Spears down."

"I can't believe my father would do such a thing," said Jonathan.

"And don't believe it!" said Harrison quickly. "Your father has earned every bit of his success and someday he will tell you all of it. I have seen your father in action, Jonathan, and he is a spirited and cunning leader and an excellent fighter. However, many men are jealous and can't stand on their own feet without putting others down. Take Captain Walker, for instance. He was in competition for assignments against your father, but both of them celebrate each other's success. They are proud of their relationship and cheer each other on. But there are some people that are so weak in character that, well, if another accomplishes something, they feel that glory and honor is taken from them. Derrick Spears is one of those types."

"Then his son, Wayne, has probably been poisoned by his father against me!' said Jonathan.

"I do believe that is what is going on," said Harrison. "And there is more. It was widely known that Derrick Spears, a widower, also claimed that a certain Miss Barbara Thompson was a love interest of his, and, well, I do believe Miss Thompson and your father are…" Harrison paused, not knowing how to continue with this sensitive bit of news.

"Courting?" suggested Jonathan.

"Yes," said Harrison, relived that Jonathan chose the

word. "And that has added fuel to the fire. Be careful, Jonathan. And don't play all your cards at once. Keep Spears guessing."

"I will," said Jonathan, and he stood for a moment, thinking of just how he could keep Spears at arm's length and still gain an advantage. Spears was a bully and bullies were usually hard to handle.

Just then, the ship's bell signaled two hours before noon. As if on cue, Sean appeared on deck, with Stewie in tow. Both paused, looked at the sun, then simultaneously stretched and yawned in a grand manner.

"Hello, Jonny Boy! G'day Mister Harrison!"

"A tough morning of duty, Flagon?" asked Harrison jokingly.

"I am on night watch and believed a little sleeping in was in order," said Sean, stretching a bit more, trying to get all the sleep out. "Besides, Stewie was not quite ready to rise and shine. I thought it would be considered rude to wake him."

"You would sleep-in even on the day of your own funeral, Sean Flagon," Harrison said with a laugh.

"'tis true, I would!" laughed Sean.

At that moment, Lieutenant Blake appeared and addressed the boys.

"Mister Harrison, Mister Moore, good day. Flagon, a good day to you as well."

"Yes, sir," Sean said.

"It seems that Captain Walker is in need of entertainment and has suggested a fencing exhibition on the poop deck. We will draw straws and the two shortest will have a go. Are you in?

"Aye, I am in, Mister Blake!" said Sean, suddenly awake and energetic. "Let me get my belt and -"

"Excuse me, Flagon," said Blake, somewhat irritated, "This invitation is not for common seamen. Officers only."

Sean was visibly deflated and started to sulking, heading for a ladder to go below decks.

"Sean!" Jonathan called. "I will exercise with you

when I am done, would that be agreeable?"

Sean stopped, turned and smiled.

"Of course, Jonny. Now go give them what for!"

* * * * * *

The officers made their way aft, back to the poop deck, and took their places in line. There was Lieutenant Holtz, with his strange look on his face, taking a straw from Captain Walker. Blake drew second, Harrison third. What was disturbing was the appearance of Spears and Lane, both getting in line right behind Jonathan.

"It seems that I have a long straw!" stated Harrison.

"And a nose to match," said Steward as he prattled by, wheezing at his own joke. Harrison only smiled.

"Steward," Harrison said, "Your humor is truly juvenile."

"Thank you," Steward said as he went down the short ladder to the main deck to watch the fencing with the other men.

"I, too, have a long straw," claimed Lieutenant Holtz as he chose one from the Captain.

"As do I!" said Blake.

"Moore, you're next! Choose carefully!" said Captain Walker, and he extended his hand to Jonathan, showing three straws left. As Jonathan reached for the far right straw, the Captain cleared his throat and slightly moved his hand to position the center choice for Jonathan.

Jonathan chose the straw in the middle. It was short.

"You are one of the first then, Jonathan!" said Harrison. The crew clapped happily. Many had seen Jonathan in action while he trained with Mister Harrison for what seemed like every minute of every day for months on end during the last mission.

"He's quite an accomplished and entertainin' swordsman!" said Garvey to some of the new crew members. "Just watch and ya will see!"

"I can almost beat him," added Sean, "and I think I

am actually quite fine. So the sure bet is on Mister Moore!"

The others who knew about Jonathan agreed.

"Step up now, Midshipman Spears, try your luck!" said Captain Walker as he held out his hand with the two remaining straws.

"Thank you, sir," Spears said, and he reached for his choice.

"It is short!" he said with a grin.

"Then it will be Mister Spears versus Mister Moore!" Captain Walker announced. With a smile, he said under his breath: "What are the odds of that?"

There was many a hand not assigned to active duty that appeared on deck once word had gotten around of the match. All watching could see that Spears was slightly larger and also had a longer reach than Jonathan. Some commented that maybe Jonathan was a little out of his class.

"Would ya like to wager on the outcome then?" asked Sean. And four or five of the new crewmen offered up a shilling to bet on Spears as the winner. Steward held the money, laughing the whole time.

"I will pay the winner, but we all know Sean will be a richer man in a few minutes," laughed Steward.

"The rules are simple, boys," said the Captain. "Today's weapons will be foils, so only hits to the front and back torso will be points. Remain on the poop deck. And no striking with hilts! Face to face is the rule of the day, do you understand? First to score three points is the winner."

"Yes, sir," they both said, and each received a foil from Mister Koonts.

"Sir?" asked Lane.

"Yes, Lane?" answered the Captain.

"I didn't get to choose a straw."

"What is the point?" asked Walker. "The two shorts have been drawn and you would have gotten a long straw."

Lane stood at attention, embarrassed, but did not yet

realize his mistake.

"Lane, you dolt!" said Lieutenant Blake angrily. "There were only long straws left! And long straws don't play. Only short straws play. No matter what, you would have gotten a long straw! All the shorts were taken!"

"But, I didn't get a chance to choose -"

"Quiet!" yelled Blake, "I'll explain it to you at a later time when you can grasp it!"

Jonathan went to the port side of the poop deck, with Spears going to the starboard.

The Captain asked the boys to salute each other, then held up his hand. "En guard! Pret! Allez!" he said and backed away quickly.

Spears, not surprising to anyone, attacked quickly and ferociously, yet somewhat clumsily, barreling straight ahead, as if to try to bowl Jonathan over like a set pin in an alley. Jonathan easily parried the thrust, stepped aside, and spun around to face his opponents back. He did not counter attack.

"Odd," said Harrison to Captain Walker, "Jonathan could have easily scored a point. Why did 'e not press?"

Walker watched as the boys lined up head to head, ready for the next action. He also wondered why Jonathan did not score the easy point. Then it occurred to the Captain that possibly, something was going on beneath all this. *Jonathan is a strategist, that is for certain,* he thought.

Spears attacked again, this time a bit more cautiously. Jonathan parried excellently, but did not *riposte,* did not counter attack. He did, however, retreat, not allowing Spears to get too close. Jonathan moved backwards, farther and farther until he was against the ship's rail. He stood still, defending himself easily against Spears' thrusts and lunges. The crowd cheered wildly.

"Have at him, Mister Moore!" many of the men said.

"Touché! Score a point!" other chimed in.

Spears was relentless in his attacks, yet he seemed to use too much energy. Jonathan was, conversely, reserved. At one encounter, after a series of attacks and parries,

Jonathan ever so slightly lowered his foil as Spears lunged at his shoulder. Just like that, Spears had a point.

"Touché," called Walker. Some polite applause came from the crowd.

Sean saw what had happened clearly and thought to himself: *What is Jonathan doing? That is a beginner's mistake, to lower the blade point like that!*

The fight continued, all around the poop deck, the two combatants weaving in and around the officers, the deck guns and the rigging. At one point, Jonathan went on the attack, but was slow to it. As he lunged, he disengaged, retreated, but again, let his point down and held it there. Spears lunged and score a second *touché* to Jonathan's right upper chest.

"Jonathan!" called Sean, "Pay attention and keep up yer guard!"

But Jonathan could not hear above the crew members who were calling out loudly, the new ones cheering for Spears as he looked like a winner, the old *Poseidons*, as they were called, admonishing Jonathan ever so slightly.

"It is now two to naught!" called Walker. "En guard! Pret! Allez!" and the boys were at it again.

Jonathan looked calm and relaxed, yet not himself. The bout continued. At one instant, Jonathan had Spears against the rigging, almost tangled in the ropes of the aft mast, and just as he should have lunged to score an easy touché, he withdrew. It was a matter of seconds for Spears to regain his balance, clear himself of the ropes, and attack again. Jonathan simply was too slow and Spears scored a lucky strike to Jonathan's chest, ending the match.

The crowd was both ecstatic and disappointed, though none more upset than Sean. Not only had his best friend lost, and embarrassingly so, Sean also lost three shillings to those who bet for Spears.

"Midshipman Spears," said the Captain. "Well done. You are the victor it seems."

"T'was easy, sir," said Spears.

Jonathan approached him cautiously and reached to

shake Spears hand.

"Nicely done Spears," he said.

Spears just shook his opponent's hand lazily. "Any time you'd like a thrashing, please allow me!" he laughed.

6
A Loose Gun

The rest of the day proceeded slowly as the crew returned to work, the officers to plotting course, the midshipmen to navigation and checking the time. Jonathan and Sean had discussed the fencing match and all Jonathan could say was "I was just not myself," and bow his head. But Sean knew there was more to it than that.

By late afternoon, the Captain called for gun practice. Lieutenant Blake supervised the manufacture of a barrel raft as a target using the few empty kegs on the ship. They were lashed together, planks of wood nailed to the sides, and a pole with a flapping red rag was secured to complete the target. Now finished with the construction, Blake called for the raft to be set adrift. Men lowered it over the side using the yard arm, then cut the attached rope as the raft touched the water.

As Walker watched the proceedings, he heard a small sound, a rattle of sorts that seemed to be coming from behind him. After listening for a few more moments, the rattling stopped altogether. He could not place it.

"Holtz," he called, and in a moment, the Lieutenant appeared before him.

"Come up here," commanded Walker.

Holtz ran to the side of the poop and climbed the few steps to reach the small upper deck. He stood at attention next to the Captain, in silence. Finally, Walker spoke.

"Do you hear it?"

"Hear what, sir?" asked Holtz after listening for a second or two.

"Blast!" yelled Walker. "It was there just a moment ago. A rattling sound, as if a board were loose."

They remained in silence, listening, but the crew's

activities were noisy. Though Walker believed he heard the rattle once again, Holtz could not be sure.

"Never mind!" exclaimed Walker, exasperated. "Begin the exercise!"

"To your battle stations!" yelled Holtz, and the crews went quickly into motion, each man knowing his place.

Sean ran down the ladder to the first gun deck and then proceeded toward the bow, past all the gold and black weapons that lined each side of the *Danielle*. He was now assigned as the eyes for the *Barker*, the same ferocious beast of a gun that was Jonathan's first assignment. He finally reached his position and climbed to the beams above the gun. It was the third gun on the starboard side, across from Garvey who took a similar position on gun sixteen, called the *Wurm*. He was delighted to see Sean so close.

"Ah, Flagon! Let us have a contest! Let's see which of us can land a ball on that blasted flag, eh?"

"I have had enough games for today and am almost penniless besides!" Sean said. "I lost on the fencing and will not recover until payday!"

The crew laughed, remembering that Jonathan had lost the fight and Sean had lost his money. No one saw that Jonathan had arrived on deck just moments before and had heard the comments. As he was noticed, the men stopped their conversations and became both embarrassed and ashamed that they had laughed at their good friend's misfortune. All hoped he would not be angry with them.

"Gun ports open!" Jonathan called. "Let us see if you can fire these guns better than I can fence!"

This caused the men to start in amazement and after a moment, all laughed heartily. They moved into their positions as they kicked open the small doors on the business end of the guns.

"Wait for my signal," Jonathan instructed, "and then fire as she bears. Starboard side, you will have the first chance, so let us teach Mister Spears and the lower deck some true accuracy!"

The men cheered and busied themselves as their

powder monkeys, the boys bringing the sock-like cartridges packed with gunpowder from the powder room, arrived at their assigned guns. The cartridges went into the barrels of the guns, the ramming poles shoved them down deep inside each, then ball was loaded and likewise rammed home. One by one, the crews were ready. All paused, deadly quiet, torches above the touch holes. The men felt the sudden change in the ship's direction, tossing them to one side as the great vessel came about, heading back toward the target raft.

Jonathan ran down the starboard side, checking the readiness of each gun and its crew, then, seeing all was well, ran back to the bow, slapping each aimer as he passed.

"On my mark!" he yelled as he peered out the forward gun port. Ahead, the raft and the little red flag appeared in the distance, the *Danielle,* pausing for an instant as the wind was now at her side. As the tack was executed, she leapt forward and raced toward the target.

Mister Harrison stuck his head down the center hatchway and called to Jonathan: "Upper starboard guns! Fire as she bears, but not too early, as we are still out of range!"

"Yes sir!" Jonathan called as he kept his eyes on the raft. Within a few moments, he called to the gunners: "Ready…ready…as she bears…FIRE!"

The sound was deafening. Explosion after explosion rocked the ship as the guns on the starboard side erupted, one after another, belching flame and smoke and most importantly, ball flying through the air, splitting the distance between the ship and raft with an audible *whoosh!*

Jonathan watched as the first ball missed, it being fired a bit too early. However, the second and third crashed into the raft and the remaining balls landed more-or-less within thirty or forty feet from the raft's debris.

"Hits!" Jonathan yelled, "Numerous hits! Well done, men!" he called, and the crews cheered loudly as they reset their guns in the blocks.

On deck, Walker watched in amazement through his

telescope as the little raft was turned into splinters. He lowered his glass and turned to Holtz.

"That was impressive," Holtz said. "But can the other crews do as well?"

"We will see," said Captain Walker, smiling. "Have Lieutenant Blake build another raft and we will go again."

A new raft was put into place and the *Danielle* and her remaining crews had their chance to fire away. Though none quite equaled the accuracy of the first deck's starboard side, the crews were close enough to please Captain Walker… for now.

At dinner that evening, Sean, Garvey and two new crew members, Nicolas and Colin Stredney sat enjoying their stew on the main deck. The Stredneys were brothers, both tall and lean, a few years apart in age. All four boys got along fabulously, bunking near enough to each other in the orlop to become close friends. They discussed the mission to the Caribbean and the possibility of finding pirates. This excited the brothers Stredney, causing them to ask questions, non-stop, for at least one hour.

"Will there be gun battles?" asked Nicolas.

"And pirates? Evil ones? Missing legs and such?" asked Colin.

"You will get your fill of pirates and gun practice, boys!" said Garvey.

"And if you are lucky," said Sean, jumping up on the table and pretending to swipe a sword at imaginary pirates, "you will face a few of them in a duel to the death!"

This caused all the boys and surrounding crew to howl with laughter and cheer Sean on to victory as he lunged and parried.

"Flagon!" a voice boomed. "What in the world do you think you are doing?"

Sean immediately got down from the table and turned to see that the voice came from none other than Midshipman Spears. He quickly tipped his cap in a salute and bowed his head in respect, as did the others. The entire deck became silent.

"I asked you a question, Flagon!" barked Spears.

"Aye sir," said Sean meekly. "Just entertainin' the crew is all. A little fun."

"On *my* table? Are you *mad?"*

"No, sir, er, I mean...y-yes sir!" stammered Sean.

"Come here, Flagon! Follow me to the bow sprit! On the double!

Sean looked about quickly, to see if he could find an officer, or maybe even Jonathan; anyone who could come to his rescue. He was afraid of Spears. Since their last tussle, he knew that going away from the eyes of others might be dangerous. Sean knew that in a fair fight, he could handle Spears easily, however, this was a ship of His Majesty's Navy, and striking an officer could bring severe punishment, even death.

"Now, I said!" yelled Spears, and Sean quickly moved toward the bow.

As they reached the sprit, Spears motioned toward a ladder leading to the deck below. Once at the bottom, Sean realized that they were alone, on an area far removed from the rest of the crew, especially at dinner-time.

As soon as Sean turned to face Spears, he was met with a hard punch to the face. He fell to the ground.

"I have had it with your insolence, Flagon!" hissed Spears.

Sean spun around on the floor and stared angrily at the midshipman. *Officer, or not,* thought Sean, *I will take him down right now and take my chances with the Captain.*

"Stand up when in the presence of an officer!" said Spears.

And just as Sean stood, clenching his fists, ready to give Spears a bit of *street justice*, as it was called, the hatch to the ladder opened.

"Hoy! What is going on here?"

It was Steward.

"None of your business, bosun," said Spears.

"Looks like Flagon 'ere 'as a red mark on 'is eye. Nasty

I'd say," Steward hissed, turning to face Spears. "And it is my business, *Mister* Spears, as I, too, am an officer o' this ship. A lowly warrant I carry, 'tis true. 'owever, I don't care much fer yer rank. My job is to watch all on this ship, and I tell the Captain all I see. And I think I see somethin' I don't like. And when I don't like something… I fix it. Do you catch my meaning *Mid-ship-man* Spears?"

Spears turned red and stared into Steward's eyes. Neither blinked. Many aboard knew that, as uneducated and at times as ridiculous as Steward could be, none doubted his strength or his ability to put a knock on an enemy. He was a veteran of numerous battles, many resolved in a hand-to-hand manner. He was not one to be trifled with. Spears finally turned away quickly and rushed up the ladder.

"Let's get ya up and to see the Doctor," said Steward to Sean.

"I was gonna knock that lout on the head, I tell ya!" said Sean angrily.

"Now, now, Sean! We all know ya could, but we also know… that ya shouldn't."

* * * * * *

Later that evening, the dark clouds that Jonathan had seen in the morning were upon the *Danielle* as she sailed westward toward the Caribbean and the Bahamas. Men felt the first drops of rain and saw the sea began to rise and fall as waves became bigger and more powerful. The wind crept up, and soon, some men were sent below to stay out of harm's way.

"Moore! Spears!" yelled Harrison above the wind, "Make sure the guns on the main deck are secured. Moore, take port, Spears, take the starboard side. Lane, join Mister Blake and check the first and lower decks!"

Jonathan and Lane ran off right away, but Spears paused, looked at the rain now falling fast, and approached Harrison.

"I am not needed, Thomas. Those two can handle the guns," he said matter-of-factly.

The wind was now rising and beginning to howl, partly drowning out Spears words, but Harrison understood them well enough.

"Spears, did you just call me by my first name?"

"Well, I-I meant -" stuttered Spears, knowing he was out of line.

"You are *not* questioning my order, are you?" Harrison asked loudly and forcefully.

"No, sir," Spears said, "I just see the rain is getting up and with only a dozen guns on the top deck, well, why get wet? Moore can handle it."

The few hands that remained on deck, Steward and Claise among them, stopped securing barrels and lines and looked up to see how the mild-mannered Lieutenant Harrison would respond.

Harrison stared at Spears for a moment, then took in a deep breath, like a small dragon, and let forth a stream of colorful expletives that rivaled Captain Walker's best explosions.

"Spears, you ignorant gull whacker! Get your blooming backside out there and secure those guns or I will have you hung off the yard arm for a week and then keel-hauled! How dare you question my orders! Of all the pretentious, snot-nosed antics I have ever heard, this takes the cake! You moronic buffoon -"

Spears was visibly taken aback and immediately turned and ran off to do his duty as Harrison continued spewing out insults and worse.

"Well," called Claise over the wind, "Seems like a bit o' the Captain has rubbed off on Mister Harrison."

"Aye," replied Steward. "If I didn't know better, and if the timbre was a wee bit lower, I'd 'ave thought it was the grand dragon himself!"

Jonathan heard none of the exchange between Harrison and Spears. He busied himself with his task, making sure the guns on the portside main deck were secure. He moved quickly and carefully, starting with the aft guns. The *Danielle* had four on each side, tied down with heavy ropes and wooden blocks that held them in place. A loose gun on deck in turbulent seas could cause great damage to the ship, any crew members and certainly, there was a danger that the gun itself would crash through the rail and be lost. As the aft guns were secure, Jonathan checked the fore and also the complete starboard side, even though it had been assigned to Spears. Once he was certain they were properly secured, he took another run around the deck, as a secondary precaution.

After a moment, Jonathan noticed that Spears had finally begun inspecting the starboard guns. *I wonder if he is angry with me, as I am also checking his side and my side as well. No matter. Never can be too much checking,* Jonathan thought. *One can't be too sure!*

Finally finished, Jonathan retired to the lower decks to search for Sean. He found him with Garvey, securing guns with the instruction of Lane. Once finished, they all planned to settle in for the wild ride that was surely to come.

"Not a big one, I can tell ya that!" Garvey said. "I've seen worse!"

"It still makes me queasy, though," Sean said, turning to see Jonathan.

"Sean!" said Jonathan in alarm as he looked at his face. "What has happened to your eye?" Jonathan moved closer to inspect the bruise. It was black and blue.

"Just an accident," Sean whispered.

"If Midshipman Spears can be considered an accident," added Garvey.

"Spears?" said Jonathan, his anger rising. "I have had it with that naughty pake! Lane! What do you know of this? Speak up!"

"I-I know nothing!" said Lane defensively.

"Not to worry, Jonathan, I can handle Spears," assured Sean.

"How? Will you strike him? An officer? I will not have him pushing anyone around! I will attend to him directly!" Jonathan ran to the top deck to confront Spears.

The Captain and Lieutenant Holtz remained on deck with Watt, ever-present at the wheel, to handle the ship through the storm. The waves rose and fell, tossing the *Danielle* from crest to trough, but she sailed smartly and actually proved to be a fine rough-weather ship. A little lightening was about, nothing serious, though all knew that the wind could get up and damage the sails and the smaller cross beams. As little sail was needed to propel the ship forward, the men were instructed to take in almost all.

Suddenly, a horrible scraping sound was heard, as if a giant was dragging a huge metal contraption across the top deck. From below, the men could hear the moaning of something. Only the most experienced knew what it was. "Loose gun on main deck!" they called, and fear for their mates was upon them.

Above, Walker and Holtz rushed forward, seeing one of the nine-pounders from the port side sliding across the slippery deck, toward the foremast. The gun crashed into it, sending splinters flying in all directions.

"Grab a rope!" called Walker as he ran forward. "Try to capture it!"

Harrison appeared on deck just as Jonathan ascended the ladder. Seeing the issue, both rushed to the gun as it wedged itself between the mast and a stack of barrels. They tried to grab the ropes attached to the rear of the gun, but just as they reached, the ship tilted to port. The heavy weapon started sliding again, this time heading straight for Jonathan.

"Get out of the way!" Harrison yelled, but Jonathan had nowhere to go. He backed up madly, slipping on the wet planking. The gun barreled towards him. In the instant right before the gun would have struck him and crashed through the rail, he leapt overboard. The gun followed.

Harrison and Walker rushed to the rail and looked over just in time to see the gun sink into the dark waves.

"Jesus, Mary and Joseph!" called Walker.

"Man overboard!" shouted Harrison.

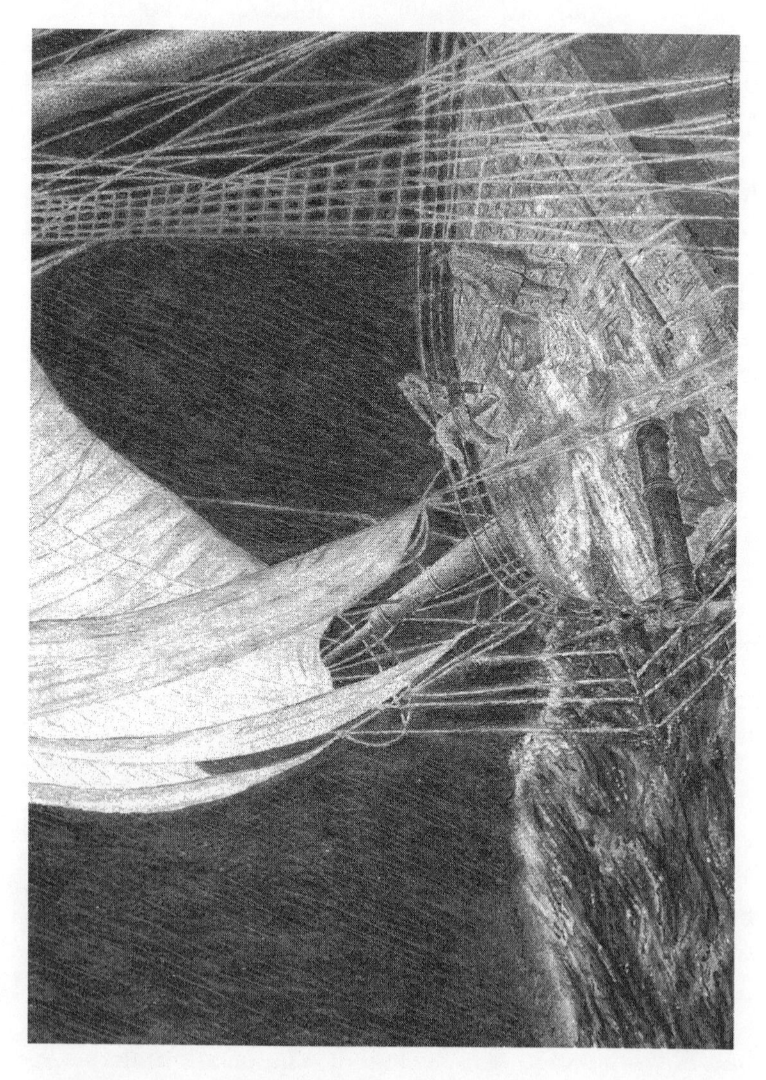

A Loose Gun

"Not quite!" called a voice from below. As Harrison and the Captain looked against the side of the ship, there was Jonathan, holding onto the anchor, dangling, with only his hands to secure him.

Mister Harrison, Jonathan and Spears were, of course, summoned to Captain Walker's cabin, all still wet from their third check of all the topside guns. They stood at attention, staring out the aft windows of the cabin, trying not to breathe too loudly and possibly raise the ire of the Captain any further than necessary. Mister Koontz and Lieutenants Holtz and Blake were also present; all sitting at the large table in the center of the room. There was a pot of steaming coffee on the table and a few bits of hard tack, some jam and the last bit of toasted cheese. Steward was clearing the dishes and as he reached for the remaining food, Holtz gave him a concerned and confused look.

"Are ya done with this here tack, Lieutenant?" asked Steward.

"Not at all, Steward. I would be happy to take it all," Holtz said.

"Aye, ya see? At least someone appreciates my cooking!" said Steward happily.

"No, not at all," said Holtz. "I seem to have a loose rat in my cabin and if I can get him to eat *this*, he will certainly perish!"

This caused many to laugh out loud, reveling in the joke. Harrison, who would usually have made the comment about Stewards lack of culinary talent, did not join in the mirth, though he greatly desired to, and just continued to stare straight ahead. Steward remove all the plates and the coffee as well, then exited the cabin, grumbling.

"Harrison," the Captain said calmly, only delaying the assured explosion to come. "What in the world is going on aboard this ship? A loose gun?"

"Aye sir, that it was," Harrison replied.

"I know what it was!" exploded the Captain, "Did you

ensure that they were secure?"

"I had…I had ordered Mister Moore to the port side and Mister Spears to the starboard," said Harrison, knowing that this fact would look bad for Jonathan.

"Mister Moore," said the Captain, turning on him. "How could you miss a gun?"

"Sir, all guns were secure when I check them and I checked them twice."

"Then you must have checked incorrectly - twice!" boomed the Captain. "What has happened to you, Jonathan? This is not what I expect from my midshipmen, especially you!"

Jonathan stared out the window as the Captain continued to scold him. But something told him to look about the cabin; a feeling compelled him to believe there was something amiss. As Jonathan scanned the others in the room, his eyes fell upon Spears, who was grinning widely. Jonathan looked at Harrison and he, too, was looking at Spears. Could it be that Spears was delighting in the misfortune that Jonathan was enduring? *Or could it be more*, thought Jonathan. *Could it be that Spears loosened the gun after I had checked it? He did come to the port side and was busy about my guns. I just know he did this to bring shame to me, though I shall bite my tongue, as I have no proof.*

When the tongue lashing was complete, they were dismissed, Jonathan sent to the crow's nest for the evening, without dinner. Spears, now hiding his glee, bowed and retreated to the cockpit.

Walker took a look at his empty coffee cup and called for Steward to bring back the pot immediately.

"Lieutenant Holtz, please attend topside and assist Mister Watt in navigation if you please. Blake, I would ask that you check all guns and supplies and make sure all are secure."

Both Lieutenants rose and nodded to the Captain, knowing full well that they were being asked to leave so as not to hear the remainder of the discussion. Possibly, it was a further tongue lashing for Lieutenant Harrison and it would be poor form for them to be present. They left the cabin immediately.

"Well, Mister Koonts," said the Captain, "How do you think all this has come to pass; the sudden degradation of Mister Moore's capabilities?"

Koonts mulled this over for a moment, then scratched his chin. "Not at all like him, Captain. Not at all."

"I agree. It seems that more is afoot than is on the surface," Walker said as Steward entered the cabin with the coffee and set three cups on the table. He began filling each with the steaming brew.

"Captain, if I may?" asked Mister Harrison.

"By all means, continue," said the Captain.

"Jonathan has had three mishaps in this short cruise, two even before we left port. He fell off the gangplank, then he participated in a shoving match with Spears, and now this gun incident."

"If I may be so bold, Cap'n?" Steward said as he poured the last cup of coffee for Koonts. "I think ya are missing a few facts. First off, I saw Spears waitin' at the bottom of the gangplank before 'e boarded the *Dani,* just a-standing there. No reason. Then as soon as Jonathan came up – Spears was right behind. I didn't see anything happen as far as I could tell, but I wasn't lookin'. Second, well, I have seen Spears beratin' Sean Flagon on more than one occasion, and a bit of pushing and shoving. Petty stuff, mind ya."

The Captain looked calm and thoughtful. "Are you suggesting, Steward, that Spears is behind all this?"

"Well, one can never be so sure," Steward said, "but I also know that Spears' father is no friend o' the Moores. I think he's tryin' to make things more difficult, that's all I'm sayin'."

"Then let's call Spears in here and get to the bottom of it!" demanded Koonts. He was now upset, his face starting to glow red. He was partial to Jonathan, as they all were.

The Captain took a sip of his coffee and held up his hand.

"Not yet, my dear Koonts. Is Spears behind this? I have thought as much, but needed confirmation," the Captain said. "What we have now is just hearsay. No real proof, no eye-witness account. However, we need to watch closely for two reasons. One, if our suspicions are correct, Spears can be dangerous, not only to Jonathan but to other crew members as well. That gun almost killed Jonathan and could have injured a handful of men. We must keep an eye on Mister Spears. As a precaution, let us put Mister Moore before the mast. Have him leave the cockpit and bunk with Flagon and the crew. He will be disappointed, but I wager he will be relieved to be away from Spears."

"I will tell him myself, sir," said Harrison. "What is the second reason to watch closely?"

The Captain smiled and took another sip of coffee. "We must watch Jonathan and see how he handles this entire issue. If we step in and solve it for him, well, that does not give him a chance to work it out. He is resourceful, so let us check those resources. I wonder what he will do."

Steward nodded and spoke with a smile on his face. "I think Mister Moore suspects Spears. If I know my Moores, which I do, 'es got something up his sleeve, Jonathan does."

Outside the Captain's cabin, Spears turned to his left to make his way to the cockpit. After a few steps, he felt a rough push from behind that sent him sprawling to the deck. Before he could react, Jonathan jumped atop him and pinned his arms to the planks.

"I see what you are up to, Spears, and if you desire to challenge me, then so be it!" hissed Jonathan.

"I don't know what you mean -" said Spears, surprised at the intensity of the attack.

"Stow it, Spears. I am warning you; leave Sean Flagon out of this!"

Jonathan stood up and kept his eye on Spears, who continued to lie on the floor, laughing.

7

One for Adventure

The next morning, Harrison informed Jonathan that he was to be *put before the mast* as part of his punishment for the loose gun.

"Before the mast? What does that mean Mister Harrison?" asked Jonathan.

"It means that you will no longer bunk in the cockpit where all the officers and midshipmen sleep," said Harrison, "Since the cockpit is *behind* the mizzen mast, you will be sleeping *before* the mizzen mast, where the common crew sleeps."

Jonathan smiled.

"I know I should be upset, it is quite a disgrace to be sure. However, to bunk with Sean and Claise again and be free of Spears, well, I can't thank you enough, Mister Harrison!"

"It was not my doing, but I am glad for it," said Harrison. "Be careful Jonathan. Sleep with one eye open, as they say!"

"I have been! And now, before the mast and amongst friends I will finally get the first good night's sleep since we left England!"

Word spread quickly that Jonathan was moving to the lower deck. Though some were shocked, none were disappointed. The young brothers Colin and Nicolas Stredney, knew nothing about Jonathan and his exploits, but were soon educated, as their crewmates told of the last mission and Jonathan's part in it.

"He is a true hero!" said Nicolas. "It will be excitin' to meet him up close!"

"I wonder," said Colin, "if he will even speak to the likes of us, lowly and basically one step above the gutter."

"But that's where he came from, lads," said Jones, "e's a street urchin himself, only being plucked up by Steward 'bout a year ago. He knows what it's like to be a poor man, yet, he discovered his father again, after being lost."

"And his father's a Captain!" said Smith. "Such an amazing tale couldn't be made up!"

Just then, Jonathan appeared, with Sean in tow. The men all rushed to him and clapped him on the back in welcome.

"Take my spot, Mister Moore, right by Seany," said Claise as he began gathering his things. "I have been sleeping in the galley anyway."

"He snores terribly and keeps many awake at night," added Smith.

"True, but not a problem," continued Claise. "I am just happy you're back with friends. And you'll have more room than we had in the closet, eh?"

"We welcome ya with open arms, Mister Moore!" said Garvey.

Jonathan graciously accepted Claise's offering and took the hammock that had been strung over a few beams, right above Sean.

Once all personal items had been organized, Jonathan and Sean left the lower deck and headed toward the cockpit to retrieve Jonathan's gear.

Upon their arrival, Spears sat up in his bed, presumably from a nap. He rubbed his eyes and spoke harshly to Jonathan and Sean.

"Well, Moore and Flagon, what are you doing and where are you going with your things?" he demanded.

Jonathan continued collecting his clothes, his telescope from his father and his small cooking stove that he received as a Christmas gift. Sean had hoisted the heavy locker and began happily dragging it out of the room.

"I asked you a question, Moore!" Spears said.

Jonathan looked at Sean; they smiled and left without a word. This caused Spears to rant all the more.

"When I left, Jonny," Sean said in a whisper, "I let go

a nasty crack in there!"

That night, as all without duty settled in, Sean began reading from his book. He read aloud, as many had been listening and were enjoying the tale of King Arthur.

"There was seen in the churchyard, against the high altar, a great stone four square, like unto a marble stone; and in midst thereof was like an anvil of steel a foot on high, and therein stuck a fair sword naked by the point, and letters there were written in gold about the sword that said thus: Whoso pulleth out this sword of this stone and anvil, is rightwise king born of all England."

Sean stopped and looked up from the book. He stared at Jonathan and smiled.

"You remind me of the young Arthur, Jonathan!" said Sean. "I picture you in my head as I read it, as if it were actually happening before me, like a play."

"First of all," said Jonathan as he stretched out on the hammock after removing his shoes and coat, "you have probably learned to drink and enjoy rum a little too much if you imagine me as Arthur. That is utter silliness, Sean."

"Well, it is my imagination and I am doing the reading, so I will be as silly as I want," said Sean. "But it makes some sense in that Arthur was destined for greatness and he just needed to prove it. Just like you."

"However do you mean, Sean?" asked Jonathan sleepily. He really didn't want to know the answer, only to sleep deeper than he had at any time since the voyage began. At last he could close both eyes and even snore if he wanted.

"You were roaming the streets, like Arthur, and you became a midshipman by your deeds -"

"And because my father is a Captain in the Royal Navy -" added Jonathan.

"And by your deeds, you were rewarded with command, you see?"

"If it pleases you Sean, you can picture me as Arthur, you as Lancelot -"

"Who is he?" asked Sean.

"You will see," said Jonathan.

Just then Steward appeared to check on the boys. "And ya can picture me as wise ol' Merlin, the wizard, as I'm almost magical in my knowledge 'n skills!"

"Steward," asked Sean, ignoring his comments about being a wizard, "How do you believe I am progressing with my reading?"

"Very well, Sean," he said. "By the time yer finished, ya'll be able to read the exam, I am sure."

Sean looked at him with a quizzical face. "The exam?"

"Why yes! What are ya? Daft?" cried Steward and delivered a stinging swat to the back of Sean's head. "The exam to become a marine! It is a written exam, at least part of it! That's why Gorman has you reading!"

"Oh, yes, I remember," said Sean. "Then I had better get to it!"

And as Sean continued reading, his voice soothed Jonathan, and he drifted off in to a deep, restful sleep. Within a few minutes, the rest of the audience, likewise, drifted off. Sean looked up, smiled, and blew out the candle.

The remainder of the cruise to Nassau, Bahamas was uneventful. The weather cleared and on the second of March, HMS *Danielle* sailed smartly into port on a calm, turquoise Caribbean Sea, with the sun glittering off the waves.

As soon as the ship was docked, Jonathan ran to his sleeping quarters. Under Sean's hammock, he had stored his locker. Within it, in a secreted area, he removed the dolphin necklace he had purchased for Miss Delain Dowdeswell, still in its fancy lace wrapping and bow.

He rushed to the main deck, ran to the port rail and searched the crowd welcoming the famous ship. There were people of all types, workmen, dock hands, ladies and gentlemen, all waving and cheering. The *Danielle* was famous, especially in Nassau, as she was first seen there after the successful mission to Skull Eye Island. At the Governor's mansion, Jonathan, Sean and Harrison had met the ladies Dowdeswell, including the eldest daughter, Rebecca, the younger daughter, Penelope, and the middle daughter, Delain. Jonathan had taken a liking to Delain and she to him, so he believed. They had toured the ship many times, had dinner with all the officers and Dowdeswell family, and upon their departing, Delain had asked Jonathan to return for tea someday. Amazingly so, it was now coming to pass.

"Do ya see her?" said Sean, who had crept up beside Jonathan.

"No, not at all," said Jonathan, somewhat disappointedly.

"I think I do," called Harrison, as he pointed to the side of the fort that sat on the northern bluff overlooking the bay. "Use my glass. Just below the parapet, almost dead center."

Jonathan grabbed the telescope and peered into it, searching the fort, and then…there, just as Harrison had said, someone was dangling off a rope, swinging from side to side, repelling downward slowly. As Jonathan looked closer, it was clearly a young girl, wearing pants, and now and again looking upward at an older man, who was fretting greatly, waving his arms. On closer observation, it was clearly Delain on the rope.

"Well, that is certainly Miss Delain Dowdeswell," Jonathan said. "Obviously, one for adventure."

Captain Walker appeared on deck with his lieutenants in tow and addressed Mister Koontz.

"Before we let out the wild beasts, allow me to approach the Governor to see if he has any special requests. I am sure he will invite us for dinner, or at least I certainly hope so."

As if on cue, a voice shouted from the dock.

"Ahoy *Danielle*, Ahoy!"

It was Rebecca Dowdeswell, with her youngest sister,

Penelope, waving to the Captain and his officers.

"Ahoy there, little ladies!" called Steward, as it was his duty to address those hailing the ship, even in such a comfortable atmosphere. "Do ya have any news fer the Captain?"

"No real news, I'm afraid," said Rebecca. "However, I have been sent by my father, the Governor, to personally request your attendance at dinner tonight at the mansion, if that is agreeable."

"By all means," called the Captain happily, "There will be eight of us, myself and the officers. Is that acceptable?"

"As long as Mister Harrison, Mister Moore and Sean Flagon attend!" said Penelope.

"Penelope!" cried Rebecca, not truly concerned. "What a caution you are!"

Jonathan and Harrison and Sean laughed out loud, but it was clear that Spears and Lane, who had appeared on deck as well, were not happy with the fact that Sean had been personally invited.

"Then make it nine!" laughed the Captain. "Moore, make sure Flagon is bathed and smelling like a lily."

"Yes, sir!" Jonathan said. "Come now, Sean, a bath would do you well. I am sure you haven't had one since we left London!"

"And you, dear Jonny, don't smell like a lily, more like a beached lobster!"

* * * * * *

Dinner was scrumptious, especially since the officers and Sean had not had fresh food for the last few weeks of the voyage. There was grilled fish, chicken in white wine sauce, garlic potatoes, fresh peas and even American corn. Fresh loaves of bread seemed to be sprouting out of the kitchen as fast as the guests could eat them and though they tried to remember their manners, the officers, more than once, had to remind themselves to slow down and enjoy the feast.

To Jonathan, the most enjoyable part of the evening was the fact that he had been *paired up*, as they say, with none other than Delain Dowdeswell as his dinner partner. She sat to his right, with Sean and Penelope beyond. To Jonathan's left, Rebecca Dowdeswell chatted with Harrison.

"I wonder, Mister Harrison," asked Rebecca, "have the heroes of Skull Eye Island participated in any new adventures? We would greatly enjoy another one of your tall tales."

"Tall tales? As if they were not completely truthful?" asked Harrison defensively.

"Most certainly are stretched more than a little bit," laughed Jonathan.

"Not as such, then, Miss Dowdeswell," Harrison said between playful frowns. "The trip across the Atlantic was quite calm and matter-of-fact. Unfortunately, nothing to tell, I'm afraid."

"We did meet the King," said Sean calmly.

The table was shocked into silence. They all looked at Sean.

"Well, we did," he said, as if he felt no one believed him.

"And how did you find His Majesty, Mister Flagon?" asked Governor Dowdeswell.

"I found him most agreeable," Sean said. "His majesty particularly enjoyed Jonathan's telling of the tale and even granted wishes!" Sean laughed. "It was like Christmas all over again!"

The table, for the most part, began asking questions and eventually demanded that Harrison tell of the entire story, from the time the *Danielle* left Nassau until they returned. Of course, with the many embellishments added to the tale, Captain Walker exploded with laughter, sending the table into hysterics. When it came to Jonathan's suggesting the gifts for each member of the crew, he shyly turned red and attended to his plate.

"So we are to address you as Lord Captain, is that

correct?" asked Lady Dowdeswell.

"*Captain* is more than adequate, Lady Dowdeswell. The title is simply honorary at best, and if I may suggest a change in topic? We have been dispatched here to deter French privateers and American rum-runners, as we have heard the activity in the area has increased."

"We have seen a few smaller ships suspiciously in the offing from time to time," said the Governor. "It has gotten to the point where we have decided to move my daughters to London for the next few years, to be schooled there. We had been thinking of the move for some time and the increased activity has forced our hand. My sister, Lady Bracknell, will look after them."

Jonathan looked at Delain. He could easily tell she was not happy about the move. Her face and brow became scrunched and she held a dark expression for a few moments.

"I, for one, am so excited to see London!" proclaimed Rebecca. "All the shops and fine ladies and gentlemen. It is the most famous city in the world!"

"And they have candy!" said Penelope.

This caused the table to explode into laughs and hisses.

"We will make sure you receive your fill, young lady!" added Captain Walker. "Miss Delain, are you also excited about the journey?"

Delain paused for a moment, looked to her father, then with a small frown, she turned to the Captain.

"I am most certainly looking forward to the crossing in some fine ship, that adventure will be extremely exciting."

Her father, the Governor, smiled slightly.

"Delain is certainly the adventurer in the family. I wonder if you may have seen her performing her latest fancy, *mountain climbing*."

"I did," said Harrison. "We could see a small figure descending the parapet wall of the fort overlooking the harbor. Mister Moore and seaman Flagon also witnessed the event. Most impressive and daring if I may say so."

"You may," said Delain, smiling now that someone recognized her as impressive.

"Well," her mother said with a slight scowl on her face, "For a sailor or a pirate, maybe those are impressive talents, but for a lady? This is one of the reasons we are sending the girls to the culture and dignity of London.

Jonathan and Sean looked at each other and smiled. They knew both sides of the great town from the posh and warm houses near the Walkers and their apartment on Charring Cross, as well as the back streets and hard cobblestone alleys. Hopefully, Delain and her sisters would be spared the latter.

"Possibly, if your next port is London, you could transport them, Captain Walker?" asked Lady Dowdeswell.

"It would be an honor," said Walker. "Though we have a four month cruise to make of the islands. Will that be soon enough?"

"Actually, it will allow us time to prepare for their departure. Thank you."

"Then it is settled. I will have Steward prepare the officer's cabin next to mine. I am sure my Lieutenants will not mind a few weeks of sleeping on the gun deck."

Looking at Holtz and Blake, it was obvious that they did mind, actually, and it was all that Harrison could do to stifle his laugh.

"Father!" said Delain, "Before the *Danielle* leaves on her cruise, would it be possible for the Captain to drop me off on Conception Island to see the turtles? Just for a day? My teacher has said they are nesting this time of year and I would love to make a few sketches and observations!"

"Delain, Delain!" the Governor said sternly. "The Captain has orders and duty to attend to. He has no time to play nursemaid to you and your turtles."

Delain was visibly crushed and looked as if she was about to cry. Jonathan and Sean noticed her disappointment and quickly looked at the Captain with sad faces, ones that pleaded for his assistance in this matter of the turtles.

Captain Walker, of course, noticed them. After feeling a bit on the spot and needing to address the awkwardness, he stammered a reply.

"W-well, a-actually, Your Lordship, it would really be no trouble. We could simply take the launch from the *Danielle* and a few men and, well, a *short* excursion would be easily accomplished. No trouble at all."

It was decided over a dessert of chocolate éclairs and fine coffee, that the *Danielle* would sail directly southeast to Conception Island, set off the launch with a small contingent consisting of Delain, her teacher, Mister Tupper, and a few others to see the turtles. The shore party would camp for the night as the *Danielle* continued to cruise the islands to the south. The next morning, the *Danielle* would retrieve all from Conception Island and return to Nassau. After re-supplying, they would cruise the islands for four months. Finally, the great ship would return for the girls before leaving for London.

As the evening progressed and all left the fine table after praise and thanks to Lady Dowdeswell, the guests retired to the balcony that overlooked the port of Nassau for after dinner drinks and conversation. Jonathan remembered that this was the very same balcony where he had first met the daughter's Dowdeswell, and also the same balcony where Captain Walker told Jonathan the welcome news of his father's fate. It was, as far as Jonathan was concerned, quite a pleasant location. Even the fact that Spears was there muddling his way about, couldn't dampen his spirits.

Delain had joined him at the railing and they both looked over the bay, observing the ships in the harbor. Lights twinkled on the few buildings next to the dock and aboard the *Danielle*. A fiddle was being played somewhere on deck and a young man's voice, probably Garvey, was singing sweetly.

"Mister Moore," said Delain, "It is with great pleasure

that I greet you. How wonderful that you accepted my invitation to tea!"

Jonathan smiled. He remembered her calling to him as the *Danielle* left Nassau for London last November and that he had promised to return.

"Yes, Miss Dowdeswell, it is a wonder. But as you know, I can only follow orders. It was a wonderful chance that brought us here."

"Are you saying it was luck, Mister Moore?" Delain asked.

"I certainly do not believe in luck, Miss Dowdeswell. It seems that will and desire had more to do with it. The more industrious and determined one is, the luckier one seems to be."

"Then you must have been quite determined to return," she stated.

"I was, Miss Dowdeswell."

"May I ask, Mister Moore, did you ever find your father? I know it was of the utmost importance to you."

She looked into his eyes, hoping they had been reunited and that all was well. Jonathan stared back and smiled broadly.

"I did, Miss Dowdeswell, thank you so much for asking. He is as wonderful as I remembered and I don't know how I survived without him. We are a small and happy family. Even Sean lives with us! Isn't that something?"

"Oh, I am so pleased!" Delain exclaimed. "What a wonderful thing it is to have a family."

Jonathan smiled again and reached into his coat pocket. He took the small box he had carried all the way from London and shyly presented it to Delain.

"Miss Dowdeswell, I – I would like you to have this small gift. It is a symbol of our friendship, I would like to think."

Delain let out a small gasp as she accepted the box.

"Mister Moore, I –I don't know what to say. You really shouldn't have!" She excitedly opened the box, removing the lace ribbon and paper that wrapped it.

"I acquired it in a shop on Oxford Street. It reminded me of you and the wonderful crystal waters that surround your home."

Delain had finally opened the box, parted the fine paper within and gazed upon the small dolphin necklace with the blue crystal eye. She immediately asked Jonathan for help in attaching the chain about her delicate neck.

What Jonathan did not see was that almost every one of his shipmates was watching. Sean and Harrison smiled in their shared joy, however, Spears and Lane looked on in disgust. They whispered something to each other, then Spears approached.

"What is all this, Moore?" he said rudely.

Jonathan just looked at him, shocked that he would interrupt them so.

"Pardon us, Mister Spears, this is a private conversation, however, to be polite, I will properly introduce you to Miss Delain Dowdeswell. Miss Dowdeswell, this is Midshipman Wayne Spears."

Delain said nothing, just looked at Spears with a blank face, waiting for him to speak. Spears smiled a bit, then bowed most elegantly.

"My pleasure, Miss Dowdeswell, certainly," Spears said. He then took her hand and kissed it most gently.

Jonathan was shocked into silence. Delain looked at her hand, then at Spears.

"Midshipman Spears," she said coldly. "It is not proper to kiss a woman's hand upon a first meeting."

Spears looked slightly surprised and instead of apologizing like a gentleman, he immediately said:

"I would assume, you being captive on this island, with no suitable prospects, that you might be happy for the attention."

Delain's eyes displayed her shock at Spears' comment.

"Take that back immediately," Jonathan stated as he stepped up to Spears.

"I will not," he said. "And just what do you suppose

to do about it? Tell the Governor? Like a tattle-tale?"

"I most certainly will, Spears. You are a sad chuff, a louse; there are no other words for you. And I suggest you take your leave now."

"Or what, Moore?"

Before Jonathan could think, his anger got the best of him. What he said was certainly not well thought out and he regretted saying it almost immediately.

"I have put you in your place once, Spears, and I will do it again if I must. In whatever manner necessary."

Spears smiled.

"Is that a challenge, Moore? Are you challenging me to a duel?"

Just then, Mister Harrison approached with Sean. Seeing a possible altercation, Sean stood right behind Lane, as if to say *if you get involved with this, I will get involved with* you!

Harrison looked both men in the eyes and raised a finger.

"One misstep, gentlemen, just one, and I will have you both before the cat, am I understood?"

Jonathan thought about the cat, the whip that was used to administer punishment to unruly crewmen. It was something he had never seen, but he had heard of the damage it could do, almost stripping a man's back to the bone. It certainly was not worth it, not even to put Spears in his place.

"Yes, sir," they both said sheepishly.

"And another thing, there will be no duel," said Harrison sternly. "It is against all things gentlemanly and against the regulations of His Majesty's Navy. I am ordering you both to forget this. Now, carry on with your evenings - separately."

Jonathan decided to take this as a chance to get away and cool his emotions.

"Miss Dowdeswell, please excuse my boorish behavior," Jonathan said. "May I escort you to the punch bowl?"

"By all means," Delain said. And as she took Jonathan's hand, she spun quickly and somehow managed to drive the heel of her shoe into the toe of Midshipman Spears. He yelped in pain.

"Oh," said Delain, "Ever so sorry Mister Spears! How clumsy of me!"

8
The Turtle and the Fiero

That night, no one sleeping in the orlop was interested in asking Jonathan about the evening he had in the mansion of the Governor. Even Sean seemed to clam up as all settled into bed. News had preceded their arrival that Jonathan and Sean had gotten into some type of altercation with Spears, and that Mister Harrison was beside himself about their behavior. As the many bunk mates settled into bed, Sean could do nothing but take out his book, curl up under a thin blanket with Stewie on his chest and mope. The brothers Stredney asked for Sean to read aloud from King Arthur, but he refused politely. And though he looked to be reading by candlelight, he mostly worried about his friend until the wick burned out.

The following morning, the entire town appeared to wish the *Danielle* good luck on her short cruise, and with the sun shining brightly upon the emerald-green sea, the ship let down her sails in a flourish of white canvass that seemed to glow in the golden rays. The breeze was warm and strong, and the *Danielle* moved smartly out of the harbor. A celebratory round was fired from the starboard side guns causing the crowd to cheer and applaud in excitement.

On the main deck, Delain Dowdeswell and her teacher, Mister Tupper, had different reactions to the explosions. Tupper, thin and frail looking in his spectacles and parson-like hat, was visibly shaken to the core and almost fell to the deck in horror and shock. He certainly couldn't stand another round and already feeling a bit dizzy from the swaying of the ship, he now felt his heart racing to escape his chest.

"Oh my! Do they do that often, Lieutenant?" he asked, shaking with worry and dread.

"No, no," laughed Harrison, who was standing beside the teacher. "We only fire the guns to say hello and good-bye, or if we see a pirate or two!"

Delain, on the other hand, was so surprised and delighted by the noise and rumble, that she immediately grabbed Jonathan's arm and simply requested for him to have the guns fired again.

As Delain waved to her father and mother, Captain Walker approached and addressed them.

"Lieutenant Harrison, will you choose a crew to assist in preparing the launch and carry the needed supplies for a single day? We will be just west of Conception Island within the hour and I would like you to supervise the good teacher and Miss Dowdeswell."

"With pleasure, Captain," he said.

"Remember, Lieutenant, there may be some pirate activity and a watchful eye would be most welcome," the Captain added.

As ordered, Harrison had the launch prepared. It was actually one of the larger boats attached to the *Danielle,* almost twenty-nine feet long and almost ten wide, with a mast that could be stood up or laid down and a sail for use if needed. There was a small cabin-like area in the bow to keep supplies dry and protect certain passengers from the weather should it turn foul. Oars were secured alongside in case rowing was in order.

Harrison then chose his crew. Though Spears volunteered for the duty and turtle watching, Harrison refused him and instead chose Jonathan and Sean, along with Hudson and Hicks, the two marines that assisted them at Skull Eye Island.

Delain appeared on deck wearing a simple dress, a light jacket, and carried a leather bag filled with drawing materials and the like. She watched the loading of the supplies by Jonathan and Sean and suggested a few improvements as to the placements of the articles in the boat.

Hudson and Hicks approached the launch, greeted Mister Harrison and thanked him for selecting them for an enjoyable duty.

"We'd be delighted to come, Lieutenant!" responded Hudson.

"But of course," added Hicks. "I'd love to see the turtles! I've 'eard the smaller ones are simply tender and juicy in a soup or just as a steak!"

Delain heard this plan for turtle soup and shrieked with horror. Even Jonathan and Sean stopped their loading and hauling to see if indeed, there would be some turtle for dinner, not sure if they would approve.

"Now, now, Miss Delain," assured Harrison. "No one will be harvesting any turtles! Isn't that right, men?"

Hudson and Hicks looked down dejectedly.

"Yes sir," they murmured, looking at their feet in embarrassment.

As promised, within the hour, the launch was steadied over the side as Delain and her crew, along with the somewhat queasy and green-skinned Mister Tupper, were lowered into the calm water. As the men erected the mast and let out the sail, she leaped away, like a small racing skiff, heading toward the sandy beach.

"Lieutenant Harrison!" called the Captain as the two ships departed on their separate missions. "Remember to post a watch, always. We will see you tomorrow by mid-morning, I suppose."

"Aye, Captain!" Harrison called, then motioned for Jonathan to set a course for the nearest beach. At the tiller, the long pole attached to the rudder that was used to steer the boat, Jonathan set a zigzagging course, heading just slightly into the oncoming wind, but a point or two to port. After a while, he came about, heading a point or two to starboard. He continued this back and forth action, *tacking,* it was called, until they were within a few yards of the sand.

"Take in sail!" called Harrison. Sean, Hudson and

Hicks hauled down the sail and the launch slowed just a bit, then firmly skidded up a few feet onto the sand before stopping. The men jumped out and pulled on ropes to move the launch even further upon the beach, then tied the ropes to two sturdy palm trees on either side of the bow.

"That should hold her," Harrison said happily, then escorted Mister Tupper off the boat and onto solid ground. "Better, Mister Tupper?"

The teacher simply nodded and dropped to his knees, exhausted and still looking a bit green.

Jonathan and the others stood on the white sand beach and observed the beauty of Conception Island. They saw white coral cliffs in a nearby bay surrounded by low rock outcroppings and scrub brush of various green hues. There was a large rise in the center of the island that certainly would command a great view of the surrounding waters. Palm trees dotted small beaches and all was outlined by calm and clear turquoise waters.

Immediately, Harrison instructed them to erect a tent with two compartments, one for Delain and the other for the rest of the party. Once completed, all continued on with their plans. Delain and Jonathan immediately began searching for turtles and their eggs. Sean and the marines climbed the small rise in the center of the island to watch the sea in all directions. It was possible that a pirate looking for a fight might choose to attack smaller ships when the odds seemed to be in their favor. After a few concerned looks about, Sean and the marines mostly spent their time sunning themselves, as Sean practiced reading from King Arthur. Hudson and Hicks greatly enjoyed the stories and corrected Sean if he had trouble with a word or two.

"You are doing wonderfully, Sean!" Hudson said.

"A regular orator if I must say so!" added Hicks. This delighted Sean, though he wasn't sure exactly what an 'orator' was, but by the smiles on both of the marines' faces, he was comfortable with the label.

Harrison explored the beaches and nearby coves,

looking for any stores used by pirates as hiding places. But there was nothing on the island except for the occasional lizard and now and again a small pig or two. He did return to the launch every hour on the hour to attend to Mister Tupper and make sure all was well. The teacher sat in the shade, unable to move, and groaned softly.

Delain, somewhat angry at the lack of turtles, continued her search, but was losing patience. She and Jonathan had been looking at every beach they could find and after seeing nothing all morning, they were beginning to think maybe Conception Island was bereft of all things amphibian. At one point, Jonathan looked up into the sky, as something caught his eye: a flock of seagulls, chattering as they flew above the next beach.

"What is peaking their interest?" asked Jonathan. "Those noisy gulls are certainly interested in something!"

"Babies!" cried Delain, now suddenly full of energy and excitement. She ran off through the brush, dropping her bag and disappearing into the flora. Jonathan paused and thought: *Babies? Human babies?*

He ran after her, fighting his way through the thick bush and sharp palm tree trunks. After a moment, he stumbled onto a small white-sand beach. There, before his feet, were hundreds of light-green baby turtles, none more than half a foot long, rushing from under the sand near the edge of the beach to the safety of the water. A flock of gulls numbering at least twelve dozen hovered a few feet above the earth. With relentless fury they swooped down upon the turtles. Several of the screaming birds actually caught a newborn in their beaks and by some miraculous ability, were able to fly away with their prize. Others kept trying and trying, lunging and crying out in an endless racket. Jonathan noticed a few of the turtles moved very quickly, probably the strongest and fastest of them, to make it safely to the water.

As amazing as the turtles were, Jonathan was mesmerized more so by Delain. She was howling and slashing her fists at the birds, jumping into the air, trying to scare them off. Her face was contorted into something almost horrible and menacing. Certainly, this was a side of Miss Dowdeswell that was not usually seen by many.

"Ahhh! Get away! Shooo!" she cried over and over again, though it was of little consequence as the gulls easily avoided her and continued pecking at the turtles.

Jonathan thought for a brief moment, hoping to find a way to assist his friend. Then he saw a long tree branch lying on the sand a few feet from his position. He quickly grabbed it, broke it in half, creating two sections of approximately four feet each. Grabbing one for each hand, he rushed to the beach, avoiding turtles as he ran.

"Delain! Delain!" he shouted. After a few more screams and swipes at the birds, she looked to him. "I will swat at the gulls! You carry as many babies as you can to the sea! Hurry!"

Jonathan now started screaming and swatting at the attackers as he ran in circles around Delain. This angered the birds, and only after a few were struck fatally by Jonathan's mad thrusts and swings, did they begin to yield. Delain was now able to snatch up six or seven of the baby turtles. Cradling them in her arms, she carried them to the surf and unceremoniously dumped them in the water, only to return for another load.

Some of the gulls, seeing that a madman was swinging at them, changed course and followed Delain. They began attacking her, pecking at her head and back as she stooped to pick up the frightened babies. Jonathan rushed to her side, but she waved him off.

"No, Jonathan! I am fine, keep swatting! Keep swatting!" she called.

The battle seemed to last for hours, as Jonathan chased gulls away and Delain gathered the frightened little ones, flapping their fins in the air. A few turtles even snapped at Delain, biting her fingers, though she paid them no mind. Jonathan had actually killed a good number of the birds and injured many more, however, more replaced them. Some moved to another area of the beach, wherever

Jonathan was *not.*

"How will we ever save them all?" cried Delain, tears streaming down her face. Jonathan felt pity for her, because he knew she must love them dearly. His heart was starting to feel heavy, knowing that many of the turtles would be killed and eaten, regardless of their actions.

"We must save as many as we can!" he yelled, "Think of the ones you are saving, not the ones you are losing! Think of them swimming in the sea, happy and growing old!"

Delain and a Turtle

Within another few minutes, it was over. All the turtles that could be saved had been, and those that were lost to the gulls were lost. The two heroes sat down heavily in the sand and Delain sobbed quietly. Jonathan held her hand and patted it gently.

"Delain, I am so sorry," he said. "But I am sure the dozens that you saved are grateful you came along. It was a kind thing you did."

Delain stopped sobbing after a moment and managed a smile.

"We did teach those birds a thing or two, didn't we?"

"Yes we did!" Jonathan answered. "They will think twice the next time they come to this beach. They will remember the day Miss Delain Dowdeswell, adventurer, came to call!"

They sat on the beach for an hour or more, until the sun began to set, saying nothing, just looking at the surf and breathing in the fine salt air. It would soon be time to return to the launch and then to sleep in their make-shift tent.

Delain leaned against Jonathan's shoulder and slowly drifted off to a deep sleep, exhausted by her task. Jonathan sat still by her side, looking at the sea, enjoying the sound of the water as it crashed upon the sand and the warmth of the sun on his face. Mostly, he realized he enjoyed the fact that Delain was there next to him. Her fine hair fluttered in the wind, sun lit golden shimmers dancing on each strand, hypnotizing him. He smiled, though soon broke the spell by turning his gaze to the bay, observing the different colors of the water: the emerald green close to shore, rich dark blue in the deep, and every combination in-between. On the far shoals made of coral, hundreds of yards off shore, the water broke into foamy white streaks that stood out like small sails on the horizon.

As Jonathan watched the white water crash and return to the blue, he noticed how some looked even more like sails than others and that a few of those seemed to have a longer life, taking more time to crash and disappear. He watched far in the offing as two of the white waves seemed to be taking a very long time to crash. He blinked his eyes, thinking the sun was playing tricks on him. Then his heart skipped a beat.

"Delain?" he said softly, rubbing his eyes.

"What is it, Jonathan?"

He quickly stood up to get a better look. Yes, it was now clear. The white waves did not disappear, as they were not waves at all. Jonathan ran to his coat he had left on the edge of the beach and pulled out his telescope from the sleeve. After a hasty focus on the spot he had seen in the waves, he cried aloud.

"Dear me!"

Delain ran to him.

"Jonathan! What is it?" she asked frantically.

There was no mistaking it. As he stared into the glass, it became clear that the waves were actually sails; discolored and dirty, even with a few holes in them. A ship and her men were now visible, a motley crew to be sure.

"Pirates!" he said. "Heading our way!"

* * * * * *

Sean stood on a low rise of the small island with Hudson and Hicks, smiling and laughing as they picked the wild strawberries that were growing in a patch at their feet. Having nowhere to put them or carry them for their later enjoyment, they simply ate them immediately.

"It would certainly be nice to have a bowl of cream with these berries, don't you think?" asked Hudson.

"Aye, it would," said Hicks. "But, alas, we 'ave none."

Sean thought for a moment as he stuffed his twentieth berry into his mouth and chewed slowly, enjoying each bite.

"Cream, yes that would be good," he said, "though we don't have any and, well, it would just get in the way of all this *strawberry!*"

Hudson and Hicks stopped their chewing for a moment, looked at each other, then nodded.

"Yes, I see your point," said Hudson.

"When ya put it that way, well, 'oo needs cream?" said Hicks.

After a few more berries were devoured, they heard a call and looked up to see Jonathan and Delain running toward them on the beach below.

"Up here, Jonny Boy!" Sean called, "And have we got a surprise for you!"

"I bet I have a better one!" Jonathan said as they climbed the short rise then sat down puffing and straining to catch their breath.

"'Have ya got any cream by chance?" asked Hicks.

"Cream? Whatever for?" asked Delain.

Sean pointed down to the ground.

"For the strawberries!" Sean answered.

Jonathan and Delain looked down and saw what remained of the patch after the three had grazed for probably a half hour, non-stop. Only a couple of small berries were visible.

"There were more a moment ago," said Sean sheepishly.

Just then, Mister Harrison appeared. He was holding two dirty glass bottles, with dark liquid in them.

"I found this rum in a nearby cave! There is much more besides, probably left here by rum runners or the last few pirates. I would think they will return for it. This is all I dared take as it is time to eat and ready our evening, lady and gentlemen. To the launch!"

"There is a small complication, Mister Harrison," Delain announced.

"I believe we may have seen the owners of the bottles. Pirates," Jonathan added.

"That is your surprise?" asked Sean. "Well, not as tasty as strawberries, but a bit more interesting!"

Jonathan took a moment to explain what he and Delain had seen and that it was unmistakable. The dirty sails, sloppy crew and hap hazard way the ship was attended to meant that it could only be a pirate ship.

"How many masts, Jonathan?" asked Harrison.

"Three with a small spanker in the stern," Jonathan said. "It looked like a twenty-four gun brig if I were to wager a guess. A fully-rigged sloop."

"Men?" asked Harrison.

"I counted less than three on deck and ten in the masts." Jonathan answered.

"Let's have a look, and for the King's sake, keep out of sight. Stay off the beaches," Harrison said as they all moved to the edge of the rise and took turns sharing Jonathan's glass.

After everyone had taken a gander at the ship, it was clear that sailing off in the launch was not going to be possible without being noticed. A single shot from one of the pirate guns, all at least nine-pounders, would destroy the boat and probably kill all aboard. Also, the possibility of hiding the launch in the brush was discussed and abandoned quickly. It was larger than a jollyboat and three times as heavy. Jonathan pointed out that maybe the pirates were coming for the rum that Harrison had found and they might leave right after obtaining it.

"Surely you are correct, Mister Moore," Harrison said. "In fact, I would think they will send a small jolly boat in to take the bottles and be off. Let us wait and see and take our chances that they will not discover the launch."

By now the sun had almost set, a few weak beams streaking through the trees of the island, and a slight wind started to gain force. Harrison watched the moves of the pirates onboard the ship, and now and again, he would count to himself and ask Jonathan to confirm the number of men he could see.

Delain and Sean went to attend to Mister Tupper, who at least was now sitting upright, leaning against the bow of the launch. He accepted the last two strawberries that Delain had taken from the patch and seemed to enjoy the slightly cooler breeze that now had reached the beach.

"I hope I never have to set foot upon a sea going vessel as long as I live, Miss Delain," Tupper said. "Though I understand some actually prefer that life, it would be the death of me."

Jonathan and Harrison, with the two marines, kept an eye on the pirate ship. They all agreed that there could be no more than forty men aboard. They had also identified one who appeared to be the captain, a tall yet slight man in a raggedy grey beard who seemed to order the others about, but with little effect. The discipline was lax at best.

"It would seem," said Harrison, "That the captain of this ship has slightly less control over his crew than even a French captain possesses."

The other laughed a bit, remembering the tales of the crew of the *Danielle* when it was a French ship of the line. The almost democratic way the ship was managed, allowing all members to have a say in what was done, seemed comical to the strict and rule-ridden life aboard a British sailing vessel.

"I am not sure what they will do, but no matter what, we can not leave until they do it," Harrison said. "We had better hope they can't see the launch, if they haven't already. The last thing we need is a fight right now."

"Maybe the *Danielle* will return early and assist us?" suggested Hicks.

"Possibly, but unlikely," said Harrison. "They must sail around almost all the islands, with tacking and such. They will be awhile yet, at least until the early morning. It would be best if we avoid detection and sleep here through the night. We can take turns watching and if the *Danielle* arrives in time, we will watch her make short work of them!"

At this point, Jonathan was watching the pirate ship through his glass. He thought that though the ship was dirty and probably ridden with rats and fleas, it deserved better. He remembered of how poorly all had considered the condition of the *Danielle* when she was won in battle and how splendid she shined when Sean and his beautification crew had spent months on her repair. Didn't this ship deserve the same attention? It was smaller by far than the *Dani* and just slightly larger than the *Paladin* and

Echo, however, it had graceful lines and stood proud and ready in the water. If he could only have a chance to clean her and add a bit of paint and sail, well, wouldn't everyone think she was pretty? And that gave him an idea.

"Mister Harrison?" he asked, "Why wait for the *Danielle*?"

"Whatever do you mean, Jonathan?" asked Harrison.

"How many men does it actually take to sail a ship like this pirate brig? Not into battle, mind you, just to sail it for a day at the most."

Harrison thought for a moment. "To sail it how far, Jonathan?"

"Let us say, just to Nassau," Jonathan said, putting down the telescope and grinning.

"I would say one to man the wheel, at least two in the sails and two more on the ropes to cast off," Harrison said, now smiling as well. "So that would be five experienced hands."

"Funny that we have five with us right now," said Jonathan.

"A-are you suggestin', Mister Moore, that we should simply take the ship?" quivered Hicks.

"J-just the f-five of us?" added Hudson, not sure if he liked the idea any more than did Hicks.

"I believe I am!" laughed Jonathan. "And each Royal Marine is worth at least five pirates, don't you think?"

"As long as the pirates know that..." added Hudson in reply.

"And I assume you have formulated a plan to get us past the *forty* pirates aboard?" added Harrison, knowing the answer.

As the stars came out and the wind settled down to a calm, cool breeze, pirate Captain Hiram Petterwick gazed at the island before his ship. It was called Conception, he remembered, and according to some of his crew, there was a great store of rum hidden in one of the caves; over six-hundred bottles to be precise. That would certainly fetch a pretty penny and go a long way to pleasing the restless crew aboard the *Fiero*. His order to wait until the morning before beginning the search was an unpopular one. But as the previous captain had explained, it was no use having the crew drunk at night, when a British warship could sneak up and capture them. Better to wait until morning, find the treasure, then get underway quickly while all were sober.

Petterwick thought that was great advice from the previous captain and he heeded it; right before he mutinied and locked him in the brig. Though the *Fiero* didn't actually have a brig, per say, chaining the old captain to an overhead beam below deck had the same effect as putting in a steel-barred cell.

As Petterwick stared at the island, he thought he saw a flicker of light coming from a low hillside. Maybe his eyes were playing tricks on him, maybe not. He raised his telescope once again and waited. After a moment, just when he was about to lower the glass, he saw it again. And this time, it was brighter and did not flicker. It remained on. It had an amber glow. And then a shadow moved in front of it from time to time. A fire?

"Porter!" he shouted. "Get up here with 'yer glass and take a look at this! Hurry now!"

His mate, Obadiah Porter, appeared after a few moments and lazily took up his glass and searched in the general direction of the island.

"And just what am I a lookin' fer, Petterwick?" he said.

"It's *Captain* Petterwick, you son of a hog! And it's a fire yer lookin' fer. Right in the center of the rise!"

Obadiah Porter adjusted his telescope and soon found the fire. He could see someone in front of it. The figure looked to be dancing.

"Looks like a party, *Captain*," he said. "And now I see another fire a bit to the left! And there are a few shadows there as well. And they seem to be drinking. Yup. They's a drinkin'."

Captain Petterwick strained to see the shadows and

their dancing, but his telescope was not as accurate as Obadiah Porter's. All he could see was the bright fire, flickering in the wind.

"What do ya suppose they are drinking?" asked Petterwick.

"I can't tell from here, *captain*, but it's straight out of a bottle, I can see that!" said Porter.

Petterwick had a cold feeling wash over him. *Straight out of a bottle?* he thought. *Is it the rum we are coming for?*

As he looked again at the island, to his horror, he saw several other fires appear on the hillside and one on the beach right in front of them. A quick scan showed that each had a man or two, swigging from a bottle, dancing and cavorting. Next to some fires, there were men passed out in the sand, probably from too much drink, and all that was visible was their oddly shaped coats. He glared at the closest of the fires, the one on the beach.

"Well I'll be cursed to coal!" he said, "There a young woman there! She's drinking from a bottle of rum! Dancing with some short fellow with blonde hair! Right on the beach!"

Porter looked to the beach and was aghast at what he saw. He found the young girl easily and as he focused the glass, he saw her take two full bottles of rum and dump the contents into the fire, sending the flames leaping high into the air.

"She's mad, I tell ya!" Porter said. "She just emptied two completely perfect bottles of rum onto the fire! It's a waste, I tell ya! A waste! But, well, it's not my rum, it's her own loss, eh?"

Petterwick looked at the scene and again had another cold chill come over him.

"I wonder," added Porter, "Why, with all these fires goin' on, there are at least twenty or more souls on that island, all drinking rum like it was going out of style. Where would they get all that rum?"

"You idiot!" exploded Petterwick. "That's our rum! The rum we came to steal from whoever left it here in the first place! I am sure they think they have beat us to it!"

"What should we do?" asked Porter.

"Get the men up! Let's get in the boats and sneak up on 'em! We can certainly take them easily as they have been a drinkin' and we have not!"

"A good point, Petterwick!" Porter said.

9
The Ghost at the Gun

From the brush on the beach, Jonathan laughed as he saw Sean, Hudson, Hicks and Delain running from fire to fire, carrying on as if they had too much to drink and dumping rum in every possible place. Hudson and Hicks certainly had taken their roles as drunken sailors *literally* and had taken a few generous swallows just to be convincing. Even Mister Tupper, now feeling almost human again, joined in. It was his idea to stuff a few jackets and blouses with palm fronds and twigs, then top them with coconuts, making a few extra bodies for the ruse.

As the party continued, Harrison joined Jonathan by the bushes next to the beach.

"The launch is ready to go," Harrison said. "Have they taken the bait?"

"Just now, yes!" said Jonathan excitedly. "And none too soon. The sun is just coming up. I can see the purple glow of night changing as we speak."

It had taken most of the night gathering enough bottles, collecting wood to build the fires, and creating the stuffed sailors to be positioned just so. Now it was time to spring the trap before the sun rose and the trick was foiled.

"I will get Hudson and Hicks," said Harrison. "You retrieve Delain and Sean and meet us at the launch!"

"Yes sir!" said Jonathan excitedly, slapping his telescope closed and taking his jacket from a tree that was 'wearing' it.

Petterwick had set both boats of the *Fiero* in the water with almost twenty men in each. That only left two aboard and the prisoner of course, however the new pirate captain determined that the more fighters on the island, the better their chances. He and Porter had only guessed at the number of men ashore. It could be twenty, forty - maybe even one hundred. Though all of his men were experienced in fighting and attacking beaches, they were nervous still. A fight was a fight and some may not return. They carried their swords, a few pistols, a dozen or so knives and certainly a few axes; all brought along for the short trip to the beach. The pirates continued their trip, rowing softly and quietly through the calm water.

Harrison, Hudson and Hicks pushed the launch into the sea and carefully assisted the others in climbing aboard. Through the pale moonlight they could barely discern the way out of the small bay, but soon, after a bit of sail was added, they were slowly moving into open water, turning toward the pirate ship.

"I see them!" whispered Jonathan, again looking into his telescope. "They are almost to the beach!"

"Then let us make haste and approach the ship from the seaward side," said Harrison. "I am sure all hands on deck are looking to the island!"

Petterwick was now at the bow of the first jolly boat and was readying himself for the jolt of the boat hitting the sandy beach. His sword was drawn and he heard the others behind him do the same.

"Remember, men, quiet and easy!" he whispered hoarsely. "Sneaky like a cat! They will probably be too drunk to resist!"

The other pirates chuckled to themselves, sure that Petterwick was correct.

The boats hit the beach, making a hushed sighing sound as their wood bows met the sand of the shore. The pirates jumped out. Each ran to his assigned fire, weapons at the ready. They were silent and swift. The pirates fell upon the sleeping forms in the sand, striking with deadly accuracy. They hacked, they stabbed and there was even a pistol shot or two. However, something was wrong.

"Got ya!" yelled Porter as he removed his sword from the head of a sleeping form. There was a coconut stuck to his blade.

"What in the stinking swamp is this?" he said surprised.

Petterwick pulled his blade from the blouse of his target and saw that no blood was upon his sword. He stood there, stunned, not knowing what was happening. These were not real men.

"By the tricks of Hades, what is going on?" Petterwick called. "These are not men! They be dummies!"

As the two remaining pirate hands stood on deck of the *Fiero,* watching the jolly boats disappear into the darkness, Jonathan, Harrison and Sean shimmied up the anchor rope, the hawser, and after much effort, reached the top. They swiftly pulled themselves over the rail and gently stepped on deck. From the launch below, Hudson tossed a rope to Jonathan who quickly fastened it to a cleat nearby, thereby securing the launch to the *Fiero.* Quite to the surprise of all, Delain made her way up the rope easily and was stunned as the boys looked at her in awe. She shrugged, remaining silent, then lent a hand assisting Hicks and finally Hudson over the rail and onto the deck.

"I am afraid I am too weak to climb!" said Tupper from the launch. "Might I stay here?"

"As you wish, Mister Tupper," whispered Harrison. "But if we are unsuccessful, I suggest you release the rope and drift back to the island as quietly as possible."

"Oh," said Tupper. "I see, well, you carry on and I will see if I can muster the strength to join you."

All knew their roles and each moved quickly to their positions. Hudson remained by the hawser, ready to cut the *Fiero's* anchor loose with his sword. Hicks gave his sword to Jonathan, then joined Sean and Harrison as they crept to the foremast. There, they began silently climbing the rat lines upward, making their way to the sails and the ropes that held them. With only the three of them to manage the sheets, it would take quite some time, sliding across the beams and letting out the sails on all three masts.

Since Harrison was the only member of the boarding party who had piloted a ship of this size, he was the designated *master*. After letting down a bit of sail, he ran to the wheel, leaving only Delain and Jonathan to do away with the two hands of the *Fiero*.

As always, Jonathan had a plan in mind and explained it to Delain, who was more than delighted to be part of the 'cutting out' of the ship, as the boys had called this small adventure.

Silently she crept up to the men looking at the island and waited for Jonathan to get into position just to the side, behind a pile of broken barrels and other debris left on deck. Delain bent her head down almost to the floor and removed the ribbons and ties from her hair. She then shook her damp locks, ran her fingers through them just so and quickly brought her head upwards. This flinging of her hair, combined with the dampness in the air, held her golden strands out straight and puffy. It was as if she had been windblown most of the day, which of course, she had. After loosening her small jacket, Delain held her arms up in the air and began rolling her head about in a strange fashion, like she was possessed by a spirit. Into the failing light of the moon she drifted. Even to Jonathan, she appeared beautiful, yet haunting and almost unreal. *A golden ghost!* he thought to himself, and stifled a laugh.

"They 'ave been gone a long time!" said one of the pirates. "I wonder if they're already looking for the rum."

"Better them then me, mate, I can tell ya that right now. Let them do the dirty work and let us take the easy duty, eh?" said the other one.

"Right on that, mate. Safe and sound I always say!"

After a moment of silence, a voice, deep and airy, cut through the air.

"Ayeee aaaaam aay loossst ssspreeerit!"

The two pirates paused for a second, then turned to each other.

"Was that you?" asked the first one.

"I thought it was you," said the second.

They both turned slowly, the hairs on the back of their necks standing on end. They beheld the ghost from the mist. They were shocked into silence, shaking in their shoes. Her hair blew in the wind and she gyrated as if containing horror and evil.

"Ayeee cooome from theee deaaad too speeek to those abooout to leeeave thee liiiiving!"

"W-what do you say, spirit? We are about to leave the living?" said the first pirate as he shook and quivered in fear.

Creeping out from behind the barrels, Jonathan slowly made his way to stand behind the pirates. As he looked at Delain he had to remind himself that she was not really a ghost. *She is really quite convincing, I must say!* he thought. Raising his sword, he was now serious with his duty. It seemed wrong to strike these men down without warning, without giving them a chance to defend themselves, yet, he had to think of the mission. If these two were not put down, then they could spoil the plan and even worse, harm himself or his friends, even Delain. He gritted his teeth and raised Hick's sword over his head.

Just then, another voice joined the conversation, this one from far off.

"Dwayne! Barnus! It's a trick! A trick!"

It was the voice of Petterwick, coming from the shore. As all looked toward the island, the sun was now seen glowing in the east and two jolly boats could easily be seen making their way back to the *Fiero*.

"A trick?" said the first pirate.

"That's what he said, Dwayne!" said the second.

"Stop them!" yelled Petterwick from the first boat. "Stop them before they take the ship!"

The pirate now known as Dwayne turned back to Delain and muttered under his breath.

"Wait a minute! Yer not a ghost, are ya?"

"In the sunlight, she looks more like … a little girl!"

exclaimed Barnus, the second pirate.

As if to answer, Delain kicked Dwayne in the nose. As Barnus drew his sword, Jonathan wrapped him on the head with the hilt of his blade, sending the pirate to the rail, writhing in pain.

"Where did you come from?" demanded Barnus as he held his bloody nose.

"The streets of London!" said Jonathan, and with that, he shoved Barnus over the rail. He turned quickly and held his blade to Dwayne's neck. "It is your choice, but you better make up your mind before I count to three -"

Dwayne did not wait for the count. He immediately jumped over the rail, landing in the water below with a great splash.

"They are on to us!" yelled Jonathan.

"Let out the sail! Slip the anchor!" yelled Harrison.

The sun now broke over the horizon and from the jolly boats, Petterwick and his crew could see the soiled sails of the *Fiero* drop slowly and unevenly, then fill slightly with the wind. A chopping sound was heard and he looked to see a Royal Marine hacking at the hawser.

"It's the British! They are stealing our ship! Faster men! Row faster!" called Petterwick, and the men began rowing with amazing fury. They were gaining on the *Fiero*, as it seemed to have trouble getting underway. Even when Hudson had finished cleaving the rope that held the anchor, the *Fiero* dawdled and barely moved.

"There is no wind!" called Harrison. "Hicks! Flagon! Let out more sail! Hudson, help them!"

With great speed and agility, the two marines and Sean climbed the main mast and hurried to let out as much sail as they could. The sun was now up completely, making it clear that the pirates were less than a hundred yards away.

Standing on the port side, Jonathan and Delain stared at the approaching boats. A shot rang out and splinters flew from a spar just above Delain's head.

"Stay down, Delain!" Jonathan called, pushing her

lower to hide behind the rail.

"What can we do?" yelled Delain. "They will be here any moment!"

Jonathan considered their situation, looking around for an answer. *What do I have at my disposal?* he thought. *What is here that I can use?*

He noticed that near the stern was a pair of portside deck guns. *Ten pounders to be sure,* he said to himself. *With a well-aimed shot or two, maybe we could slow down the approaching boats.*

"Wait here! I will find powder for those guns!"

Jonathan disappeared below decks, using a hatch and ladder near the stern rail. It was hard to see in the dark, though as his eyes became adjusted, he searched the hold quickly. Being such a small ship, with only a single deck below, he soon found small cartridges and a few balls. Then he paused. A sound. Jonathan believed he heard laughing, laughing up close, but after a quick look around, he dismissed it as one of those strange creaking noises that ships made in the water. He ran to the upper deck as fast as he could, carrying his supplies. Once in the brighter light, he waited for his eyes to adjust, and there was Delain at the guns.

"Hurry, Jonathan! Hurry!" she called.

"Excuse me, Miss Dowdeswell," Jonathan said firmly approaching the weapons. "Guns are very dangerous. Please stand aside." He handed her his sword, then positioned her at the center of the deck, out of harm's way.

She nodded, saying "By all means, Mister Moore, please continue."

The wind began to pick up and the ship began moving ahead, though pitifully slow. Harrison seemed to struggle a bit at the wheel, but he held on, concentrating his energy.

Jonathan quickly grabbed a ramrod and shoved it down the barrel of the first, then the second gun. He then rammed a cartridge into each and lastly a ball. Next, the touch hole needed cleaning before he could light the gun, however, there was no touch hole. *Odd,* he thought, *how does one light it?*

"The chain on the back, Jonathan!" called Harrison, still at the wheel, "It sparks when you pull on the chain!"

"Ingenious!" exclaimed Delain, now fascinated with the entire process of cleaning, loading and hopefully firing the gun.

"I see!" called Jonathan, and he turned to aim the first gun at the approaching boats.

"Now Miss Dowdeswell," he said, "Please stand back as I can tell you-"

There was a scream.

It was Delain. Jonathan looked at her face and noticed it was a strange shade of white, her eyes were wide open, her mouth as well. She seemed unable to speak, so finally pointed behind him.

Jonathan spun around right as a sword blade fell inches from his head. It was Dwayne, bloody nose and all, still dizzy from Delain's kick, but aggressively slashing at Jonathan, who backed away. *He must have made his way up an errant rope,* thought Jonathan, *and now I must deal with him again!* With no sword, Jonathan was certainly at a great disadvantage.

"The boats, Jonny Boy!" called Sean from the tops. "They are almost here!"

"Busy, Sean!" he called as he ducked from a wild slash by Dwayne.

"Ya snotty brat!" Dwayne called. "Ya got the drop on me once! How do ya like a bit o' yer own medicine, eh?"

Jonathan crawled backwards, dodging thrusts and swipes by the clumsy pirate, slowly making his way to the center of the deck. He was hoping Delain would kick his sword to him, yet she seemed too excited to do anything but gasp in fear.

"Miss Dowdeswell, my sword if you please!"

"Oh!" Delain said. "So sorry. By all means Mister Moore." And with that she retrieved his blade and after some inspection of the situation, tossed it toward Jonathan's general direction. After its short flight through the air, the sword spun perfectly to land point downward, the tip firmly driven into Dwayne's right foot.

"Owe! Oh! By the saints!" he cried out.

Jonathan swiftly lunged forward and yanked the sword out of Dwayne's foot, then quickly stood up, composing himself for the duel.

"Make short work of him!" called Sean from the tops as he and the marines let out additional sail, "They are almost upon us!"

By now, Dwayne was bloodied and hurt, but he was still dangerous. Besides being quite a bit larger than Jonathan, he fought like a wild beast, not as sophisticated as the French spies or British officers who trained Jonathan. This time, the midshipman had his hands full.

Delain, on the other hand, took one look at the boats, another at the guns and said to herself, *Well, there is no time like the present to learn a new trick!*

She approached the first gun and looked down the barrel. *There must be a way to aim it*, she thought. *Maybe one just guesses. It looks as if I were to pull the chain, the ball would land right in front of that first boat!*

She took one last look down the barrel.

"Stand to the side!" called Jonathan as he glanced her way. "Stand to the side of the gun! Not behind!"

"Oh! Thank you, Mister Moore. That makes perfect sense," Delain replied.

She stepped to the side of the gun and pulled the chain.

Petterwick saw the flash from the gun, only forty yards away. He had just enough time to duck as the ball sailed over his head, a mere foot from his scalp. It struck the other boat that happened to be directly behind, exploding the bow into a cloud of splinters and smoke. The men fell into the water as the jolly boat quickly sunk.

"Dear me!" exclaimed Delain. "That was not where I was aiming, however, one must make due. I did not compensate for the fact that they were moving toward me. This next one should be just a bit lower!" She moved to the second gun and began her aiming ritual.

Jonathan finally had an opening and with a few quick feints and a lunge, had wounded Dwayne and swiftly kicked him in the buttock, sending him over the rail. He turned to Delain as she labored over the gun.

"Delain! Wait! I will take the next shot!"

"Nonsense!" Delain said. "After I have now got the hang of it?"

She pulled the chain. A puff of smoke and flame shot out of the end of the gun. The ball raced through the air with a *whoosh!*

Petterwick saw the second flash and thought to himself in an instant: *The last one just missed, I will not be so lucky this time!*

"Abandon ship!" he yelled, and jumped over the side into the cool water. The men aboard scrambled about, trying to get away, but the ball struck dead center, sending men, wood and hopes up in smoke.

Jonathan ran to the rail and looked at the pirates in the water, all swimming madly back to the island. They appeared to him as angry kittens, all wet and eyes wide with fear. They were quite a way from the beach, but with some effort and determination, they could make it to the shore safely.

"An excellent display of shooting, Miss Dowdeswell," Jonathan said. "It's as if you have been doing it your whole life!"

Delain smiled and curtsied ever so slightly. "One never knows what one can do unless tested, as Mister Tupper always says!"

As the sun continued its rise in the east, the wind finally appeared, modestly filling the sails. The *Fiero* moved slowly but steadily east into deeper water toward the nearby island of San Salvador with Lieutenant Harrison still at the wheel. He laughed aloud in joy.

"We did it! We have captured our first prize!" he called out. Sean and the marines came down from the tops and joined Harrison at the wheel, all clapping their hands and congratulating each other.

Hudson and Hicks took some time to complete a thorough search through the holds of the ship, starting at the bow, as Jonathan, Sean and Harrison became familiar with the sails and rigging. Delain even received a fast lesson at the helm and within a minute or two, she was at the wheel, guiding the ship south toward home.

"Amazing!" she said repeatedly, fully enjoying the thrill of moving the ship through the water, "who would have reasoned one could actually sail *into* the wind and make progress!"

Sean, on the other hand, was not so easily impressed with their new means of transportation. He surveyed the ship and shook his head disapprovingly.

"Aye, it's a wonder she even floats!" said Sean. "So many leaks and broken pieces, I'd think it will take months to make her sea worthy!"

"You have experience with this type of renovation, Seaman Flagon," Harrison said. "I am sure the Captain will have you in charge of the *Fiero's* repairs when we get to Nassau!"

They all laughed again as Hudson and Hicks appeared on deck with worried looks on their faces.

"Hudson! Hicks," said Harrison fondly, "Report!"

"Aye Captain," they said.

"I like the sound of that!" said Harrison.

"That is right!" beamed Jonathan. "Since you are in command on this ship, that makes you her captain! Congratulations, Mister Harrison - er, I mean *Captain* Harrison!"

"If the *Captain* would like to know," interrupted Hudson, "We found something of interest below deck."

"Maybe more accurately, *someone*," corrected Hicks.

"Someone?" asked Harrison.

"Yes sir," replied Hudson. "It seems that this ship has more than Miss Dowdeswell as a ghost. There is a gentleman below, clapped in irons as there is no brig. 'says he's an American."

"He says his name is Kozak," added Hudson.

As they all wondered about this new development, they were interrupted by a swooshing sound that grew louder and louder. Immediately, the sailors and marines recognized the noise and crouched to the ground instinctively. Jonathan reached for Delain and pulled her to the deck. The deep swooshing sound could only mean a gun shot, a ball shooting across the bow of the Fiero.

Quickly, Jonathan and Harrison took up their glasses and looked toward the east, away from the many islands to starboard. It was a large warship, bearing down upon them.

"Oh my, my!" said Jonathan. "It is the *Danielle*!"

The others looked as best they could, but even to Delain, the great ship was easily recognizable, though many yards away. She was approaching fast from the northern tip of San Salvador.

"Why are they shooting at us?" asked Sean.

"Oh!" Harrison cried. "Look atop our main mast! How could I be so stupid?"

As they looked up, there was nothing to see, because it was not something they were looking for; the mistake was that something was *missing*. There was no flag flying. No colors.

"Aye, they think we're a pirate!" said Hudson.

"Not good," said Hicks. "And bad luck to be blowed out of the water by your own mates, eh?"

"We must think of something!" said Harrison.

"Can't we just turn toward them, so they can see it is us?" suggested Delain, now equally concerned.

Harrison looked worried and took the helm from Delain. He shook his head.

"Turning toward them might be seen as an intent to

engage, to attack. We must drop sail, showing we do not mean to give chase, but with this little wind and only a few hands, it may take too long!"

Suddenly a voice from below rose up.

"Pardon me," it said.

They all became startled. They had forgotten that Mister Tupper was alongside, a few yards astern, in the launch.

"I have an idea" he said. "Miss Dowdeswell, may I have a private word with you?"

Aboard the *Danielle,* Captain Walker and Lieutenant Holtz stood on the bow, as the men aboard raced to battle stations. The ship always came alive at times like these and if one didn't mind his steps and position, one could easily be trampled as the hands rushed to guns, sail and rope.

Lieutenant Blake had spotted the small ship just a minute before and alerted the captain to the two large sails and a small mizzen at the stern.

"A twenty-gun sloop, sir," he said. "No colors at all. If I didn't know better, I'd say she was a dead ringer for HMS *Drake.*"

"The *Drake*?" said Captain Walker. "That was lost almost...twenty-five years ago. Though there are many like her, a good size for rum runners and aspiring pirates. Let's send a shot across her bow so she knows we are here."

With that, Blake attended to the deck guns on the bow and had one readied with powder and ball. Mister Watt, ever present at the wheel, came slightly into the wind giving Blake the chance to aim just a bit ahead of the smaller craft.

"Fire!" he yelled, and the ball headed toward its mark.

Walker continued to stare with his glass at his prey. After a moment, he could see the ball strike the sea a dozen or so yards ahead of the sloop, sending up a small fountain of water. By now, he could also see there was no flag atop the main and that certainly meant a pirate, and more importantly, a nice prize for himself and the crew. Any ship captured by a British captain was to be sold at action, or purchased outright by the Royal Navy itself. The monies collected were then split, somewhat unevenly, by the officers and the crew. The Captain received the lion's share, followed by the lieutenants, other officers, midshipmen, and finally the members of the crew. Even the Admiral that was above Captain Walker received a share. Walker thought of how easy it would be, as the *Danielle* could pull alongside this smaller ship and literally take all her guns repeatedly and not even show a scratch.

"Easy money and a nice barky as well, if she is cleaned up!" said Steward, who just happened by.

"Possibly," Walker said calmly. "Let's keep the men at their guns, Mister Holtz."

Spears and Lane now appeared on deck and reported to the Captain that all guns were manned and ready.

"Excellent. Keep watch on them boys and listen for the command to fire." Walker lowered his glass and turned to Holtz.

"It seems Mister Moore will miss another battle! Ha! Can you make out anything aboard her, Lieutenant?"

"No sir," Holtz said, looking through his eyepiece. "Not really, however, I do see someone climbing the main mast, possibly to display their colors?"

As he watched, he could barely make out a small form ascending the main mast. He focused his glass and saw that the man had finally reached the top, and had pulled a fabric of some sort from within his blouse. As they sailed closer still, Holtz could see that the man atop the sheets was blonde haired. He frantically tried to attach the fabric to the head of the main mast, and after a moment, the breeze kicked up and unfurled it just enough to be seen. Holtz had to look twice to be sure he was certain.

"What is it, Holtz? What is the flag?" asked Walker, impatiently.

"Well, sir," Holtz said, "not a flag, really."

"Then what in the bloody blue blazes is it, man!?" exploded Walker, now impatient and eager to engage his ship.

"They have raised no flag, but, well, it's bloomers, sir. A ladies bloomers."

Indeed as they neared the *chase*, the ship they were pursuing, it could be seen that it had taken in all sail to show the intent not to fight or flee. Even the old eyes of Captain Walker, who had seen everything there was to see on the blue ocean, had now admitted to himself that this was certainly new: a ship flying white ladies bloomers from the main mast. As he continued to observe through his glass, some figures came into view, waving and jumping at the stern of the brig. He could not hear their cries, but he didn't have to. As he adjusted the glass on his 'scope, he brought into view the recognizable crew of his prey.

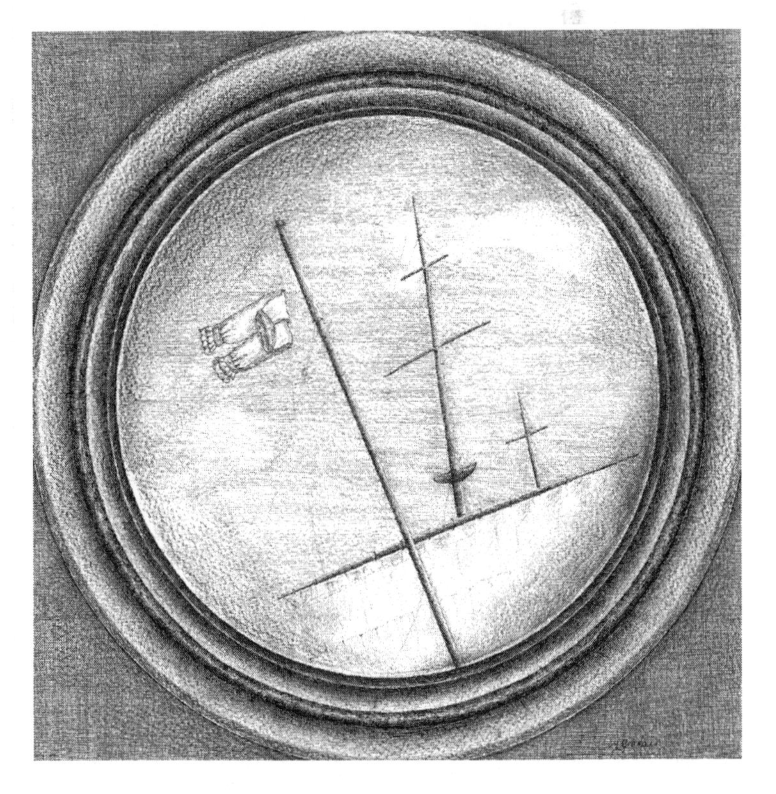

Not the flag of a pirate

"Have the men stand down, Lieutenant. Secure the guns. She's a friendly."

"A friendly? With such a strange flag?"asked Holtz.

"Yes, Lieutenant. It seems the prize has already been taken... by Mister Harrison and his band!"

"Harrison?" blurted Steward. "His first prize and only a wet-eared lieutenant? Oh, by the saints, there will be no living with 'em!"

Walker laughed loudly as the *Danielle* closed her gun ports and signaled her intent to come along side.

10

Finally, a Pirate

As the boys were welcomed aboard the *Danielle* to the cheers of the crew, Jonathan, Sean and Harrison beamed with pride. The marines and Delain also were applauded and immediately invited to the Captain's cabin for toasted cheese, coffee and the like. Mister Tupper excused himself and went to find a cool place to lie down and hopefully sleep a little of his sea sickness away. He was happy to be on a much larger ship, as the launch seemed to accentuate each wave and swell. The *Danielle*, on the other hand, was like a small city, sailing through the calm Caribbean waters, barely a tilt or a slant to be felt.

A party of marines boarded the *Fiero* to catalog all the wares and stores aboard. They even removed the prisoner and placed him in the brig aboard the *Danielle,* as he was considered a pirate. He was fed a small fish sandwich, a bowl of Claise's stew and a streaming cup of coffee. A marine was posted outside the door, just in case. His fate, said Captain Walker, would be decided after he had heard the complete tale from Harrison.

As the new heroes entered the Captain's cabin, Steward was laying out plates, cups and saucers, and a variety of treats he had created. As this meal was a special occasion, Claise was serving as well. He had been asked to *assist* Steward in the preparation by the Captain himself, though all knew he did almost all the cooking. There were small, puffy rolls with sugar and cream on the inside, toasted cheese of course, and tea and coffee. There also were fresh eggs, cheesed and peppered, and some sliced ham as well. Jonathan and Sean looked at each other and smiled, as they did whenever a wonderful meal was placed before them.

All officers and midshipmen were in attendance, as well as Sean and Delain, making the room crowded once again. Even though all windows were opened, it remained a bit stuffy. Hudson and Hicks, who had never seen the Captain's cabin, were delighted to attend and stood at attention, away from the table, until they were invited to help themselves to the fare.

"Well, well, well," Walker said. "It seems –" and he stopped. The Captain turned his head slightly to one side and closed his eyes.

"Sir?" said Harrison. "Are you well?"

"Shhhh!" snapped Walker. He listened for a long moment. "Do you hear it?"

Jonathan listened intently. And then … there was … a faint rattling.

"A rattle?" he asked.

"Yes!" cried Walker, happy that someone else had heard the noise. Each night, as he stood on the poop deck, he would hear the scraping from time to time and believed that he may be going mad. Unable to find the cause, he walked about the deck, listening. "Do you hear it, Mister Moore?"

Jonathan listened again, though he now heard only the sounds of the busy ship.

"I do not, now, sir," he said. "It could just be my ears ringing. I was very close to the guns aboard the *Fiero*."

Walker seemed to frown at Jonathan's lack of confidence in his hearing and waved his hands in the air in dismissal. He would continue to listen by himself, later.

"Miss Dowdeswell!" boomed Captain Walker, wanting to change the subject. "Are you comfortable? Do you require anything at all?"

"Not at all, Captain Walker," she said eyeing the table's fare and taking a napkin for her lap. "How very kind of you to ask."

Jonathan marveled at Delain. How she could be firing a gun at pirates one moment, then thirty minutes later, was a lady with the most proper manners and delightful way, sipping tea and eating finger cakes. As the Captain asked the other officers to sit at the cramped table, Jonathan moved to sit to Delain's left; however, he was rudely and literally elbowed out by none other than Spears, who grinned as he sat down next to the Governor's daughter.

"Spears," said Harrison, "have you tossed the log as of late?"

"Tossed the log, sir? Why, not since last night," said Spears. He had a questioning look on his face, as if to say *why would I need to toss the log to check the ship's speed at this moment?* "We are just cruising a few islands under minimum sail," he added, as if to question Harrison.

"Is that what we are doing? Lord, I assumed we were on a merry-go-round at the fair," said Harrison sharply, yet calmly. "Please take Lane with you and report the ships speed back to me immediately, thank you. You are dismissed."

"Aye, sir!" said Lane, who quickly grabbed a handful of the peppered eggs and marched to the door. As he left the cabin, Spears glared at Jonathan who took the seat next to Delain.

Mister Harrison caught Jonathan's eye, smiled and winked. "Always good to know a ship's speed, Mister Moore," Harrison whispered. "A critical element in the calculations of position upon the sea."

"I agree, Mister Harrison," said Jonathan, smiling.

"Now then," said the Captain, eyeing Harrison, "since the seating arrangements have been adjusted to please the young at heart, I would like to make sure that Miss Dowdeswell is perfectly well and if she suffered any injury in her adventure?"

"I am as perfect as can be. No injuries whatsoever, Captain," she said, taking a small bite of the sugar puff. "It was most exciting, I must say. I never had an opportunity to fire a cannon, or as you say in naval terms, a *ship's gun*, as cannon are for...how did Mister Moore say it? For *cretinous land-lubbers of the army?* Ah, that alone was worth the effort."

"You fired a gun?" said Walker, taken aback. "Mister Harrison, details if you please and hurry."

Harrison then began the tale of finding the rum stored in a cave and then Jonathan's report of seeing a small pirate brig just off the outer reef of Conception Island. Sean interrupted just long enough to explain his discovery of strawberries and how all the evidence of his find was devoured by the marine detachment.

"Not that I need to ask, but protocol requires it," said the Captain. "Whose idea was it to take the *Fiero*?"

"Jonathan's, sir," said Harrison. "It was his idea and his plan. Quite ingenious, I would say!"

Jonathan just smiled and blushed, then took over the tale. He explained the stationing of their small party among the bon fires and Mister Tupper's idea of stuffing a few jackets and blouses with palm fronds and coconuts to increase their numbers. He also mentioned, much to the mortification of Steward and a few officers, how they *wasted* a large amount of rum in an obvious manner to entice the pirates ashore.

"'Tis a sin to waste, Mister Moore!" exclaimed Steward.

Koonts laughed his squeaky cackle as Jonathan continued, explaining Delain's part as a ghost and her firing of the deck guns.

"It was really quite simple," Delain said, "once Mister Moore had prepared them for me. His advice to stand to the side of the gun was well received, as I could have been horribly injured had I stood behind."

"He has great experience there," added Harrison with a laugh, referring to Jonathan's mishap and near injury when he first fired a gun aboard HMS *Poseidon*. Harrison had saved him by knocking him out of the way. Only Jonathan's pride was seriously injured.

"I remember that lesson well," said Jonathan, flush with embarrassment.

"If I may ask, sir," said Harrison, "how did the *Danielle* come about Conception Island? We didn't expect you to be coming from the north."

"Ah, it was fortuitous," answered Walker, taking a bite of a large piece of toasted cheese, "we made our tour of the waters to the south past the Turks, and as we sailed northwards, we saw flashes of light in the morning sun as we past east of Rum Cay. Guessing they were a ship's guns, we stayed to the east and headed to San Salvador to hide ourselves. We spied a slow moving vessel, the *Fiero* as we now know, and decided to engage from the north and trap our prey as she approached. We had all guns ready to fire. Quite a close call."

"The bloomers certainly were...unique," added Koonts. "Bravo, Miss Dowdeswell."

Now it was Delain's turn to blush.

"Ah, but all's well that ends well," said Sean. "And we had strawberries to boot!"

The ship sailed on to the south, lazily as the wind was sparse, but the turquoise water and golden sunlight flickering off the waves made the crew sigh in relief, as indeed, it was a beautiful day. They also smiled as they talked about how the prize money would be split and the probable selling price of the *Fiero* was guessed at by many.

In the galley, Sean engaged in a conversation with Claise and Steward. He was surprised that he would even see a shilling of the prize money.

"Aye, you'll get a penny, Flagon," said Steward as he rummaged through Claise's pots and pans for an implement of some kind. Claise didn't mind - the pots, pans and spoons that made up his galley supplies were actually the property of the *Danielle*, not his own. He could always borrow them back when Steward was busy with other business besides cooking for the Captain.

"I figger the *Fiero* will present itself decently in prize court. Should sell fer almost two-thousand pounds, and after all the officers and leeches ashore take their *undo share*, we should see, oh . . . a couple 'o pound or there about. Not a fortune, but a few days o' comfort at some interesting port-o-call!"

"I'd like to buy some spices, if I can," said Claise. "Before he left with Mister Langley, Gallotta suggested that I obtain some oregano and fennel, and basil as well. He gave me his mother's tomato sauce recipe. He swore it was *authentic Italian*...whatever that means, but it must be good!"

"No doubt, Gallotta was a fine cook and his days aboard the *Poseidon* were filled with stories of his mother's sauce and her pasta dishes. 'used to make me stomach growl just hearin' 'em," added Steward, finally pulling up a small metal spatula from a drawer. "Fer the toasted cheese. Mine is worn to a nub and nothin'."

"Pardon me, Steward," Sean asked, "Did you say one or two pounds would be my share of the prize money? That's a lot of money. I've never seen so much as that!"

"Aye, it's a small fortune, accent on the *small*, but, better than a poke in the eye it is," Steward said, laughing. "I remember when I was on the *Troy* with Jonathan's father. We captured a Spanish galleon, an old one mind ya, but a beauty. Over eighty guns it had and some gold pieces as well. I believe my share as bosun was over seventy-five pounds. Oh! I remember a long and comfortable Christmas that year. And being a bachelor, as I was and am still, well, I went through it fast, but it was worth it!"

"What did you spend it on, Steward?" Sean said, giving little Stewie a scratch on the head.

"Ah! Oh...well," stumbled Steward, "just some nice evenings with some new friends is all! But no time fer that tale now, Flagon! Captain wants ya to board the *Fiero* with a crew and get 'er cleaned up as best ya can. The sail master will inspect the sheets and see if he can repair or replace. So get a move on!"

Sean and his crew of at least a dozen of the *Danis* hurriedly set about their work of polishing, painting, sweeping and straightening the *Fiero*. Others, the team of carpenters mostly, inspected and probed the old ship and made lists of all the heavy work to be done. The officers had another chore. As they gathered on the stern deck, the poop, as it was called, Walker called to Hudson, who was standing just below on the main deck.

"Hudson, have the pirate brought to me immediately."

"Yes sir," Hudson said, and sharply saluted and turned, quickly walking across deck and disappearing down a ladder to the brig.

"Captain," said Harrison, "Do you think he is really a pirate? I mean in the truest sense?"

"We shall see," Walker said. "There is something about the *Fiero* that is out of place. Holtz here thinks it resembles HMS *Drake*, lost in the American War of the colonies. If so, it may actually be British property and that would make our prisoner an enemy of the King."

Jonathan and Delain were standing by the rail and inched their way closer to listen in. They could see Hudson now on deck with two marines escorting an interesting person to the stern. The prisoner wore a black coat; one that looked like a tattered officer's uniform from years gone by. The blouse underneath was stained with heaven-knows-what, appearing almost brownish and mottled with bits of red as well. His pants, also black, were ripped and dirty, and his shoes mismatched. One had a buckle, the other a single bow, wilted and grey. However, in contrast to his garb, his hair was clean and flowing about his shoulders, a dark brown with some streaks of grey, and looked as if it was in many small waves, like the ocean itself. One wave was in the center of his forehead and as Jonathan stared, he believed the pirate had purposefully positioned the curl just so. His eyes were blue, like the Captain's, and he smiled broadly.

"The prisoner, as you requested, Captain," said Hudson.

The prisoner bowed elegantly and then straightened himself to his full height to look Walker directly in the eye.

"Captain Walter Kozak, at your disposal, Captain Walker," he said, smiling.

His accent is a strange form of English, thought Jonathan, *It sounds, well, funny. He must be speaking American. How very odd it is!*

Walker looked Kozak in the eye as well and didn't blink. They held the gaze for a moment; Kozak finally looked away, nodding at each of the officers.

"Gentlemen, a fine ship, very fine. Seventy-two guns, is it?" Kozak asked as he surveyed the main deck and the massive sails above.

"Did you say your name was Kozak?" asked Walker.

"Yes, Captain Walter Kozak, of the privateer *Fiero,*" he answered. "Then there must be seventy-four guns if there is a one, eh?"

"And under what flag do you sail?" continued Walker, not even acknowledging Kozak's questions.

"Flag?" asked Kozak. "None really. I am an *international citizen,* Captain Walker. I work for many nations, though I do reside in the Caribbean, mostly, at times as far north as Virginia and as far south as the Lesser Antilles."

"So how did you become chained to the overhead beam, *Captain* Kozak? Odd place to command a ship, isn't it?" Walker asked.

Kozak seemed slightly put off guard, but after a moment, he smiled and nodded knowingly.

"Yes, it is odd and unfortunate as you can imagine. I was the object of a mutiny, can you believe that?" Kozak said.

Walker smiled. "No, actually, I don't believe it."

Kozak continued, "Dear Captain, what a horrible thing to say! My men are not of the disciplined sort such as yours! I must pick them all as volunteers - no press gangs in America, I can tell you that! Each man comes under his own volition and unfortunately, under his own desires. One little disagreement and a mutiny is brewing."

"What was the disagreement?" asked Walker, calmly. He was watching Kozak's eyes, looking for a sign that might show a lie. Kozak knew it. He took a deep breath and exhaled loudly.

"If you must know, it was over rum. The crew wanted to change our plan and pick up a few hundred bottles some of them had buried on Conception Island. They wanted to make a quick penny selling it to the locals in the Bahamas, Jamaica and the Tortugas, maybe a few other small settlements. I disagreed."

"So they locked you in irons?" asked Walker.

"Extreme, yes, however that is the first thing the scum did when they took my ship."

Walker knew this was true and wanted Kozak to feel safe in his story. But now it was time for the real questions to begin.

"I wonder about the *Fiero*, Captain Kozak. If memory serves me, it was a Spanish ship, yes?"

Kozak nodded.

"And as I remember, the *Fiero* was sunk before the war with America, by the British ship HMS *Cloud*. Could this be the same *Fiero*, raised from the deep?"

"Indeed, the *Fiero* was a Spanish ship originally," Kozak added. "But this *Fiero* could not be the same one you mention, could it? Just a name my employer chose, I assume."

"I wonder. It resembles HMS *Drake*, wouldn't you say Lieutenant Holtz?" Walker said.

"Yes sir, I would," answered Holtz.

Kozak was now without a smile. "I was assigned this ship by my employer. An American business man named Rockwell. He hired me to transport some goods -"

"Did you know that the *Drake* was captured by the Americans in 1778?" interrupted Walker.

Kozak now seemed absolutely pale.

"That is an interesting fact, Captain Walker. I had not known that." Kozak said.

"Surely, you know of the American Naval hero, John Paul Jones? He captured the *Drake* and then sold her at auction in New York. I would wonder if we remove the plaque across the stern, if we would see her original name."

Just then Sean called out from the *Fiero* and held aloft a plank of wood that read *Fiero*. He tossed it to the deck and looked over the stern with Hicks at his side. They stared for a moment, then called to the Captain.

"Aye Cap'n," called Hicks. "As ya said. The original plaque reads *HMS Drake!*"

Kozak was slightly stunned, but he had figured he couldn't play ignorant any longer.

"If I can explain, Captain," Kozak said.

"Take him to the brig, Hudson."

Assisted by two other marines, Hudson grabbed the prisoner roughly and began *escorting* the struggling man below.

"Wait! Captain Walker! At least hear me!" Kozak pleaded.

Walker just stared at him with contempt, his steel blue eyes squinting in the sun.

"You are in possession of a stolen British ship, Kozak. You will hang after your trial in London, no doubt."

Kozak managed to halt his departure for a moment and turned to face the Captain.

"Captain Walker, I have news of something that might interest you. At least hear my story, then hang me by the yard arm, keel haul me or simply set me adrift on a plank if you must. But I guarantee you will want to know what I have to say. It can aid you in the war against Napoleon and the French!"

Now, Walker was interested.

* * * * * *

The *Danielle* sailed into Nassau harbor right as a noon bell was ringing, most likely from a church or schoolyard. Many townspeople came to see the strange sight of the great ship now accompanied by the smaller *Drake*. The ships then anchored in the harbor and Walker sent Steward and Claise ashore with a team of men to report to the Governor and to escort Delain back to her parents.

Jonathan and Sean stayed aboard to complete work on the *Drake* and tell the story of their adventure and capture of their new prize to all who would listen.

"Sounds like a great amount of luck to me," said Lane as he supervised a painting crew aboard the *Drake*. "There is no way scabs like you could even catch *a cold* if you tried, much less a pirate ship!"

"True," added Spears who was doing nothing that Jonathan or Sean could discern, except wandering about the ship, adding his opinion when it was not asked for or useful. "They must have all been drunk to allow you to get the drop on them. Luck, pure luck," he added.

Sean bit his tongue, not wanting to anger an officer. Though he tried to remain close to Jonathan whenever possible, he could not avoid Spears all the time. He kept his head down when the Midshipman was about. Sean remembered their altercation below deck at the bow; and there were other times when Spears would bully and insult him. It was best, for now, to avoid any confrontation.

Jonathan, being a midshipmen and the same rank as Spears and Lane, however, could say and do as he pleased, as long as he remained professional.

"There *was* some luck in the capture of the *Drake* and our party meeting up," Jonathan said, "however, when presented with the opportunity; we used our wits and courage to take advantage. A lesson you could learn, eh Spears? But I am sure you need to get back to work. By the way, what *are* you doing besides sucking up air?"

Spears grinned and stood toe-to-toe with Jonathan. "I don't have time to waste on your fairy tales, Moore," Spears said. "Someday we will all see the truth about you!"

"And I," said Harrison who again came by to keep the two midshipmen from injuring one another, "I will be there to substantiate Mister Moore's story. In the meantime, Spears, get some cats from the *Danielle* and put them aboard this scow. We need some rat catchers!"

As Spears left in disgust, Sean stood up and grabbed Stewie from the nearby rail.

"Stewie is already full, as he's been ratting all day!" said Sean, giving the little tabby a scratch on the head for good measure. "Some rats are even bigger than he, so maybe he could use some help!"

Later in the day, Walker, Holtz and Koonts sat at the Captain's table with coffee and some stale bread that had been sugared by Steward. The midshipmen were in a row behind, standing at attention. Across from them, all alone on the opposite side of the table, sat Kozak. He daintily dipped his bread in his coffee and tried to keep the dripping to a minimum. Walker started the conversation.

"Captain Kozak, tell me the details of this information you mentioned."

Kozak smiled, patting his chin with a napkin, then dipped a large slice of the delicious sugar bread into his coffee, smacking his lips as he ate the last bite. He leaned back in his chair and wiped his mouth one last time.

"It is the original mission I was hired to perform that will be of great interest to you, Captain Walker," said Kozak.

"Yes, that much I have heard. What is it?" said Walker impatiently.

"I must start at the beginning, then," said Kozak. "Please indulge me as I tell the tale. Now, the Spanish and the French, as you know, are allied against your King, isn't that right?" asked Kozak.

"It is common knowledge, yes," said Walker.

"So, enter into this tale a few hundred Chinese iron workers. The Chinese make beautiful silk and have wonderful spices and exquisite artwork. They also have invented a thing here and there, including…the cannon. They make them in China, as they have been making them for centuries."

"All common knowledge, Kozak," puffed Walker. "Where is this going?"

"Just setting the stage, Captain, please! Here is the gem: The French Navy has by now, already picked up a large amount of Chinese cannon. They need to deliver them to the French army, now in northern Africa. And the fastest and safest way is not via the Mediterranean Sea – too many English ships cruising about! The best solution is to deliver them to a point in *Africa*.

"Chinese cannon?" said Koonts.

"Not all in China, with its many families and factions, are completely, how shall I say - *comfortable*, with the English and the East India Company that manages trade. I am sure you have some knowledge of the unrest there?"

"Yes, yes, continue with your tale," said Walker.

"Now, a new player enters," continued Kozak, performing the tale as if it were a great play, and so it was for many in the room. "Generalissimo Miguel Aguilar, a Spanish arms dealer, really, is in such a position to receive these cannon and arrange for their delivery."

"This Aguilar is to arrange for transport of the cannon to the French *through Africa*? Impossible! It is a wild jungle!" said Koonts.

"Not as wild as you think. And not all will go over land. Some will be sent on smaller ships, in disguise, a few here, a few there. "

"And how does this involve you, Kozak?" asked Walker.

"Almost there, Captain," said Kozak. "The Generalissimo, being a greedy little fellow quickly determined he could shave a few cannon off the top and make a fast fortune selling them off in the new world. Since my normal career involves moving goods of a *delicate nature*, I was to outfit the *Fiero*, meet with a small transport ship or two, collect Aguilar's cannon and sell them off to buyers in South America. All this before the French Army even knew they had arrived. "

Walker stood up and walked to the stern windows and looked out upon the sea. He didn't think he could believe Kozak and as of yet, there was nothing in the tale that interested him. At best, he could find out exactly where the French were going to deliver the cannons and perhaps try to meet them for a fight. But if all he wanted was a fight, he could sail to any number of French ports and have it out. No need to find this particular ship. *Why is Kozak telling me this?* he thought to himself. *Just to buy time? To delay my delivering him to the authorities in London?*

"Captain Kozak, you are telling me that the French are delivering a few cannon to the Spanish and a corrupt Spanish general is going to sell them off instead of giving them to his army? It actually sounds fine to me, meaning there will now be a few less cannon firing upon British soldiers."

"Ah, but there you are wrong, my dear Captain," said Kozak, excitedly. "There are not *a few* cannon, unless over *one-thousand* are considered a few! They are sailing in a squadron of at least six merchant ships, all full to the gills! Why, Aguilar's skim alone amounts to over one-hundred! Wouldn't that be a pretty thing if you were to send them all to the bottom of the sea?"

Walker was now interested. He reasoned that if this outlandish tale could even be true, stopping a thousand cannon from reaching Napoleon's army would indeed turn the tide of the land war in Britain's favor. But he was not quite ready to give in to Kozak just yet.

"If this outlandish tale could even be true," said Walker, "it tells me nothing. It is a shot in the dark, with no detail or time table; just hearsay. And a squadron of merchant ships carrying so many cannon would surely be protected by a dozen or so French battle ships."

"Ah! Now I will sew it all up nicely with two more facts!" exclaimed Kozak. " Fact one: the French are running short on ships, as you must be aware, in fact, you are sailing on one now, isn't that right?"

Walker did not answer, but all knew it was true.

"This squadron only has *two* frigates of thirty-six guns for protection!" exclaimed Kozak. "They are no match for the mighty *HMS Danielle* and the cunning Captain William Walker! And fact two, my dear captain: I know exactly *where* this small squadron of ships is to meet Generalissimo

Aguilar and approximately *when*."

"How do you know this?" asked Koontz.

"I have seen the manifest! The shipping order that lists the items on the ship and *when* and *where* they are to be delivered. Are you now interested?" asked Kozak, the pirate already knowing the answer.

"If this is true, then yes, I am interested," Walker said, turning back to Kozak. "However, considering your position as a pirate, I am not sure you can be believed at all."

"Oh, Captain!" Kozak said, feigning insult. "We are cousins, we Americans and you English! How can I make you believe me?"

"Tell me where the manifest is. Do you have it on your person?" asked Walker.

Kozak laughed aloud.

"Captain Walker, if I had it on my person, you would have found it by now. I have been searched thoroughly by your marines. No, I do not have a copy. As I said, I have only *seen* a copy."

"Where is it now?" demanded Walker, quickly losing his patience. "I have a mind to string you up the yard arm, which is very much in my right as a British Naval Captain, and toss your body to the depths of the ocean."

"Now, now, now, let us not be too hasty!" said Kozak, quickly. "Captain! We need to make a deal. I tell you these things not from the goodness of my heart, but as you have now confirmed, for the purpose of sparing my skin! I want to be freed. Then, I will tell you where the manifest resides."

Now it was Walker who laughed.

"My, my, Kozak, are all Americans as amusing as you? We are on the horns of a dilemma, aren't we? On one hand, you might be telling the truth and you do know where the manifest is. But once you tell me, I have all I need and you have only my word that I will set you free."

"No disrespect meant to you, Captain Walker," said Kozak. "I am sure you are a gentleman of the best sort, however, I trust no one."

"And I don't trust you, Kozak. I think this is a tall tale and you are lying to save your skin," said Walker. "The best I could do for you would be to speak of your assistance when we reach London. I could convince the court to spare your life."

Kozak frowned.

"That won't do, Captain Walker. A life in prison will be as much a death as the gallows or the guillotine."

"It is not up to me to free you," said the Captain. "That is for the authorities in London. There is no manner in which this deal can proceed without your story being proven. Give me the location of the manifest. If I can obtain it and it matches the list of ports you allege to know, I will speak for you myself. To the King if necessary."

Kozak hesitated. He thought for a full minute and stood to walk about the cabin. He stared out the window and tapped his foot, thinking if he could trust Captain Walker. *My other choice is the gallows and death, and most possibly in the next few minutes if the Captain does intend to use the yardarm of this ship as a gibbet,* he said to himself. *I have no choice and no other prospects yet. For now, I will go along with this until I can find a way out!* Finally he sighed loudly and turned to face the Captain.

"Well then," said Kozak, nodding his head. "Will you at least promise to keep me until you return to England then?"

"I have said as much, Kozak."

"Here, then," Kozak said softly. "Do you know of the Spanish colony in Africa by the name of Rio Muni?"

"I have heard of it," said Koonts. "It is at the nook of the continent, on the western seaboard just south of Bioko Island; a terrible, dangerous place, nothing of value at all. Slave trading is its main business. It is surprising the Spanish continue to hold it."

"Surprising, yes, however understandable," said Kozak, pausing for effect, "if one needs a suitable port to conduct *discreet* activity, and yes, as you mentioned, slave trading. But also other items need some special handling, items such as cannon."

"And this is where the manifest is now?" asked Walker.

"Indeed. The manifest is currently in the newly constructed *Fort de la Selva*. I was to meet Aguilar there on or about the fifteenth of May to take on my cargo. The manifest is in his office. It will tell you all you need to know."

"We will discuss this privately, Kozak," said Walker. "Take him back to the brig. For your sake, this tale had better be the truth."

As Kozak was led to the door, he turned and addressed the captain one more time.

"The tale is as true as your word, my dear Captain Walker."

"Then you have nothing to worry about," Walker said with a smile.

11

Planted Seeds

At the Governor's mansion on the second evening of their return, the officers of the *Danielle*, complete in their best cleaned and brushed uniforms, dined with the Dowdeswells and a few of the more affluent citizens of the port of Nassau. The dinner was superb and even Spears seemed to behave himself, avoiding Jonathan and Sean completely, and somewhat politely listening as Harrison told the tale of the capture of the *Drake* to great effect. The guests were astonished at the idea of a handful of men and two boys taking a ship away from "at least fifty pirates" according to Mister Harrison's ever expanding count. Most amazing and shocking to the Governor himself, was the role Delain played. As usual, she was calm and reserved about the whole affair, only saying "It all came quite naturally to me. No trouble at all, really."

As the dinner went on and dessert was served, Jonathan noticed that Delain was becoming ever more silent and even refused her strawberry tart and chocolate sauce.

"I am feeling a little under the weather," she said to Jonathan softly. "It must be all the excitement of the last few days."

Jonathan at first felt sorry for her, however, the more he considered her comment, he concluded that it made no sense. *Delain seemed fine during all the doings with pirates, turtles and even when under fire from the* Danielle. *Why was she suddenly ill from 'excitement'?* he thought to himself.

As the plates were being cleared and the after dinner drinks were passed to the older men and officers, Governor Dowdeswell offered a toast to the Heroes of the *Drake*, as they were now known to all of Nassau.

"A toast and salute to Lieutenant Harrison and Midshipman Moore! Along with Seaman Flagon, it is a wonder the French have not yet surrendered!"

There was a general laugh and many cheers and applause for the boys. Even Harrison blushed for an instant this time as Jonathan and Sean nodded to each other, glad that they could assist their friends in any way.

"I am certainly comfortable that my daughters will be in safe hands when they depart on your ship, Captain," said the Governor. "We wish you all a safe voyage and the best of luck."

"Excuse me," Captain Walker said, trying to politely interrupt the Governor. "A small change of plans, Your Excellency. Some recent developments require me to transport the ladies immediately aboard the *Drake* with Lieutenant Blake. I know that shortens your time with them. One could always await another transport."

"Really? Well, I would rather put them on a fighting ship than a cargo clipper. At least the Navy is filled with gentlemen, eh? Captain, I will hasten their packing. We will have them ready tomorrow morning."

"I appreciate your understanding, Governor. I must take the *Danielle* immediately to Southern Africa, I am afraid."

"Africa?" blurted Delain. "How exciting!" She had suddenly a wild look in her eyes as she imagined how wonderful and exhilarating a trip to Africa must be. Certainly, the lions, tiger, elephants and rhinoceroses would be endlessly more fascinating than the polite society of London.

"Delain!" scolded the Governor. "Please do not interrupt! You see, this is why sending the young ladies to London is in order! They are in dire need of some culture and could practice their manners. Pardon the outburst, Captain."

"Not at all, Your Excellency. As a Navy man yourself, I am sure you understand the temporary nature of all plans when it comes to the war."

"Indeed I do, Captain," said Governor Dowdeswell.

"I will instruct Lieutenant Blake to do everything in his power to assure the comfort and safety of your daughters," said Captain Walker, nodding in respect. "I am sure he will be honored to turn over his cabin for their usage. I will assign a top notch crew to assist him. Is that still to your liking?"

"If you assure me it is a safe option, then yes," said the Governor.

"The safest available," answered the Captain. "We plan to depart tomorrow morning, so we must thank you for this beautiful evening and return to our ship. We have much work to complete before we set off again." Walker turned to his officers and Sean: "Gentlemen?"

All rose to bow to Lady Dowdeswell and her daughters, and after a moment, all rose to leave the table and say their good-byes. Jonathan stood and pulled out Delain's chair, a very gentlemanly thing to do; however, as she stood, Delain swooned and dropped toward the floor. Sean was there to catch her before she could injure herself. In an instant, all crowded about, offering to assist in any way.

"Dear me," cried Lady Dowdeswell. "Whatever is the matter, Delain?"

Delain blinked a few times, looking about as if lost.

"What happened?" Delain said, looking to Jonathan. "How did I get down here?"

"You fainted, Miss Dowdeswell," he said, though to Jonathan, she seemed a little too animated, almost as if she were *acting* a part of an ill person. Not being a doctor, he really couldn't say how sound she was, however, he had his doubts. "Are you alright?"

Delain assured everyone present that she was just fine, however, in the end, her father had a servant carry the girl to her room and another was sent for a doctor. The evening was over.

The next morning, both ships completed the final

preparations, loaded stores of food and water, and crew members that were chosen to sail with the *Drake* moved their gear to their new ship. The officers met in Captain Walker's cabin for a breakfast of eggs and bacon, toasted cheese, and finally, to the joy of primarily the Captain, oil-fried anchovies appeared on a platter from Steward's small galley.

"Spa-len-did!" exclaimed the Captain as he took notice of the crispy fish. "And to think that in these warm waters they were available!"

"Truly a gift of heaven, sir," said Steward. "Must 'ave swum all the way from Peru. Got 'em in the nets early this mornin'."

Spears was disappointed to learn that Lieutenant Blake would take no midshipman with him aboard the *Drake*. At the end of breakfast, he thought to suggest to the Captain that sending Jonathan would be satisfactory.

"If I may Captain," Spears asked, "I'd like a word with you about the assignments you have chosen for the *Drake*."

The Captain simply looked up from his last anchovy and began turning from his normal pale white to a deep crimson.

Anticipating an outburst of tremendous proportions from the dragon, one after another all quickly blurted out excuses to leave, saying: *Much to be done, Captain*, or *Begging your pardon sir, some bookwork to complete*, and even *Pardon me, Captain, time to inspect the deck.* With those words the guests began running for the door, all except Holtz, who decided he would stay for the show. He grabbed a last cup of coffee, leaned back in his chair, and at last glace, Jonathan could swear he was grinning.

"Yes, Captain," Spears continued, "I believe sending Mister Moore with the *Drake*, since he seems to have gotten credit for the capture, would be -"

"How dare you question my orders!" Walker roared.

"But Sir," came Spears feeble whine, "I was just –"

Those were the last words anyone heard from Spears, as Captain Walker, now a ferocious, fire-breathing dragon yet again, let fly with a stream of colorful expletives, vivid metaphors and vicious insults that even had Steward cringing.

"Ouch!" he said as he closed the Captain's door and stepped quickly outside. "Cap'n's in rare form today! 'aven't 'eard those words since I was a young pup, in the boarding school. It takes a talent to wax so expressively!"

"Yes, Steward," said Harrison, "the Captain is truly a wizard with words. We can only aspire to be so grand when it is our turn to lead!"

Jonathan laughed nervously, though he remembered being in front of the dragon on more than one occasion, and though his dislike for Spears was almost as great as Captain Walker's wrath, he still could not listen and moved with Koonts to the gangway to offer his assistance.

Sean was already making his way up the plank, carrying additional supplies with a few marines, mostly powder in small kegs and boxes of lead for bullets. He was working quite hard, sweating in the sun, so Jonathan removed his coat and assisted in the lifting. Koonts opened his great book and began tallying the items that were coming aboard.

"Yes, Sean, come right up," he said, "let's get these last supplies aboard and cast off as soon as we can. Don't want to upset the Captain."

"Seems like he's already upset to me!" said Sean, putting down the last of his boxes and removing his cap to wipe the sweat from his brow.

A voice called out from below. The Ladies Dowdeswell had appeared in their best clothes, though it was clear that Delain was still ill and leaned on her sister Rebecca for assistance. They were accompanied by several servants at the foot of the dock, carrying their many bags, packages and even more boxes of supplies and possessions.

"Ahoy, Lieutenant Harrison," called Rebecca. "Is there any offer of assistance we can receive? We do not know our way around the *Drake* and could use your guidance on the storage of our belongings!"

"Ah," said Harrison softly, "ladies in distress! Come Moore, Flagon. To the rescue."

They left the rest of the supplies to the marines and hands and began down the gangway, happy to be off the *Danielle* for a few minutes to escape the Captain and to also spend a few last moments with the Governor's daughters.

The girls were pleased to see that the *Drake* had undergone a somewhat miraculous change, now being almost presentable as a ship of His Majesty's Navy. It was far from being the shining example of cleanliness and efficiency as the *Danielle*, however, many men were still working, cleaning, mending and polishing the small ship.

"By the time you reach England," Sean said in his most proper English, trying to imitate the King, "she will look *spa-len-did!*"

Jonathan led the way to what used to be Lieutenant Blake's cabin. The sisters selected a few of the essentials from their packages and bags, and dismissed the servants to store the rest below. They all moved excitedly except for Delain, who immediately sat on a make-shift bed that had been created from spare lumber and covered by a small mattress made from sailcloth and stuffed with extra fabric. She seemed sleepy and even looked about nervously for a while. As the others chatted and chirped with excitement about the ship, the journey and of course, the wonderfulness of soon living in the largest city of the King's empire, Delain sat quietly.

"Miss Dowdeswell," Jonathan said as he stood by her side. "I am concerned about your state of health. Are you well enough to travel? You are so quiet and still. It is not like you, I must say."

"I am sorry, Jonathan," she said. "I just feel a little under the weather."

Jonathan nodded and smiled a bit.

"Maybe a last stroll around the *Danielle* before we must leave would do me some good, I love her so," Delain added. "Could that be arranged for my sisters and me?"

"Of course!" said Jonathan. "However, we had better hurry, as the *Danielle* is set to cast off within the hour."

The ladies accompanied Jonathan, Harrison and Sean about the deck of the *Danielle*, enjoying each other's company and watching the crew work quickly to prepare the ship for the open sea. After a few minutes, however, Delain said she was feeling refreshed and better, though still a bit tired, and begged leave to go back to the *Drake* and sleep. She had Jonathan and Penelope escort her to the gangway. Before she turned to go, she asked her sister for a *little privacy*. Penelope smiled and obliged by walking down the plank to wait silently by the last few boxes and crates sitting upon the dock. Mister Koonts stood nearby checking his giant book, making sure all was accounted for. He noticed Jonathan and Delain, nodded his head, and also turned about, heading back to the wheel to discuss something of obvious importance with Mister Watt. Now and again he would look back at Jonathan and Delain and smile. Watt actually cracked what could be mistaken for a grin as he also glanced at the couple.

"Well then, Miss Dowdeswell," Jonathan said.

"Please call me Delain," she said. "It seems that we have been through so much together, I would think we can progress to first names, don't you?"

"One never wants to be too forward, Miss Dowdeswell, and of course, I am in uniform and must display some sense of decorum in front of the crew. But, as you wish, Delain."

This made them both smile and Jonathan almost reached for her hand, yet stopped, realizing that no fewer than one-hundred people were most likely watching them as if they were on stage in an outdoor theater. A quick glance about showed him that it was difficult to find a face *not* staring at them. Even Steward was watching, like a proud mother goose. The only faces he did not see, to his pleasure, were those of Midshipman Spears and Captain Walker.

"I wonder when the *Danielle* will be back in London. Do you know?" asked Delain.

"I am not sure. Our mission has not been announced to me, so I have no way of knowing. It is at this point a mystery, but involves the pirate Kozak, I am sure. Assuming the worst, I could only hope to return by autumn at the latest."

"A long voyage. I wish you luck, Jonathan," said Delain, somewhat sadly. She pouted ever so slightly.

"If it would be agreeable, I would like to call upon you when I return, Delain."

Delain smiled once again and fingered her necklace, playing with the beautiful dolphin dangling on a silver chain that Jonathan had given her.

"Possibly we could try iced cream?" she asked. "I have never had any."

"Absolutely, Miss Dowdeswell."

"I look forward to it with great anticipation, Mister Moore," she said as she lightly brushed his hand with hers. With that she turned away, and Jonathan, not wanting her to see the redness in his face, also turned and walked back to his duties.

At the bottom of the gang plank, Penelope awaited her sister with a smile.

"That was a pretty scene, Delain," her sister said. "Did he agree to visit you in London?"

"Of course!" Delain said happily. "He is a gentleman and a wise one at that."

"You are a caution, Delain!" Penelope said. "Back to the *Drake*, I presume? You *do* look a little flushed."

They both laughed as if this was a joke of which only they were aware, and after a quick look around, Delain said almost too loudly, "Oh, dear me! I have forgotten my brooch! I will retrieve it from Rebecca and meet you back on the *Drake*."

"I will prepare your bed, dear sister," said Penelope.

With that, the girls parted, Delain returning to the

Danielle amidst the hurry and the activity, and Penelope to the *Drake* and the confines of the captain's cabin.

* * * * * *

Captain Walker called for a discussion with his officers in his cabin during the final few minutes before the ships were to depart Nassau. Specifically, they discussed the mission of both the *Danielle* and the *Drake*. Steward laid out a bit of fresh milk for Jonathan and Spears, along with coffee and a few plain cakes on a platter. No anchovies could be seen by the Captain and he frowned, saying:

"Where are the anchovies, Steward?"

"Sorry, Cap'n" Steward said. "We had a few, as ya know, but they're all eaten. No more around these parts today. Must 'ave returned to Peru, or they're hidin'."

Harrison smiled as he bit into one of the cakes from the platter.

"There *is* a foul taste in these cakes; maybe they are hiding in here?"

Jonathan tried not to laugh, yet a burst did escape his lips and this made Steward frown all the more.

"And now to the business at hand," continued Captain Walker, seriously. "Lieutenant Blake, is the *Drake* ready to sail?"

"Aye Captain," Blake said. "Stores are loaded, the crew is accounted for and I have Smith, Jones and Johnson inspecting the guns as we speak. We have ammunition enough if we require it."

"Speed is your best weapon, Mister Blake. Remember that you have the daughters of the Governor to deliver as your primary mission."

"Yes, sir," Blake answered, now assuming his part in the discussion was over and that he could now attend to the plates of cakes and cups of coffee. He was quite hungry, as he had been up most of the night preparing for the voyage and had only a few short naps in-between duties, though no food whatsoever.

"Now onto the mission of the *Danielle*," said the Captain, and all ears perked up. "As you may have heard, our guest, Captain Kozak, has told us that a French fleet of merchant ships are sailing from the Far East with a very large cargo of cannon for Napoleon's army. He states they are accompanied by only two thirty-six gun frigates. We need to confirm this story."

The Captain paused to refill his cup with more of the hot steaming brew and also to at least take a cake, as he finally had come to accept there were not to be any anchovies.

Jonathan wondered just how they would confirm Kozak's story. He was a pirate, after all, and probably a criminal in many other ways. How could he be trusted? As if to answer, Walker continued.

"Kozak claims there is a manifest in a fort at Rio Muni, on the western coast of Africa. Our mission is to locate the manifest, confirm the story and if true, we will proceed to intercept the ships. Steward! Is there at least any toasted cheese?"

As Steward magically appeared with a steaming plate of toasted cheese, Koonts set his cup down and cleared his throat. "If I may, Captain?"

"Please," Walker replied, taking a bit of cheese to his plate and slicing off a small piece to nibble.

"Thank you," said Koonts. "I do recall that Kozak mentioned there were at least six merchant ships in the fleet? Even if we can defeat the two frigates, which I have no problem agreeing that it is in our favor to accomplish, the merchant ships will scatter! It will be near impossible to find them after engaging the frigates."

"True," said Holtz. All waited for him to say more, however, he did not.

"That is where Lieutenant Blake comes in," answered the Captain.

Blake looked up from his cake and coffee and the one piece of toasted cheese he dared take, surprised that he was still in the conversation.

"As the *Drake* sails toward England, she will alert any British ships she encounters to tell of our mission and ask them to assist. Meanwhile we will sail southeast, to resupply in the Cape Verde Islands. We may find some assistance there as well."

"Cape Verde?" asked Koonts. "Are we to bypass the Canary Islands? They are much closer, as the Captain is aware."

"Thank you, Mister Koonts," said Walker, only slightly irritated at being questioned. "The Cape Verde Islands are in a more direct line than the Canaries, as we are heading to the central coast of Africa. As well, Marine Captain Gorman is possibly still there and we can always use his assistance."

"I am sure Gorman can assist us in locating the manifest at Rio Muni," added Harrison. "That would substantiate Kozak's story."

"Precisely," said Walker. "We can combine with whatever assistance we find at Cape Verde or that which Lieutenant Blake sends our way. We attack the frigates while our sister ships either sink or take the merchants. Do you understand your part, Lieutenant Blake?"

"Aye, sir," Blake said. "I will look for assistance as I sail on to England and refer them to the Cape Verde Islands."

"Yes. We will anchor off of the port town of Ribeira Grande, on the south side of the Island Santiago," said Walker. "If we are not there, Blake, instruct all you meet to proceed down the coast of Africa to the Cape of Good Hope. That is where I expect to meet the French and their Chinese cannon by the strait."

"Yes sir," Blake said. "I will alert all to your need."

This all seemed to make sense to Jonathan, except the part about the fort and the manifest, the list that would prove Kozak's story. How were they going to get into the fort? And then, as he remembered, into the office of the Generalissimo?

The officers continued discussing particulars of the

plan as they ate, and as the food ran out, so did the conversation. Finally the Captain spoke, dismissing all.

"Then let us hope Lieutenant Blake encounters a few fast ships and the word is spread quickly to the fleet. If there is nothing else, then let us delay no longer. Holtz, please ring the bell. Good luck and God's speed to all."

On the main deck, the bell rang just as Jonathan and Harrison joined Sean and the remaining Dowdeswell girls.

"Is Delain feeling better?" asked Jonathan.

"Oh, much better, Mister Moore, thank you for asking," Penelope answered. "She is sleeping like a baby."

Just then Steward happened by, calling orders out to a few of the crew and then addressing the Governor's daughters.

"Ladies, it's time to depart! Board your chariot to London, HMS *Drake*. We all hope to see you there soon, right boys?"

The boys all agreed and walked the ladies to the gangway, avoiding the last few crates and barrels being loaded by the crew.

"Aren't we missing one?" asked Steward innocently. "I don't see Miss Delain."

"She is already aboard the *Drake*, in a deep slumber, Mister Steward," said Rebecca. "We will make sure she is tucked in. Please be careful and return safely to port. We wish you all farewell."

They all shook hands politely and even Sean held Penelope's hand for an extra moment or two, smiling and looking at the deck in embarrassment, shuffling his feet.

"Mister Flagon," Penelope said, "I will see you in London, I hope?"

"Oh! By all means!" Sean said excitedly. "Though I am originally from Ireland, London *is* my home town! I will be glad to show you around upon my return."

"And hopefully you will show her some of the *finer* areas, Flagon," added Harrison, who smiled deeply at Rebecca, causing her to turn almost as red as the Captain did from time-to-time, though in joy, not anger.

"Until our reunion, Miss Rebecca?" Harrison asked softly, boldly holding the eldest Dowdeswell's hand.

"Until then," Rebecca answered, and touched Harrison's cheek ever so gently.

As the ladies left, Steward just shook his head.

"Ah, Cupids arrows strike deeply upon departure, the poets say!"

HMS *Danielle* departed Nassau to little fanfare, as did HMS *Drake*. The Governor wished his daughters well from the dock, Lady Dowdeswell blowing kisses to Penelope and Rebecca and worrying visibly about Delain, who was still ill.

As the sun washed golden sparkles along the top of the calm sea, the *Drake* and *Danielle* let down all sail, *sheeted home* by tightening all attending lines, and within a few minutes were racing eastward with a strong wind at their backs and nothing but open sea ahead. It seemed a contest to all who watched the ships from shore, though within a minute or two, the *Drake,* with its much lighter load and smaller draft, surged ahead, and within another few minutes, it was gone from sight.

Walker stood on the poop deck and enjoyed the sunshine in his face and the breeze at his back. Alone at last, he could take pleasure in some solitude and be with his thoughts. Now in the midst of a real mission, he was content and engaged.

Click... click... clickity-click... came the sound of rattling.

"Good Lord!" he exclaimed aloud, scaring a few crew members, even the stone-like Mister Watt who was nearby. "Where in the bloody, blue blazes is that coming from?"

So he stood still once again and listened. The sound was clearly louder than it had ever been before and now it was unmistakably coming from behind him. Walker turned and walked to the stern rail, closed his eyes and listened.

Click...click...clickity-click...

He looked down as the sound was coming from right below him. There he saw nothing out of the ordinary. He could make out the windows of his cabin and the rudder deep below. There were no ropes or loose boards he could see. Then he heard the sound again.

Click…click…clickity-clickity – click – click – click.

"Blast it!" he yelled, then noticed movement. A board was separated an inch or so from the stern of the ship. *The placard?* he said to himself. *That infernal plaque reading* HMS Doggard*? It is loose, in fact, very much so. It looks like one side is about to fall off!*

As he stared at the board he could tell that it had been placed over the original '*Danielle*' plaque and was held on by only four wooden screws. And as he leaned over the side to take a closer look, he saw there were scrapes and gouges about the corners of the plank, as if someone had been trying to unfasten it, or chip it away.

Someone is defacing the ship! the Captain thought. *They must be stopped! Of all the outrageous behaviors! It is truly juvenile! I must have the carpenter fix that plaque before it falls off!* And then he caught himself. *What am I thinking? I hate that infernal name! Should I ignore this… it will probably fall off in a few days and we will be the* Danielle *outwardly as well as inwardly. Though I do love a mystery, I will keep this one to myself and avoid solving it!*

Something else that was kept a secret was the fact that there was a stowaway aboard HMS *Danielle*, and of course, only one person knew of that fact: the stowaway. Hiding in the larger of the two jollyboats at first seemed like a good idea. It was spacious, bigger than most bedrooms in houses, though not quite as comfortable. There was no bed, no linens and no pillows. There was, however, rope and tarp and even some small tools that were probably needed by the men who used the boats.

The Still Secret Stowaway

And that raised a concern. *What if they needed this boat?* thought the stowaway. *I would be discovered directly and it is not time yet for that! We are too close to the islands and I would be put off in a day's time. I must wait until we have been at sea for at least... three or four weeks. I believe it should take that long to reach Spain and then make a good distance to the south along the African Coast. Amazing, even if my first view is from peeking under this tarp! But it keeps me dry and reasonably warm. This rope, if I take time, can be fashioned into a bed of sorts, and maybe these tools can be of use.*

The stowaway knew that silence must be kept and most importantly, food must be acquired as soon as the meager rations brought from Nassau were exhausted. *I will attempt some scrounging tonight, when the activities slow and darkness can conceal all.*

At seven days from their departure from Nassau, the *Danielle* was still heading southeast toward the Cape Verde Islands. Tossing the log revealed she was making barely eight knots, simply an average feat for such a large ship. This process of measuring the ships speed was performed by Jonathan and Lane, and observed and supervised by Mister Harrison. Using a prepared rope with knots tied at approximately fifty-foot intervals, a triangular plank of wood was tied to the end. Jonathan tossed it over the side into the swiftly passing sea.

"One…two…three…" Lane announced when each knot banged against the side rail as the passing ocean pulled the rope and board into itself.

"Five…ten..." Jonathan said as he watched his thirty-second sand glass trickle the time away.

"Thirty!" called Jonathan after the glass had emptied.

"And…eight!" called Lane after a short pause.

Despite this fine accomplishment of mathematical measurement, the Captain was hoping for a bit more speed, at least ten knots, but the winds would not comply. The crew sensed his foul mood and seemed to lapse into complacency, carrying out their tasks routinely as they had thousands of times before. The only respite from the daily grind was the afternoon foil matches between selected officers and a few marines. As usual, when Harrison was chosen, he always won, unless he fought the Captain. The biggest excitement and most wagering came when on this particular day; Wayne Spears and Jonathan Moore *mysteriously* drew long straws yet again and performed a rematch of their earlier contest. Unfortunately, or possibly not, Spears was the easy victor.

At this point in the journey, Steward had noticed a few *odd occurrences*. As he sat in the main galley, enjoying a cup of coffee and nibbling on soft tack, he discussed these with Claise, who was now accepted gratefully as the ship's official cook.

"Tis a good cup o' coffee, Claise, there is no doubt yer a master at the grinder!" complimented Steward.

"Aye, Steward," answered Claise. "I thank you for the compliment. But I notice you are not taking your usual cream in the cup and us just a bit from our last port. The cream is alright, isn't it?"

"Ah. That's the issue! I do like cream, when I can get it. But I can't get it," answered Steward.

"Out? Then take some of mine for you and the Captain. I have a small urn, but the men don't use it and I can drink my coffee as dark as the night and still enjoy it. Please."

Claise stood and went to his larder. He unwrapped his bundle of cool, wet-wrapped rags from about his small cream urn, the rags used to preserve delicate items for as long as he could aboard the ship. He opened the small lid and looked inside to check on the freshness.

"Dear me!" he said to Steward. "It's gone!"

"I thought as much," Steward said as he sipped his coffee and nodded. "Mine as well."

"We will have to milk the goat then," said Claise.

"It will be of no use. The goat is dry. I checked this mornin'."

They discussed the oddity of this and a few other strange events they had both noticed. It seemed there was also missing loaves of bread and salted pork. Claise even admitted to losing a small cherry pie he had baked for Mister Harrison; it had disappeared over night. It was on the table in Claise's small cabin in the evening and gone the next morning before he woke.

"A ghost, possibly?" asked Claise.

"Or a thief," suggested Steward. "There are near three hundred men aboard the *Dani* and many come from a, well, *less than pure background,* if ya catch my meanin'."

Claise shook his head. "I assume Captain Walker must be told?"

"Aye," said Steward as he stood up and drained the last of his coffee. "I'll inform 'em. But keep an eye out, Claise, and two ears besides. If someone is stealing food, they will continue. Look fer evidence. Ask around those ya trust. See what ya can see."

12
Planted Weeds

In the lower depths of HMS *Danielle*, usually a happy ship in all respects, existed a gloomy place. There was little light there, both in the way of illumination and spirits. The few rats that remained on board found its dark and dank spaces enjoyable. There was rarely anyone present, and now and again the rats could drag a bit of discarded food down to the creaky depths and enjoy it in peace.

This day, however, there was an unexpected guest, a large one, and the rats stayed hidden, only venturing out to the gloom if it was clear that the intruder was asleep.

This place was called the *brig*, by the crew, an area that was made up of four small cages, each being the size of a small closet, each with bars for a door. There were no windows or comfort.

In one of these cages, sat Captain Walter Kozak.

He knew the ship was moving, however, he could not ascertain if it was going straight to London and most certainly his public execution, or going to Rio Muni and the *Fort de la Selva.* He wondered, as he sat on the hard floor and tried to rest his head against the hull of the ship, if Captain Walker had believed his story of the manifest. If so, he had a chance to save his own life. *If not,* he thought, *I need another plan and maybe some help as well. There must be a way to escape.*

He sat staring into the gloom for what seemed like hours, when suddenly a shaft of light pierced the darkness and two figures appeared on the stair-like ladder that led down from the upper decks. The figures were soon discernible as small officers and within a moment, as his eyes adjusted to the light, he could see clearly that they were midshipmen – and one looked familiar. He carried a platter of what Kozak hoped would be some food; he was starving. The other had a large cup of what he thought could quite possibly be coffee, as the slight breeze caused by the opening of the hatchway had blown the smell of rich beans directly to his cell.

"Captain Kozak," Jonathan said, "some breakfast for you." With this he slid the tray and food under a space in the barred door. Kozak nodded and slowly took the tray. It was filled with some stale cakes, a bit of cheese and something else that looked like it may have been an egg at some previous time.

"Coffee as well," added Spears. He set the cup next to the bars and the boys turned to go.

"You, I recognize," said Kozak, causing both boys to stop and turn back. "You are the one who stole my ship."

"You mean the ship that was stolen from the British Navy? Yes, that was my friends and me," said Jonathan.

"You're welcome," said Kozak after a moment. "I am sure you will be congratulated by your King, if you were ever allowed to meet him."

Jonathan smiled, but decided that speaking to Kozak would do no one any good. Certainly saying he had already met the King and that the King actually owed Jonathan a favor, would just not be believed.

"Now, you," said Kozak, motioning to Spears, "You I have not seen. You are a midshipman as well?"

"No, I am the Queen of England," snapped Spears angrily.

Kozak laughed a bit.

"And I am the President of the United States! A joy to meet you, your Highness."

"We must go," said Jonathan, "Come, Spears."

"Come yourself!" said Spears. "I do not report to you!"

"Not yet," said Jonathan quickly, and he turned to go. "Captain wants no discussion with the prisoner, that's orders."

Spears stood still now, defying Jonathan and also the

Captain, however, it's all he could do. If he followed Jonathan, it would seem as if he actually *did* report to his rival, so he stayed, watching as Jonathan walked out and climbed the ladder to the main deck.

Kozak now knew that these two boys were adversaries and that maybe, just maybe, there was a way to use that to his advantage. He needed to escape and that meant he needed someone to break him out of the brig.

Could one of these boys be persuaded to assist me? Kozak said to himself. *Could I learn something about them and use it to my advantage? Maybe I can get information from this remaining boy. Spears, I believe the other one called him.*

"Your name is...Spears, is that correct?" asked Kozak.

"Yes," snapped the midshipman. "What is that to you?"

This boy is nothing to me, thought Kozak, *but I need to gain his confidence. A common cause? A common enemy? Yes, that is it!*

"Oh, nothing," said the pirate, "though I think I have heard of you... in America. The Spears are a well to do family, correct? Most in America are poor, as you know, and we desire to learn of those who actually have a better life."

This seemed to spark interest from Spears, and Kozak noticed his flush of excitement at the compliment. The pirate was gambling, of course, and tried one more lie. He knew a bit about the British Navy, and that only privileged families could receive an appointment for their son to become a midshipman.

"Your father? He is a Lord? Or a captain in the Navy?"

Spears wondered how this man knew of him and also his father. *Maybe the family Spears* is *news in America. And why not?* Spears thought.

"Yes, he is a Captain. And we are well to do. What is that to you?"

"I was just wondering why someone with your stature and family name would have someone like that *boy*," and Kozak said *boy* as if it were a derogatory word, "as your superior officer."

"He is *NOT* my superior in any way!" blurted Spears, now exposing his anger once again. "Jonathan Moore is a spoiled brat and before that he was a common street urchin!"

Kozak could now tell there was a hatred deeply seeded in this Spears character. He also knew the other boy's name. *If I could use that to my advantage,* thought Kozak, *maybe I could sway Spears to free me.*

"Midshipman Spears, your first name wouldn't be the same as your father's would it?"

"No, he is Derrick, I am Wayne. And another thing," Spears quickly added, "the Captain seemed to have bought the idea that Jonathan Moore is something special! His capturing your ship, certainly the work of Lieutenant Harrison and the two marines, was credited to Moore! It's a conspiracy!"

"I see," said the pirate. "You do all the hard work and studying and get no notice, no reward."

"Exactly!" cried Spears.

"What you need is a chance to prove your worth," said Kozak, "without this Moore *boy* getting in the way, correct?"

Spears agreed and continued explaining how the Moores were nothing but worthless, money grubbing opportunists, gaining advantage by keeping others down.

"Why, even after I pushed Moore off the gangplank to teach him a lesson or two, he was coddled! Like a baby!"

"You pushed him off the plank? When was this?" asked Kozak, laughing.

"Just before we left dock at London!" laughed Spears, bragging. "It was enjoyable I can say! But in the end, Moore continued to receive favor, attending the Governor's dinner, being applauded for his action aboard the *Drake*, and even making his way toward the Governor's daughter! It will improve his station to marry into the Dowdeswells, as if he needed more assistance!"

"Outrageous!" said Kozak in mock concern. "It must

be a hard thing to live with, Wayne, seeing that sort of scandalous behavior being rewarded."

If I could offer the promise recognition and fame to Spears, thought the pirate, *at the expense of Moore, then maybe, just maybe Spears would team with me. At least long enough for me to use him to effect my escape.*

"A hard thing indeed," said Spears. "And as his father did to my father, young Moore will surely stand in my way for promotion. The British Navy is wrought with favoritism and privilege."

"Ah," said Kozak, "as it is the American Navy as well. That is why I left -"

"You were in the American Navy?" interrupted Spears, interested.

"Yes, and being in a like situation as yours, my friend, having others pass me by for favor and promotion because of their name and position, well, I decided to use my experience at sea for my own gain! I became a privateer, a merchant seaman, captain of my own ship. It is a respected career in America and I have never regretted my decision. Adventure! Riches! Why, I was on my way into a very lucrative deal when your Mister Moore decided to ruin my plans! Wayne, it seems we both owe him a thing or two!"

"But I heard your crew mutinied," said Spears warily.

"Of course they did," laughed Kozak, "Once they heard of the money to be made on this venture, they decided to change the game and take it all for their own. My share as captain was much larger than theirs, so they jailed me. They probably planned to kill me at an opportune time. If I only had a right-hand man that I could trust! One with some experience and discipline. Like yourself, a military man."

Spears now seemed to feel slightly more comfortable with Kozak and even smiled as the man continued telling him of his pirate adventures, the riches to be had and the fame that Kozak had obtained as a business man, *a privateer,* in America. Spears even thought that *he* could be the trusted, right-hand man that Kozak needed. After all, he had experience in military matters.

However, unbeknownst to Spears, the pirate was a born liar and a good one at that. He was not always successful swaying others' opinions and cheating people out of their fortunes, but with a young boy, one with a chip on his shoulder, Kozak was a master of turning a phrase. He found it easy to prey on the weaknesses of the boy's simple mind. After a few more minutes, Spears would see Kozak as the only one who believed in him and one who shared a mutual hatred for their mutual enemy, Jonathan Moore.

"Yes, in America, a man with some backbone and industry can rise above his station easily, as a privateer, a *sea-going business man*. A man with experience, like you, who knows the sea, well, where I come from he is *valued*. All one needs," said Kozak, "is a chance to prove oneself."

Kozak could see that Spears was thinking this over, putting himself in a place of splendor, as a respected man. Kozak's seed of discontent had been sown and was quite possibly taking root in the young mind of Spears. It only needed time and some care to flourish.

"However, for you," said Kozak, "this Moore character must be dealt with. He is obviously plotting against you."

"I am being watched by Moore's cronies, Lieutenant Harrison for one and his silly Irish friend, Flagon. Gaining retribution is nearly impossible!" continued Spears. "I have even challenged Moore to a duel!"

"Indeed?" asked Kozak, surprised. "Certainly justifiable, considering the circumstances."

"It will never come to pass," continued Spears bitterly. "He is too well protected."

"As it may seem," said Kozak, standing and leaning close to the barred door. He now had something with which to bait the hook and catch Spears. "But there are ways to make things come to pass, to *urge them along*."

Spears looked Kozak in the eye and a questioning look came across his face.

"How can I duel with Moore? You know of a way?"

Kozak smiled, knowing he was leading the dull-witted Spears along to a predetermined conclusion.

"I believe I can devise a plan for you," said Kozak. "I have been in numerous duels myself, as they are common place in America. But I will have to think about it for a day or so. Will you be back?"

Spears frowned and squinted eyes at the pirate.

"You can't tell me now?" asked Spears, now annoyed and impatient.

"Now, now, Wayne," soothed Kozak. "These things take time. I need to recall all of my own duels and see which situation is most appropriate. We may need more than one attempt. Patience!"

With that, Spears stomped out, slamming the door, plunging the pirate into the dank gloom once again.

Kozak laughed inside knowing that the idea of revenge would eat at Spears. In a day or two, as he thought it over and over in his mind, the young man would become incensed, and it would not be long before Spears would willingly do anything to get at Moore.

The stowaway stirred from sleep in the jollyboat that was tied to the main deck, right across the beam. It wasn't comfortable there, even with the fashioned rope-bed. But the tarp that was always pulled tightly over the boat kept it dark and private. As long as no one actually needed the boat, its occupant was safe and out of the way.

Food was now a simple issue. Earlier, to get cream and milk, the stowaway struggled, sneaking into various places, the galleys in particular, in the middle of the night, hoping to find something reasonably fresh. During one forage, a goat was discovered in the lowest deck. With a few tries, milking was accomplished that supplied a generous amount of goat's milk from time to time. To remain concealed on these night missions, the stowaway would don a small coat that had been left in the boat and ever so slowly sneak into one of the two galleys. The one that was manned by the quiet gentleman, the one in the center of the ship, had certainly more food than the one back by the Captain's cabin, though not as good of quality. It was easy to wait until the cook fell asleep, then sneak inside, close the door ever so gently and take a few things that were easy to get. There were biscuits, some salted pork, and even at times, some stew that had been left over. One evening, the stowaway even found a small cherry pie and cream.

Tonight, though, the stowaway needed some fresh eggs and maybe a bit of cheese. Goodies such as those could be found only in the galley near the Captain's cabin. That was dangerous, as the Captain always seemed to be awake, and if not, he was being awakened by a lieutenant or midshipman, who brought him news about the ship and its position. The stowaway had listened to some of the conversations by hiding in the shadows. *Why not just wake him if something is wrong? Why wake him to say 'all is well, go back to sleep?' It seems ridiculous.*

Making way to the galley was difficult, as one could not just stomp across the deck. There was always someone at the wheel, someone walking about, maybe even a marine or two on deck, looking and watching. It was much easier, the stowaway found, to just sneak out of the boat, slip down a ladder and sneak along the passageways to the rear of the ship. It was only a second or two of nervous terror to slip past the captain's door and into the galley.

Inside, it was dark. The cook was never there and the stowaway deduced that he must sleep elsewhere. As silent as a mouse, the stowaway gathered a few eggs that were in a cupboard and some fresh cheese that had been wrapped in a damp towel and kept in a box with a tight lid. Also, there was a small bit of fruit. Reaching for a plum, a noise came from outside, just to the other side of the door.

"Captain," came a voice. "I just checked on Mister Moore. Sound asleep, I tell ya!"

It was the Captain's cook. *He is back,* thought the stowaway. *Would he check on the galley? It is best if I leave now, while the cook's back is turned.* Peeking out the door, it was obvious that the cook, halfway into the Captain's cabin was facing the other way.

"Good," said the Captain sleepily. "Carry on, Steward."

"After I check my stores!" he said. "Seems that some things get out of place during the night!"

He turned and opened the small door to the galley.

The stowaway had just slipped past and down the ladder. *Ah, just made it!* the stowaway thought. *I need to make my way back carefully and enjoy my bounty!"*

Within a few minutes, after finishing the plum, the intruder was back in the jollyboat where the tarp was pulled down tightly, locking out the wind and the salt spray. But there was suddenly a sound coming from the deck outside: footsteps.

Just a few yards from the jollyboat, the footsteps stopped. It was Steward. He had taken to searching the ship at night, looking for clues to the mystery of the missing stores. It disturbed him greatly that, firstly, someone was stealing food, and secondly, that he did not know who was responsible. It was suspected by the crew but still an unsubstantiated fact that Steward was one of Captain Walker's secret *sets of eyes and ear*s and that he took great pride in informing the Captain of the goings on aboard the ship.

After searching the stern and seeing nothing out of the ordinary, Steward took a few more paces toward amidships. Then, *c-r-a-c-k!* He heard a crunching sound as he stepped on something very hard. Looking down, he moved his foot and saw a roundish shape on the deck in the darkness. Upon further investigation, he could see that it was a plum pit.

The following morning in the damp brig, Kozak watched as his breakfast was brought on a tray by none other than Midshipman Wayne Spears. There was a little small talk between them and after a while, Spears brought up the subject of the duel. Kozak smiled inside, knowing that his trick was working and that Spears needed his advice.

"I did give it some serious thought, Wayne, and I believe I have a plan for you. A public duel is never going to happen, as you say, Jonathan is being watched like a baby by doting parents. No, there is no way to arrange a public duel. However, there is another way to achieve the same purpose."

"And what is that?" asked Spears, now almost aching for the answer. He had indeed thought about taking revenge upon Jonathan all night long. He slept very little and then only fretfully. Every idea he had come to him, about how to get ahead of Jonathan Moore, seemed to be a dead end.

I can not pass him in the eyes of Captain Walker, thought Spears. *His father is now an adjunct and in the King's favor! With his capturing of the* Drake, *he will probably be knighted! All is a dead end!*

"It will take courage, Wayne, and absolute determination on your part," Kozak said, almost like an army major addressing and testing the resolve of his troops before a great battle. "You must be as ruthless as the Moores have been in their quest to keep you and your family down."

"I will do anything for my honor and name," said Spears, equally serious and determined.

"I know you will, Wayne Spears," Kozak said. "I have seen few men with your determination and guile. Those characteristics will serve you well. So…here it is…you…must murder Jonathan Moore."

"Murder him?" said Spears, now taken aback.

"You tried before, didn't you, but it didn't work, when you pushed him off the plank, to be squashed between the ship and the quay."

"I wasn't *really* trying to -"

"Yes you were," snapped Kozak. "And a great plan it was, my boy! No one saw, it was perfectly done! If it wasn't for his handlers, those that assist him in his climb to the top – the climb made on the backs of the hard working Spears Family, he would already be gone!"

"I didn't know that he could have died!" blurted Spears.

"Yes you did!" continued Kozak, almost pleading with the boy to agree. "However, as in all great execution, we, we men of action, we focus! We focus on the task at hand, not the result!"

"But murder?" whispered Spears, now almost mad with fear and excitement as well.

"Why not? He has effectively murdered you! And his father did the same to your father! The Moores have plotted against you ever since…well before you were born! You said yourself that his father had used favoritism to keep your family down. Now his brat of a son is joining the farce! But you can stop them! This is your chance!"

Spears slumped down to the hard deck, just outside of the barred door. He looked to the ground, stunned and dizzy. He thought to himself that there must be another way. But as in his dreams of last several nights, there was no answer. Spears kept running over all the possibilities in his head as the two sat in silence. Kozak never took his eyes off the boy. He reached out and touched Wayne's sleeve, patted it gently, then sighed. Spears finally looked up into the kind, understanding face of the pirate Kozak.

"How?" was all Spears said.

13
Rendezvous Incognito

Upon the deck of the *Danielle*, the ship's bell rang twice, signaling the hour of one o'clock in the morning. Jonathan ascended a ladder from the dimly-lit lower decks, then paused, once topside, to wait for his vision to adjust to the deeper darkness. The night watch was usually quiet and calm, and as expected, he could see and hear no one present, though he was sure there had to be at least a dozen men at work, silently attending to sails and rigging, or watching for other ships from high in the tops. A slight sound of wind rushed easily through his ears, and the splashing of waves against the side of the ship drowned out any voices, even if there were words being said. After a few more moments, his eyes became accustomed to the night and he could now see that the heavens above shone brightly, not just with white stars, but with stars of all colors, glittering on both sides of the ship, fore and aft, and due to the reflection of their light off the water, even below. The sea and sky had merged together, the horizon impossible to discern. The stars gave off light enough to cause a few shadows to be cast on the deck. To Jonathan it was dreamlike, almost magical and truly amazing, even though at times, disorienting. Mister Watt, however, seemed untroubled by this condition. The ship sailed straight on through the speckled, multicolor star field as if moving within the heavens themselves, no longer earth bound.

A pair of eyes peeked from under the tarp of the jollyboat, watching as Jonathan walked the deck in a circular fashion. After his third time past, the *somebody* that belonged to the eyes quietly slipped out of the boat, dropping like a cat to the deck, scurried away to the nearest ladder and down to the deck below.

Jonathan continued onward, only hearing a few sounds of creaking wood behind him. This was no cause for alarm, as the great ship groaned and grumbled constantly, reminding all aboard of her tireless task, and that indeed, she was hand-made.

About an hour later, Jonathan walked to the beam and looked up to the main mast. No one was aloft. All seemed quiet. A quick glace around with his glass showed that they were alone in this sparking world where both the sea and heaven held stars. The rushing sound of the water racing along the side of the *Danielle* seemed steady and strong.

As he turned his gaze back to the deck, Jonathan looked astern. In the darkness, he thought he saw a shadow move. *A crewman?* he wondered. *But why skulking in the dark?* Steward had told him of a food thief, responsible for an ever-growing list of missing items. *Could this be the thief?* Jonathan stared in the general area he had seen the shadow and after a moment…there! He saw a stooped shape sprint across the ship and disappear behind the jolly boat.

He moved quickly to investigate.

"You there! By the boat! Show yourself!" he called. There was no answer. As Jonathan approached, he decided to move to the port side and walk around the boat. *Maybe this person was hiding behind,* he thought, *and I need to move fast to see him!* He quickly ran about and jumped behind the boat – but no one was there. Even after circling twice, he saw no one.

Someone is here, he thought, *and their skulking leads me to believe they are certainly out of place.*

Though he continued his search, he saw no more shadows nearby and decided to move toward the bow. Then he paused. He thought he saw something move by the portside deck guns. *Could the shadow have moved that far so fast?* he thought, and again, Jonathan moved to investigate.

As he came upon the deck guns, a shadow arose to face him and took the shape of a man. Jonathan stepped back, afraid and stunned. He let out a gasp as the shape moved quickly toward him. The person had smeared something black across his face, maybe ash or paint it seemed, as all Jonathan could see were two shining white eyes. The figure grabbed at Jonathan, clutching his hand around his lapel.

He tried to wiggle away, but he was collared tightly and in a second he was pinned between his attacker and the foremast. He couldn't run.

"It ends tonight!" seethed the man, through gritted teeth.

Out of the man's coat came something gleaming in the starlight. A knife. It was quickly brought down in a murderous arc. Jonathan parried with the telescope and moved to the side. But the powerful push of his attacker caused them both to tumble backward, falling in a heap. Rolling, Jonathan added distance between himself and his adversary.

The man rolled to his left and stood up hurriedly. He raised the knife again and flew at Jonathan. Moving aside just enough to miss the stroke, Jonathan extended his foot to trip the attacker and then spun, striking the knife from his hand with his telescope. It fell to the deck.

As the man stumbled, Jonathan reached for the blade and brought it up quickly. The attacker turned and charged again, then gasped, noticing his own knife was now turned against him. In trying to ward off the blow, he caught the blade in the lower arm. In pain, he spun quickly, sending the blade into the air and over the side. As Jonathan watched the knife disappear, the attacker ran head down into his chest, knocking the wind out of him and dropping him to the deck. Shocked, Jonathan lay motionless for a second, then quickly regained his senses and struggled to his feet. He looked about frantically. The fleeing attacker was nowhere in sight.

The next morning, the Captain's cabin was a hive of activity as land had been sighted. To plan and discuss, all the officers were in attendance for breakfast at the Captain's table, awaiting orders, but more importantly, awaiting a decent meal. Now that the ship had reached the outer Cape Verde Islands, they would surely take on new supplies, mostly water and possibly even some fresh meat. Though there were still a few eggs left, they had just eaten the single remaining chicken for dinner last night, so there would certainly be no more of those. And almost always in abundance while at sea, fish was at best, *tiring.* Approaching a friendly port meant more food variety and quality and also meant they could finish up any perishable food left from the voyage.

Additionally, the Captain had now officially informed them all that someone was stealing food, and that meant fruit was in short supply and all the sugar was gone.

"At least whoever is pilfering has no taste for wine or rum," said Steward.

"Unfortunately," said Harrison, "The thief also has no taste for the food you have cooked, as I see it here in inglorious abundance!"

This caused all to laugh, except Steward, of course. He just shook his head and muttered something about disrespect for elders and the ungratefulness of youth.

"Any idea as to the identity of the food thief, gentlemen?" asked Koontz.

Holtz and Walker shook their heads to say 'no', as did Harrison. As their eyes trained on Jonathan to hear his response, he realized that he must say something about last night. He did not want to alert anyone to his *knife fight,* as certainly that would make Captain Walker become over protective. He would be moved from the orlop, possibly into the Captain's cabin and probably not allowed to leave until they returned to London. True, it was now not a game, it was serious. Someone had tried to kill him. He of course suspected Spears. *I will wait a bit longer before I ask for help,* he thought. *Probably a mistake, but I desire to figure this out by myself. And I do have a trick or two up my sleeve.*

"Sir," Jonathan began. "I believe I ran into the food thief. I had him cornered and he lunged at me. Luckily, no harm but a bit of bumping as he ran off. I could not see in which direction he escaped."

This seemed to cause great alarm with all in the room.

"Did you see the scoundrel's face?" asked Walker.

"No sir, he had blackened it with ash and the like."

The officers asked for details and for the story to be retold from the beginning at least three times. During the tale, they continued eating the last few eggs and cheesed toast, and drinking coffee.

Just as Jonathan was about to mention the knife, a knock came upon the door.

"Enter," called the Captain, and in walked Lane followed by Spears.

"Midshipmen Lane, Spears! Thank you for joining us," said the Captain sarcastically. "Is there anything I can get for you?"

"I am fine, sir," said Spears, oblivious of the rub as he sat immediately at the table and began taking food and drink for himself. "So sorry I am late. My blouse was not up to snuff. I needed some pipe clay and powder to whiten it. Lane was assisting me."

"It looks presentable now," said Holtz matter-of-factly as he took some cheesed eggs, "except for that spot on your wrist cuff. You should attend to it after breakfast."

Jonathan couldn't help but look at Spears' wrist. There he saw the spot, though it was really more of a line. In the next second, he also saw that this thin line, about three to four inches long, had a dark brown, almost reddish tint to it. As Jonathan stared, it seemed to grow, as if something underneath was feeding it. Suddenly, Jonathan shuddered, as he realized it was a wound, bleeding underneath the cloth and still fresh.

Immediately, Spears caught Jonathan looking and

adjusted his coat to cover the blood.

"There," said Spears, "All proper and prim."

Now Jonathan knew with absolute certainty that Spears had tried, once again, to murder him, the wound surely coming from the knife used in last night's altercation. He wrestled with telling someone, maybe Sean or Harrison. *What then would happen next? I have no proof it is Spears. Do I tell the Captain? He already seems disappointed in me, so would he even* believe *the accusation? It would only be adding more fuel to the fire of hatred Spears has for me,* he thought, and with that he made up his mind. *I will deal with him myself. These friends have already done much for me. It is time to stand on my own, as I have done on the streets and as I have planned.*

Eventually, the talk moved to the duties at hand, about loading supplies and taking on additional water if any were to be had. The Captain also reminded Steward and Holtz, who were to go ashore immediately after the meal, to pass the word of their mission to any other British ships at dock or in the bay and see if they could arrange additional company.

As Steward left with a few dirty dishes, Garvey approached the captain's door and was shown to the table to report his urgent news.

"Beggin' your pardon Captain, sirs," Garvey said, bowing.

"Go ahead, Garvey, but have you eaten?" replied the Captain.

Garvey looked at the officers sitting at the fine table and was taken aback at the invitation. The Captain's table was for the elite aboard, not a common seaman. But Captain Walker had shown before that he broke a few rules and bent etiquette from time to time. Sean Flagon, a mere seaman, had been to dinner numerous times with the Captain, so it was not all that out of the ordinary.

"Eaten, well," stumbled Garvey. "Is this fare from Claise or Steward?"

"Steward," chuckled Harrison, knowing what was

coming next.

"I have eaten my full, Captain, though many thanks for the generous offer," answered Garvey. "Just thought you might like to know that I have just come from the crow's nest and I got a good look at the harbor."

"Ah! *Spa-len-did*!" said Walker, "And how many of our sister ships are in attendance?"

"Unfortunately, only Mister Harrison will be pleased," Garvey said. "Just the Periwinkle is in port."

Indeed this sent Harrison into high spirits, as it was well known by all aboard, even Holtz, that he fancied HMS *Paladin*, also called the Periwinkle, affectionately, due to its strange but colorful purple stripe painted the length of the sleek brig-rigged sloop. She was famous, of course, being both beautiful and known as the fastest ship in the fleet. With only eighteen guns, she was used primarily for delivering messages and a few important passengers from time to time, rarely for action. There had been a few instances where the guns were fired, however, the true weapon of the *Paladin* was her speed, and it could be used to great effect by a smart and able captain.

"I assume, Mister Harrison, that you would like to visit the *Paladin* and speak to her commander personally? Ask for his assistance in at least spreading the word? It would be foolish to add those guns to our battle, if there is one to be had. But the speed of the *Paladin* can alert many a ship."

So excited was Harrison, that he stood without answering, grabbed Jonathan by the collar and dragged him out of the Captain's cabin, heading for the main deck.

Walker, Holtz and Koonts all laughed aloud, leaving Spears and Lane to wonder what was the attraction to the small ship.

Harrison approached the port side rail amidships and was soon joined by Jonathan and Sean, who had just come down from aloft, as he and the others had expertly taken in sail to ease the *Danielle* into the small harbor.

"Good mornin' sir! G'day to ya, Jonny Boy!" Sean said as he stretched and yawned. "It is a pleasure to see land once again. I even heard Garvey say your girl is here, Mister Harrison."

"Yes he did, Flagon. And this time I propose to see not only her beautiful, sleek lines from the outside, but I am going *aboard* and hopefully will see *the inside* as well! I have heard she is all teak on deck and in the cabin, and the finish shines like a mirror. More a pleasure boat on the inside than a naval vessel, but we will have to see."

"How was breakfast?" asked Sean. "Claise had no eggs, but he did make us salted pork sandwiches and a tasty lime tart with the last bit of sugar. His coffee is quite excellent, I must say."

"We had Steward's scrapings from the bottom of the pan, it seems, but he can finally make coffee almost enjoyable," said Harrison. "But Jonathan's description of his adventure last night with the food thief was the most interesting part of the meal."

"You saw the thief? Who is it then?" Sean asked, shocked.

Jonathan reluctantly counted the tale once again, remembering to leave out the part of about the knife.

Inside the jolly boat, someone listened to this conversation and held a breath for what seemed to be close to ten minutes. Any noise might cause the three boys to investigate.

The *Danielle* glided into port, and to greet her, was none other than the *Paladin.* Harrison was speechless as he beheld her again. Even Jonathan and Sean could not take their eyes off the graceful ship with her striking raked masts. She was tied up tight, all neat and proper, seeming to sun herself like a beautiful mermaid, lying in the turquoise shallows, her deck glowing in the sun, like rays off her golden hair. She wove a spell over the boys and they were happy to be under it, each dreaming of the great speed at which she would carry them into adventure and fame.

"Ahoy *Doggard!*" came a familiar voice. "Ahoy Lieutenant Harrison!"

The boys all snapped out of their dreams and looked down upon the dock, now almost directly beneath them. As the *Danielle* daintily slid to a stop and hands tossed lines to secure the ship, the boys noticed a tall marine. He was dressed in his best uniform, red coat and gold sash, and removed his hat to expose his white wig as he bowed elegantly.

"Captain Gorman!" they yelled. Undeniably it was their friend and compatriot.

"So good to see you, sir!" called Harrison. "And I would stow that name. We are the *Danielle*, regardless of what the plaque says, and if you desire to test any other designation, you will witness the Captain's wrath."

"Ah! I appreciate the warning," Gorman said. "Then, ahem, Ahoy *Danielle*!"

"Are you available for breakfast?" called Harrison. "The Captain would love to entertain you; I am sure, though there are no cheesed anchovies, I am sorry to say."

"One can't have all one desires I fear," said Gorman. "A cup of coffee and one of Steward's hard rolls will have to please."

With that the plank was lowered and Gorman marched aboard, being greeted by most of the nearby crew and of course, all the marines. Hicks and Hudson were extremely glad to see their former commander and snapped the best of salutes.

Sean escorted him aft.

"Before you sneak away again, Captain Gorman, could you find some time for me? I have been wondering if you could teach me a little more about the Marines," Sean said quietly.

"Then I will make sure we spend a good amount of time together. I am unattached *now,* as it were. My *sneaking* is finished. It was a great joy to sail aboard the

Periwinkle all the way from London. I had a feeling I could gain news of your whereabouts, and at last, some luck, as I have found you. Have you been reading, Sean?"

"Yes sir!" Sean said excitedly. "Jonathan and Steward have been teaching me and I have already finished half of King Arthur. It is quite thrilling!"

"Excellent," said Gorman as he patted the boy on the head. "Have you been keeping Hudson and Hicks in line?"

"They are a caution, there is no denying that, but, well, I will let them tell you all we did after we had a mid-day desert of strawberries and stole a pirate ship!"

Gorman laughed as they reached the jollyboat in the middle of the deck.

"And I hear we are off to Africa," added Sean. "That is exciting, don't ya think?"

"Africa? Whatever for? I assume I will know shortly," Gorman said as they had now reached the Captain's door. "It seems," the Marine said, "that there is mischief and adventure even when I am not around to orchestrate it all!"

Even though the deck was alive with men now running and calling out to each other, the someone beneath the tarp in the jolly boat ventured a quick glance out from underneath and saw the small island clearly. *This must be Cape Verde, the islands I heard the crew speak of,* the stowaway thought. *And they said we are heading to Africa? How far is that? Will there be enough time to go ashore and get some real food? This salty pork and dried bread is not pleasing at all. As I remember from geography, Cape Verde is far from England – but usually filled with British ships! If I popped out now, I would be sent home aboard the next ship heading north! No, I will wait a while longer, when it is too late to turn back! Ah, to see the coast of Africa!*

Down in the brig, Kozak noticed the mooring of the *Danielle*, as he could hear the calls of the men and sense that all motion had stopped save the gentle lapping of waves against the side of his cell wall. He wondered where he was. Surely not back in England. He had counted the days as best as he could since they departed Nassau. He had made eleven marks on the wall of his cell with his finger nail, one for each day.

"Too many days for the Canary Islands," he whispered to himself. "And we are not far enough for Ascension. This must be Cape Verde! Not the best location for an escape, if one is to be had. But if careful, a boat could be stolen, maybe at night."

With that, the hatch above the ladder was opened and down came Midshipman Spears, with a tray of food. But Kozak could not look at the fare. He was most interested in the outcome of the previous evening. Did Spears actually try to murder Moore? Was he successful? If so, then it was time to spin the next lie and slowly trick Spears into believing *he had been seen* and that the Captain had only a few more ends to tie together before he found out who had murdered Jonathan Moore. Once Spears was sufficiently petrified, Kozak would explain how they both could escape and live a life on the seas together; become rich and respected in America.

All Spears would have to do is release Kozak.

"Ah, Wayne!" Kozak said. "And how did you fare last night?"

Spears set the tray down slowly by the opening beneath the bars and pushed it gently inside. He looked up to Kozak, tears now running down his face.

"I failed," Spears finally got out.

"H-how? Did you follow my advice?"

"Yes," said Spears.

"To the letter?" asked Kozak.

"Yes!" yelled Spears. He settled down quickly. "To the letter. But Moore was lucky once again and struck me with a staff of some sort. I was so close! But I was rewarded once again by the boot of injustice!"

"Did he see you? Could he recognize you?" asked Kozak, hoping that the answer was yes. Then it would be as good as having committed the actual crime and the pirate could continue his plot to scare Spears into helping him.

"No," said Spears. "I was disguised. A larger coat. I blackened my face with ash and water. Moore might have seen my small scar upon my wrist, but they can't prove anything. Many of us have scars like this."

They remained in silence, both lost in their own thoughts. Spears was thinking about the unfairness of it all and the idea that Moore most assuredly knew it was him. *What would they do with this knowledge?* he thought. *Who would he tell?*

Kozak was feeling sorry as well, but not an ounce was wasted on Midshipman Spears. He felt sorry for himself. This latest failure spoiled his escape plan and unless Spears could be sufficiently *motivated,* he would not assist. Not after this botched attempt.

"Lord," said Kozak, somewhat angrily. "Isn't there anything you can do better than Jonathan Moore?"

And that stopped Spears cold.

Yes, he thought*, there is one thing that I can do better than Moore. I have proved it time and again in front of the whole crew. And it could be turned into a deadly talent!*

"Of course," said Spears, now standing. "I can out fight him with a sword. I will challenge him again, ashore and away from prying eyes."

"How?" asked the pirate. "He will never agree! You said so yourself!"

Spears just laughed.

"No, I said it would never happen, because Lieutenant Harrison has gotten wind of it. The duel was actually Moore's suggestion! If I can get him alone…ashore…he will accept. Especially if I goad him."

"And how will you accomplish the goading?" asked Kozak, now beginning to see that Spears may play into his hands once again.

"I will tell him the truth about a great many things! About how I accosted his father and how *my* father called in a favor from a few friends in the Admiralty!"

14
The Duel

Those many members of the crew who were given leave to go ashore in Ribeira Grande lined up in front of Mister Koonts to receive their pay and be dismissed into the port city. They were reminded that the stay was for one night only and that anyone not reporting back at sunrise would be severely punished. But even this threat could not dampen their spirits. Santiago Island was a popular destination for ships of His Majesty's Navy and Ribeira Grande was the largest city of all the surrounding islands, thereby presenting the most entertainment. All knew it offered hearty food, beer and the like, and soft beds that didn't sway from side to side throughout the night. The day was warm and the breeze pleasant, the small streets beckoned the sailors to explore and enjoy.

Jonathan and Sean were given leave to go ashore and with Garvey as their guide, they explored all the favorite places. He showed them, first, his favorite pub that had the most amazing goat sandwiches and suggested they each order one with a glass of tea.

"Goat?" said Jonathan. "I don't know. The meat is grey, isn't it?"

"Now Jonny," Sean said. "We have gone over this before. You have had it!"

"No, I have not," Jonathan said quickly.

"Yes, yes, in London on White Chapel Street, remember? There was that pub owner who had offered us a bowl of goat stew for hauling coal! You loved it!"

"It *is* tasty, Mister Moore," added Garvey with a smile.

"I did not love it, Sean," Jonathan said. "I had been smelling coal ash and sweat all day, I hadn't eaten in what seemed like a month. All I remember was looking at the empty bowl when I was done. I tasted nothing."

Garvey and Sean continued badgering him until Jonathan agreed to try just one bite. If he didn't find it to his liking, they would pay for anything else he wanted. With substantial reluctance, Jonathan finally, cautiously and gingerly took a bite.

"Oh," said Jonathan, tasting the meat and spices along with a sauce that could only have been olive oil and some kind of ground pea, "Dear me! It is wonderful!"

"If it can't kill you, you should try it, my Da always says!" Sean added as the boys laughed.

The remainder of the day was spent climbing the few small hills on the outskirts of town and doing a little shopping. Garvey led them to a small shop where they discovered a variety of cooking oils, spices, salts and even a few herbal remedies that greatly interested Sean. Jonathan had picked a few bottles to assist in his cooking when his eyes fell on a bracelet, a silver affair with a small charm on it. A charm of a sea turtle.

"Will you take a look at this!" he said, and Sean and Garvey came to see his treasure.

"A turtle, I believe?" said Garvey.

"It just happens to be Miss Delain Dowdeswell's favorite animal," said Sean. "And I would say that Miss Delain Dowdeswell is Mister Moore's favorite as well!"

This sent Sean into fits of laughter and even Jonathan chuckled a bit.

"Then I must have it!" he exclaimed, and collected all his goods and carried them to the counter. The shop woman wrapped the turtle in some fine cloth and tied a ribbon around it, then placed the items in a sack. She collected a few small coins and smiled brightly at the boys. After thanking her, they walked out into the bright daylight, ready for their next adventure.

Unfortunately, it was Midshipmen Lane and Spears who first caught their eye. The two miscreants walked from the other side of the street, directly toward them. They seemed to be nervous, looking from side to side.

Jonathan was also nervous, so much so that Sean noticed he kept his hand at his hip near his sword, ready to fight if need be.

"Gentlemen," said Jonathan cautiously. "I hope you are having a pleasant day?"

Spears ignored this and immediately bent in close to whisper.

"Moore, it is nice to see you with only two body guards instead of the entire ship."

"How is your wrist? Still bleeding?" asked Jonathan with a twinge of venom in his voice.

"Yes, it was me, Moore. I only wonder why you haven't called on your personal Captain and told him all about it."

"I have my reasons and they are my own. Besides, I can deal with *you* myself. What is it you want?"

Spears laughed and looked around again to make sure there were no officers about.

"Send Garvey on. I want to speak to you and Flagon. Alone," he said.

With a nod from Jonathan, Garvey went on ahead full of suspicion, turning back to look at the two midshipmen and wondering what was being discussed. He didn't trust Spears, as he had seen him berate and bully Sean on a several occasions and a few other crewmembers besides. Most of the men despised him and the talk was always about the desire for him to be transferred or promoted off the *Danielle*.

Strange, thought Garvey, *the idea of Spears and Lane confronting Mister Moore and Sean is disquieting! I think I should inform someone.*

Spears now waited a minute or two for Garvey to be out of ear shot, then addressed Jonathan angrily.

"Moore, can you stand for yourself, by yourself, or will you always have your handlers about you?"

"I was alone when you tried to kill me on deck the other night," answered Jonathan, "and that ended up with you on the wrong end of a knife, or did you forget that?"

Sean could not stand silently. He now realized that something went on between Jonathan and Spears that he was not privy to, and that angered him. A knife fight was fought and luckily his friend was not hurt, however, he felt it was his duty to watch and protect Jonathan. Now, his temper was near its limit. Sean boldly stepped in front of Spears and looked upwards the few inches into his eyes.

"If I were there on deck instead of Jonathan," he said coldly, "that knife would have been planted more permanently, I can assure you. And I may do it just the same."

With that, Sean reached to his calf and retrieved his *letter opener* from the sheath around his ankle, bringing it up quickly. With a flash of sunlight glistening off the blade, he had the edge against Spears' throat. The Midshipman quickly grabbed Sean's hand, pushing the blade away just a few inches to protect himself.

"As usual!" Spears cried out, laughing. "Your personal valet comes to your rescue, Moore!"

"Sean," said Jonathan coolly. "Please calm down. And put that away."

Sean removed the blade and stepped back, his anger still at a dangerous point.

"You Moores are all alike. Always collected and polite. Using your connections and favors to get ahead! Bringing your own protection, even if in the form of a pip-squeak like Flagon. Never standing on your own two feet! Being propped up by others!" continued Spears, getting more heated by the minute. Jonathan watched him closely.

"I do believe you are insane, Spears," Jonathan said. "Come on, Sean, let us find better company."

Spears reached out to stop Jonathan, grabbing him by the coat lapel.

"And you should learn to tie down your deck guns! Yes, I was behind that as well!" laughed Spears.

"As if I didn't know? You are a fool, Spears. Now move your hand," Jonathan said softly but firmly, "or I will move it for you."

"Ha! The last time you said that, you challenged me to a duel! And you ran off, afraid."

Jonathan slapped Spears' hand away, but stood his ground, eyes narrowing and anger rising.

"I am certainly not afraid of you!" Jonathan hissed through clenched teeth. "However, I do not wish to throw away my career over a duel with a useless, insolent and cretinous cod fish."

"You sound like your father, with your boyish insults!" said Spears.

"A brute like you could never be so lucky as to hear his words, let alone meet my father!" snapped Jonathan.

"Ah," said Spears laughing again, "But I did! And I almost knocked him on the head, just last Christmas Day, at the docks!"

Jonathan quickly remembered the story his father told him and how he suspected the attacker was Spears. It was now confirmed.

Sean could see that Jonathan's temper was rising. It looked dangerous to him. Not sure of what would happen next, he kept an eye on Lane who also seemed on edge, looking about and even breaking into a mild sweat. *This could get out of hand,* thought Sean, still holding his blade in plain sight. *Jonathan is always polite and always a gentleman. But I know his one weakness: his temper.* There were times on the streets of London, when Sean remembered bullies trying to take their food or blankets. Out-numbered and undersized, it didn't matter; if Jonathan's temper heated up, he could become dangerous. It served him well at times, and at others, his pride and sense of protection for his friends might have gotten him a few bruises from the bigger boys, bruises that he could have avoided.

"I owe you a knock or two," Jonathan said angrily.

"Or maybe even four or five!" Spears said giddily. "Oh, I have been sitting on this for the longest time! I have been dying to tell you this one, *Jonny Boy!* You see, your family is not the only one with friends in high places. The Spears have a few as well. One close friend of the family is

Admiral Worthing! And my father called on him for a favor. Yes, you are seeing it now! Even your dull-witted mind can follow that my father orchestrated the blocking of your father's promotion to admiral!"

Jonathan swung, but Spears saw it coming and leaned back, avoiding the blow.

"You grobian!" Jonathan yelled. "I will cut you down myself!"

"Excellent!" said Spears. "That is exactly what I had in mind! Since there are no pistols to be found, the duel is with swords. Agreed?"

"Absolutely!" called Jonathan, now writhing with anger. "Where and when?"

"Jonathan!" cried Sean.

"At the park," snapped Spears. "Just south of the church on the edge of town. Sundown."

"I will be there!" Jonathan yelled, enraged and seemingly out of his mind.

"Wayne," said Lane meekly. "I think this has gone too far -"

"Shut up!" Spears said, now grabbing Lane by the arm and turning away. They stomped off, Lane quite nervous and Spears laughing.

Sean was certainly not laughing.

"Jonathan! What were you thinking? You can't fight him! One of you will be killed! It is murder! If the Captain finds out, that will be the end of you!"

Jonathan watched Spears and Lane disappear around the corner of the small shop, and as they did, he seemed to calm down considerably. He took a deep breath and relaxed his stance.

"It will not be the end, Sean! Have some faith!"

Aboard the *Danielle*, there was a meeting of the minds in Captain Walker's cabin. Mister Koonts was there, sampling the few delicacies a ship's officers could enjoy while in a port with fresh food. There were eggs, of course, chicken, fresh fruit and even cream for the coffee. Joining

Koonts was Lieutenant Holtz, sitting with his surprised look as he contemplated a berry of some sort that Steward has acquired from a rushed trip to the grocer. Captain Walker was sitting at the large table across from Marine Captain Gorman, both sipping coffee and studying a large map of the islands off the eastern coast of Africa.

"So you see, Captain Gorman, our guest, Kozak, has told us the manifest is here, in the fort De La Selva," said Walker.

"Yes," said Gorman. "I have heard of Kozak and of the fort, and also of its frequent guest, Generalissimo Aguilar. It is well known he arranges arms for South American colonies and also that he has been profiting from his dealings since the war began. He agrees to transport weapons to Napoleon's troops through various networks, though always after he takes his share of the goods. If there is a manifest, then it is surely in his fort. "

"I am not sure if Kozak can be believed," Walker said. "He could be lying to save his skin. We will need to confirm this story of his and the manifest would prove it."

"Let me have some time," said Gorman. "I may be able to get some information out of him. A small threat, a slightly veiled ultimatum can do wonders."

"Are you suggesting torture, Captain Gorman?" asked Walker.

Gorman smiled. "Only if completely necessary, however, I think the threat of the noose will be enough to get him to talk. But no matter what, we should proceed immediately to Rio Muni."

"Gentlemen," said the Captain, standing to signal the end of the conference. "We are taking the word of a pirate who is most probably lying to save his skin. To be sure, it is critical that we obtain that manifest."

"I will develop a plan for that," said Gorman.

All were dismissed. Gorman headed to the brig to interrogate Kozak.

* * * * * *

A small park with short green grass surrounded by tall trees and thick bushes seemed to be the most private place on the island. There were no benches, no wandering couples, no statues for viewing or fountains for wishing; just the grass and a small path that led across the center. It was like a shallow dinner bowl with the trees for the sides and the lawn the bottom. Thin beams of sunlight streamed through the leaves, striking the park with sparkling sunrays as the evening came on.

In the middle of the park stood four young men. Two were removing their dark blue naval jackets, the others inspecting two swords recently purchased from a local armorer. Neither combatant wanted to use his own blade as these new ones would be thrown into the sea to destroy any possibility of connecting them with the duel that was about to take place. It had been also agreed upon by all parties that the loser's body would be dragged into the woods and buried in the soft loam. A story could then be told about how he had been last seen in the company of a few local merchantmen and was last seen heading for their small ship. This way, desertion or foul play could be assumed by Captain Walker and the others.

Sean, of course, thought that all this was absolutely ridiculous and the falsehoods would be immediately seen through by even the numbest brains of the crew, let alone the officers. Jonathan would never desert and certainly was known to be too intelligent to be tricked by anyone. However, Sean was made to agree to the plan at the behest of Jonathan. *He is clearly out of his mind!* thought Sean. But no amount of talk or threat could convince him to abandon the idea.

"I believe we are ready, Gentlemen," said Lane, quite nervously, yet politely.

"Agreed" said Sean, still not believing the madness of this. Though Jonathan was an excellent swordsman, it had been seen again and again aboard the ship that he, for some reason, did not pair up well against Spears. Was it just a bizarre circumstance? Were their fencing styles simply just so that Spears would be favored to always come out on top?

Sean and Lane then each chose a blade and took their selection to their masters. Upon inspection, both Wayne Spears and Jonathan Moore each held their sword in front of their face in salute of the other.

"En guard!" called Lane.

The sun was beginning to set on Ribeira Grande. The sailors where all, by now, in their favorite pubs, entertaining themselves, stuffing their faces and cavorting like bands of roving lunatics. Most of the fun was light hearted, however, there were a limited number of instances of poor behavior and a few minor arrests by the local law officers. This was fully expected when any ship's crew arrived in town.

At the port dock, Lieutenant Harrison exited the small cabin on the stern of HMS *Paladin*. He looked as if he had been smitten by one of cupid's arrows, the smile upon his face from ear-to-ear. His feet seemed to barely touch the deck as he lazily sauntered to the gangplank and then off to the dock, now and again spinning to look back at the sleek and handsome craft.

"Just as beautiful on the inside!" he said aloud to no one in particular.

Shortly, Garvey approached him and tipped his cap.

"Ah, Garvey!" Harrison said. "Have you come to gander at the most beautiful vessel ever to grace the ocean waves?"

Garvey scratched his head in wonder, trying to decipher Harrison's words, then after a moment, realized that the Lieutenant was under the spell of the Periwinkle.

"Aye, Lieutenant," he said, "She's a barky, that one is, but no, that is not why I am here. I am looking for you."

"You have found me and found me in a delightful mood! I have just spent an hour with Lieutenant Sutton, the current captain of the *Paladin*. He has agreed to sail straight to England and alert any ships he sees to our mission. With the speed of that graceful lady, it would surprise me if he did not gather us one-hundred ships! Captain Walker will be pleased as punch! Did you know, Garvey, that the teak wood on the inside of the *Paladin's* hold is varnished? Amazing! It glows like honey!"

"Aye, sir," Garvey said impatiently, "I am sure it is most satisfying. However, I have a dire need. Urgent I would say. Life and death, sir."

Harrison's smile was now fading from his face. He looked at Garvey and held up his hand.

"Let me guess. Jonathan and Spears?"

"Yes sir. Seems the duel they are not supposed to have, well . . . they are having."

"Where?" asked Harrison, visibly shaken by the news, his anger and concern growing.

"The park at the edge of town," Garvey said hurriedly. "I can't be sure, but they certainly didn't want me to hear what they were plotting. Sean and Lane are there as well!"

"Blast!" said Harrison. "They are there as seconds, to make sure all goes according to plan! We must run, Garvey, double time!"

Harrison remembered the fencing matches that Jonathan and Spears had aboard the ship. He believed Jonathan was not fighting to his full potential, losing on purpose, laying a trap for Spears. However, he also knew that sometimes things could go wrong, and sometimes fatally. He followed Garvey, both running as fast as they could into town, hoping to reach the park before it was too late.

As always, Spears began his attack by charging heavily, lunging at his foe constantly, expecting him to retreat. However, somehow, Jonathan kept to his seemingly improved footwork and moved out of the way easily. Spears spun and renewed his attack, lunging and swiping with great fury. He was powerful and certainly seemed bent on killing Jonathan. His beats were strong and the swords clashed loudly as every advance was parried by Jonathan. Back and forth they moved, around the center of the park, at times into the trees, Spears beating and attacking, Jonathan parrying and slipping to either side to avoid Spears' blade. It was frightening, and Sean was worried that this fight would end up just like all the others, with Spears as the victor. This time, however, the loser would be dead.

This may be the last time I see him alive, thought Sean. But then he noticed an odd thing. As the swordsmen seemed to pause, Spears looked drenched with sweat and quite red in the face. Jonathan, on the other hand, didn't even seem to be flush or tired. In fact, his face was the absolute picture of calmness and serenity.

"How long have we been at it, Sean?" called Jonathan.

Sean had no real idea, but gave an estimate.

"Five minutes, maybe a bit more! Be careful, Jonathan!"

Spears now took advantage of Jonathan's distraction caused by his asking for the time. He completed a quick stutter step attack with a quick lunge, aiming directly for Jonathan's heart. Jonathan moved quickly to his left, avoiding the attack, causing Spears to stumble past. Not even turning, Jonathan lifted his blade above his head, flicked his wrist backward and extended his arm behind his own back, catching Spears as he passed, the point scoring between his enemy's shoulders.

Spears toppled over into the grass and grimaced in pain. A small amount of blood could be seen through his white blouse.

"A point, Jonny Boy!" said Sean, happily. He could not believe it. In their previous matches, Jonathan scored less than a handful of points against Spears, and this one, well, it was quite amazing to both Sean and Lane, and even more so to Spears.

"Lucky!" said Spears as he stood up.

"Must be," said Jonathan. "But I find, the more skilled and talented one is, the luckier he seems to those who are unaware and of lesser skills."

"Really?" said Spears angrily. Like a wild beast, he charged, sword swiping. When he was but a few feet from Jonathan, Spears dove through the air in an attempt to tackle his opponent. Jonathan doubled over and squatted. As Spears was in mid-air above him, Jonathan quickly stood up, his shoulders striking Spears in the legs, causing him to spin end-over-end and land harshly on his back in the soft dirt. Jonathan then spun about, advancing quickly. He took a fast swipe with his sword, cutting off the majority of Spears' hair tail precisely above his collar.

"Arrrr!" yelled Spears. He stood and raised his sword once again.

"Just lucky, I guess!" said Jonathan, smiling. "Your hair does look better neatly cropped I must admit. Now, as we are almost eight minutes into the contest and the sun is setting quickly, I think we should end this. I am getting hungry!"

"You cad!" said Spears, his anger suddenly renewing his energy. He went after Jonathan again and again, relentlessly and viciously.

But to Sean's surprise and joy, Jonathan continued to repel all attacks and scored a few quick hits to each of Spears arms and quite humorously, one to each buttock. Neither wound was fatal, however, Spears was soon gasping for air, almost completely exhausted.

Could it be that Jonathan was not really trying all those times he faced Spears on the Danielle? thought Sean. *Maybe he was waiting for an opportunity to trick Spears?*

"You know, Wayne," said Jonathan as he easily executed his defense, "I knew it was *you* who pushed me off the plank in London. I saw your now shortened pony tail as I fell. You could not help looking over the side, could you?"

"So what?" said Spears, huffing and puffing. "You deserved it!"

"Did I, Spears?" Jonathan said as he easily parried a misaimed slashing attack. "Then that is the crux of this whole issue then, isn't it? You think I deserve blame for your misfortune. I know you hate me and my father. But I will tell you something. With God as my witness, we have never even *concerned* ourselves with your existence. This hatred was created by you. There is no basis for it."

"Liar!" said Spears between labored movements. "You have kept us down!"

"Why would we care, Wayne? We stand on our own and you should too. Can't we forget this duel? Let us go have a nice dinner and return to the ship. I am extending the hand of friendship -"

"And I will cut it off!" yelled Spears, and he lunged wildly, almost barreling into Jonathan in a desperate tackle. Jonathan expertly met Spears sword, and in a twisting motion, spun his tip into the hilt and flipped his opponent's blade into the air, to land lost somewhere in the wood. A side step and a thrust foot by Jonathan sent Spears falling, tumbling onto the ground with his face slamming flat in the dirt. He spun over laboriously to his back and tried to rise up to stand on his feet, but Jonathan advanced on Spears, backed him up to the edge of the lawn, until he positioned him against a tree, unable to move. The blade of Jonathan's sword rested upon the neck of Wayne Spears.

"Kill me, then, you spoiled brat!" said Spears. "Take my future and my life! Use it to embellish yours!"

Jonathan smiled a bit, then a feeling of absolute pity came over him. He realized that Spears would never get past his jealousy, his misdirected anger, and that was a shame. He would always be a danger to him and his father; however, he could not take his life. No matter what he was now, Spears had once been an innocent child and the influence of his father made him what he was today: a disgruntled malcontent with a chip on his shoulder, put there by a parent who saw the world through faded glasses.

"Jonathan! Stop!" called Harrison as he reached the clearing. He and Garvey had finally arrived, winded and panting. Jonathan turned to regard them, then quickly looked back at Spears. His eyes narrowed and his voice was firm and strong.

"Spears, I offer you this: I will not kill you, though I will regret this decision, I am sure. But you will pay me for your life with a simple deed. You will request transfer off the *Danielle* as soon as we return to the ship. If you do so, I will mention nothing about what you told me, or this duel. You will never speak to me, Sean Flagon or my family again, or interfere with our lives."

Exhausted and spent, Spears considered this. Soon the weight of his absolute failure rose within him to spill forth in the form of tears. As they began to stream down his face, he thought about all that had happened. Had he really tried to murder this boy? Had he really sank to such a despicable low? Maybe it was true; that his troubles were not the fault of anyone but himself. That notion would be hard to accept. And now, here was his enemy, offering a way out. The humiliation of it all was clearly becoming realized and the thought of living with such defeat was certainly going to be unbearable. Though there was no clear answer, he did know one thing: that he did not want to die.

"You can resign from the Navy," said Jonathan, "If that suits you. Or, kill yourself. But your death will not be at my hand. Are we agreed?"

Spears thought for a moment longer. All he could feel was his utter exhaustion. He was physically weak from the fight and mentally drained from the years of anguish he believed caused by the Moores. It was dawning on him now through pangs of realization, that possibly his view on this matter had been all wrong.

"Agreed," said Spears, finally.

Harrison now approached as Jonathan lowered his sword and backed away.

"Spears," Harrison said. "I, too, will ignore this entire fiasco, if you are true to your word. And at this point, your word and its value and quality, is a great foundation with which to begin a new life."

Harrison extended his hand and assisted the boy to his

feet. Together, Harrison and Spears walked back to the *Danielle*, and as night fell, they quietly and secretly walked up the plank, and into Harrison's cabin, where Spears' wounds were attended to.

"Timothy Lane," Jonathan said, dusting himself off and donning his midshipman's jacket. "We are going to a quaint pub in the center of town to enjoy goat sandwiches and I suggest you join us."

Lane looked at them suspiciously, then slowly smiled, knowing they were sincere in the invitation. He thought the evening was getting a bit cool and as all the excitement had worn off, he was looking for some peace and relaxation. And why not?

"Goat?" Lane said with a wry smile. "Sounds disgusting. I accept."

The four sailors laughed, then arm in arm headed for the center of Ribeira Grande.

15
The Mouse Takes the Bait

The *Danielle* had sailed quickly out of the harbor before noon on a strong breeze through calm water. Conversely, the crew moved a bit slower than usual. The previous evening spent ashore had most likely involved a bit of liquor, and the skills of the men seemed greatly diminished. The Captain had even *commented loudly* about the sloppiness of the letting out of sail and expressed his utter horror at the haphazard way the crew attended to their duties. He assigned extra work to all and even ordered Lieutenant Holtz to add as much sail as possible and to be "quick and ruthless about it." Nevertheless, the *Danielle* was soon miles away from the Cape Verde Islands and headed southeast to Rio Muni and the fort that hopefully contained the manifest.

Before breakfast, Spears had his meeting with the Captain. Mister Harrison accompanied the midshipman for support, however, the private conversation was really no shock to the Captain. He somehow knew of the duel and knew of its outcome, though Spears and Harrison could not figure out how he had gained this knowledge. Walker agreed that the best course of action was for Spears to request transfer. The Captain agreed to assist him in receiving an assignment on another ship. There was a brief discussion about absolute resignation, but the Captain would not hear of it.

"That is a discussion between you and your father," he said, "and I will speak to him directly when we return to England. Until then, you are a midshipman under my command and you will act accordingly, as will those around you."

As Spears exited the Captain's cabin, it seemed to him

there were many eyes trained upon him. Some seemed to sneer, some faces seemed to laugh at him, and he even thought a few heads just shook in disgust. It was clear that the word of the duel and his defeat had spread throughout the crew. A cold chill now ran down Spears' spine as he realized that once the *Danielle* returned to London, the entire Navy, maybe even the whole city, would hear the tales of awful deeds. His mood became dark and he retreated to his cabin, asking Lane to please leave him alone in his misery.

The next day, Jonathan and Sean were at the bow looking ahead as the *Danielle* sailed southeast. In the afternoon sun, the sails above their heads seemed to glow almost a golden–amber color and the top gallants seemed to scrape the silver clouds as the ship flew across the deep waves. Jonathan had guessed the *Dani* had obtained almost nine knots and was surprised to hear from Lane that they had reached almost eleven, certainly quite a feat for a ship as large as theirs. The guns were glistening as they had just been polished, the deck secure and freshly holy stoned and washed, and even the hands and marines seemed to be cleaner than usual. Jonathan could not help but smile as everything seemed right. Even Sean's reading seemed to be greatly improved as he sat nearby, going verse by verse in his book.

"...so Arthur pulled the sword as hard as he could..."

Sean stopped and closed the book. He looked to Jonathan and smiled.

"It seems, Mister Moore," said Sean, "that everything is working out for us, just as it did for the young King Arthur in these stories Captain Gorman has given me."

"Yes, Sean," smiled Jonathan, still looking out over the waves, feeling the warm sun on his face and cool breeze at his back. "It seems that with Spears at bay and Lane realizing what a *spe-len-did* group of friends we can all be, this trip is almost enjoyable!"

"Aye," said Sean. "What could possibly ruin it?"

At that moment, Steward approached them from the stern, carrying two cups of steaming hot cocoa. He smiled at the boys and handed them each a cup.

"Compliments o' the Captain, lads," he said.

"Bless you, Steward!" they said and began sipping.

"Aye, but thar's a catch," said Steward, now frowning. "'Seems there is planning afoot, a plan to prove the pirate Kozak right or wrong. And as it is a plan made by Captain Gorman, so it involves sneaking, involves skulking and probably a good chance of danger."

"What else could one expect?" said Sean. "It *is* a Gorman plan."

"So what *is* the catch, Steward?" asked Jonathan.

Steward smiled. "The plan involves you! Back to the Captain's table with the both of ya, on the double!"

With that the boys quickly stood and marched back to the stern to join the officers in the Captain's cabin.

Jonathan and Sean entered the room, and as their eyes adjusted to the dark, they could hear laughing and the clinking of plates and cups. As usual there was food present, and the main dish, seemingly piled as high as was safely possible, was a plate of fried and toasted anchovies, complete with lightly-browned cheese and some type of dipping sauce in an adjoining saucer. Captain Walker and Gorman were sitting at the table, close to the fish, and were happily selecting one at a time, dipping their choice in the sauce and then devouring the fish in what seemed to be a single bite. Koonts was there, sipping coffee and enjoying a small cake of some sort. Holtz and Harrison also sat at the table and mostly looked at the others as they ate. To the boys, the Captain's and Gorman's fascination with anchovies was a mystery, a conundrum and also at times, quite disgusting to watch. No matter how many napkins and 'pardon me's accompanied their feasting, many others in attendance had to often turn their heads.

Jonathan and Sean stood at attention, waiting to be addressed, asked to sit or even to be dismissed. And after a moment or two, Steward appeared with a plate of small ham sandwiches and a tub of fresh mustard. This sent Holtz and Harrison into action as they each took a portion for themselves.

"Ah!" said Walker. "Moore! Flagon! About time! Please be seated and we can begin. I heard you have tried goat and find it agreeable, so I would assume an anchovy would be acceptable?"

After a pause and a look into each other's eyes, the boys squirmed. Both remembered their first experience with the little creatures and it was *not* pleasant.

"Thank you, no, sir," Jonathan replied respectfully. "Sean and I just finished a buttered egg sandwich with pepper from Claise. Most enjoyable."

"Oh?" said Walker, as if he could not comprehend any situation where one would refuse one of the delectable tiny fish. "Maybe next time, yes?"

The boys sat down as the Captain selected another fish.

"Gorman," he continued, "what have you ascertained?"

Gorman stopped eating, blotted his lower lip with a napkin and took a quick sip of coffee before beginning.

"Thank you, Captain. Yes, I have spoken with Kozak over the past few days. He is a more devious character than I had expected. Some of what he says seems truthful, some does not. But I do know this: the only way we can proceed is to take a look at the manifest and determine if Kozak is telling the truth."

"Yes," said Holtz, with no intention of adding any additional content.

"The manifest is most likely where Kozak has stated, in El Forte de la Selva," said Gorman. "I have seen the fort myself, not a large one at all with maybe a dozen or so guards. It lies at the entrance to the river."

"We may be seen by any number of small ships, some maybe even Spanish," said Koonts, warily.

"True, Mister Koonts," said Gorman, "However, I do

believe we can sail in the dead of night, Captain. There will be a moonless night on eleventh. If we drop in a jolly boat while in the darkness off the coast, Mister Watt can stay a dozen or so miles north and avoid detection. The landing party can row eastward to the fort."

Captain Walker shook his head and leaned back in his chair. His eyes wandered the room and finally rested upon the main lantern hanging above the table in the beams.

"It is risky," he said taking a breath and letting it out slowly. "And once we arrive there undetected, if at all possible, we still must sneak into the fort and obtain the manifest."

"I have a plan for that," Gorman continued. "Some sneaking and tight spaces at the end through a few windows and gutters, but not impossible - if we remain unnoticed."

Walker seemed to think hard, his face turning from frown to grimace and he wrestled with the plan and its chance of success. Eventually his eyes fell to the boys.

"Moore? Flagon?" the Captain said. "Captain Gorman once again needs assistance from a pair of *smaller* crewmembers to squeeze and skulk and commit a little burglary on foreign soil. If caught," Walker said, pausing for effect, "you will surely be executed. The choice is yours."

Jonathan and Sean again looked into each other's faces and soon two smiles appeared. They had been through so much together, and since the '*taming of Wayne Spears*', as they called their last adventure, life was getting a little dull aboard the *Danielle*.

Do you have an appetite for some excitement? Jonathan's expression seemed to say to Sean.

It's what I live for! Sean's face seemed to say.

"This is strictly voluntary," said Walker. "If you do not agree to it, no one will think any less of you."

"*We* would think less of ourselves, Captain," said Jonathan. "Please inform us of the details!"

* * * * * *

As the day wore on, Spears was summoned by Steward to the galley by the Captain's cabin and was given a platter with left over fish and a piece of hard tack, the stale bread that seemed to appear at almost all of the prisoner's meals. Coffee was also readied and the food was carefully carried by the young midshipman to the brig.

Wayne Spears had mixed emotions about facing the pirate once again. He was both ashamed at his failure and was also angry with Kozak as it was appearing to the midshipman that possibly he had been ill-advised by the man. It was Kozak that mentioned the murder; it was Kozak that seemed to push him toward the desperate duel. With these thoughts, Spears finally decided that he would simply drop off the food; ignore Kozak's comments and questions.

He quickly opened the hatch from the main deck, descended two levels to the bottommost hold and then into the dark and lonely brig.

"Ah! Wayne! A feast you bring me to celebrate your success?" said Kozak. Spears just slid the plate under the barred door and turned to walk away, not even looking Kozak in the eye. The pirate realized in an instant that Spears had somehow lost the fencing match, and that somehow, Moore had again come out on top.

Maybe Spears is in very deep trouble, maybe he has been suspected of the attempted murder thought Kozak. *And maybe he needs a way out. The game is not finished yet!*

"So things did not go as well as they were planned, Wayne? It is not your fault. It is no one's fault but my own."

This comment caught Spears by surprise. Kozak was not blaming him, not chastising him. He was accepting the blame himself.

"Yes, I have been thinking of the bad advice I gave you, and frankly, my dear boy, it was not sound council. The more I thought about it, the more I realized that there is a better way to prove one's self."

"I need to prove nothing to you or anyone else," growled Spears. "Just leave me alone. I will figure this out on my own."

"Of course you will," Kozak said. "I am just happy that you seem to be all in one piece. And I hope Mister Moore is likewise well?"

Spears turned to look at the pirate with a scowl on his face. "Spin your webs somewhere else, Kozak!" he snapped. "You are nothing but a despicable lout. How I let you talk me into this foolery, well, it has caused enough trouble for a life time. I need not your help or suggestions!"

Kozak turned his hands to the sky in surrender and bowed his head deeply.

"Of course, Wayne," he said softly. "I am truly sorry and I know you will think of something to make it all right again. And when you do, I wish you the best of luck. Hopefully, an opportunity will arise, one with which you can take advantage. Opportunities can be long in coming, as life aboard a ship of His Majesty's Navy turns slowly. It could be a year or longer before you return to London, where I am hopeful something will come your way."

Spears thought of these words. Indeed life aboard a ship did cause the world turn slowly. At times, the monotony of the waves, the chores, and the endless bells tolling each hour bled together; days turned to weeks and weeks to months; and soon, one lost all track of time. It seemed to Spears that this journey had lasted several years already, with no end in sight. Would an opportunity to prove his worth arise soon? Or would there be months after months of nothing but waiting and disappointment?

Kozak watched the boy and could tell that he was thinking over his options. It was time to spring the trap and see if the mouse took the bait.

"I was only wishing," said Kozak, "that I had told you of my other plan, instead of the ill-advised debacle I presented to you. I should have known you were a man of determination and industrial spirit, not a fool bent on revenge."

Spears now thought that listening to another plan might not be a bad idea. He would only *listen* to Kozak and certainly think deeply about the consequences that any success or failure might bring. Waiting for another opportunity could take years and maybe Kozak could present a way out.

"And just what is this plan you have kept for yourself?" asked Spears.

Kozak now knew that he had Spears at his lowest low, with no way out. Anything, no matter how drastic, that offered a glimmer of hope to regain his honor or prestige would be acceptable. The pirate sprung his trap. And the mouse took the bait.

HMS *Danielle* sailed on into the night and all the next few days toward Rio Muni and the Fort de la Selva. Watch replaced watch and crew members attended to the sails and ropes with extra care. Lookouts were posted in the tops and the crow's nest. All knew they could encounter Spanish ships at any minute, so even the guns were prepared for action; the gun crews sleeping by their battle stations. After the sun set, no lights were allowed on deck that might alert the enemy as the *Dani* slipped silently southward.

Colin Stredney, in the crow's nest, had spotted the few lights of Rio Muni and at just a few minutes past midnight, Captain Walker had ordered all sail taken in except the spanker.

"Why is it called the spanker?" Sean asked Harrison as they watched the sail being tightened.

"I really have not a clue, but I remember it because it is on the *rear end* of the ship, and like a bad child-"

"That's where you'd get spanked!" interrupted Sean. "I get it! *Spa-len-did!*"

The ship more-or-less drifted for two hours in the darkness. Mister Watt, with Captain Walker at his side, could see the faint lights of the Rio Muni settlements a few points off the port bow. They drifted past dark Bioko

Island and continued east toward the mainland. There, they could see a stubby outcropping of land where the fort resided. The plan was to release a small boat, row to the rocky beach, then come ashore just a short hike from the fort.

16

El Fort de la Selva

At just two hours after midnight on the twelfth of April, Sean and Jonathan were awakened by Steward and after some groaning and yawning, the boys arose. They gathered their swords and a few other effects, then allowed Steward to lead them silently out of the orlop and up the ladder to the main deck.

The moon was not yet up and the stars shown brilliantly white. There were so many, seemingly millions upon millions of sparkling lights, that Jonathan and Sean gazed in wonder.

"You can see the light they shine on our faces, Jonathan!" said Sean.

Jonathan smiled. He remembered his recent night watches when he would marvel at the stars and planets. Even Mister Watt, usually silent and grumpy, would sometimes tell Jonathan of their names and colors, and how he used them to guide the ship. Jonathan could even see the milky-like stripe that spanned the sky on extremely clear and calm nights, and he wondered if each of those stars had planets like earth and if there were strange seas and lands to explore.

"I love the night watch, Sean," was all he could say.

The Captain, Gorman, and Koonts were on deck watching Hudson, Hicks, and Harrison attending to the jolly boat amidships. With the help of Steward, they angled the boat over the side and manned the ropes.

"Good-morning, boys!" whispered Harrison. "Or maybe it is still good-evening. Either way it is dark and it seems that this is becoming a standard of your service in His Majesty's Navy! How many early morning boat trips have you taken with Captain Gorman?"

The boys smiled and looked at Gorman as he checked his own supplies: his sword, two pistols, a telescope and a small pouch that hopefully contained food. He was not in his uniform, but had donned dark trousers and a dark shirt, and had even obtained a black cloak that he wrapped around himself.

"Once again into the breach, dear friends, once more!" Gorman said, silently laughing. "Yes, we do seem to repeat our means of success; however, this one is slightly more dangerous than the last two. Steward, do you have the clothes for the boys?"

"Aye," said Steward, "I do. Jonathan, Sean, if ya please!"

With that, Steward stripped them down to their undergarments, dressed them in dark outfits just like Gorman had donned, and even coaled their faces for good measure.

Suddenly, a loud scraping was heard coming from over the stern rail. Immediately, a faint splashing sound as something hit the water. All froze.

"What was that?" exclaimed Harrison.

"Something fell overboard!" said Steward. "Let's have a look!"

Walker, knowing full well that his desire for the plaque to finally stop clicking and clacking and depart for good, held up his hand.

"Let us stay focused, gentlemen," said the Captain. "I have it all under control."

"But sir," said Koonts.

"That is enough!" Walker said raising his voice just a little. Eager to change the subject, he addressed the boys. "Moore, Flagon, do you have the plan in mind?"

"Yes sir," they said.

"Then listen to Captain Gorman and do exactly as he instructs. No room for error. And be as quiet as mice. You can gain more treasure sneaking in the back door than stomping through the front. There will be tight spaces and guards at every turn. Hopefully they will be sleeping, eh?

Good-luck boys. Into the boat you go!"

"Don't forget to bring back some souvenirs from your African holiday!" laughed Harrison quietly as the boys and Gorman entered the boat with Hudson and Hicks. It was slowly lowered over the side and into the dark waters.

"We will meet you off the coast at the appointed time, Captain Gorman," said Walker somberly. "Good luck to you all and speed as well."

With that, the boat gently touched the sea and the ropes were released. Oars were positioned allowing Hudson and Hicks to begin rowing away from the *Danielle* as the great ship let out minimal sail and tacked away through the darkness into deeper waters.

Jonathan and Sean looked back at her. They could see the Captain, Holtz, Harrison and even Steward standing at the rail, telescopes out, watching them depart. Although a drizzling rain began almost immediately, Sean waved and smiled as they drifted away into the night.

The boat continued on. Shortly, Jonathan could make out the rocks and rough shoreline of the point. By starlight he could see the land was lush with plants and tall palm trees. They moved inland using the Muni River as a guide, trying to peer as deep into the jungle as their eyes would let them. The boys seemed to think that at any minute a lion or tiger would appear, however, all was calm and silent save a few bizarre insect noises and the lapping of the water on the boat as it moved through the dark.

Beyond the water's edge the point was only slightly higher than the sea itself and on a very slight rise appeared a dark stone fort, small, but frightening in the eerie mist. There was a single tower in the center, with a dim light visible through a window most likely from a lantern. The sides of the structure was made of a gray stone, but there were also parts of the roof and a few other areas that were made of wood and tarpaulin. On one side of the two-story structure facing the river were several tall windows, now dark. To Jonathan, it looked like a great haunted house.

Hudson and Hicks silently continued rowing as Gorman's eyes scanned the fort and surrounding areas. He checked and rechecked his weapons, then looked to the boys.

"Gentlemen, let us review the plan. Hudson and Hicks will stay near the boat, just ashore, rifles at the ready. They will fire a single shot if we are in trouble of being discovered and two shots if the *Danielle* is, for some reason, early. We will approach the fort from the southern edge; you will scale the outer wall by the small scrub bushes. I believe your small hands can fit in the cracks and with some effort you can pull yourselves up to the window. You will fit through it. But I will need a larger entrance. The window should lead to a hallway, close to the Genralissimo's study."

"Is that where the manifest is?" asked Jonathan.

"I presume so," said Gorman. "There should be a desk or a closet with rolled papers, much like the manifests Mister Koonts has shown you. But that is of no concern. Once inside, you will make your way down to that doorway to the far right by the corner. Can you see it?"

The boys looked at the fort, in the direction Gorman was pointing and easily made out the doorway.

"Yes," they both said.

"Good, then make your way there and open it for me. I will then have you go straight to the boat and join Hudson and Hicks. I will retrieve the manifest. If you hear two pistols shots in direct succession that is your signal to leave and row to the *Danielle*. Understood?"

Jonathan furrowed his brow as he thought of his part in this plan. He didn't like it.

"Do you mean to say that you brought us along just to open a door for you?"

"Jonathan," Gorman said. "This is very dangerous business. If we are to be caught, it will surely be death as a reward. Even more importantly… I promised your father I would not endanger you or Sean and I am arguably doing that as it is."

"But we can keep watch for you as you search!" said Sean.

"And three swords are better than one!" said Jonathan.

"And swords are more silent than a pistol!" said Hudson.

"Shut up, Hudson," said Gorman.

"I told ya," said Hicks.

"This is not open for debate," hissed Gorman in a hoarse whisper. "We will follow the plan! Not another word!"

Through the drizzling rain and fog they rowed in complete silence, save for the swishing of the oars in the water and the gentle tinkling of the last drops of rain. The drizzle was all but gone, leaving nothing but a thin fog about them. After a few more minutes they were touching a small, rocky area that was tame enough to facilitate their landing. Hicks and Hudson silently replaced the oars in the bottom of the jollyboat, then stealthily hopped over the side into the shallow water.

"We will assist you to the shore, then hide by those dark rock outcrops just up the path, rifles pointed at the fort," Hudson whispered.

"Boys, let us proceed," said Gorman softly as Hudson grabbed each boy and handed them to his captain, now standing on the dark, rocky beach. They were now crouched low and followed Gorman through the boulders, around the scrub bushes and over a series of rises. The marines went about their duty as the plan dictated. After a moment or two, Hicks was in position by the path.

"I see 'em," said Hicks as he peered through the darkness.

"And I have tied up the boat so she won't make any noise," said Hudson as he joined his friend. "Hopefully all will go as planned. I will watch to the east, you to the west." The men settled in and kept a sharp eye on the fort.

What the marines didn't notice was right behind them, however. The small tarp that was in the bow of the boat was moving. Silently, and ever so carefully, a hand and then a leg appeared in the starlight. Had they been looking, Hudson and Hicks would have seen a small delicate face appear over the side, peering out, green eyes flashing in the starlight.

Forte de la Selva

My dear! thought the face that belonged to the stowaway. *If I have ever heard of a more ridiculous plan, it certainly is lost to my memory. Going in the fort alone? There must be fifty guards if there is a one. As the boys have said, the Marine captain will need help and I am certainly not going to sit here and not do a part. After all, I am now experienced in these sorts of things!*

The stowaway slowly began exiting from the boat, a feat that had been practiced time and time again as discovery and capture aboard the *Danielle* had been avoided. Silently, the stowaway found a way through the shallow water and up onto the rocky land of the point. Carefully, the stowaway approached the position of the marines.

At the edge of the gate to the fort, Gorman held up a hand to signal the boys to stop. As they peered through the fog past the low stone wall that surrounded the Fort de la Selva, they observed two guards walking along the building's edge, then turning toward the main entrance. They waited and watched until both guards were inside; through the darkness they could hear the clanking of the big door.

"There should not be any more guards for a while," said Gorman. "They are either already asleep or about to be very soon. Let us wait a minute or two and then we will go on."

The three waited and watched. After a few minutes of seeing no one, Gorman whispered:

"I will go first. Wait until I motion for you." He rushed quickly to the side of the fort. After covering the short distance to the building, Gorman turned with his back to the wall, then slide sideways until he was near a scrub bush directly beneath a second story window. He signaled for the boys to follow with a wave from his hand.

With only a slight hesitation, Jonathan ran first. After a few beats, Sean followed. They copied Gorman's movements to the letter, and unseen, they joined him under the window.

"Up you go, Jonathan," Gorman whispered as he

made a step with his hands. Jonathan placed his right foot in the marine's grasp and after being lifted, began his climb, now and again looking upward to the window, but never back down to the ground.

It was over twelve feet to the upper window and though not as scary as caulking the side of the *Danielle* while she was underway, there was no rope or platform to offer assistance. As difficult as it was, Jonathan pressed upwards, slowly moving his left, then the right foot, then his right hand and finally the left hand, each finger or toe finding a crack or small hole in which to grip. It was slow moving, but the wall was only slightly slippery from the light rain and only once did he slip a bit.

Sean was right behind, just to the left. This made sense to Jonathan, as if he were to fall, there would be no sense in landing on Sean on the way down and injuring both of them. Both boys gritted their teeth and concentrated on the task at hand.

Gorman waited below, mostly looking up, and positioned himself under the boys just in case one might fall and he would need to make a desperate catch. He watched as they slowly but steadily made their way to the edge of the window. He noticed Jonathan listening intently at the ledge, then grasping the sill and peering inside.

Just then, Gorman heard a crunching sound of a boot on gravel. He quickly crouched down by the bush. To his right, a guard was plodding along, approaching their position.

Sean looked down to see a man staggering toward them. He froze then tugged gently on Jonathan's trouser, alerting him to the danger. Jonathan turned his head out of the window and stopped all movement. He held his breath.

Gorman reached into his boot and silently removed a short bladed knife. He waited for the guard to move close, almost on top of him. He then he positioned himself for the killing thrust. As he was about to attack, the guard belched so loudly, that the boys became startled and almost lost their grip on the wall and window.

The stench from the wine the guard had been drinking overwhelmed Gorman and it was just powerful enough to stay his hand. He stared at the guard, who obliviously continued staggering past. Soon, Gorman relaxed. *He is so drunk he didn't even see me, nor the monkeys on the wall,* Gorman said to himself as he watched the guard turn around the corner of the fort to disappear in the dark.

* * * * * *

Upon crawling through the open window, Jonathan and Sean found themselves in a dark hallway. The walls were unadorned, except for the few candles that glowed dimly in lanterns every few yards. There were no tables or chairs about, and most welcome was the absence of Spanish guards. They stood still for a long moment, peering both left and right down the hallway, considering the several doors along the corridor.

"The stairs downward must be behind one of these doors!" whispered Jonathan.

"So we will have to peek into each one!" replied Sean softly, his hands shaking in fear.

The boys walked to the right, moving silently toward the first door. On each side they stood and drew their swords. Jonathan opened the door a crack and Sean peered inward. He could see that the room was lit by a small lantern and though still dark, Sean could make out three sleeping men. He motioned to Jonathan by holding up three fingers, then making a pillow with his hands and tilting his head down, closing his eyes. Jonathan nodded and closed the door ever so gently.

They moved to the second door and repeated the process. It was a small closet, with some rifles and a few other shorter guns. A third door at the far end revealed a stack of lumber and some lantern fuel.

Knowing they must go the other way, the boys tip toed through the gloomy hall and paused just a moment by the window to motion to Gorman their intention to head the other way.

Continuing on, the first door on the left side was locked. The second door revealed a staircase leading downward. The boys smiled, then slowly proceeded, closing the door behind them. A few creaks and cracks later, they reached the bottom and peeked left and right, making sure no one was present. When all looked clear, they chose to walk to the right, as that was the direction the door to the outside would be located. They stepped cautiously, swords still drawn. After a few moments reached another hallway. It, too, led both directions, though it was obvious that the exit to the outside was to the right. That hallway was shorter and darker. They could see the iron handle and old wooden planks that made up the door, though at its base, there was something crumpled in a pile.

As they moved closer, a bit of light fell through a high lantern and they saw that the pile was actually a man, the drunken guard. He had fallen asleep against the door, wine bottle still in hand.

The boys warily moved away, back down the hall where they had come, and tried to decide how to deal with the situation.

"He is blocking the door! How will we open it for Gorman?" whispered Sean.

"We can't just kill him - he may cry out!" said Jonathan.

"Then let us return to the window and speak with Captain Gorman," Sean suggested, and the boys crept back down the lower hall, up the stairs, and paused once at the top, as a guard was walking past. They hid in the shadows and watched as he drearily moved on. Once he was out of sight, Jonathan looked out the window as Sean kept watch on the hallway. He looked left and right, but saw no one. Not even Gorman.

"Captain!" Jonathan called as loud as he felt safe, however, no one replied.

"Gorman is not there!" he said. "He must be at the door, waiting. We have to alter the plan. We must find the manifest ourselves!"

"But how?" whispered Sean. "Where is the desk of the Generalissimo?"

Jonathan remembered Gorman saying the office was most likely on the second floor. They had checked all the doors save one.

"The last door, Sean!" Jonathan said softly but excitedly, and pointed to the door to their left.

Again, they took positions on either side, swords ready. Jonathan slowly opened the door. He peered inside and smiled. He could see a large, heavy-looking wooden desk and shelves behind holding books, papers and a few boxes. He opened the door a little wider, just enough for himself and Sean to slip inside. They did, and the door closed behind them.

The room was dark, though there was a sliver of light from a flickering lantern hanging in the center of the room. There were a few chairs about the desk, a great globe on a stand, and a wall of maps. As the boys explored, they looked for anything resembling a manifest, papers rolled like the ones Koonts had shown them earlier aboard the *Danielle*. Nothing remotely resembled a manifest.

Just when all seemed lost, they noticed a thin door against the wall opposite the desk. Upon opening it, they saw a large closet with hundreds of shelves of a peculiar shape: all like little boxes and each containing several rolls of paper. It was obvious on further inspection of a few rolls that they had found the manifests.

"Oh no!" said Sean. "How will we find *our* manifest? There are probably hundreds of rolls in here if there is a one!"

Jonathan randomly selected a roll from a box for inspection. "We will use our heads to narrow it down!" he whispered to Sean. "Look at this," he said, spreading the rolled paper out on the floor. Sean knelt and held one side as Jonathan held the other.

"It looks like the manifests on the *Danielle,*" Sean said.

"Yes," said Jonathan as he studied it, "and Gorman said that the Spanish word for cannon is *cañón*. That should be easy enough. C-a-n-o-n, and the 'n' has a funny little swirl above it. The 'o' has a slash. All we need to do is find a manifest with that word."

"Jonathan," Sean whispered, slightly irritated, "I can barely read English and now I need to read Spanish?"

Jonathan stifled a giggle. "He also said 'ship' is *barco,* or we may even see *barco mercante* for the merchant ships."

They both took a section of the page and searched. After only a few minutes, Sean had found a word that looked like *barco,* and Jonathan confirmed that it was *barco mercante,* followed by the words *San Elena,* possibly the ship's name. It was the line right under the date, clear as a bell, on the upper right hand side of the first page. Under that, a few lines of words and then rows, with three columns across, containing letters and numbers that could only be a listing of goods aboard.

"Finally we have figured it out!" Jonathan whispered, "Now all we need to do is find one that says *cañón*. Here! This one refers to cannon in the column, but the numbers are too small."

"Yes," said Sean, "I would think we are looking for a ship with a number near one-thousand! But where do we begin?"

They began by looking at the shelves, and though not labeled in English, they found that all the manifests in a particular area all had similar words inscribed on the outside of the roll. The first shelf they inspected had rolls that read *Diciembre* or *Noviembre.* After some discussion, they realized that these were for December and November. They continued checking month by month, trying to translate in order. It was easier than they thought. Even though *Enero* had them stymied, *Febrero* could only be February, and soon they arrived at *Marzo, Abril* and *Mayo:* March, April and May.

"Kozak said he was to meet the French ships here by

mid-May," Jonathan said. "Let us check the columns on the manifests from both April and May, just to be sure."

Outside the fort, Gorman waited by the door behind a small pile of boxes and barrels. He wondered what could be taking the boys such a long time and soon became worried that something had gone awry. He returned to the window to see if maybe they would re-appear, but after what seemed to be a half an hour, he realized they were probably either captured or lost. He couldn't just barge in, screaming their names, hoping to find them: if things were still in order and all was well, he would just wake up the Spanish guards and that would be unpleasant. He moved back to the door and decided to put his ear against it, hoping to hear something, anything that would help him. As he pressed his ear to the wooden planks, he could make out a small rumble that would start and stop on a regular basis. After a moment, he smiled and shook his head.

Snoring, he thought. *There must be someone asleep near the door. The boys must have seen this and will soon be back at the window. I will wait there and devise a new plan.*

By the boulders at the beach where the jollyboat had been secured, Hudson and Hicks waited, their eyes on the fort. They had seen the boys climb the wall and the drunken guard stagger past. They had seen Gorman move to the far door, then return. They had even seen the boys reappear at the window. All this made them believe that something was not right.

"They should have let Captain Gorman in by now," whispered Hudson.

"True. But they 'aven't," said Hicks.

"They might be in trouble," suggested Hudson.

"Could be, but probably not. Not yet at least," said Hicks.

"How do you know that?" Hudson asked.

"No yelling. No gunfire," said Hicks. "We would 'ave 'eard something. After all, it is a calm, silent night."

After a brief moment of silence, they heard the gravely soil behind them *crunch*. The sound made their eyes open wide and they quickly spun around rifles at the ready. Hicks peered into the darkness and could see a shape that he hadn't noticed before. It looked as if there was a rock about the size of a human head, balanced atop a large boulder. He was sure that it wasn't there when they first took position. Then, the rock moved, descending behind the boulder.

Silently he motioned for Hudson with his hand then pointed to the boulder. Hicks then waved to the left side. Hudson nodded, understanding the signal, and moved to the left. Hicks took the right. This way the marines were able to explore the boulder from each side and not let whoever was hiding behind it escape.

They crept as silently as they could. Then the sound of footsteps came once again from behind, crunching lightly on the rocky soil. The marines rushed to the other side of the boulder. There they saw a small figure rush just past the boat and duck behind a small bush.

They slowly aimed their rifles and proceeded toward the water. Their prey had nowhere to go.

"No shots now!" whispered Hudson.

They moved closer and closer. Finally, just a few feet away, they could see a shape behind the bush.

"Show yourself!" called Hudson as loud as he dared.

The figure of the stowaway stood up slowly and put two hands on hips in a show of defiance. The starlight cast just enough radiance on the face that features could be seen.

"It's you!" they both said, lowering their rifles.

* * * * * *

Jonathan and Sean knelt on the floor of the closet in the office, studying manifests. The lack of proper lighting made the task difficult, but they continued on, now sure they would find the correct one. They were through the rolls from April and were now looking into May. The word *cañón* was seen on only a few manifests, but as Jonathan pointed out, the numbers were too small.

After another five minutes, Jonathan replaced the rolls they had looked through into the shelf they came from and reached for the next pile. As each shelf seemed to represent a week, as they could tell by the dates on the manifests, he was startled by the next shelf. This one had over two dozen rolls. *That is a lot of ships for just one week,* he thought.

Jonathan held up the rolls he had taken from the stuffed shelf and presented it to Sean as if he were bowing. The boys smiled and each opened a roll. They poured over the details.

"Listen, Jonathan! 'Expected on the fifteenth of *Mayo, el barco mercante Orléans'*, with one-hundred fifteen cannon," said Sean.

"Here is another: 'Expected on the fifteenth of *Mayo, el barco mercante Rodez'*, with one-hundred and twenty-nine cannon of various sizes!" said Jonathan excitedly.

Each of the next several rolls they examined had similar listings. The boys determined that they should take all the manifests listed for the month of May, just to be sure, and gathered all the rolled manifests and set them into two piles. Nearby, they found twine to bind the rolls and make them easier to carry.

"Let us take these to the window and get out of here!" Jonathan said and the boys reached for the closet door handle. But as they reached, the handle turned by itself and the door swung open from the other side.

"¿Que es esto?" said a short, squat man. He had a beard and was wearing a long nightshirt. He held a lantern high above his head to shed light on the boys.

"Ah…Buenos dias, senor!" Jonathan blurted out.

"Buenos dias?" the man yelled, anger showing on his face. "Es la noche! ¿Quiénes son ustedes muchachos? ¿Qué están haciendo en el armario?"

Jonathan looked to Sean and shrugged. After a moment, he charged past the man using his fear to propel him. Sean followed as they both ran to the door. But the man was fast for his size and beat them to the exit, blocking their way.

"Swords!" said Sean.

"Of course!" said Jonathan. They dropped the manifests and unsheathed their weapons. They smiled, knowing that they could easily handle a man in his night shirt.

"En guard!" Sean said.

"If you dare!" said Jonathan.

The man smiled, set down the lantern on the desk and reached to the wall behind him, taking a beautifully crafted bejeweled sword from its mount.

"So, you are Eeeng-leesh? And you think you can beat the Generalissimo, a Spaniard, with those leettle blades? Ha!" he said.

"So you are the Generalissimo?" asked Jonathan.

"Si," said the man, and then shouted loudly: "Guardias! Centinela! Espías en la oficina!"

"What did he say?" said Sean.

"I have no idea," Jonathan said, "Though I am sure it will not help us."

Outside the doorway to the fort, Gorman heard the shouting. He knew Spanish and quickly translated the words: *guards, a detachment! Spies in the office!*

Time to go, he said to himself. *Sorry to wake you!*

Gorman took ten steps back, lowered his shoulder and ran at full speed into the wooden door. It gave way, not coming off the hinges, but splintering. Gorman sailed through, rolling over the broken boards and the sleeping guard. He ran down the hallway and turned left at the first junction. He knew there had to be a staircase leading up to the second floor and he needed to find it before the hall became filled with guards.

In the office of the Generalissimo, the boys raised their swords. They were the first to press their attack.

It was a short attack, however, as the man deftly dropped his sword and produced a pistol from under his shirt. He aimed it at the boys, smiling.

"Not fair!" yelled Sean.

"Wee have a saying in Spain, my Eeeng-leesh friends: 'La vida no es justa'. It means 'life ees not fair!' Put down your blades!"

As the boys bent to place their swords on the floor, a voice was heard at the door.

"We have a saying in England," said Gorman as he leveled his two pistols at the Generalissimo. "Dos pistolas son mejores que uno'. It means 'two pistols are better than one.' Drop your weapon."

The Generalissimo did as requested, setting the pistol on the floor.

"Gather your things, boys. Time to leave," said Gorman. Jonathan and Sean retrieved the rolls of manifests and their swords, then moved to the door. Then they stopped, shocked at what they saw.

"Will this never end?" said Sean, exasperated as all saw two Spanish guards enter through the door, rifles leveled at Gorman. They cocked their flintlocks. Gorman, knowing the sound, stiffened. He raised his hands above his head.

"Now who has thee advantage, you Eeeng-leesh pigs?" said the Generalissimo. He reached for his pistol once again and aimed it at the boys.

Another shadow appeared in the doorway and moved slowly forward to stood behind the guards. Jonathan, Sean and Gorman could not believe what they were seeing.

"Who eez thees?" said the Generalissimo.

The guards turned their heads to look, leaving the rifles pointed at their prisoners.

"Allow me to introduce myself," came a female voice as a young lady stepped into the full light of the room. "I am Miss Delain Dowdeswell, adventurer. And you will release my friends now or suffer the consequences."

"Delain!" said Jonathan, now in utter bewilderment.

"I have now seen everything there is to see in this life," muttered Gorman, astonished.

"Totally at a loss," said Sean.

The Spanish were also stunned at this appearance of the young girl. Then they started to laugh.

"What are you going to do, niña?" said the man. "You are hardly a match for my guards and their rifles!"

"That is correct," said Delain, "however, my two friends are more than enough."

Stepping into the doorway, Hudson and Hicks each fired a shot, hitting both of the guards; one in the hands, the other in the shoulder, knocking their weapons to the floor. Gorman now leveled his pistol at the Generalissimo.

"So sorry to leave you in such a condition, Señor," said Gorman.

"What condition ees theez?" asked the Generalissimo.

Gorman struck him hard on the head with the butt of his pistol, sending him to the floor.

"That condition."

The marines likewise used their rifle butts against the two injured guards and Gorman quickly rushed everyone out the door.

"Hudson, Hicks, take the lead. Get us to the door. Miss Dowdeswell, in the middle. Boys, help me watch our rear. Hurry now!"

In this single line they hurried down the stairway and turned right after Hudson had called "all clear." As they approached the junction nearest the exit, they heard a commotion outside. Hudson peaked around the corner and saw guards rushing in the door. He fired a shot. Hicks leveled a round in the same direction.

"That will hold them for a moment," Hudson said. "We need to find another way out."

"The window!" suggested Jonathan.

"Men, hold them here," said Gorman. "We will exit the window, then draw their fire so you may affect your escape."

Gorman led the boys and Delain up the stairs once again. Once at the top, they startled two new guards, who they quickly dispatched with fast sword play and a few well-placed kicks by Miss Dowdeswell. Rushing to the window, they saw three more guards below.

"The area will soon be swarming with men," said Gorman. "I will go first and move behind the large boulders on the left. I will fire a few shots at the guards to distract them. The rest of you will head straight to the boat, do you understand? Get her ready to depart!"

Gorman slipped over the window sill and hung by his hands for a moment. He made his way downward quickly and after a few feet, he let go, falling to the ground. In a flash, he was up, limping, but heading to the boulders, pistols drawn.

"I will go next," said Sean.

"And Delain, you follow immediately. I will keep watch. Hurry now!" said Jonathan.

Sean slipped over the sill followed by Delain, and like Gorman, both precariously moved from stone to stone, getting as low as they could before letting go. Sean dropped only a few feet and landed unhurt.

"That's not too bad!" he said, standing and brushing himself off.

Delain then dropped, landing directly on Sean.

"Owe!" came his cry.

Jonathan leaned over the edge of the window and saw the tangled heap of his friends.

"Sean, stop your silliness and take these!" he said, tossing the manifests out the window. He then slipped over the edge of the sill and began his climb down. After a few moments, he heard shots coming from around the corner. He turned to look and saw Gorman firing at the Spanish guards from behind a pile of boulders. In a moment, there were more shots fired in Gorman's direction and then so many shouts, screams and gun fire that it was hard to tell exactly what was happening.

Jonathan dropped to the ground safely and together

they ran toward the boat. Keeping their eyes on Gorman's position, they hoped to see all three marines running to meet them. As they ran further on, they could now see the boat in the gloom on their right and the fort door to their left.

"Wait," Jonathan said. "Look! Gorman is vastly outnumbered. We must help somehow!"

"All we have is our swords. They are no match for so many guns!" said Sean.

Jonathan looked about, as he always did when in trouble, looking for something he could use. *Nothing but sand and bushes and…rocks!* he thought.

"Rocks!" he yelled and picked up one the size of his fist, then another. Sean and Delain joined him and soon they had a dozen or so each.

They ran toward the fort, keeping low and out of sight, and when they were within twenty or thirty feet, they found a small tree to hide behind. They could see Gorman loading his pistol, and six or seven guards now leaving the protection of crates and barrels, approaching his position.

"On three, and don't stop throwing until you are out!" Jonathan cried. "One… two… three!"

With that, they stood and threw the rocks with great force at the approaching Spaniards. As there was no noise, the guards were not alerted to the incoming projectiles, and though two missed, a third struck one man hard on the chest. The man fell. Soon, other stones rained down upon them, many finding their mark. Confused, the soldiers turned and ran back to the crates that surrounded the door.

"Hudson! Hicks! Now!" cried Jonathan, and the barrage of rocks continued, joined by Gorman's pistols, now reloaded.

Within seconds, Hudson and Hicks exited the building, firing a few last shots into the backs of the guards and rushed into the safety of the darkness. Gorman retreated as well, and quickly, all were running as fast as they could to the jollyboat.

"Rocks?" said Gorman as he assisted Delain and the

boys into the boat. "Clever, Jonathan."

"We really had no other options," he answered. "But it did the trick."

"I used to throw rocks at squirrels as a kid," said Sean, "and a few at bullies on the streets of London when need be. A cheap and reliable weapon, I'd say!"

They were soon all in the boat. Hudson and Hicks immediately manned the oars and rowed hard and strong. Delain even placed her hand over the side and paddled.

"Any little bit can help," she said, smiling.

Gorman watched the shoreline, and as he suspected, they were not out of danger just yet. A few of the guards must have alerted others, and now a score more men were seen at the edge of the fort, running to a stretch of beach to the north.

"I think we are about to have some company," Gorman said.

Just as the moon rose from behind the low hills to the east, Jonathan and Sean turned to see several boats being launched, now visible in the new light.

"That is not what we needed right now," the Marine Captain said. "It must be later than I thought. Our delay may make this interesting!"

"I believe it has been quite interesting already," said Delain.

The enemy continued to gain on them, as there were at least four oars for each of the Spanish boats compared to only two oars manned by Hudson and Hicks. All knew it was a long way to row to meet the *Danielle*, wherever she was, and their chance at escape was slipping away. To make matters worse, some of the Spanish boats had riflemen, and soon shots were ringing out, splashing in the water nearby.

Jonathan turned and looked out to sea, hoping to catch a glimpse of the *Danielle*. He saw nothing but a fog bank.

"Captain Gorman, there is a fog bank ahead! We can hide within it!" he suggested.

"Row!" Gorman yelled to his marines. "Row yourselves to exhaustion or you will die at the guns of our enemies!"

This seemed to spur them on, as the boat lurched ahead.

"They are still gaining on us!" said Delain.

And just then, the first wisps of fog spilled over the jollyboat. After a few moments, it was hard to make out their pursuers.

"Keep rowing!" said Jonathan. "We are now hidden from their view! But we must keep a sharp eye out. The fog may dissipate and expose us again!""

For the time being, they were completely covered by the mist and could not see more than a few feet in front of their faces. Jonathan peered ahead, hoping the fog remained thick and would continue to conceal them.

After a few moments had passed he suddenly gasped aloud. There, dead ahead, rushing up quickly at their boat, was a great black shape in the water, towering dozens of feet into the air. The boat slammed into the object, jarring all of them from their positions and almost throwing Sean into the dark sea.

"Dear God!" shouted Gorman as he spun around to see what they had struck. "What is this?"

"This is HMS *Danielle,*" came a voice, "and I suggest you row about to the starboard side, as we are about to liven things up just a bit!"

They all turned to look at the ominous shape. As the fog rolled in and out, they could now make out the side of the great ship, two decks of gun ports open. One by one, the golden circles of the weapons being rolled into firing position. Out of one port appeared Harrison, smiling widely.

"You are late, Captain Gorman, so we thought it best to drift in for a better look. Handy, this early morning fog, isn't it?" he said. "Pardon me for a moment, will you please? Oh, you should now *duck!*"

Harrison disappeared into the ship and all heard his

voice loud and strong from the other side of the hull.

"Fire! Fire! Fire!" he yelled, and the world erupted in a great noise as thirty-five guns exploded in unison sending ball and grape shot toward the pursuing Spanish boats.

17
The Stowaway

HMS *Danielle* finished her bombardment quickly, just a single reload and fire as sails were let out immediately after the shore party was safely aboard. Holtz had observed many small boats being turned into splinters and many Spanish guards floundering in the water. The fog had rolled in thicker and thicker and the morning sun was still many minutes from appearing. Walker seemed pleased with the result and ordered Lieutenant Holtz to make sure all sail was let out and all hands remained at their fighting stations. They were in enemy waters. Walker knew that not only Spanish ships were prowling about, but French squadrons could also appear at any moment. He did not want to risk a fight. The *Danielle* needed to escape to deeper waters, far from the unfriendly coastline and continue her mission.

True to expectations, the crew let out all sail, tightened lines and secured all cargo below and on deck. The *Danielle* caught a friendly breeze and slide away at approximately eight knots, or possibly nine, as Steward had suggested was the current speed after Lieutenant Harrison had announced his lesser estimate for the Captain.

Captain Walker settled in on the poop deck, observing the crew and advising Mister Watt on his duty. Harrison appeared on deck and stood properly next to the Captain. He had a wide smile on his face.

"Report, Mister Harrison!" commanded the Captain.

"Yes sir!" Harrison said. "The shore party is aboard and reports that they were successful obtaining the manifests, as well as . . . *another surprise*."

"Another surprise?" asked Walker. "Whatever do you mean?"

We have a… new *passenger* sir," Harrison continued. "It seems the thief is also a stowaway and has been found. She was in the jollyboat that rowed ashore."

"*She?* Did you say *she?*" asked Walker.

In the Captain's cabin, all the lieutenants were present, along with Mister Koonts, Jonathan and Lane. Spears was reporting ill, and all assumed it better that he be with his thoughts and tend to his future plans. The only other officers not in attendance were Mister Watt, ever present at the wheel, and Gorman, who would join shortly once he completed pouring over the manifests.

The table was set with only coffee and Steward was sternly dismissed the minute he finished pouring the Captain a very large cup. Steam rose from the hot drink, swirling up into the beams overhead, however, all who had been in similar discussions knew that the wisp of vapor was nothing compared to the venting of anger that was brewing within the dragon they all called Captain Walker.

He glowered as he stared at his cup, teeth clenched and hands in tight fists. He mumbled a few disguised expletives and as the tension rose in the room to an almost unbearable point, he turned his gaze upon the one person in the room that was *not part of the crew*. He drew in his breath and unleashed a tirade that even Koonts, who had known and sailed with the Captain for the longest time, over ten years, found truly astonishing. The eruption was not spectacular for its ferociousness (which it certainly was), nor its volume (it was certainly louder than a hurricane), nor the fury that was evident in the Captain's voice. It was spectacular because of what it did not contain: swearing.

"Miss Delain Dowdeswell!" the Captain began in an enraged tone. "Did it ever occur to you that this ship was involved in a war? And that at any minute we could be engaged in a life and death struggle that would possibly result in your own demise?"

"Well, sir," she began.

"Silence!" Walker boomed. "I do not need to hear your foolish responses to my rhetorical questions! Stand at attention when a ship's captain addresses you!"

Delain snapped as straight as a rod. Jonathan, as well as all the lieutenants, also bolted to an even tighter state of attention. They all realized that Delain was not a member of the crew, in fact, not even part of the Royal Navy in anyway and therefore she was neither subject to naval protocol nor its rules. Unsurprisingly, none of them made an effort to point out that small fact to the Captain, who was now roaring like a typhoon at the young girl. To her credit, she stared straight ahead, looking out the stern window, just like Jonathan and the Lieutenants. After a few more minutes of "did you even think before you took this course" and "do you not believe your father and mother will die of heart failure once they hear this tale," Captain Walker calmed only slightly and then turned to Jonathan.

"Mister Moore, please tell me your part in this idiocy!"

"He had no part in it, Captain Walker," said Delain, meekly.

This set the dragon at it again, spitting venom and fire.

"Is your name *Moore*, young lady?" he blasted. "Did you not have enough of my tongue? Only a foolish, impudent, deranged, cretinous -"

The Captain went on for a full minute without ever stopping, never repeating the same insult twice. Delain was now silent as a statue. Jonathan assumed she had used her mind to shut out the verbal thrashing as she stared directly ahead, looking out the window. *We must look ridiculous,* Jonathan thought, *all standing like statues and only the Captain breathing!*

"Mister Moore!" the Captain said, now shocking Jonathan from his thoughts. "I asked you, what was your part in this farce?"

"I had no part, Captain. I was as shocked as anyone to see Miss Dowdeswell appear in the *Fort de la Selva*."

The Captain rose from his chair and stomped over to

Jonathan. He placed his eyes directly even with the boy's and stared at him menacingly. *Like looking into the eyes of one of Sean's serpents from King Arthur,* Jonathan thought.

"Am I to believe that this *prissy little girl* boarded the ship all by herself and was never noticed?"

"I never left, your honor," said Delain.

The Captain stomped to Delain and took up a threatening pose.

"Never left *what?*" he demanded.

"I never left the *Danielle* after the final tour," Delain answered.

"But you returned to the *Drake,* you left with Penelope..." blurted Jonathan, who received an evil glare from the Captain, as if he was saying: *Did I ask you to speak*?

"Yes, I did walk to the deck with Penelope, after feigning my illness, however, when no one was looking, I hid in the larger jollyboat."

"Lieutenant Blake said you were in your cabin aboard the *Drake,* asleep, when we departed Nassau!" bellowed Captain Walker.

"A sack of rags," Delain said, almost appearing happy as she now was telling of her ingenious plan and at the same time entertaining the Lieutenants and Jonathan, who seemed totally engrossed with the tale.

"A sack of rags?!" roared the Captain.

"Yes, sir. If I may explain. I announced to my tour guides," Delain said, pointing to Jonathan and Harrison, "that I was feeling poorly and would return to the *Drake*. Penelope returned alone and prepared my bed with a sack of rags and pieces of our luggage, then covered them with blankets to replicate my shape. Rebecca was also an accomplice and was instructed to continue the ruse whenever Lieutenant Blake or anyone else, for that matter, inquired about my state of health. I would assume that by now the truth is out aboard the *Drake.*"

The Captain simply shook his head and turned his back to the girl.

"The jollyboat was actually quite comfortable," Delain

said "and food was easy to come by. I borrowed some from Claise, though mostly from Steward, as I found he had better fare, fresh eggs and even some delicious little fish that he would toast and cheese. I took a few as they cooled in his galley. Quite delicious if you haven't had any; I thoroughly recommend them."

Walker exploded.

"You were eating my anchovies? Of all the gall!" His tirade continued for a full five minutes, and only after that did he calm down once again to only a howl.

"What is God's green earth ever possessed you to do this?"

"Boredom, for one," she said. "As exciting as some may find London, I knew that all awaiting me there would be school, and books, and work, work, work. Proper parties and engagements with grown-up, uninteresting people who never laugh - or have adventure!"

The Captain stared at her, not laughing, looking older than dirt.

"Once you announced that the *Drake* would be taking us to London, I knew the *Danielle* was off to something more exciting than tiresome dinner parties and school lessons," Delain continued as the Captain turned about and moved to his throne. "Besides, I so much enjoyed the cutting out the *Drake* and disposing of the pirates, I thought along with my adventure, I could lend a hand at the guns!"

"Dear Lord," said Walker, dropping into his chair.

"How did you get about for three weeks without being seen?" asked Koonts.

"The night watches made it simple," Delain continued, "especially when the fog was about. It was no trouble at all sneaking where I needed. I even remember almost being caught a time or two. Very exciting. I even overheard the crew discussing Africa and the cape, so I knew I was in for some excitement! Africa? Lions? Tigers? A wild primate or two? That's for me!"

The Captain slumped into his chair completely. He seemed spent and alone in his thoughts as he stared at the decking. No one stirred for a full minute.

Then a knock came at the door.

"I assume this will be one of your sisters, Miss Dowdeswell?" the Captain mumbled. "Enter!"

All turned to see that it was not a Dowdeswell at all, but Marine Captain Gorman, and in his hands he held a rolled manifest.

"Ah," Gorman said happily, "I see Miss Dowdeswell has been entertaining you with her tales, eh? Well, so sorry I missed it. Maybe we can hear it again over breakfast? Is that to your liking, young lady?"

"Indeed," said Delain with a small curtsy.

"If we can all attend to the business of the war?" asked Walker, still angry. "Miss Dowdeswell, you will be restricted to my cabin. You are not allowed out under any circumstances; you will dine and sleep in here as well. Lieutenant Holtz, with Blake gone, I shall bunk with you."

"Yes sir," said Holtz.

"We will alter course and return to London immediately. After *disposing* of Miss Dowdeswell, we will re-supply and depart as soon as possible, understood?"

"Begging your pardon, sir," said Gorman.

Captain Walker paused, looking at the marine with slight irritation. It was unthinkable to interrupt the Captain, especially after he had given an order. The only thing that kept *the dragon* from another explosion was the fact that he respected Gorman greatly, knew him to be proper and respectful, and more importantly, a spy for the Navy. If Gorman had information, he needed to share it now.

"Captain Gorman, continue," said Walker.

"Thank you, sir," Gorman said, approaching the table and unrolling the manifest he carried. He used the Captain's coffee cup and the saucer to weigh down the edges of the paper to prevent it from rolling back to its tubular condition.

"Jonathan and Sean correctly acquired the proper manifests, and many contained valuable information. I have found that this particular manifest happens to be the most valuable. It contains three important pieces of information. One, it certainly corroborates Kozak's story. There *is* a fleet of French merchant ships carrying supplies and cannons; over nine-hundred as of my last count. They are accompanied by only two French frigates, as Kozak had said. The manifest also states that the ships are bound for Rio Muni and Aguilar is to receive them as Kozak has claimed."

"So Kozak was telling the truth," said Jonathan.

"Indeed," said Holtz, and all paused, then remembered that as usual, he had nothing to add.

"Secondly," continued Gorman, "there is reference to the *Fiero,* or as we know it, the *Drake*, on this particular manifest. It is to collect, as is stated, *'several tons of general supplies'* from Rio Muni for delivery to a point unknown."

The Captain thought for a moment and stared at the manifest, following all the points made by Gorman. "We need to get to them before they unload the cannon at Rio Muni."

"Aye, but here is the *rub*," said Gorman. "If we head immediately for the southern tip of Africa, we should meet them on or about April the twenty-sixth. They are due in Rio Muni after that, of course, about mid-May." He paused to let the information sink in.

"Our trip to deliver Miss Dowdeswell to London will be over…" Koonts calculated the numbers in his head and his face turned pale. "Dear! It will add almost ten-thousand miles to our journey!"

"At seven or eight knots on average, if we have favorable winds … that will delay us…" the Captain calculated the numbers in his head, then after a moment, " …almost two months!"

"We will miss the French squadron if we sail to London first," said Gorman.

The room fell silent as all considered the situation and the fact that they might not even present themselves for battle.

"We are past the point of no return," managed the Captain as he sighed heavily. He shook his head as he realized that not only was it true that a trip to London would destroy their chances of meeting the squadron, but that any other course would leave Delain on the ship and put her in danger of losing her life. Additionally, her father was a very influential governor, who also happened to be a retired naval hero. The fact that Delain had stowed away aboard the *Danielle* could not have made for a more dismal dilemma.

One by one the officers in the room realized what was happening and how Delain's presence was a hindrance to their mission. All eyes trained on her, even Jonathan's, though reluctantly. Delain uncomfortably noticed the glances and realized her prank to enjoy a little more excitement before school in London was possibly not her most well thought-out idea. Finally, even the Captain turned his stern gaze upon her. After a few moments of uncomfortable silence and clearing of throats, she spoke.

"You seem to have some serious business to discuss, gentlemen, and possibly I should take a stroll about the deck to give you some needed privacy."

The Captain held her gaze, sternly and unchanging.

"Or," she said meekly, "I-I could just sit quietly."

Walker turned his gaze to Gorman.

"You mentioned three points you discovered looking at the manifest. The number of ships was one, the delivery to Generalissimo Aguilar at Rio Muni was the second. What is the third?"

"There is other cargo being transported," Gorman said. "One of the merchant ships carries over sixty of Napoleon's generals."

It was now clear to the Captain what course he should take. He stood up and walked to the window to look out on the rising sun as it danced among the waves. The *Danielle* was under full sail, heading south as she left the coast of Africa, Bioko Island now slipping away astern.

"Lady and Gentlemen," he said, turning to address the group. "We will proceed directly to engage the French along the coast of Africa and even around to Madagascar if we must. At the most opportune time, we will place Miss Dowdeswell ashore with an escort and proceed to engage the squadron. If we are successful, we will return for her. If not, we will leave them with supplies and a means of signaling ships for rescue."

Delain gulped and thought to herself: *stranded on the African coast? Though it sounds exciting, it may be a little too exciting, what with lions, tigers and elephants! I may see a turtle or two, though I may also be eaten alive by snakes!*

Thoughts were also running around in the head of Jonathan Moore. He knew that Miss Dowdeswell's escorts would not be common seamen, or a Lieutenant for that matter. *They will need a gentleman or two who can look after her, not make any advances, and ones that can survive in harsh environments,* he thought. *And that most assuredly means Sean and me. Once again I will miss the battle action, as I did on the last mission!*

"Captain," said Koonts softly. "Not to question your decision, but just as a reminder, the African continent is wild at best. It is quite dangerous. And the addition of slave traders, certainly not the best of God's creations, well, is it really safer ashore?"

"I hear your concerns. And I have considered them before I made this decision. On Isla Sello, just to the southeast of the Cape, there is a grand old Portuguese fort where they can find shelter."

"The Castelo de Fogo? It is quite a sight! Are you certain it is uninhabited, sir," added Harrison.

"I have heard through some of my fellow captains that quite recently it has been confirmed as being *abandoned.*"

The Captain continued giving orders as the others seemed to relax a bit, now having something to do besides just standing about, praying for the dragon to cease his fire-breathing before he found reason to target them.

"Our mission is to sink as many French ships as we

can," Walker said, "be they laden with cannon or generals. Hopefully the *Paladin* and the *Drake* have informed some of our sister ships, so we will not fight alone."

* * * * * *

The *Danielle* sailed on to the south, the sea relatively calm and the winds moderate but steady. The log was tossed and revealed that the ship was barely making eight knots. Swift by most respects, however to Captain Walker, not swift enough.

At times, one could look to port and see glimpses of the wild continent. Somehow Miss Dowdeswell had learned of this fact and through incessant pleading, convinced Captain Walker to ease her confinement. He agreed to allow her out for an hour in the morning and another in the afternoon, though only under the watchful eye of Mister Koonts and from time to time, either Jonathan or Sean. During one of these tours, Jonathan had an opportunity to speak with Delain about all that had happened as they strolled along the port side heading toward the bow.

"Your duel, Jonathan!" said Delain, breaking a short silence. "Please tell me about it! Where you afraid?"

"How did you know about that?" asked Jonathan, somewhat shocked.

"As I am sure you know," said Delain, "if one keeps an ear open on this ship, obtaining news and gossip is easier than reading the paper!"

This was true and Jonathan had often heard that the officers used this network to gain and disseminate information. *No wonder Captain Walker knows all and sees all, as some say,* thought Jonathan. *Tongues wag constantly on this ship. There are few secrets.*

"To answer your question about the duel, Delain, I was not afraid," Jonathan said sadly. "I certainly wasn't looking forward to it, however, I knew I could best Spears. When I fenced him previously, I had played the fool, all the time studying his style and ability. At the same time, I made sure he never saw any details of my own habits and skills."

"I must say," Delain said with a wry smile, "that you are quite devious and cunning, Midshipman Moore. I wonder if you can be trusted. And where would one learn such a talent?"

"On the streets of London, Miss Dowdeswell."

Delain eyed him suspiciously and paused for a moment.

"Whatever do you mean, Jonathan?"

He considered explaining his entire past to her. He knew she had some understanding of his separation from his father and his mother's passing, but she knew no details of his years on the streets, living as an orphan and fighting day to day to survive.

"Let us just say that Sean and I had a rough few years and though unhappy and strenuous, we gained some knowledge and skills that seem to be necessary in His Majesty's Navy. Could we leave it at that?"

"If you promise that someday you will tell me the entire tale?" Delain asked.

"Surely, it would be my pleasure," Jonathan said. "Possibly once we are all back in London. You had promised that I could show you some of the finer sights."

"Then it is a date then," Delain said. "If I am not in school!"

"And is that really why you chose to become a stowaway? To avoid a few weeks in a classroom?"

Delain reflected upon this question as they rounded the bow and proceeded aft along the starboard rail. The sun was now beginning to head downward and the breeze that brushed them gave the entire scene a dreamlike quality as the waves sparkled, sea birds darted between the sails and flew swiftly alongside the *Danielle*.

"Partly, yes," she stared hesitantly. "I did not feel that after all my adventures on the beaches with turtles, climbing the fort to the highest parapet, exploring the marshes of the islands, that I could just sit in a room and memorize lessons. After the winning of the *Drake* and the firing of those guns...well, I suddenly thought that all of it was...unfair."

"Unfair?" asked Jonathan. "To use your phrase, whatever do you mean?"

"Being a girl, Jonathan," she said. "We are expected to be proper, polite and tranquil. Do as we are told, be models of perfection and grace. And I think you know by now that I could never be one to follow that path. I actually wanted one more great escapade before I was expected to *act grown up* and be *properly Brit*ish. The idea of heading to sea..."

Jonathan thought of his possible future and all the choices and adventures that surely remained ahead. He had never realized that these were endeavors that were reserved for men and not for women. *But didn't all women enjoy being, well, women? And having their sedate, polite and planned lives spelled out for them by society? Obviously not* this *girl,* he thought as he looked at Delain. She had her own ideas. And that was what made her interesting.

"Maybe things will change, Delain," Jonathan said, hopefully.

"Not unless I change them," she said quietly. "That is why I came. I want to control something about my life. And I did."

They remained silent for a while, taking in the scene and enjoying their stroll. Jonathan thought of what she had said and wished he could help her. But of course, he realized that Delain would control her own destiny.

"Well, it is going to be a little more adventurous, Miss Dowdeswell," Jonathan said. "I am sure your escorts will be Sean and I, and together we will have some areas to explore. Are you ready for that?"

"Yes," she said, smiling. "Can you imagine the animals we might see? I can't even comprehend the possibilities!"

"Maybe you will see some of your special friends, the

turtles," Jonathan said, and quickly held out the beautiful necklace with the jeweled turtle he had purchased in the shop at Ribeira Grande in the Cape Verde Islands. "Please accept this in memory of our adventures."

Delain smiled even brighter, if at all possible, and gently took the necklace. She examined it closely and held it up to the sun to see how it sparkled.

"Mister Moore," she said coyly. "You shower me with gifts quite often. A turtle and a dolphin. People will start to think there is something between us, won't they?"

Jonathan looked deep in her eyes. They were emerald green, and he found that they held an element of adventure and promise in them, and a cunning that was un-nerving, yet attractive. Staring into them was like seeing a rare gem of unusual depth and quality.

"Let them," he said. And for some reason, he moved his head close to hers, and as their eyes met, he felt the need to...

"Aye! Thar ya are, Mister Moore! Cap'n needs to see you about your upcoming escort duties!"

"Steward!" Jonathan said surprisingly as he retreated from the proximity of Delain Dowdeswell's lips.

"And I am to take the little lady back to the Captain's cabin before dinner. Hurry on, Mister Moore, he's waitin' fer ya in his new quarters!"

As Jonathan bowed to Delain and shot Steward a look that if not able to kill, would surely maim, he retreated below decks in search of Walker.

As Steward escorted Delain to the cabin, she smiled and took a deep breath.

"Adventure, Mister Steward! It can't be beat!"

"Aye, Miss Dowdeswell, and a bit o' romance is not bad either!"

Also allowed on deck each day for a much briefer time than Delain, was none other than Walter Kozak. He was watched by two marines, ready with loaded muskets, and escorted by Midshipman Wayne Spears. The crew watched the two oddballs, one because of the tales they had heard about him, his strange accent and his peculiar dress; the other because of the full details of the extremely *one-sided* duel. Since then, Spears had kept a low profile, not attending to any duties other than his basic watches and his delivering of food to the prisoner.

Kozak, for his part, was not yet done conniving. The opportunity for him to converse with Spears was welcome as he continued his effort to convince the boy to do his bidding. He had already proposed his idea to Spears a while ago, after the boy's defeat in the duel, and though Spears had agreed, it had been more than a few days since they had spoken. It was obvious by the look on Spear's face that he was apprehensive about the arrangement, yet the fact that he was now escorting Kozak about the ship meant he was still in the game.

Kozak desired to assure the boy that the plan would benefit both of them: for Spears, a way out of an embarrassing situation, for Kozak, a means of escape.

"My dear boy," Kozak said as the two strolled around the deck, "It is joyful to breathe the fresh salt air after being cooped up like a laying hen in the bowels of this ship! Freedom is the most precious gift of God. Being captive like a caged animal is disquieting to the soul."

Spears thought of these words as he gazed out to the sea, the continent barely visible. He, too, felt like a caged animal, caged not by iron bars, but by his past actions and his future disappointments. He had agreed to transfer off the *Danielle* when the ship returned to London and he continued to believe that retiring from the Navy completely was really his only choice. *Better to abandon my career,* he thought, *than live with ridicule and discrimination.* At least Kozak's plan was a way out. He mulled it over in his mind as they strolled, Kozak going on and on about freedom, the bright sunlight falling on one's face and the virtues of the American way of life.

"The future is always bright in America," Kozak said softly, "every man having the ability and opportunity to succeed. And in certain ventures such as trading and sailing, well, the world has endless possibilities. A man with talent and industry, such as yourself...well, to be young and have a bright future!"

Spears continued half listening. He knew Kozak was still trying to convince him to carry out the plan, and he had actually already agreed. It was a simple task, really: at the right moment, when the *Danielle* was in the midst and confusion of battle, Spears was to release Kozak from his cell, secure the larger jollyboat, and the two would make their escape. Hopefully, they could find a French colony along the African coast and gain passage on a larger ship to America. There, as Kozak had promised, he and Spears would become a team, gain employment in the growing shipping business, and become Captain and First Mate of a trading vessel. They would share command of the business and the profits. Spears had thought that if indeed this could happen, it would only be a matter of years before he became well-to-do and a few more before he became rich. And that sounded considerably better than being disgraced and forced out of the His Majesty's Navy.

"Kozak, begging your pardon," interrupted Spears with a harsh whisper, slightly irritated at the non-stop selling of the idea. "I have previously agreed to the plan and my word is my bond. I will carry out my part accordingly. When Captain Walker is busy fighting the battle, we will take a boat, preferably at night, and be off. Pray, let us not speak of it again," he continued, shooting a quick glance at the marines following too closely behind them.

The two continued walking to the nearest ladder that led below decks and soon disappeared out of sight. The marines followed, desiring to put the bird in his cage, as it were, allowing them to attend to more appealing duties.

Life aboard the *Danielle* was never truly easy. The continuous workings of a large ship in His Majesty's Navy was complicated and at times wrought with physical exertion. This trip was no exception. As the ship sailed southward along the African coast, the crew's duties were mostly set about preparing for a battle that was sure to come. Sails were repaired, even the slightest hole patched. Rope that seemed to most to be completely sound and in excellent condition suddenly required replacing.

And of course, there was gun practice. The men enjoyed this duty. Normal practice was to build a raft out of barrels, lash and nail planks to the side, maybe even attach a pole and flag, and then drop it over the side. The *Danielle* would then reverse course, let one side have at it, and then reverse course again and give the opposite side a chance. Unfortunately, since time was of the essence and the Captain wanted to make sure they located the enemy squadron as soon as possible to create a better chance of sinking them, he would not slow down or reverse course. Losing even precious minutes could devastate the mission. The gun crews were instructed to fire at targets on shore, as Mister Watt steered the *Danielle* a bit closer toward land. The port side had certainly more opportunities, as they faced the continent. They fired at clumps of trees, open spots of beach, a few outcroppings of rock, and tangles of floating debris. The starboard side, however, had slightly less at which to shoot, and was able to only target small islands that Mister Watt could safely maneuver into position.

Jonathan and Harrison stood at attention on the poop deck and waited to be addressed. The Captain was discussing some matter with Mister Watt and seemed to be at odds with the helmsmen as to what course to take. Finally, after much discussion, both men nodded their heads in agreement. The Captain turned and took his position on the poop, staring forward, now and again looking upward at the sails and rigging. The ship was moving along at almost eleven knots, amazingly fast for a vessel the size of the *Danielle*, but it was clear to all who read the face of Captain Walker that it was not fast enough.

Jonathan suspected the reason he had been

summoned, and as he contemplated his response, he saw Steward and Marine Captain Gorman escorting Sean Flagon to the stern. When they arrived and took their silent positions next to Jonathan and Harrison, it was clear what was to happen.

"Gentlemen," the Captain said as he stared upwards, trying to find an extra bit of wind or think of another way to power the ship onward, "we are approaching the tip as we say, on the southern coast of the continent. In less than three days we will be around and heading northeast. Hopefully, we will not see our prey before then. I would like to bottle them up in the strait between these islands and the continent. That way they can't maneuver and scatter."

The Captain then turned his gaze to the crow's nest and to Garvey, who seemed to be living up there permanently these past few days. He indeed had sharp eyes, almost as sharp as Harrison's. In a dire situation like this, Captain Walker usually sent Jonathan and Harrison to look out, but it was clear that they were important officers on the *Danielle* and were needed to manage the crew and relay orders.

"Garvey," the Captain called, "Anything to be seen?"

"Just clouds and deep blue sea, Cap'n! Nothin' yet in any direction!"

Certainly the Captain was asking unnecessarily. If Garvey had seen anything, he would call out immediately. It was proof that even the Captain was nervous.

"No sign of any enemy to the south and no sign of assistance from the north," muttered Walker.

"I had thought that with the *Paladin* and the *Drake* sounding the alarm, we would have at least a few smaller ships attending!" said Koonts in exasperation.

"Possibly they were successful," said Harrison, "though any aid is still in route. We are moving at quite a clip and it may take some time for anyone to catch us."

"Let us hope that is the case and they meet us before we begin to dance," said Captain Walker. "We must do away with the frigates quickly, at least get them out of the picture long enough to chase down as many merchant vessels as we can. Mister Moore? Flagon?"

"Yes sir," they said in unison.

"I have called you here to give you important and specific orders."

I knew it, thought Jonathan; *we will be set aside once again, missing the action.*

"You will miss this action, boys," the Captain continued, "and be set down with Miss Dowdeswell on Isla Sello, *Seal Island* in the King's English. It is located at the entrance to the strait, so at least you will have an excellent view of the battle from there. You will do all in your power to make Miss Dowdeswell comfortable and safe. We will provision you with food and water enough for many weeks. Hopefully we will be successful and return to you when all is clear. If not, we will also leave powder, a few barrels, so you can make fires to possibly signal another ship that will pass by. No matter what the nationality, you should signal and try to gain passage back to Europe. Do you understand?"

"Yes sir," they both said. It was no surprise to the boys this was coming. They had already begun packing a few essentials of their own: their blades, Jonathan's telescope and compass, Sean's knife, a few remedies he had received from the doctor, and his book. Even Stewie appeared and jumped at Sean, making sure all knew that he was ready to accompany them.

"Captain, if I may?" asked Jonathan, respectively.

"Continue, Mister Moore," the Captain said, now looking the boy in the eye.

"Thank you sir," Jonathan said. "I strongly request that I be allowed to remain aboard, as the only actual experience with true battle was -"

"Thank you, Mister Moore for your opinion," interrupted the Captain, somewhat annoyed. "Duly noted. You have your assignment."

What the Captain would not say, was that he was

sorry to lose Jonathan for the upcoming fight. His ingenuity and creativeness would surely be an asset in the coming fray, and certainly the men loved Jonathan and would fight for him as much as for their own lives. They considered him their good-luck charm and his past activities had made some of them a few pounds and a notoriety worth at least a drink or two in any port tavern. Jonathan was uniquely considered both "one of us" to the crew as he had come from the rough streets of London, yet, also rightfully promoted officer with a family history steeped in Navy traditions. He was, to all aboard, a gentleman and a commoner, the best of both worlds. No one wanted him off the ship when the going was tough.

However, Captain Walker had promised Nathaniel Moore that he would do all in his power to return Jonathan to London. To keep him safe, the best place for him would be off the ship completely. Yes, there was a risk of being marooned there on Isla Sello, however, chances were that a ship would happen by almost weekly, as the strait was the only way around the tip of Africa. If the *Danielle* was unsuccessful, Jonathan, Sean and Delain would have a good chance of survival and rescue.

"Captain, I must insist -"

"There will be no insisting, Mister Moore!" the Captain said, now showing anger. "You are dismissed!"

* * * * * *

The weather became noticeably cooler over the next few days as the *Danielle* traveled south, then turned east with a strong wind at her back. The ship's crew was busy preparing for slightly rough seas as the ocean about them had turned quickly from pleasant to more than slightly agitated. Jonathan walked the deck alone, thinking of what dreadful events could transpire at his next stop. As he stared to the sea, he imagined that like a real person, the ocean had its own moods and purposes that were only slightly understood by those that sailed its waters. At times, it was calm and pleasant company, even welcoming in its beauty. Then, at times of storms, it could be horrible and angry. In the waves, Jonathan could swear he had seen monstrous shapes, sometimes looking like shadowy sea serpents rising and falling, beating down upon the ship mercilessly. Many men aboard believed there were truly evil creatures in the sea, giant whales and monstrous squids with tentacled arms that could sink a ship by grasping it and dragging all to the dark, cold depths. Some believed in sirens that would appear as beautiful women swimming in the water only to change into hideous apparitions that would drive the crew insane with their screeching and wailing, until they were mad and dove into the sea to drown.

At one point, after reaching the southern-most tip of Africa, the water stirred most unusually, and though not as active as in a great storm, there was still a warning of sorts in the sickly, gloomy-green water: *Beware! A ship had best be careful, for I will not make your voyage through these waters agreeable.* As if by command of the sea, an eerie haze rolled in from the continent and soon obscured their view of all except the few hundred feet dead ahead.

Midshipman Spears was actually now more active than he had been since the duel at Ribeira Grande. He busied himself with his assigned tasks and watches, and Jonathan even noted that he refrained from annoying almost everyone. Even Sean seemed to escape his ridicule. Presently he was attending to the larger jollyboat, tightening its tarp and securing the ropes that held it firmly to the deck. Jonathan thought that possibly he should approach Spears and try to converse in a friendly manner. It would be difficult, but Jonathan thought it should be attempted. Maybe a friendship could arise between the two of them, as seemingly had been done with Lane, who now ate and worked with Jonathan and Sean whenever possible and had become particularly fond of Garvey. The two shared stories and jokes, and even had maneuvered themselves onto the same gun crew. Garvey remained the eyes and Lane lit the beast they both called *the Dragon,* presumably in honor of the Captain and his more colorful and active tempers.

"Hullo, Midshipman Spears," Jonathan said as he approached, "Is the day to your liking?"

Spear looked up for an instant, then quickly turned his eyes to the deck. He mumbled something under his breath that sounded something like 'agreeable'.

"It seems I am to be put ashore once again, missing all the fun," Jonathan said.

"I hear that as well. Good luck to you," Spears answered and finished lashing the final rope to the tarp.

"I was wondering, Wayne, if you might be available for some lobscouse this evening. Harrison is a fine cook and has assured me it will be well worth it."

Spears looked up for an instant, then again, hid his eyes and murmured something along the lines of "Can't. Busy." And with that he was hurrying aft to check the smaller of the jollyboats.

Sean had watched the whole exchange from the first yard of the main mast, only a few feet above Jonathan's head. He could tell something wasn't right about Spears, and at the same time, he welcomed the fact that his one-time thorn had seemingly been clipped.

"Tis a mystery, Jonathan," Sean said. "And I still don't trust him."

"Something is amiss, Sean," Jonathan said as he watched Spears attend to the tarp of the small boat. "Maybe it is just his realization of what he had brought upon himself. Maybe he is trying to sort it out."

"And maybe," Sean said as he returned to his duty of lashing sails to the yard, "the snake has one more bite left. Never let your guard down. That one still has some teeth."

At that point, Miss Delain Dowdeswell appeared on deck, accompanied by Midshipman Lane.

"It seems, Mister Moore," she said as they approached, "that it is Mister Lane's duty to complete my tour of the ship today. Were you assigned another stowaway?"

Jonathan chuckled a bit, then became stern in a comical way. "Miss Dowdeswell, though Mister Lane is escorting you, there are many watching your movements. Stredney and Garvey up in the crow's nest, Holtz next to the Captain there," Jonathan said pointing aft, "even Smith and Jones by the deck guns are watching you closely. Not only are you a young woman onboard -"

"Most consider a woman onboard bad luck, may I point out," added Lane.

"A capital point," said Jonathan, "and even more so the fact that technically you are a criminal of the highest degree, a stowaway. They can be dangerous and even unpredictable. Are those characteristics of yours that you deny?"

"Certainly!" exclaimed Delain, alarmed. "I am most undoubtedly not a criminal nor a dangerous person!"

"Aye, but ya notice Miss Dowdeswell didn't say she was not *unpredictable!*" said Sean as he continued his work from above.

"Oh!" said Delain, noticing Sean for the first time. "Well…I must admit that I am somewhat… *impulsive*."

This sent the boys laughing hysterically as Mister Harrison approached with Steward.

"Have we missed the show?" Harrison said. 'What is so funny?"

"Mister Harrison," Delain said. "As you notice I am the only one not laughing. Is it true that women aboard are considered unlucky?"

"Yes, by the crew at least," he answered.

"Is it also true," she continued, "that many are watching me because I am a criminal and a stowaway?"

"Hmm," Harrison said as he thought a moment. "I would think so. I have not been assigned that duty, but I am sure the Captain takes your offense most seriously indeed."

"Do you think I am dangerous and impulsive?"

"I am sure the pirates aboard the *Fiero* believed you were dangerous, so I would have to agree. Also, you do fire a deck gun with amazing accuracy. The fact that you have stowed away aboard this ship may lead one to believe you are impulsive as well."

Delain seemed shocked as the others roared with laughter. It was Steward who broke the mood.

"Now, now, little lady," he said in a fatherly tone. "The boys are having a bit o' fun with ya. Don't mind them! Brutes at the core and no manners b'sides. I am sure the only one really watching you is Mister Moore, and he has been doing that since, oh, last October I believe, when he first met ya!"

This sent even Delain laughing. All joined in except Jonathan who merely put his head away to stare overboard, embarrassed.

"Land ho!" came the call from above. It was Nicolas Garvey from the crow's nest. "Isla Sello! One point off the starboard bow, Captain!"

The Captain immediately ordered a reduction in sail. As the *Danielle* slowed to only a few knots, the haze cleared ahead and a massive darkness slowly appeared in the gloom. All on deck could see Isla Sello rise from the waves, its jagged coastline wrought with white foam as angry waves splashed and churned at its base. There was no beach, no inviting palms or fruit trees. Just a hard-looking, sheer black volcanic mass that rose from the surrounding dark green water. It continued upwards almost two-hundred feet, narrowing as it reached into the low clouds, its topmost point hidden from view. There could be seen in the water the triangular fins of great sharks.

"Now that is foreboding!" said Steward unnecessarily.

"Are you all packed, Miss Dowdeswell?" asked Harrison, his tone now sad and serious. "The Captain will need you and your escorts to disembark immediately. Meet us on the port side by the small jollyboat in a few moments. Lane, assist with Miss Dowdeswell's luggage, if you will."

Delain took one last look at Isla Sello, turned, and slowly made her way with Lane to the Captain's cabin. She now realized this was no longer a simple and enjoyable adventure. Her stowing away had now turned a lark into a possibly dire situation. She and her friends could be marooned on the island to only await their death from starvation eventually, or worse. And it was her doing that now placed Jonathan and Sean in peril.

As the ship's bell rang twice, signaling one hour past the midday watch, Jonathan, Sean and Delain were standing at the port side of *HMS Danielle,* watching the island just a few hundred feet away, across a dangerous sea. Their supplies were being loaded on the boat that was hanging securely off the yard-tackles. Smith and Jones and a few other hands attended to the proper procedures as the Captain, Gorman and Harrison looked on. Even Koonts was there, and Doctor Hoffman, giving last minute advice to Jonathan and Sean.

"Stay away from three stemmed plants, Sean," Doctor Hoffman said. "Only eat fish that are bland in color that you catch fresh. Cook them thoroughly! There are many snoek to be caught here, though they have a poisonous bite, be careful!"

"Find the Castelo de Fogo, Jonathan," said Koonts. "It looks to be completely shrouded in clouds at the moment, but it is there. Explore it thoroughly and carefully. Then survey the island and look for hazards to avoid. The weather is cooling off rapidly. In a month it may be bitterly cold!"

"Winter begins in June south of the equator," explained Harrison. "Let's hope we are united long before then."

"Take this olive oil and this pan," Claise said as he approached. "And here are some simple spices: salt, pepper and some lime rind. Always good with fish. I also have a few potatoes as well in this sack. They will keep for a few weeks if kept dry and away from nibbling creatures."

Jonathan hugged Claise, who seemed near tears, and thanked him for the supplies.

Lane appeared and handed Jonathan his small cooking stove that he had received as a Christmas present from Steward.

"Don't forget this. And best of luck, my friends," he said.

"Mister Moore," the Captain called after he had inspected the boat and made sure all supplies were aboard, "a word with you. Sean and Miss Dowdeswell, time to board."

With that Delain and Sean took their places in the jolly boat, Stewie tucked deep in the folds of the blankets Sean was holding. Smith, Jones, Garvey and Harrison also boarded, manning the oars. Jonathan approached the Captain and stood at attention. Walker turned to the boy and bent down slightly, to look him eye to eye.

"Jonathan, firstly, let me assure you that the island is safe. The birds nest here because there are no predators. Just stay out of the water. There are many sharks. Great Whites. The most dangerous kind."

"Yes, sir," Jonathan said, bravely.

"Secondly, you have enough supplies to last you months if need be, though I suspect your stay will be much less than that. Eat the perishables first, the fruit, the salted pork, hard tack. But save the limes and use only a little slice every few days. There are fish lines and hooks as well. We have included many lengths of rope, a saw, hammer and nails, some spare lumber…if you need to build a semi-permanent structure. A boat will not be left. There is nowhere near which to row, and the continent is, well, *less than friendly*."

Walker turned his gaze to the island. He was not one to second guess himself; however, this seemed barely the lesser of two evils. Kept aboard, Delain could be killed by cannon fire or drown if the *Danielle* was sunk. Set ashore on this island, she could starve to death or become injured. However, if the *Danielle* was defeated, it was more than probable that other ships would pass by, however... He wrestled with the thought of calling the entire plan off and giving up on the mission altogether.

"As soon as you can, cautiously, and I repeat, *cautiously* explore the Castelo de Fogo. In English, that means *Castle of Fire*. If you are fortunate to have a clear afternoon, watch the castle as the sun sets. You will see how it got its name. I have seen it only a few times, and even then, it has been mostly covered with fog and clouds. Tales tell that it is a large castle and is partly carved out of the stone that makes up the mountain in the center of the island. It is, as Mister Harrison says, *quite a sight*."

"I will explore it, sir" said Jonathan, wondering what all the mystery seemed to be about the castle. From his point of view aboard the ship he could see nothing, only a bit of a wall possibly, when the clouds shifted just so.

"Jonathan, here is my plan. Mind well," Walker said. "We will search for the French around the southern tip of the continent and possibly up the eastern coast for a few hundred miles at the most. Once we spot them, we will turn and lure them back here. Hopefully, we will engage the frigates once we have them in the strait."

"If you can disable them," Jonathan asked, "will you go after the merchants?"

"It will be difficult," said Walker. "Engaging with two ships at once is tricky and takes time. Without the help of our sister ships, it will be difficult. However, we will try."

"I wish, sir, that I could do something to help!" exclaimed Jonathan.

"You can, Mister Moore. If you see any English ships, signal by starting a fire and inform them of the plan. Have them wait past the tip of land there," he said pointing.

Jonathan turned and saw a glimpse of the mainland and a protruding piece jetting out into the sea. Certainly ships could hide there, then with a keen eye, pounce at the right moment, coming to the aid of the *Danielle*.

"One last item, Mister Moore. Today is the twenty-sixth of April. We should catch sight of the French and return for you within the week. If for some reason we don't return, save yourselves. Look for an English ship, however, don't wait too long. If we do not meet again in one month…we are lost."

The weight of the situation now hit Jonathan hard. This could be the last time he ever saw Captain Walker and all his friends from the *Danielle*. If marooned on Isla Sello and left to starve, it would also mean the death of Sean, Delain and himself.

"I will use the gunpowder and fire starters to create an explosion to signal other ships," Jonathan said slowly, now staring at the ground.

"Yes," said Walker, forcing a smile. "That should be easily done with Sean. He knows full well how to create a bomb. Good luck to you, Mister Moore. It has been a pleasure to serve with you in His Majesty's Navy."

"Thank you, Captain Walker, for all you have done for me," answered Jonathan in a quivering voice. "If for some reason I do not return to England, and you do, would you please tell my father… I loved him so?"

The Captain nodded and put Jonathan aboard the jollyboat. Hands lowered the craft into the churning sea and with a fine salute from the Royal Naval officers, Gorman and all marines; the jollyboat disappeared into the mist.

18

The Castle of Fire

On the north side of Isla Sello, the jollyboat crew found an excellent landing area: a large rock shelf that had a near-flat top rising above the water almost two feet. Once the boat was secured, Harrison commanded the others to move the supplies higher and inland, away from the sea, as it was important to secure food and other goods from a rising tide. As a final bit of advice, Harrison told them all: "Remember - your mind is your best asset. It has gotten your through much. Rely upon it. We will see you all soon."

Jonathan, Sean and Delain stood on the low rock shelf, dressed in their heavy woolen coats and gloves. Even Delain wore a *Dani* cap, looking much like a young seaman, except for her long dress, now stained and slightly damaged. Jonathan wore his midshipman's uniform; however the bicorn hat was exchanged for a woolen cap. Stewie had his own fur coat, of course. He nervously looked to the water, amazed and frightened by the fins of sharks that could be seen just a few yards off shore. After a long moment, they waved a final good-bye to the jollyboat and turned their backs to the sea.

The weather was cold and the fog remained about them, still covering the upper portion of the small mountain in the center of the island veiling the Castelo de Fogo. As they surveyed their surroundings, Jonathan glanced up at the shrouded crest and wondered what the castle looked like and how large it really could be. However, for now, he tried to concentrate on his command of the shore party, as much as one could command one's best friend and Miss Delain Dowdeswell. *Maybe Stewie would be easy to control,* he thought, and that made him chuckle inside.

"What is our first order of business, Jonathan?" asked Sean as he patted Stewie on the head.

"We need to explore our surroundings," Jonathan replied, "and find our way up to the castle, though I still can see none of it through the clouds."

"I would prefer if we stay together as a group," added Delain, and all agreed.

Slowly, the three friends began a clockwise search of the island, looking for useful items and possibly a way to scale the mountain and climb to the castle. The terrain was rough at times and the dark, volcanic rock cut their hands or scraped their knees as they scrambled up and down the many formations and cliff walls. The island had very few trees upon it and some small plants sprouted from between cracks in the many boulders. The only living things they saw were the many birds on the leeward, or calmer, side of the island, and in the water, the sharks that seemed to follow them as they made their way about. After two hours of searching they had returned to the landing area, discovering very little that would assist them in any way.

"Well," Sean said, "there is nothing around the base of this mountain. No shelter, no water, no stairs and no anything. Just rock. And what can you do with rock?"

"Let us stay here for tonight," Jonathan said, "and build a tent for shelter."

With Sean's assistance, they strung rope between tree stumps and boulder edges, then slowly lashed tarpaulin to their make-shift rigging.

"If we can make a house out of broken barrels and crates in an alley," said Jonathan laughing, "we can make a tent out of all this!" Eventually the rope, tarp and supply boxes left by the crew of the *Danielle* came to resemble a tent.

Delain sat still on a nearby boulder in silence. The omnipresent fog unnerved her as did the thought of *The Castle of Fire,* just looming over her head. She shivered and couldn't help but think that this predicament had been all her making. If she hadn't stowed away, Jonathan and Sean would be aboard the *Danielle*, with their friends, doing what they loved. However, they would be in danger aboard the ship or on this island. *No matter now*, she thought, *we are here and I must make the best of it*.

As Jonathan and Sean continued to wrestle with the shelter, Stewie sought out Delain to curl up in her lap as she sat. Her head moved about, left to right, looking for something that she could do to assist the boys, though they assured her the final construction of their shelter was well in hand. In time, she looked upward at the mist surrounding the mountaintop.

"Maybe if the fog would clear," she said out loud, "we could see the top of the hill and therefore a way upwards."

"Possibly," said Jonathan as he concentrated on his work. "We are not the first ones here. Someone must have climbed this hill in some manner."

But the fog was unyielding, and it continued its slow rolling as the sun, somewhere above, began to set. The grayish glow of light slowly darkened as it settled lower in the hazy sky and soon fell the night.

In the darkness, a little scared and quite uncomfortable, the three friends and Stewie sat leaning on one another and staring out into the nothingness. The tent was low, only a few feet from the ground, and for a floor, there was only the hard stone with a single remaining tarp spread across it and a few blankets to shield them from the cold earth. Jonathan and Sean had piled the crates of food and powder close together, creating a wall of sorts. This blocked the cool wind that was almost constant. No fire had been attempted – they were all too tired to try. It was in this state that they fell into an uneasy sleep.

Sean, as usual, snoozed like the kitten next to him, unperturbed and for the most part comfortable. Jonathan slept as well as could be expected, rising twice in the middle of the night to leave the tent and survey the surrounding area for danger. Seeing all was safe, he returned to the tent and an uneasy sleep. Though somewhat comforted by the closeness of her friends, Delain never nodded off for more than an hour at a time. She thought she heard animals in the night tearing at the tent and howling, and she would shake herself awake to find that they were only dreams. Eventually, she would drift off, exhaustion taking over her fear. At least by early morning, she had finally managed a few uninterrupted hours of slumber.

A bit before noon, she woke fully, though tired and a little cold. The boys were still fast asleep, however, Stewie was awake, lying in the sun at the edge of the tent floor. Rays of sunlight made their way through clouds as they rolled by and past tree branches as they waved gently in the breeze. The cat playfully swatted as the shadows danced on the blanket. *It looks warm in the light,* she said to herself. *I shall join him in a moment.*

Delain crawled out from under the tent and immediately stood in the sun, warming herself. She could see that the mountain in the center of the island was barely covered in a light fog. It was quickly fading away with the aid of the hot sun and revealing areas that could not be previously observed. There were a few trees, gnarled and twisted, yet they did have some leaves upon them.

Jonathan and Sean were now awake and joined her in the study of the mountain. Eventually, the sun showed itself stronger and brighter and before their eyes the fog was slowly melting away. Gradually, more trees were revealed, green grass in patches grew. Even birds could be seen flying about, great boobies and frigate birds, black and brown, with long, slender tail feathers that splayed outwards. As the sun continued to dissolve the fog, a wind picked up and blew from the ocean, across their camp and upward to the hilltop. The breeze now pushed the mist away from the land until it reached the top. They gasped aloud.

The Castle of Fire

There, several hundred feet above them, was revealed a massive castle made of huge, blackened stone blocks. At least four separate levels could be seen, with parapets, balconies, and a domed enclosure. There was a chiseled stairway that almost reached directly from the fort down to their waterside camp. With a few barrels piled atop one another, they could easily reach the first step.

"The Castelo de Fogo!" said Jonathan.

"The Castle of Fire," translated Delain.

"Well," said Sean. "That a fine good-morning to ya, no matter how ya pronounce it!"

No other words needed to be spoken as the three began rolling barrels and stacking crates in which to use to reach the first stone step.

After having a quick meal of hard tack and some cheese, they began the climb as the afternoon sun began reaching for the west. The going was not difficult from the point of safely ascending the stairs; it was difficult due to the effort it took to consistently climb upward. Each took a turn carrying Stewie, who simply meowed from time to time and dug a claw into an arm during some of the more steep sections. There were a few respites now and then carved into the stone steps, flat areas some three or four feet wide where the steps became large enough to allow all three to stand, or sit, side by side in relative comfort. After resting and taking a sip from a water bag that Sean had thoughtfully remembered to bring, they would take a deep breath, transfer the cat, and resume the climb.

"And I thought climbing the rat lines was difficult. I am completely done!" exclaimed Sean as they rounded a corner only to find yet another series of ascending steps in front of them.

"Just a bit longer Sean," Jonathan said. "I am sure it will be worth it."

"Do you think the castle is… is…occupied?" asked Delain as she froze in her tracks. This stopped the boys for a minute. "As much as I desire improved accommodations," she continued, "and maybe even a better view, I don't want to have to fight for it!"

Jonathan and Sean glanced at each other and simultaneously drew their swords.

"Just to be safe," Jonathan said.

"I feel better already," said Sean with a smile.

It had been just a little over an hour since the

beginning of their climb when Jonathan, Sean and Delain had finally scaled every one of the steps that were hewn into the stone walls of the mountain. The sun was beginning to fade and all were aware that within an hour, it would set. The wispy clouds were already turning from white to slightly orange. As they cautiously peeked over the edge of the last step, the amber sunbeams fell softly on the hard stone of the towering Castle of Fire. A few birds swirled past the outer walls, seemingly too scared to light upon the shadowy structure, let alone enter the few arched openings that were set in the third story of the fortress. The massive outer curtain made of huge wooden timbers surrounded the castle at its base. The inner curtain rose at least fifty feet above them, dark and mystifying. The Castel was certainly strong enough to repel all but the most concentrated cannon fire. *Could a ship's guns even scratch it?* thought Jonathan as he stared in wonder. On the corner of the topmost level, facing the sea below was an impressive part of the castle, a cathedral-like structure with a domed roof made of lighter-colored rock and crowned with a stone spike and a cross. The sun was now turning the castle itself almost red in color, and along the upmost wall where large notches had been made, the stones glowed from the light as if on fire.

"Something is missing," Jonathan whispered.

"Whatever do you mean?" asked Delain quietly.

"I am not an expert on castles," said Jonathan, "but that tower and those notches up there -"

"You mean the watchtower and the embrasures?" asked Delain.

"I assume so," said Jonathan. What are they for?"

"Mister Tupper and I studied castles last year and I recall the fact that castles were built for defense, primarily. The watchtower, on the corner was used for viewing. Those tall thin openings there are used for arrows."

"The view must be extraordinary from the top!" said Sean.

"Then inside the belly of the beast we go!" suggested

Jonathan.

They took the last few steps remaining, legs still aching but curiosity driving them onward. Finally they stood before a massive wooden door set in the strong timbers that made up the castle's outer wall. It was slightly off hinge and sitting askew.

"Let us take a peek inside," said Jonathan and all cautiously took hold of the edge of the door. Unfortunately, rust and age had done more than its part in securing the entrance. No matter how hard they pushed and pulled, the door barely moved. After an hour of effort, Jonathan finally suggested that they use their heads instead of their backs.

"Let's try to pry the hinges with our blade tips. There may be a decent angle at which to apply pressure."

With some effort and a variety of approaches, they manipulated their sword tips like awls and pry bars. Finally, after another hour or so, the door was shifted aside just enough to allow them to access.

Inside the Castle, it was almost completely dark, only some faint sunlight high above them streaking in from an unseen opening. They felt about with their hands as their eyes were unable to see anything in detail. They remained quiet.

"I feel something like a twig or small branch," said Delain softly after a few moments. "Oh, there are many of them about the floor."

"A coconut?" asked Sean as his hands bumped into an unseen object.

The light from above suddenly intensified as the sun shifted and the room immediately became bathed in a deep red light, as if a great lamp had been lit. Through the crimson haze, all could see they were in a large room with a ceiling over twenty feet high, containing many archways and stairways leading to halls and rooms with closed wooden doors. There were few tables and chairs about, mostly smashed and ruined. As their eyes adjusted further, the red glow of fading sunlight now revealed that what they thought to be branches and coconuts on the floor was clearly exposed and the true nature realized.

"Bones!" exclaimed Sean in a hoarse whisper.

"Skulls!" said Delain, "Oh! And we touched them! *I* touched them!"

They all shuttered and shook uncontrollably for a minute or two. Delain was quite shaken to the point of tears, and let out a few screams as she beheld more and more of the corpses. She finally shut her eyes and sobbed. The boys immediately rushed to her, and as best as they could, assured the girl that, as frightening as the scene was, they were all perfectly safe.

"Better dead than alive, Miss Dowdeswell!" said Sean.

"Totally harmless," added Jonathan. "Delain, there was a battle here. See the arrows and swords?"

Though shocked and frightened by the sight, Delain finally realized that though eerily disgusting, the dead were quite harmless. To prove this, Sean stood and comically performed a mock fight with one of the larger skeletons, that included much tripping, hand-to-hand combat and in the end, an easy victory for the Irishman.

"Victory! He was a tough one, but just a bit stiff in his moves, eh Jonnyboy?" chuckled Sean as he held his sword above his head in an overstated pose.

Laughing now, the three inspected the grotesque scene about them. Jonathan figured that possibly a hundred or more skeletons lay about and many weapons of many types.

"What if the victors are still here?" asked Delain.

"If they were, they would have certainly cleaned this mess," said Jonathan. "These bones have been left to rot and I assume it takes a long time for them to reach this point of decay. I am almost positive we are alone."

"I can make sure," said Sean. He jumped up on the top of a half broken table and called out.

"Long live Ireland and the glory of the Emerald Isle!"

"Sean, wait!" Jonathan, but it was too late. The call could not be taken back.

All waited for something to happen, possibly for a host of ghosts to drift in on an eerie green mist to take them prisoner, or for some strange witch to fly from the shadows, casting spells and scaring them half to death. However, after a few moments and a few more calls… nothing happened; not sound nor stir. Now, somewhat braver than before, they explored the large hall. No recent signs of activity were found; no smoldering fires, no leftover food, no footsteps on the dusty ground. They were truly alone.

Each of them chose a door or a stairway to explore, always calling out to one another from time to time to make sure they were safe and to boost their courage. Sean searched upwards to the second level after ascending the main stone staircase in the first hall. Delain remained on the first level, though she shrieked often as that seemed to be where most of the skeletons had found their final resting place. But as dim as it was, the light was brightest in the main hall, so she chose to continue on.

Jonathan had also taken the main staircase, and after leaving Sean on the second floor, he continued upwards to the third and fourth. Mostly there were rooms within the stone castle that contained nothing but broken furniture, rotting tapestry and a few pots and pans. Now and again a small mouse was found and the occasional ancient warrior in his decomposed state. Anything of value had been taken by whoever had been the victor of the last battle and nothing but useless scraps of the lost occupant's possessions remained. *Not much treasure in this castle,* Jonathan thought.

He continued onward to the topmost floor and after climbing a ladder he found himself outside, standing in the center of what he could only describe as the *deck* of the castle. Like the deck of the *Danielle*, it was about the same size, yet not made of planked wood. There were no masts of course, and no guns about the edges. Along one side, there was a building, long and narrow, with many doors. Each was secured with a rusty chain and a keyed lock.

"I wonder what could be in there?" said Jonathan to himself, but after shaking and straining the chains, he ascertained that without a pry-bar, the locks were too strong to break. He turned his attention to the low walls along the edge of the roof. The notches he saw from below along the edge appeared larger than he originally thought, each notch looking like one of a giant's teeth set on an immense lower jaw. There in the corner was the domed watch tower he had seen from below, and as he approached the structure, he noticed a small set of stairs that rose several feet higher than the roof of the castle. *I'll bet the view from there is incredible,* he thought, and he walked quickly to the watch tower, up the steps and went to the short stone wall that was built at the edge.

Jonathan gasped for breath as he beheld the view. Before and below him was the strait of the Cape of Good Hope and beyond that, the southern tip of Africa, with the entire continent stretching forever to the north. All was bathed in the redness of the sunset, but most notably the Castle that seemed to glow as if the stone itself was on fire. He could now understand what the Captain had said about how the castle had gotten its name, the Castle of Fire.

In this place, he thought the curve of the horizon could be seen. Ahead sat the Dark Continent crowned with towering white clouds trimmed in orange and gold. They seemed a little less unreachable, as Jonathan was surely a thousand feet above the level of the sea. For a full ten minutes he stared in awe at the view, spinning about to look in all directions. Finally he whispered, when he could find his voice, "Harrison was right. It is quite a view. As if in heaven itself!"

Eventually, Jonathan made his way back down to the third level and continued his search of rooms and hallways. Upon opening a heavy wooden door of one room near the center, he found a large space that would suit them well as a sleeping chamber. He noticed a long, sturdy table in the middle of the room and a few unbroken chairs about the floor. There were also two doors along a back wall.

Maybe a closet or two? he thought. *Sean and I can sleep here in the main room, but what of Delain? A lady needs her privacy, so another room nearby would be best.*

Jonathan opened the first door on the rear wall. Inside on a work table was a pile of tools. Many were large brushes and files of various sizes. There were also long poles that looked like the rods used aboard the *Danielle* to clean out the guns before firing, though some had spikes of a sort, bristling at the tip. *Probably used to clean something,* Jonathan thought as he started to the next door.

In the second room, he saw an opening high on the back wall that let in just enough light to illuminate a large table to one side. Along the walls, Jonathan could see small boxes of nails, wooden pegs and other carpenter-like supplies. Saws and awls were also present in various sizes. This was obviously a carpenter's room, but also would make an excellent chamber for Delain.

After a few more minutes inspecting the contents of the last room, he made his way downward to the main hall and waited a few minutes for Delain and Sean to appear.

"I explored this entire first level," Delain said. "There are many empty rooms and an old kitchen, but also a large sleeping area for the soldiers who must have been alive here at one time. There were almost one hundred beds with straw mats that have been mostly eaten by mice."

The word 'mice' seemed to appeal to Stewie, who woke up from his slumber by the main door and scampered deeper into the castle.

"I guess Stewie has a job after all," Sean said. "The level I searched was mostly empty, no one home. I found a few storage areas and a small forge. Whoever built this fort had to be self-sufficient. I tried to open the doors to a few storage rooms, but, well, each has a rusty chain and lock, so a long bar would be great. We will need all three of us to pry them open."

Jonathan told them of his find in the upper levels and agreed that they should move their supplies in as soon as possible.

"It will take a long time to get the gunpowder up those steps," Sean said. "Must we haul it all the way to the top? At about twenty pounds for each barrel, it will take weeks. Maybe we just leave it be and retrieve what we need when we need it?"

"I think we will need it all and very soon, I hope," said Jonathan.

"Why is that?" asked Delain.

"Remember when I mentioned that something was missing?" Jonathan said.

"Something besides a warm bed and some of Claise's curry stew?" suggested Sean.

"Follow me," Jonathan said, and they made their way up to the top-most level. Jonathan led them out to the watchtower and allowed them to take in the panoramic view of the world.

"Lord," said Sean. "One could see the entire English Fleet from up here!"

"Or a French one," added Jonathan.

Eventually, after much pointing, gasping and even cheering in joy from the amazing sight, Jonathan pointed to the embrasures, the notches in the parapet walls.

"The gaps in this wall, you see?" Jonathan continued, pointing. "Why would someone building the fort leave the walls so? Something is missing and I now know what."

"Guns!" said Sean and Delain.

"Cannon, as they are called in this case, as we are on land," Jonathan said.

"But where are they, Jonathan?" Delain asked.

"And why do we care?" asked Sean.

"I presume they are nearby, most likely in these chained rooms to the rear," Jonathan said. "Unless someone took them down those stairs."

"That would be a long and treacherous task," Sean said. "I would venture the forge I found was used to make the cannons right here at the castle.

"Brilliant," said Delain. "I am sure you are correct."

"And I believe we should care," added Jonathan.

"But why? What could we possibly do with cannon all the way up -" Sean paused. A smile slowly spreading on his face as his eyes met Jonathan's. "Oh, I like *that* idea, Jonathan!"

Delain looked at the two boys and then at the spaces where the cannon were to be in the wall.

"What idea?" she asked. "What would you possibly do with cannon while we await the return of the *Danielle*? Oh, I see! I see now! You mean to join the battle!"

"Yes," Jonathan said. "If we can find the cannon and set them correctly so they overlook the bay, we could maybe take out a few French frigates."

"That sounds like fun and something to keep us busy!" said Sean, eager to get started. "I will start hauling up the powder!"

"Wait a moment," Jonathan said. "Let us find the cannon and test a single one first. And for that, we will have to wait until morning. There is not enough light to make it down. It would be best if we sleep as best as we can in here."

"I am not sleeping *in here* with all those dead coconuts about," stated Delain, and the three gathered up and cuddled against the outer wall of the castle, across from the main gate, and fell into a tired and uneasy sleep.

The next morning they were awakened by the sun, a bit of fog still creeping about but nowhere near the amount they had seen the previous day. Without breakfast they immediately cleared the main hall of corpses as Delain insisted they make their new camp 'for the living only'. After Jonathan and Sean completed this gruesome task, they began working on their plan to find and restore the cannon.

They retrieved the long iron rods Jonathan had found and moved to the first locked door, where all pried and pulled until the rusty lock was broken. Slowly they opened the heavy door allowing sunlight to spill inwards. There before them sat over one dozen cannon. All were old and dirty, and the iron wheels almost rusted into place.

"You were right, Jonathan! And at least a dozen or so!" said Sean excitedly.

"Now we need something to load them with!" said Jonathan.

In the next room, after repeating the prying and pulling, they found the armory. There were a few rifles and pistols and swords, ancient as they were, and of no use. However, what did interest them were the hundreds of cannon balls that were stacked neatly in pyramids, slightly rusty but still mostly round. Also, there were empty barrels that probably had at one time contained gun powder, along with a box of what remained of empty cartridges. Their stocking-like casings were tattered and almost fell apart when Delain simply touched them.

"These cartridges will be of no use," Jonathan said.

"Maybe we can find a way to make new ones," suggested Delain. "I will rummage through the sleeping rooms and look to obtain better cloth!"

As Delain ran off to search the areas by the lower hall, Jonathan and Sean selected one cannon close to the door, and using the long prying pole, set to loosening the wheels. They wedged the tip of one end of the bar under the back wheel and then with all their might, pushed the bar forward, moving the cannon a few inches with each thrust. It was hard work and they had to stop and rest every few minutes. At one point, Sean suggested pouring water on the rusted wheels, then banging them with the iron balls to unbind them, as his father had done to wagons on their farm.

Excitedly, they ran down to the landing area and retrieved a small barrel, then filled it with seawater. The boys took turns carrying it all the way to the top, splashing and sloshing the entire way. Though a good amount spilled as the bucket journeyed upward, enough remained for their use. Pouring it on the rusty wheels and banging them with an iron ball loosened the rust, and after much effort, they managed to move the cannon about fifty feet and into position.

Next, they gathered the spiked poles and brushes Jonathan had found and used them to clean out the cannon's barrel and the touch hole. All this work took most of the day, and by the time they had finished, the sun had set once again and the Castle of Fire glowed red.

"Boys!" called Delain from the stairway. "Please join me at the *Café de Fogo* for dinner?"

"Pardon?" said Jonathan, looking up from his work. He and Sean were sweaty and dirty, hands full of rust and grime. They had been working so hard they had forgotten about eating altogether.

"Supper!" Delain called, and motioned for them to join her below in the main hall. "I used that small stove you thoughtfully brought from the *Danielle,* Jonathan."

"It was a gift from Steward," he said. "I am glad it could be of use."

Upon entering the hall, the boys observed that they were not the only ones who had been busy. Delain had apparently been up and down the stone stairs numerous times, for many of their clothes, food and other goods were now present in the castle. The main room had been swept and most of the debris had been cleared out. The rope rigging from the camp below had been re-strung into two hammocks, one in each corner of the main hall. Delain had even traded her long dress for a pair of pants she had been given by Steward before they left the *Danielle*.

"More comfortable and less likely to get caught on things," she explained.

The most amazing change for the boys, however, was that in the center of the room, the table had been set for dinner. There was a lit torch in the corner and a blanket draped across the table. On the table in the center, Delain had set a half of a wooden crate, and inside it on a small cloth, was salted pork and hard tack from their stores. There were cups set about as well, each containing a golden liquid.

"Rum," Delain said as if reading their minds. "I know

we are quite young and not used to liquor, but honestly, it is all we have. Tomorrow we should look for a fresh source of water, but for now, *bon appetite, messieurs*!"

The three sat around the table in the center of the room and enjoyed each other's company.

"A hard day's work and a just reward!" said Sean as he bit a piece of the hard tack.

"All that is left is the construction of the cartridges and the cleaning of a few cannon balls. We should be able to test sometime tomorrow," said Jonathan.

"I get to light it. I have experience firing guns, you know," said Delain smiling. "It only makes sense."

All laughed and agreed that Miss Delain Dowdeswell would have the position of powder monkey and igniter.

After finishing dinner, it was decided that a good night's sleep had been well-earned and an early rising was in order. Before retiring, Jonathan and Sean double checked Delain's sleeping chamber to ensure the room was devoid of skeletons and vermin. She politely requested that the boys please leave her door open to listen for any strange noises, even though they would most likely be asleep. The boys jumped into their hammocks and Sean read from his book that he had somehow brought along, thinking if they were to be stranded, at least he would have something to read.

"I haven't heard you read in a long time, Sean," commented Jonathan as he lay down.

"We have been busy, Jonny boy. With a midshipman and a stowaway, duels, invading forts…well, I just haven't had the time. But as we are here," he said, thumbing through the pages, "I have decided upon the place in the story…where Merlin and Arthur find the Lady of the Lake. Hmm… 'So they rode till they came to a lake, the which was a fair water and broad, and in the midst of the lake Arthur was aware of an arm clothed in white samite, that held a fair sword in that hand.'"

"That is what we need," said Delain from her

chamber. "A lady in the water to signal the French ships to come to our precise point where we have the cannon aimed."

"Let us think on that," said Jonathan, and Sean continued the tale, until they all fell asleep.

* * * * * *

"Sails, sir! Sails!" came the call from the crow's nest.

Captain Walker ran to the poop immediately upon hearing that ships had been spotted. It had been almost three days since leaving Jonathan, Sean and Delain on Isla Sello, and they had finally found the prize, or so he hoped. Watt was at the wheel and even his stone-like countenance seemed to show some concern.

"Orders, Captain?" said Holtz, still standing at attention.

"Garvey!" the Captain called looking up at the crow's nest, "Details! And a count, if you please."

Garvey searched the horizon with his telescope as Harrison quickly reached the top and immediately took his glass and turned it on the approaching ships. After a moment, he spoke to Garvey and pointed to the enemy.

"Captain!" Harrison called, "It is hard to see. There are at least two frigates in the lead with possibly thirty-six guns, and well, at least four other vessels. I assume they are the merchants, however, I can not be positive unless we move closer."

"As long as we get them into the strait," said Walker, "we can easily take them. And if our greeting party has arrived, we should make quick work of the entire squadron. Bring us about, Mister Watt. Mister Holtz, hold a speed that puts us just ahead of them, out of their sight, until we near the straight. Then we spring our trap."

"Aye sir!" Holtz called, and after enlisting the services of Lane and Spears, the crew set about adding all sail, setting stays and as a caution and readying the guns.

As the *Danielle* turned and ran to the west, Harrison and Garvey kept a sharp eye on the French from the great height of the crow's nest. At first they could see several ships clearly, though once sail was set, stays tightened and the *Danielle* had completed her turn to the west, the enemy ships seemed to slip away, falling behind the *Danielle* and out of sight. They would alert the Captain and some sail was reduced, until they could just barely see the lead ship behind them.

"Hold this speed, Captain!" called Harrison, "We are just a wave to them sir, unless they can see better than I."

Walker laughed, as it was well known that Mister Harrison's eyesight was the sharpest in the fleet and his telescope was a device of exquisite make and quality. If he could barely see the enemy, it was almost certain that they could not see the *Danielle*.

"Thank you, Mister Harrison, we will," said the Captain. "Mister Watt, Mister Koonts. Mind our position and hold course for the Cape. Set and strike sail as necessary."

"Yes, sir," they both said.

The Captain retired to his cabin.

Up in the crow's nest, Garvey and Mister Harrison kept their scopes trained on the enemy behind, now and then losing them, only to suddenly be able to make them out between the waves. Their sails were the same color as the crashing whitecaps that were all about them, and the trick, as they both knew, was to watch for the white-tipped shapes that *didn't* fall.

"It's a dance of sorts," Garvey said as he peered into his borrowed scope. "We move in, we move out, we twirl and spin. Surely their smaller ships could move faster and catch us."

"Yes," said Harrison, "though they must stay together and therefore must travel as slow as the dullest ship in the squadron. Also, I do not believe they have even seen us. It's a wide ocean and we are quick to move out of their sight. We must be diligent, Garvey, and make sure to alert the Captain of any movements. Take a gander ahead and see if there are any other ships about. We wouldn't want to miss a friendly!"

"Or a not-so-friendly!" added Garvey, and they continued their watchful duty.

It was now the third evening the trio had spent on Isla Sello. Jonathan sat on the wheel of the first cannon they had resurrected from the armory. He and Sean had worked for a full two days repairing the cannon, assisting Delain in manufacturing powder cartridges, and cleaning over a dozen rusty cannon balls. They had rigged a few heavy timbers behind the cannon with sturdy wooden pegs that were driven into cracks in the stones that made up the floor, hoping the weapon would be held in place. It also took over two additional hours to haul a small gunpowder keg up the many steps; exhausting work, to say the least.

As he rested, he examined his hands. They were scraped, swollen and dirty; looking as if he still lived on the streets, digging through the alleys and backyards, searching for food and anything that could sustain his life. However, as he looked at his hands this cool evening on an island just off the southern tip of the African continent, he couldn't help but smile. *Amazing,* was all he could think. *How can one go from nothing to all the adventure I have had and see half of the world in the process? And what have these hands done in the last year or so? Learned to sword fight, fire a gun, tie a sailor's breastplate, cook spotted dick, salute, and now, repair cannon that have to be older than Steward and Captain Walker combined!*

Though it was only a single cannon, they had learned so much about the tools and processes for restoring these monstrous weapons. All agreed that they could repair two or three guns a day and maybe have several working by the end of the week.

After retrieving a powder cartridge from her *laboratory,* as Delain called the room where they filled the cloth tubes with explosive powder, she appeared with Sean and joined Jonathan atop the castle. They were ready to test the cannon.

"No use repairing all of them if we can't make this one work!" said Jonathan.

"And we must make sure," added Delain, "that these cartridges will satisfy. I gathered material from old sheets and bandages that I found. Sean helped me stuff them with powder, so I am sure they will work."

"These are larger guns, Jonny, so I used a *little extra* powder," Sean explained.

"He is an expert with explosives," said Jonathan smiling. "He actually damaged the *Danielle* once with a home-made bomb."

"I remember the tale," said Delain, "and though it didn't sink, it was crippled. Let's make sure this time we actually sink something."

"Then we will need a few of these," Sean said holding up a cannon ball that he had scraped and chiseled back to an almost perfectly round condition. "Let's give it a ride!"

The sun had set almost an hour ago, however, the sky to the west still showed a faint glow of purple. Stars winked to the east and above their heads, and the moon made an appearance in the southern sky as if to witness the firing of the cannon.

From their elevated position in the fort, they had seen the strait below and believed that Captain Walker would more than likely sail between the island and the mainland, leading the enemy frigates right past them.

"Let us aim in the center of the channel," Jonathan said, and Delain and Sean began to discuss in a lively manner how best to accomplish this.

"I believe it is pointed too high, Mister Flagon," Delain said. "On the *Fiero*, I was too high with my first attempt and certainly I can see that, here, we are in the same condition."

"With all due respect, Miss Dowdeswell," said Sean with a frown, "I have fired a few guns aboard the *Poseidon,* rest her timbers, and even the *Danielle*. I think we are perfectly directed at the center of the channel."

In the end, after a heated debate, Jonathan decided that the most important achievement would be to make sure the gun would fire without exploding into a thousand pieces and killing them all. As long as it worked, and the ball left the barrel with the velocity required to damage a hull of a ship at four hundred yards, it would be a success.

"Aiming can come later," he said, and moved the gun to an angle of approximately fifteen degrees, and rammed the cartridge and ball home. The cannon was surely longer than the guns aboard the *Danielle,* at least nine feet long, and by the weight of the ball, Jonathan assumed it was a twenty-four pounder. He cleared the touch hole.

"Miss Dowdeswell, if you would light the beast?"

"My pleasure!" she answered.

Jonathan lit a small torch they had prepared and handed the flame to Delain. He and Sean then moved to the left side of the cannon and covered their ears.

After a pause of a few seconds and a fast prayer, Delain set the torch to the cannon.

B-O-O-M! The blast was enormous, the noise truly deafening. As Jonathan held his ears, he saw the flame discharge from the huge gun with an amazing fury that lit up the entire center of the strait. The monster rocked backwards, yet the bracing held.

All three ran to the embrasure to see where the ball would land. To their surprise, the moon's glow had illuminated a white streak in the air as the disturbed moisture marked the path of the projectile. The trip ended after the ball travelled *all the way* across the water and slammed into the side of a cliff *on the main land,* over eight hundred yards away. They could barely see black rock exploding as the ball struck, sending dust and debris into the air. A second or two later, they heard a strong *BOOM - CRACK!* from the amazing force of the impact.

"Whooo!" said Sean laughing. "That went a bit too far!"

"Almost twice as far as needed!" added Jonathan.

"I do believe, Mister Flagon," said Delain, "that we have made the cartridges a bit too powerful, yes?"

The Cannon of the Castle of Fire

They all laughed, agreeing that maybe *a little less* gunpowder would do the trick well enough. With several cannons aimed just right, and a bit of practice they all looked forward to, the Castelo de Fogo, the Castle of Fire, would regain its namesake and could be a key element in the pending battle, if there was to be one.

Now that the first gun had been tested successfully and found to be more than satisfactory, the trio spent the next few days alternating between fixing and moving cannon and finding and preparing food. Jonathan had found the fishing line and hooks in their supplies and rigged a simple pole with an old broom handle he located in a small store room. After using a little salted pork as bait, he was more than triumphant fishing, pulling in six or seven snoek and avoiding their nasty bite to easily clean them for meals. Delain, using the small stove that Steward had given them, fried the fish nicely in some olive oil. Sean, when he was not cleaning and repairing cannons and balls, found a tarp in their supplies and had rigged it as a rain catch. Soon, they would have water, as it seemed that almost every night, it rained for at least a few minutes.

The main thrust of their effort had been the cannon, and they were proceeding nicely. Soon they had four additional guns ready and tested, and Jonathan had perfected the aiming. He knew that sailing ships would not be able to stop quickly one underway, and once they committed to a course, it would mean they continued in basically a straight line. Even hard course corrections would take a few moments to execute.

"If we can aim all the guns in the same spot," he reasoned, "and apply our firepower in a concentrated manner, we can do considerable damage. Since we only expect two frigates, we should have a good shot at disabling at least one."

"I am sure the *Danielle* will take care of the other!" Sean said laughing.

They continued working diligently and at the end of their first week, they had water, fresh fish, shelter, and eight twenty-four-pound cannon in the north wall embrasures, all aimed at the center of the channel, all within a few feet of the same target area. Every one of the eight cannon had been tested and a special routine was rehearsed that allowed them to reload and fire another series of eight if they had the chance. Of course, all the cannon would be loaded at the first sight of any sail. Then, after the first round, Jonathan would clean and dampen the cannons one by one, running down the line. Sean would follow, ramming cartridges, then Jonathan would come a second time and load a ball in each. It was to Delain's great delight that she was to clear the touch holes, and on Jonathan's command, light them as fast as she could.

As they stood, looking at their battery of cannons, Jonathan suddenly seemed worried. Sean noticed the change in his demeanor.

"What is it?"

"We need to create the signal, our Lady of the Lake, as we discussed."

"Yes," Delain said, "What can we do to make sure Captain Walker knows we are ready to fight and that he needs to bring the ship close to us? *I* am surely not going to tread water and wave him to my position!"

"I think I have an idea," said Jonathan. "Sean, get the hammers and nails. I will get the rope."

19
Point of No Return

Late the next afternoon aboard HMS *Danielle,* the sailing was swift and certainly easy for the crew to maintain. They had finally adjusted their speed so the enemy was just barely visible when the air was clear. On a few occasions, Captain Walker thought he had been spotted and that the French ships may slow down or spin off on a slightly different course to avoid a confrontation, but soon it would not matter. He was nearing the strait and was confident that he could engage them soon enough.

"Do you think," Koonts said, standing next to the Captain, "that any assistance has arrived?"

"I am not sure," said Walker as he gazed ahead.

Meanwhile on Isla Sello, two rafts had finally been completed. Jonathan, Sean and Delain had fashioned them from the lumber they had found in the storage rooms and from some of the larger barrels they had been given for supplies. They supplemented this by finding and using additional barrels they had in and around the fort. One of the rafts was about the size of the targets they regularly built and launched off the side of the *Danielle* for target practice. About twenty feet across and ten wide, the raft looked quite sea worthy and even had a tall mast of sorts, with a flag on top.

"Here is our Lady of the Lake!" said Delain happily. "Captain Walker will surely see it!"

"This flag will do the trick, Jonny Boy!" Sean said, laughing as he climbed aboard. "And I think it is *big enough* to be seen!"

"How rude, Mister Flagon!" said Delain. The bloomers were hers, of course; she had removed them the night before when the idea had been suggested by Jonathan.

"I was only kidding, my dear Miss Dowdeswell," Sean said as he tied Delain's bloomers to the pole aboard the larger raft.

The second raft was considerably smaller, about five feet by five feet, and Jonathan manned that one, complete with two paddles and a rope attaching it to Sean's raft.

"Let us make sure we stay aboard," Jonathan said. "I think those sharks we have been seeing are looking for a free meal and I'd rather not be it!"

"Do be careful," said Delain. "I can't fire all those cannon without you."

"We will, Delain," Jonathan said. "And thank you for the flag! It will do the trick."

"It is tested and true!" she added as the boys pushed off and paddled out into the channel.

The sea was a rough and still a sickly green. The boys had a difficult time, as the rafts seemed to want to float somewhat submerged, and move differently in different directions. More than once, just within the first few yards off shore, one or both of the rafts would pull the other to such an extent that they would almost capsize, causing water to rush over the low boards making up the decks.

"Lord!" cried Jonathan, "We must be careful, Sean."

"We have company, Jonathan," Sean said as a few shark fins broke the surface. The monsters swam by, looking, it seemed, right at the boys as they splashed and floundered in the water. More than once, Jonathan appeared to be sinking, and at one point a large grey-eyed shark actually swam up and placed its toothy head on deck, further tipping the raft. After a scream or two from Delain, who watched in horror from the shore, and a quick jab with the paddle from Jonathan, the shark retreated.

"This is not in any way enjoyable," Jonathan said.

However, after a few more tips and a few more paddle whacks to the trailing shark's noses, the boys settled down and worked together, both paddling at the same time.

After thirty minutes they had reached the center of the channel.

"Drop anchor, Sean!" Jonathan said.

Sean set his paddle down and pushed their make-shift anchor over the side, slowly feeding the rope into the water.

"I hope we have enough, Jonathan!" Sean called as the line slipped through his fingers.

"Proceed slowly, Sean. We don't want the anchor tipping you over!"

Luckily, and through some accurate guesses, they had figured that the channel couldn't be more than a dozen fathoms deep. They remembered that Captain Walker was somewhat worried about bringing the *Danielle* about the shallowness of the channel. He had anchored with little difficulty and though neither boy could remember how deep Watt had determined the bottom to be, they assumed that sixty feet was probably a decent approximation. The rope they had was just over one hundred feet, and finally, as Sean and Jonathan just thought it would run out, Sean felt the rope slacken in his hands.

"We've hit bottom!" Sean called happily, "And with a few fathom to spare to account for tides!" Quickly he tied off the rope on the cleat they had fashioned out of spare metal parts found in the castle. Jonathan maneuvered his raft closer to Sean by pulling easily and carefully on his rope.

But as Sean stepped from the target raft, he somehow ended up with one foot on each of the jostling crafts. He was for an instant, stranded between.

"Be careful, Sean!" cried Jonathan.

At that instant the boats pushed aside, as if some force from below was rising in an attempt to separate them. And indeed, it was true.

An enormous shark, its dark gray fin now cutting the surface of the water just to the side of the target raft, had wedged its gaping, toothy maw between the boats. This caused Sean to fall back to the target raft, his legs splashing in the water, inches from the great shark's mouth.

Horrified, Sean screamed as the cold murderous eyes of the beast glared at him. Raising its head to the edge of the raft, the brute began to chew as if Sean was already within the its grasp. To make matters worse, the behemoth began thrashing its fearsome head from side to side, further upsetting the raft. Sean kicked at the brute, trying to scramble away.

Jonathan grabbed one of the make shift paddles and began beating on the intruder's sides and head, but it was of no use. *What can we do?* he thought. *We need something with some* sting *to it! I should have brought my sword!* And then he had the answer.

"Your letter opener, Sean! Steward's knife!"

Sean had finally made his way to the pole atop the target raft as the shark continued to advance. He reached desperately to his leg, retrieved the blade from the leather sheath, and attacked the shark's snout repeatedly. After a moment, the shark retreated, nose bloodied, but still with an empty stomach.

After a brief rest and much encouragement from Jonathan and the nearly fear-paralyzed Delain, Sean cautiously made his way to Jonathan's raft. Quickly severing the ropes that held the two crafts together, the maneuvering became easier and they were able to make it safely back to the rock landing.

"I don't like small boats," was all Sean would say about the matter.

"Captain!" Garvey called from the crow's nest, "We have been seen! The lead French frigates have added sail and are heading straight toward us!"

"Captain," added Harrison, "there is another warship directly behind them. She is also adding sail!"

"How many guns?" shouted Walker, anxiously.

"Looks like our sister, Captain! I count over seventy!"

Walker took up his glass and looked back at the enemy. It took a full minute for his old eyes to see, but it was clear. Watt confirmed it: a French seventy-four with all sail and two frigates now racing ahead.

"I believe the seventy-four it is the *Bordeaux*, Captain," said Harrison as he appeared at their side and lowered his glass. "I am not sure of the two frigates. Can we make the channel before we run out of light?"

"I believe we will hit its center before the sun flashes out. We will still have some light for a half-an-hour or so," said the Captain. He ordered Watt to keep his course true and then ran to the bow, Harrison at his side. Both peered into their glasses as they searched ahead and prayed for some sign of British ships.

"I see no masts, Captain," Harrison said dejectedly from the bow of the *Danielle*. "I believe we are on our own."

Walker realized that if his lieutenant was right, they were alone in the battle against three ships with almost one-hundred and fifty guns. That would mean little chance of success. The *Dani* could add all sail, lighten the load by dumping some supplies and guns overboard to gain extra speed, however, they would still quickly be caught by the two frigates and delayed until the seventy-four could engage.

"We must decide soon, sir," said Harrison quietly.

Walker continued searching the enemy position and then the channel, looking for some sign of help. But as the sun set further, so did his hope of aid.

Exhausted, the party on Isla Sello climbed the stairs to the Castelo and sat down to a dinner of fresh fish, potatoes and some extra rum. They did not like the taste especially. The rum was used more to celebrate their success with re-igniting the cannons. The water was most welcome as well, even though warm. All three ate upon the parapets of the fort, looking out upon the world below as the sun began to set.

"The cannon may need some re-aiming," said Jonathan. "I think the raft may be a little out of place."

"From the landing," said Delain, "you seemed in perfect position. But let us see."

To the enjoyment of the boys, Delain, by herself, loaded a cartridge and a ball into the first cannon, cleared the hole, and set the torch. The shot roared out in a fiery *BOOM!* and landed about twenty feet to the west of the raft and a little beyond.

"Close enough!" the boys laughed and Delain sat back down after a brief curtsey and a smile.

"Captain!" called Garvey, "They are almost in range!"

And we are almost in the channel, though Walker. *Time to dance or flee.*

Just then, a thundering boom was heard. All on deck turned their heads to the bow. Searching, Garvey called out.

"Captain! Gun fire! From Isla Sello! I saw the flame! A single shot!"

"We saw it as well, Cap'n!" said Smith and Jones, who were on the port side near the bow.

"Jonathan!" exclaimed Harrison.

"He has guns, at least one!" said Walker. "That does it! We will delay our plan to run until we see what Jonathan has up his sleeve. Ready the guns!" he shouted. "Clear for action!"

Back on Isla Sello, the shore party was almost finished with their meal. It had satisfied them and they relaxed for a moment. Before long, Sean stood, took his plate with him and headed down to the lower levels of the Castle. "I will find Stewie and if he is not too full on mice and the occasional booby, I will see if he would enjoy this last bit of fish!" He winked at Jonathan and left. Now and again, he let out a little whistle and a call for the cat.

"If I wasn't so worried," said Delain as she sat down on the wall next to Jonathan, "I could enjoy the view. I have to say, I have gotten a bit more than I bargained for."

"As have I," said Jonathan. "Captain Walker had told

me once that sometimes, missions and assignments are actually quite boring, but I have not seen a dull minute. Ever."

"How London will ever hold your interest again, I wonder," said Delain.

Jonathan smiled a bit and blushed. "I think with my father, whom I miss terribly, Miss Thompson, and now the Ladies Dowdeswell in town, London might be as interesting and even as dangerous as my life at sea!"

"So your life is at sea, Mister Moore?" Delain asked with a comical and over exaggerated frown.

"Now, Miss Dowdeswell," Jonathan said, faking a huffy voice and a proper tone, "I believe a man can serve his interests on the waves and on land if all understand his purposes."

"And am I one of the interests on land?" she asked.

Jonathan again felt as if Delain was asking him something more, and in the setting light and the soft breeze, she looked beautiful and sweet. He admitted to himself that he had been thinking of her and even of what a future together would be like. Yes, he had much to do and accomplish, and he needed to learn more about the world and his place in it, but maybe they could learn together. And certainly nothing had to be settled right here, right now, on Isla Sello.

"You are the best reason I can think to ever come ashore, Miss Dowdeswell," Jonathan said, and once again he thought that a simple kiss might be welcome. And as he stared into her darting eyes, he saw her smile fade and her face become alive with surprise… and alarm.

"Mister Moore!" she cried.

"I- I am sorry, Delain," he said, suddenly concerned that he had somehow upset her. "I meant to take no liberty at all -"

"A sail! A sail!" she cried!

"Oh!" cried Jonathan as he stood and turned to the entrance to the channel. Quickly he took up his telescope and looked into the fading light. "Oh dear!" he yelled,

"Sean! Sean! It is the *Danielle*! And the small frigates we expected have been joined by a seventy-four to boot!"

"A seventy-four?" said Sean as he ran to join. "Kozak said there were only…"

"He's a liar!" said Jonathan. "I never liked him!"

Aboard HMS *Danielle,* Lieutenant Harrison spoke quickly to Spears and Lane as they came on deck for duty.

"Spears, take the lower deck, Lane, you have the upper. I am not sure if those thirty-six gun frigates will catch us, but you had best be prepared. Open the ports immediately!"

"Yes sir," both midshipmen said as they ran off to their duty. It seemed that Lane was excited and almost happy to take control of the guns, however, Harrison believed Spears was distracted, and though he looked into Harrison's eye, he seemed to be in deep thought, miles away.

"Anything on your mind, Midshipman Spears?" Harrison asked.

After a mumble or two, Spears simply replied "Eager to do battle, sir, that is all."

"Well then, do your duty," said Harrison, "and we may all live see another day."

With that, Spears tipped his hat and moved on.

He did indeed have a few things on his mind. Though he knew it dangerous to neglect his duty, he realized that after maybe a volley or two, he could abandon his post unnoticed and use the key in his pocket to release Kozak from the brig. In the confusion of battle, he may not be seen. As he ran to the upper gun deck, he sought out Smith and Jones as he pretended to check each gun crew for readiness. As he approached gun twenty, the *Banger*, Smith and Jones were rolling her into position. They were very experienced and had their weapon ready before the others, as usual.

"Smith! Jones!" Spears called.

"Aye sir!" they replied in unison.

"A special assignment. The smaller jolly boat needs to be slid into position over the side. Do not lower it, just secure with side lashings and remove the tarp."

"Yes, sir, though strange isn't it?" asked Smith.

"Is the Captain going to send someone off before the battle, like he did Jonathan and Sean and Miss Dowdeswell?"

Spears picked up on their concern right away and used it to his advantage.

"Not that the orders of an officer are presented for your approval," he snapped, "However, I am assuming that Captain Walker may wish to retrieve Jonathan and his party as soon as possible should the opportunity arise. Positioning the smaller jollyboat for that purpose would be thoughtful, yes?"

"Actually," said Smith, "It makes perfect sense."

"And we meant no disrespect, sir," added Jones.

Spears smiled. "No offense was meant or taken. Please attend to the boat immediately and return to your posts."

"Aye, sir!" they said and ran up the nearest ladder.

Below deck in the dim and gloomy brig, Kozak heard the scurrying and call to battle stations clearly. He quickly moved to the edge of his cell and looked up. Through the crack in the floor by the door he could usually see some daylight, however, none could now been seen. *It must have been several hours since my meager lunch,* he thought. *Good, then night is falling! So much the better to conceal our movements. It now comes down to the final test of Midshipman Spears. If he has the key to my cell and has prepared the jollyboat, then all we need do is slip away. I must be ready, but then again, I have nothing to prepare but my wits.*

On deck, Captain Walker barked commands to adjust sail and rigging, then ran to the bow one last time. Harrison joined him and gave a report.

"Guns are at the ready Captain," he said. "We are

cleared for action."

"Good," replied Walker nervously.

"However," Harrison added, "we have spotted two French forty-fours. They are far behind the *Bordeaux* and the two small frigates, and are in full sail. I believe they are heading to the south of Isla Sello."

"Two forty-fours speeding past the island?" exclaimed Koonts. "They mean to block our escape to the west and bottle us in! Captain, we will be between them!"

"I am sure of it," said Walker. "Blast! Whatever Mister Moore has in mind, it had better be effective. With the addition of these forty-fours, a fight may be out of the question. Ideas, gentlemen, and be quick about it!"

"We could try to beat the forty-fours coming around the island and escape north," suggested Gorman.

"The smaller thirty-sixes will meet us within ten minutes, I presume," said Harrison. "Jonathan may slow them if he has more than one cannon."

"If he can hit them," said Walker. "He is a marvel, however, that is a difficult shot to make even for an experienced hand. If he misses, the thirty-sixes will eventually catch us and delay us long enough for the *Bordeaux* and her seventy-four guns to engage. Mister Koonts? Your advice?"

"Run like the wind and avoid battle," said Koonts. "Toss cannon and supplies overboard to lighten our load. We may be lucky and cripple the two thirty-sixes if they come alongside us. We then may have enough time to head north and seek aid before the forty-fours catch us."

Mister Holtz returned and reported that all possible sail was out and that he, too had seen the appearance of the two forty-fours. He was quickly informed of the possibility of guns in the castle.

"Interesting," was all he said.

"We can not turn back to fight, that is clear," Walker said to himself, though all heard.

"True," said Holtz, then, as usual, he said nothing.

"For the love of God, man!" Walker bellowed, "Stop

doing that! If you take in a breath, you had better expel it and announce a viable solution! I have been tolerating your idiotic intrusions, all of which have no merit or intellectual thought! So pipe down or speak up!"

This explosion took all by surprise, as in the heat of battle, Walker had never lost his temper. However, this was a different situation entirely. The Captain rarely bet on luck and he was now on the losing end of his wager. He had hoped that some aid would arrive in time and now he realized that all hope was dashed. He was soon to be surrounded by over one-hundred and forty guns to his rear and eighty-eight directly ahead, with no possible maneuvering room.

Holtz stood at attention and at first seemed unnerved by the Captain's outburst, then he thawed.

"Of course Captain," he replied, and just when it looked as if he was about to clam up once again, he took a deep breath and spoke.

"Doing the math, sir, it would seem that we have a good chance against the two forty-fours coming around the back of the island," he said. "I favor some limited aggressiveness. If I were captain, I would head directly at the pair of forty-fours at best possible speed, trying to split right between them and give them both sides as I pass, pouring all shot into their stern quarters to damage steering. *If* we are lucky, they will be out of action as we sail past."

"That leaves us against the *Bordeaux* that we can easily outrun and the pair of thirty-sixes which we can not," said Koonts.

"After we cripple the forty-fours," continued Holtz, "We do as Mister Koonts suggests and get the dickens out of here. If Jonathan has something prepared… it may just slow the thirty-sixes enough for us to escape; not north along the coast, but out to sea. We head into the night and we extinguish all lights. We become lost in the dark. Sir."

Walker, astounded at the frankness and ingenuity of the plan, couldn't speak for a moment. All the officers nodded in approval. Finally, the Captain smiled.

"Mister Watt? Execute Mister Holtz's plan. Have the gun crews ready, Mister Harrison."

"Captain!" called Garvey from the crow's nest. "Something in the distance, in the center of the strait!"

"A British ship?" called Walker, hopefully. He put his glass to his eye and tried to focus quickly. He noticed a shape bobbing erratically in the water, he was sure of it. But if a ship, it was certainly a small one.

"A raft!" said Harrison, looking in his glass. "What is a raft doing in the inner channel?"

"And sir," said Holtz as he joined in the gazing, "I believe there is a flag on it. It's…ladies bloomers! Again!"

Walker could now see it clearly. Just like the flag hoisted on the *Fiero* so many weeks ago, the small target raft had a pair of ladies bloomers as a flag.

"The same bloomers as before!" Holtz said. "Whatever does that mean?"

"Why would someone do this?" asked Koonts.

"Not just someone," Walker said, lowering his glass with a smile, "Jonathan Moore. He is trying to tell us something."

Harrison scratched his head and thought hard. *Why would Jonathan set a target raft in the middle of the channel?* The bloomers surely stated that the raft was there on purpose, by Jonathan's doing, and certainly with the cooperation of Miss Dowdeswell.

"The thirty-sixes are in range, Captain!" Steward called from the stern rail. "The one coming to starboard is the *Petit Chaton*, the other is the *Bleu Fille.* Just thought ya would like to know!"

Walker glanced astern. There was the pair of small frigates gaining fast. Behind them in the distance, the *Bordeaux* sailed onward.

"I've got it!" said Harrison, "It is a target raft! A target!"

Walker paused, then realized what Jonathan had done. The bloomers were his signature. He had used them on the *Fiero* at the suggestion of Mister Tupper. The raft was set in position on purpose, and a target raft was clearly just that: a target.

Walker turned his eyes and glass to the island. After adjusting his scope and running it to the topmost peak, he saw the Castelo de Fogo, its parapets now a glowing reddish-orange in the setting sun. Moving aside, he spotted three figures leaping up and down as they looked over the embrasures; the embrasures bristling with several cannon pointing almost directly at the raft. Walker smiled and joy rose within him.

"I think Mister Moore is directing traffic in the strait!" he said. "Mister Watt, on my command, we will temporarily turn hard to starboard toward the target raft and fire any guns that can bear on those thirty-sixes! Then we will turn to port after leading the French to the killing zone. Once in position, we will split the frigates as Mister Holtz suggests."

"When our starboard side fires on the thirty-sixes," said Holtz, "they will have to re-load quickly, in less than a minute, if they are to rake the forty-fours!"

"Then get down there and drive those devils!" screamed the Captain and both lieutenants rushed to command the crews.

The *Danielle* executed a slight turn to starboard, toward the raft, and fired several rounds from the rear most guns. Light damage was done to the *Petit Chaton*, who returned a bow chaser to no effect. The *Dani* then went straight at the bloomered raft.

As the Captain looked to the island and to the target, Smith and Jones skillfully moved the jollyboat from its resting position and secured it over the starboard side. Looking for Midshipman Spears and not finding him, they returned to their gun.

* * * * * *

"We are committed!" called Walker. "Steady, Mister

Watt, Steady!"

A crash was heard as the *Danielle* rammed the small target raft, sending spars and barrels into pieces, some tossed wildly into the air, most splintering and falling into the dark water. Steward looked over the side and saw the bloomers sinking into the waves amidst the debris of lumber and rope.

"Now, ya don't see that every day," he said to himself.

At the Castelo de Fogo, Jonathan took up his glass and stared at the remains of the raft. The *Danielle* rushed past, then headed straight on.

The *Petit Chaton* and *Bleu Fille* continued west, sailing in line. Within a moment the *Chaton* had reached the exact spot where the target raft once floated. Jonathan paused for a second, lowered his scope and yelled aloud.

"Fogo!"

"Pardon me?" asked Delain.

"Fire!" Jonathan yelled.

"Oh!" she said. "By all means!"

Delain set the torch to the first cannon. It exploded with a bellowing roar, flame lighting up the twilight. She did not stop to look. She ran to the second and third cannon. *BOOM! BOOM!* the monsters snarled, *BOOM! BOOM! BOOM! BOOM! BOOM!* as each gun discharged in a powerful fury.

Captain Walker turned to watch as ball after ball blasted from the castle into the sails and decks of first the *Petit Chaton* and then the *Bleu Fille*. The force was amazing, certainly more powerful than he thought could come from such old cannon. Rigging of the two small frigates was torn, the masts shattered, main sails ripped and spars rained down upon the deck. At least two monstrous holes appeared in the starboard side of the *Petit Chaton*. A fire erupted as the last shot ignited at least one keg of powder aboard the *Bleu Fille*. The French ships began to spin crazily in the water and were now heading almost backwards, to the east.

"Again, Mister Moore comes through!" Walker called and the crew erupted in cheer.

"Hard to port, Mister Watt! Run hard to the south! We will surprise those forty-fours as they clear the island! Ram them if you must to split them apart!" Walker ran to the aft hatch and yelled to the gun crews as loud as a hurricane:

"Aim for their sterns and rudders, men! Hold fire until you have a clear shot!"

The *Danielle* responded quickly as Watt turned the great wheel, the ship heading almost directly south to engage the enemy.

Jonathan watched as the action unfolded. He and Sean had reloaded their cannons and Delain stood ready to ignite another barrage. He could see the two small thirty-sixes, damaged and almost colliding as their westward motion halted and the current quickly pushed them eastward, back the way they had come.

"They are drifting into our line of fire once again! Prepare to fire, Miss Dowdeswell! Sean, lower the cannon by five degrees! I will assist!"

He quickly ran and adjusted the farthest guns as Sean worked hard on the first in line. They met in the middle in less than thirty seconds.

"How do we look, Delain?" Sean said.

"Let us see!" she exclaimed, and ran down the line, igniting each cannon once again.

Two shots sailed high, into the sails and did little damage, however, the last six from the fort struck hard on the stern of the *Petit Chaton* and into the bow of the *Bleu Fille* directly at her water line. A gaping hole at least twenty feet wide appeared under the figurehead. All knew that both ships were headed for the bottom.

The *Bordeaux* after seeing the destruction of the small frigates, quickly adjusted course and followed the forty-fours to the south of Isla Sello.

"What is this?" screamed Jonathan as he looked through his telescope, "There are two forty-fours coming around our island!"

"They will be after the *Danielle!*" Sean added, "She is still greatly outnumbered!"

"What will Captain Walker do?" asked Delain.

Jonathan thought for a moment, wondering what options were available. Walker could continue on and fight, his single ship against three, or he could run to the north and put distance between himself and the enemies. But running was not something Captain Walker would do.

"I believe he means to engage, as he is heading right at them. He will most likely then head due north, to meet with whatever aid is on the way," he finally said.

"He is leaving us?" asked Delain, shocked.

"Unless he is sunk," said Jonathan as he lowered his glass. "Then we are left just the same."

Their hearts raced as they ran to the far side of the fort to watch their friends and their ship engage with the frigates. They couldn't help but be worried, as the *Danielle* was still outgunned over two to one.

Aboard the *Danielle*, Captain Walker and the officers took a few seconds to watch the small thirty-six gun frigates disappear below the dark waves.

"Bravo, Mister Moore!" Harrison said.

"Now on to the newest pair!" called Walker. He had prepared his crew, had positioned the ship as best as he could, and had instructed Watt to try to sail between the two frigates so he could give them both sides. Of course, as he sailed through them, they would also turn their sides to him, bringing as much damaging power to bear as they could.

On the parapets of the Castelo, Jonathan raised his telescope to get a better view of the battle below. The *Danielle* successfully split between the two frigates directly before her, then all three ships fired simultaneously. Ball went forth splintering masts and men, marines were firing from the tops, sail was ripped and rigging torn. The entire scene was soon half-hidden with smoke, though through the haze, the two frigates emerged.

"The French are badly damaged, barely able to steer. They are out of it for a while!" Jonathan said.

"And the *Dani*?" asked Sean.

"She is hurt, but still sailing and steering! She is … heading out to sea."

"Oh," said Delain.

In the brig, Walter Kozak waited impatiently. He wondered if Spears had decided against the plan and was instead attending to his duties. Or possibly he had become injured during the last volley. It was hard to tell from his position aboard the ship how much damage the *Danielle* had received. He felt the ship shudder and could hear the calls of men suffering above decks. Just as he had resigned himself to either dying here aboard a sinking ship, or hanging from the gallows in a London executioner's square, the door above opened. Light from a nearby fire streamed in. Legs descended the ladder. It was Spears.

"My boy! I knew you would come!"

Spears quickly inserted his key in the lock, pulled on the base, and removed the restraint from the door. Swinging it open he looked at Kozak and smiled.

"I am throwing in with you now, Kozak. I can not look back. It is my decision."

"And I will honor it," said Kozak as he reached to shake the boy's hand. "Is the boat ready?"

"If it is not destroyed, yes," said Spears. "It is now dark enough and the Captain is busy. There is a little more than he bargained for. A French seventy-four has appeared and a few extra frigates as well."

"Then we best hurry before all the sea is filled with obstacles!" said Kozak, and he followed Spears to the top deck and hid behind a fallen spar until the coast was clear.

"Damage report!" called Walker as Harrison and Holtz approached. They seemed in one piece, yet Holtz limped a little.

"Sails are in decent working order, Captain," said Holtz. "Though the foremast and spanker have issues. They are both unusable. Some other sail is torn, but all the men are still in position. We have lost a few guns on each side. They gave us a good licking, sir, but we can at least steer."

"Both forty-fours are injured, Captain," said Harrison. "Our gunners blasted both sterns with excellent effect! They are out of it for the time being."

"Captain!" came a voice from the tops. "Two more sails to the east at the mouth of the strait!"

All looked off the stern. Barely visible in the waning light, the shape of a pair of ships could be seen.

"Good God!" Walker cried. "Will this never end? Curse that pirate Kozak! Two frigates, he said! Of course the manifest would not list all the strength of the protecting force! If we make it through this alive, I will hang him myself!"

"They must have been guarding the rear of the merchants," said Koonts. "They have been called up!"

"Both are forty guns at least!" called Garvey from the top. "They are in full sail and moving fast!"

The French had held this last card for the final round and now Walker realized that he was still between a rock and a hard place. There were now two fast frigates and a seventy-four to deal with. It was only a matter of time before the forty-fours they had split and damaged would return to action. Options and light faded quickly. His only hope was to disappear in the darkness, but the approaching forty-fours had a bead on him, and it was only a matter of time before he was surrounded. *Must I strike colors? Surrender?* he thought.

"We will be surrounded in a few moments, Captain," said Koontz weakly. "We have taken more damage by splitting the forty-fours than we expected. I beg you,

William. It is time to strike colors. We have lost."

Walker knew that it was now undeniable. They had been trapped by a superior force. He could take on one, maybe two of these enemies, but not all five. And at what cost?

The newest forty-fours did not go unnoticed by the shore party in the Castelo de Fogo.

"Jonathan!" Sean called. "Two new ships! In the strait!"

"They obviously do not know about us! They must have missed our sinking the two small frigates!"

"And it is too dark to see the surviving men and flotsam in the water!" added Sean.

"What are we waiting for?" called Delain, who was already running back to the cannon. "The Castle of Fire has one last punch to throw!"

"Or maybe eight punches to throw!" said Sean as he ran after her.

Within minutes they had re-aimed the cannon and stood at the ready. Jonathan gazed into the failing light. In the center of the strait he could see the tip of a mast breaking the water, certainly from one of the frigates that had been sunk. He moved his 'scope wider. There were the two new forty-fours, heading directly toward the wreck, right where the target raft once floated.

"Steady!" said Jonathan. "Steady…"

"If we were any steadier, we'd be statues!" said Sean.

"Fogo!" Jonathan called.

Once more the Castle of Fire erupted with eight deadly shots. Flame belched forward and the sound was like thunder, echoing booms and cracks across the waves. For a moment, the French aboard the two new forty-fours looked up at the Castle and thought it was on fire, spewing lightning toward them.

As dark as it was, Jonathan, Sean and Delain could see that at least a few masts were hit aboard one of the enemy ships, however, little damage was done.

On the *Danielle*, Walker and Koonts stood at the wheel by Mister Watt and tried desperately to invent a solution. It was soon apparent that with the introduction of the last two French ships, it was hopeless. "It is suicide," Koonts added. "Mister Moore has done all he can. Our luck has finally run out."

"Very well," said Walker almost breaking down, unable to accept the hard pill of defeat. "Harrison, please strike our-"

Suddenly, Garvey called again from the tops: "Captain! Sails! Directly astern! To the north!"

Walker ran hastily to the stern, out pacing his much younger lieutenants, and turned his glass to the north along the coast of the continent. The light was almost all gone. A rising moon was now clearly visible in the low sky. And there, in a mist that rolled across the cool sea, he saw masts. At least six, possibly seven, then more.

The other officers joined him at the bow and soon, they saw the ships as well.

"Good Lord! I hope there is a Union Jack on the top," said Holtz.

As the ships came closer, there could be seen one, then two, then many colors gently waving in the breeze. And in an instant, Walker caught a clear sight of the first ship's colors as its flag unfurled: a red Saint George's Cross on a white field with the Union Jack in the upper canton. The flag of the Royal British Navy.

"Our sisters!" cried Harrison.

"The first is…the *Trident!*" said Holtz.

"Langley, bless his heart!" exclaimed Watt.

All turned and marveled at the outburst.

"He speaks!" blurted Harrison.

"And I thought, quite honestly, that he was mute!" exclaimed Holtz.

"Captain!" came Garvey's voice from above, "I see the

Proteus, the *Erinyes* and the *Drake*, heading toward us! And two fast brig-rigged sloops, breaking from behind the pack, heading… for the French seventy-four!"

"I think," Steward said to Harrison, "That your girlfriend 'as arrived and is about ta need some rescuin'!"

"Pardon?" said Harrison. "My girlfriend?"

"The sloops are the *Echo* and… the *Periwinkle!*" called Garvey. "Look at them fly, sir!"

"Oh dear!" shouted Harrison as he stared through his telescope at the racing *Paladin*, her crew visible on deck at her eighteen guns. "She will be cut to ribbons!"

"Turn us hard to assist the young ladies, Mister Watt!" called the Captain with renewed energy and determination. "I believe Mister Langley and company will take care of the four frigates."

Watt muscled the great ship to port and cut deftly before the two British sloops, who immediately cheered as they recognized their sister ship. Together, HMS *Danielle*, escorted by HMS *Echo* and the famous HMS *Paladin*, pursued the now panicked French seventy-four *Boredeaux*.

What was not seen by any of the officers of the *Danielle*, or by the shore party on Isla Sello, was the lowering of the jolly boat, the expert dive into the water performed by Midshipman Wayne Spears and the completely ungraceful flop performed by Walter Kozak. Spears had crept with the pirate along the deck, and amidst the confusion and noise, he chopped both ropes holding the small craft, watching it fall to the water below. Next, he shoved Kozak overboard, then performed his dive. Both men swan madly to the boat and scrambled inside. They raised the small mast and sail and as a fair wind caught them, it pushed the two escapees steadily toward the coast of the continent. Within a minute, they had disappeared into the night.

Aboard HMS *Trident*, Captain Langley stared into his telescope and looked hard at the deck of the *Danielle*. His second in command, Lieutenant Joshua Gray, stood ramrod straight by his side, awaiting orders.

"Odd," said Langley. "I know that to be HMS *Doggard,* as it was renamed. I see William Walker aboard. However, the plaque reads the original name, HMS *Danielle*."

"Are we to engage, Captain Langley?" Gray asked as he took up his glass and surveyed the positions of the many ships now in play.

"In a moment, Lieutenant," Langley said. "I have been sailing with Captain Walker for many a year and as I owe much of my present position and fortune to him, it is only polite that I should allow him to choose his quarry first. Ah, there he goes! He has chosen the seventy-four! The *Bordeaux,* I believe it is. Well, it won't be for long."

"He is preparing to fire, sir!" said Gray.

"I see," said Langley as he lowered his glass and watched as the *Danielle* closed alongside of the *Bordeaux* and loosed a blistering broadside of over thirty guns. The two British sloops also poured a broadside each into the sails of the French seventy-four. As the smoke cleared, Langley saw the French ship strike her colors, surrendering by taking down her flag.

"Mister Gray, signal the *Drake* to engage the two damaged frigates directly ahead," commanded Langley. "I am sure the *Dani* and the two sloops will assist. We will take on the two forty-fours emerging from the strait, with the help of the *Erinyes* and the *Proteus.*

"That is if they don't run away, sir," replied Gray. "It looks as if they are trying to come about."

"Add sail! Ready both sides!" called Langley, "Let's give them what for!"

The battle that raged on that early evening was witnessed in absolute splendor from the fort on Isla Sello. At first, it was difficult to see, but Jonathan, Sean and Delain took turns with the telescope. As guns were ignited, they trained their gaze on the ships, being lit for brief moments by the belching fire as it roared from each gun. Jonathan was near tears of joy as he watched his friend, Captain Langley, and the crew of the *Trident*, come to the rescue of the *Danielle*. Sean cheered as the Englishmen and their wonderful ships battled on until one by one, the French ships struck their colors. The loudest cheer was for the *Drake*, as she put on all sail, ran past the *Proteus* and the *Erinyes*, and engaged the first of the damaged forty-fours, now seen as the *Avignon*, destroying her main mast and damaging the foremast severely. She sailed onward and headed for the merchant ships that were now approaching to the south of the island. Seeing the mayhem ensuing in the strait, changing course, the merchants were attempting to come about and flee.

"I wonder," said Sean as he watched. "Which of the merchant ships has the cannon and which has the generals?"

"Mister Holtz!" called Walker. "You are senior Lieutenant. Take the large jollyboat with Steward and a handful of stout men and marines and take command of the *Bordeaux*. We will stay alongside and pour our starboard guns into the damaged frigate drifting by the island."

"Yes sir!" he said, and happily ran to gather his boarding party.

Harrison stood at attention, but was certainly put aback as he was almost sure he would receive the honor of commanding the captured vessel. It was true that Holtz was a senior officer, yet, not by more than a few weeks, and it was Harrison who had previously sailed with Captain Walker, and that should count for something.

As if being able to read the youngster's mind, Walker turned to Harrison and smiled.

"Don't fret so, Thomas," the Captain said. "There will be at least one or two more before the evening is done. Have the men prepare the guns for another engagement. Have Spears and Lane attend to it. Command the men in the tops. Mister Watt, after we engage the damaged frigate, let us come about to the east and finish the damaged forty-fours!"

"I wonder," said Harrison. "Which ship has the generals aboard?"

"That is easy," said the Captain, smiling. "It is the one that is running away the fastest."

"Then it has my name on it, sir!" laughed Harrison.

As they sailed on, the *Paladin* and the *Echo* came astern of the *Danielle* and all men on the decks of all ships cheered aloud. The two smaller ships, beautiful in the moonlit night with their large white sails and combined thirty-six golden guns, raced onward, passing the *Danielle* as if she were standing still. They moved swiftly to engage the almost gun-less, defenseless merchant ships with the *Drake* momentarily in the lead, before their quarry disappeared in the darkness.

20
The New Marine

As predicted, there were enough French ships captured that night for Harrison to become a captain once again and for certainly more than the few hours he commanded the *Fiero*.

Though the going was difficult due to the darkness and expanse of the ocean, the merchant ships, in their haste, forgot to extinguish all the lanterns on deck until it was too late. The *Echo* followed one such light and was rewarded with capture of the French merchant *Orléans* after only a few shots across her bow.

Also that evening, Captain Langley commanding the *Trident*, along with the *Proteus* and *Erinyes* had made quick work of the two forty-fours in the strait and only one, having been severely damaged by the *Proteus*, had to be scuttled, sunk on purpose, as she was not fit to sail. The *Trident* and the *Erinyes* then moved on to the two drifting frigates that had been hammered by the *Drake*, the *Paladin*, the *Echo* and finally by the *Danielle*. Both French ships struck colors immediately.

"We will run out of lieutenants soon," said Langley. "Who will captain these French prizes?"

"I am willing and available, sir," said Lieutenant Gray.

The *Paladin* had a more difficult time. She had found the large French merchant *Rodez*, however she failed to surrender, and after a long barrage from *Paladin*, circling the near defenseless merchant, she was sunk quickly and went fast to the bottom, no doubt filled with heavy cannon.

It wasn't until the early morning of the next day, after zigzagging in the night, that the waking beams of sunlight illuminated the sails of a four-masted merchant, the *Saint*

Annie. As Walker moved to engage, he could see military men, French Generals as it turned out, scrambling for cover on deck. He fired a starboard broadside into their sails and the French merchant captain immediately struck colors. As promised, it was Harrison that received the new command, escorted by Gorman and a detachment of all the remaining marines to guard the unruly French generals. Some insisted on fighting a bit, just to make a good show of it, though Hudson and Hicks, along with their friends, quickly disarmed the few who resisted, and Harrison took command of the *Annie* with dignity after the formal surrender. In a quick survey, they had counted over two-hundred cannon below decks and almost the same number of French generals and high-ranking officers.

"Such a beautiful ship, the *Annie* is," Harrison commented. "She will bring an admirable price as many will desire to own such a smart looking barky!"

It was at approximately nine bells after dawn that HMS *Trident,* with a captured French merchant in tow, rendezvoused with HMS *Danielle,* just a few miles south east of Isla Sello. After a call from captain to captain, Langley was invited aboard the *Danielle* for breakfast, and within minutes, he was seated at his familiar spot to the right of his mentor, Captain Sir William Walker.

"Interesting," said Langley as he sampled the toasted cheese-bread and scrambled eggs immediately after Claise had placed them on the already crowded table. "The entire time I was your first lieutenant," Langley continued, "I never took command of a captured vessel. Today, after four French frigates have been taken and a handful of merchants to boot, I still have never commanded a captured ship!"

The two captains, along with Koontz, laughed heartily.

"Some things never change," said Walker as he reached for his coffee.

"And gladly, some do," said Langley. "I see that the

name of the ship is back to the *Danielle,* as the plaque now reads the original name. I could have sworn I saw the idiotic name, the *Doggard,* affixed as we warped out of London. Was the name changed back?"

"This breakfast is exquisite, I must say!" said the Captain quickly, ignoring the comment.

"Yes," said Langley with a laugh, figuring out that Walker knew *exactly* what had happened to the plaque, however, he did not want it known to others. "I understand Steward is captain of the Lyon. Who is responsible for such an outstanding meal?"

"That would be myself, Captain Langley, thank you," Claise said somewhat nervously as he set down a platter of custard filled puffs. "It is nice to have you aboard again."

"Though we are all spread far and wide, we will soon be reunited once again," said Koontz. "We are en route to collect Midshipman Moore, Sean Flagon and Miss Delain Dowdeswell. "

Langley was aghast.

"*Miss* did you say?" Langley blurted, almost spitting out his coffee. "Dowdeswell? As in *Governor* Dowdeswell's daughter of Nassau?"

"It is a long story and we will all have to recount the tale for you at a later time, possibly over dinner if you can attend."

"Since the *Trident* received no damage in the dancing last night," Langley said, "I will gladly appear. I would not miss any tale involving Jonathan Moore and the trickster Sean Flagon. Not even for a chance to captain a captured French frigate!"

"Then assist us in collecting him on Isla Sello," said Walker. "I am sure he will be glad to see you."

"Ah, I think I know a little of the tale already. As we closed in on the strait, I saw cannon fire from above the horizon. The light was fading; however, I could ascertain that the barrage came from the old fort on the island."

"That was Jonathan Moore's surprise, and to be honest," said Walker, "I do not know all the detail, but we will soon hear all sides."

With that, a knock came at the door and Midshipman Lane appeared. He marched in after being welcomed and stood at attention, staring out the rear window of the Captain's cabin.

"Report, Mister Lane," said the Captain, retaining his good mood.

"Yes sir, I...ah...the ship is in excellent shape considering," he stammered. "A-and repairs are p-proceeding nicely on the d-damaged m-masts and rigging."

Walker looked up from his plates and quizzically stared at Lane for a moment before speaking.

"Midshipman Lane? Is there a problem?"

Lane looked like he was about to either be sick or cry. The Captain wanted nothing of either.

"Speak up, boy!" he snapped.

"It's Midshipman Spears, sir."

"What of him?" asked the Captain, now concerned.

"Ah...he...is missing, sir."

Walker stood immediately and wiped his chin of some stubborn egg and coffee.

"Could he have been lost during the battle? Blown overboard?" asked Koonts, also standing.

"Can't be sure, sir," answered Lane, "But...oddly... his gear is missing. His sword and telescope. A few blankets."

"Lord," said Walker.

"Also, sir," continued Lane, "Two other things are also missing."

"And what would they be?" said Walker, now irritated and getting angrier by the moment. It was obvious that a dead midshipman doesn't run to his locker, take his valuables, and then jump ship. Something was unsavory here. "What else is missing?"

"The small jollyboat, sir," said Lane, taking a deep breath. "And the pirate, Kozak."

On all three decks of the *Danielle*, and in the tops high

above the busy sea, all hands heard the roar of the dragon.

By noon, a longboat from the *Danielle* was launched and Langley, along with Lane, Smith and Jones, and the brothers Stredney rowed to the rock landing on the north shore of Isla Sello. There they were greeted by none other than Jonathan Moore, Sean Flagon and a slightly more svelte looking Miss Delain Dowdeswell.

After a hearty greeting and congratulations, all returned to their assigned ships and proceed directly along the West African coast. The *Danielle* sailed in the lead, followed immediately behind by HMS *Proteus,* HMS *Erinyes,* the captured French frigates including the *Lyon,* with Steward at the wheel, the *Avignon* captained my Lieutenant Gray, and the *Saint Annie* captained by acting Commander Thomas Harrison. They were in turn followed by the other merchant vessels then HMS *Drake,* formerly known as the *Fiero.* The *Bordeaux* with Holtz on the poop was followed by the *Trident,* last in line and protecting their rear.

On May the fourth after a day of easy sailing, the ships anchored in a most pleasant location near Saint Helena Bay. The emerald water was cold, yet the air seemed warmer than it had been and colorful birds flew about constantly over a single white sand beach. Here, the continent was devoid of thick dark jungle and low hills could be seen past fields of green grasses and light brush.

Repairs were made to damaged ships and men assigned appropriately to whichever vessel needed their talents. As the sun set, the fiddlers of each ship struck up their tunes, lanterns were lit and cooking fires began the task of feeding the over two thousand men about the many ships. Some danced, some sang, and some stared at the wild continent, just a few waves away to the east.

Bay of Saint Helana

Later that evening, the remaining midshipman of the *Danielle*, as well as Sean and Delain, were in attendance for the feast in Captain Walker's cabin. Mister Harrison had left control of the *Saint Annie* to Smith, Hudson and Hicks after locking the French army officers below decks. He anchored alongside the *Dani* and was transferred aboard with Gorman. Steward, Langley, Holtz and Blake also attended. With the addition of Mister Koonts it was now truly crowded, necessitating a few windows to be opened a crack, to allow a gentle breeze to waft in and keep all jolly and comfortable.

After a bit of joking and singing, mostly by Sean and surprisingly by Delain, all settled in to celebrate their success. The dinner that evening was most enjoyable. An appetizer of toasted cheese and anchovies to start, with small rolled pork slices that had been grilled and stuffed with the last few plums that Claise had pickled months before. Then fresh loaves of bread and small dinner rolls with salted butter that somehow had been kept all this time since the stop at Ribeira Grande. For the main course, the goat and two chickens had been dressed for dinner and Claise used the last of his curry for the goat. The chickens were grilled slowly over a small flame in Steward's cabin, with rosemary, lime juice and olive oil being basted on the skins every few minutes. Pepper was added making the birds not only beautiful, but mouth-watering as well. There was also a small plate of green peas. After the officers all wagered and guessed as to how he had come to possess such a rarity, Claise finally told them. A plant he had purchased in Nassau had been tended to and hidden by his small porthole in the main galley. It had recently given quite a bit of the green gems in just the past few days.

On deck, the men had extra rations of rum and some of Claise's fine curried fish stew, now cooked by the brothers Stredney, who seemed to enjoy the making of large quantities of food, yet ate very little of it themselves.

"I don't really like fish" said Colin.

"And I don't enjoy curry at all!" laughed Nicolas as they served up bowl after bowl to the crew. The men aboard the *Danielle*, however, thought it was almost as good as when Claise would make it.

In the Captain's cabin, Walker demanded happily that it was time for tales to be told.

"And where to begin?" asked Gorman. "Do we tell of our trip around the cape, or do we ask for an account of the party on Isla Sello and the Castelo de Fogo?"

"I must know, first," interrupted Koonts, who was on his third helping of rum and a fourth serving of cake, "how Captain Langley became aware of our dire need!"

All agreed that would be an excellent place to start and Langley began happily.

"I was ordered to guard the southern coast of Gibraltar, along with a dozen other ships including the *Proteus* and the *Erinyes*. It was ghastly boring if I must say so. We were sailing under Admiral Kennison who had taken up residence aboard the *Leviathan*."

"There was an admiral in your squadron?" asked Jonathan.

"Yes, the *Leviathan* drew the short straw, as we say, and the Admiral sailed with its captain. Kennison is quite wizened and almost as ancient as the sea itself. He slept most of the time, I was told, but we all remember him from the history books as a young captain and a brave sailor. One evening, as we were bringing up the rear, we were visited by the Periwinkle-"

"*Paladin*," said Harrison, defending his girl.

"Excuse me," said Langley, "the *Paladin* and Commander Sutton told us of your plight. I immediately came aboard the *Leviathan* and requested permission from Admiral Kennison to leave the squadron and come to your aid. During my explanation, well… he simply fell asleep! Seeing fate was in my hands, I informed his Captain that the Admiral was now resting, but previously had agreed to my request and suggested that I take the two forty-fours *Erinyes* and *Proteus*."

All laughed at the tale and wondered how the *Drake* and the *Echo* came along.

"We received no assistance from London," Blake said. "We left immediately as few real fighting ships were without orders. We headed in your direction and after a few days of bad hunting, we spied the *Echo* near Sierra

Leone, on the North African coast. We all sailed as quickly as we were able and it seems we were possibly a *little* late, but only just enough to make a dramatic entrance!"

Again laughter ensued, then Harrison told of the finding of the French squadron by the *Dani* north of the Cape and the spotting of the *Bordeaux* and considerably more than just a few small escorts.

"It seems maybe Kozak may have misled us," continued Harrison. "He must have known there were more ships escorting the merchants, but no matter - we would have done them all in with or without you late-comers!"

This sent the room into boisterous guffaws and chuckles and Delain had a hard time regaining her poise, contracting a severe case of the hiccups.

"As we entered the strait," continued Harrison, "we saw someone's bloomers atop a target raft that had been anchored to the channel. This underwear thieving, being a standard trick employed by Mister Moore, had us perplexed for an instant, but we soon figured it was a sign and sure enough - well, maybe Jonathan should tell what went on once he secured the Castelo de Fogo."

Captain Walker briefly explained the situation with Miss Dowdeswell's stowing away and as he became stern in the telling, Delain became slightly afraid he would begin another famous outburst. Suddenly, at the thought of this, her hiccups were gone.

"We decided to put the Governors' daughter ashore and leave her with an escort. Mister Moore and Sean did an admiral job of containing the wildest of the Dowdeswell sisters. I assume they were perfect gentlemen, Miss Delain?"

"Until they asked for my bloomers, yes!" said Delain, and that again sent the room into hysterics.

Jonathan then took up the tale, explaining how he and his band found the castle, noticed the embrasures void of any cannon, and the fort void of any human soul.

"After careful exploration," he continued, "we found

cannon, cleaning and repair equipment, and even a large quantity of shot. The guns were quite heavy! It took a day or two to move them into position and another few to clean them. In the end we were successful, as you all know, and after some needed practice -"

"Which was quite exciting!" interrupted Delain.

"-we realized that our plan to assist in the battle would actually be possible!" laughed Jonathan.

"Then we made rafts!" said Sean, and he explained how they created the larger target raft, yet had to have another to take them safely back to the island. "The sharkies followed us every bit of the way and one tried to make me a little snack. I thought surely I was going to join old Champagne in the belly of a beast! But Steward's letter opener saved the day."

"Poor fish got a few pokes in the nose, eh?" asked Steward, pleased as Sean thanked him for the wonderfully handy gift.

"And that," said Delain, "is when we prayed that you would see our target, Captain Walker, with its *conspicuous* flag, as it were, and allow us the opportunity to fire our eight cannon."

"Amazing, I must say. You are all quite inventive!" said Harrison. "Let us hope that on our next mission, sadly but preferably *without* Miss Dowdeswell, we can have a spare set of bloomers to signal one another, just in case!"

Lane then recalled his realization that Spears had departed and the pirate too. All were shocked, but none surprised.

"Maybe it is better this way," said Koonts.

"He could be hunted like a criminal," suggested Holtz.

"If one had the time and the inclination," added Blake.

"In the end," added Jonathan, "he has his own life to deal with, and we ours. I hated to see him so angry and defeated; however, he was fatally poisoned even before he boarded the *Danielle*. As his actions did not affect our success in the least, I would like to wish him good luck . . . and hope our paths never cross again."

"He had best be wary should his path cross with *mine,*" said Walker suddenly angry, though it was short lived and he quickly raised his glass in a toast. "However, be that as it may, a *spa-len-did* job, one and all. Again, the *Poseidons* emerge victorious!"

"To our lost home," Jonathan said, "HMS *Poseidon* and our lost brothers who perished in her last defense."

All raised their glasses and remained silent for a moment, remembering the final battle and the winning of the *Danielle,* at the great cost of their former ship and many of their friends.

With that Claise entered the room with more food and a few desserts. All applauded him and his efforts, but soon, it was noticed he was sobbing.

"Here, here, Claise, my good man!" bellowed the Captain. "I am sure you have been chopping onions? Or did you bump your head?"

Claise stopped his sobbing, then, as if a young midshipman, turned to the window and stood at attention.

"No onions or bumps, sir!" he said firmly. "I must admit to a serious crime. And I might as well confess in front of all my brethren and friends…and officers. May I beg for leniency!"

Claise started bawling once again causing the Captain to stand and escort him out of the cabin and up to the poop deck. He calmed the man down again and then urged him on.

"What horrible crime is this, Claise?"

"The plaque, Captain," he finally blurted out.

"The plaque?" Walker repeated, surprised. "You?"

"It was I that loosened it! While you were all eating I would chip and poke at it. I couldn't stand the name, *Doggard!* Who would do such a thing to our lovely lady?"

Walker laughed long and hard, clapped Claise on the back and told him that he would tell no one of the serious crime – if Claise would keep it to himself as well.

* * * * * *

The *Danielle*, with her sister ships and prizes, sailed onward to the north for almost five weeks, only stopping for a single day to re-supply in Gibraltar. On the thirteenth of June just after breakfast, they spotted the shores of the Isles of Scilly and from there navigated easily east to Chatham.

At the port side rail stood Jonathan, Sean and Delain. The warm wind of summer now blew about them and the late afternoon sun warmed their backs as they smiled. For a long moment they stared in silence as England became larger and therefore, more real.

"We have been at sea for a long time, gentlemen," said Delain finally. "I am not sure I want to return to land."

"I know the feeling, Miss Dowdeswell," agreed Jonathan.

Sean only smiled at them both.

Shortly, Lane appeared to take a place at their side, and the conversation turned once again to Spears. Each wondered if he would go to America and what life would be like with Kozak, living with their shared fate.

"He will forever be looking over his shoulder," said Lane solemnly. "A result of his decision to lead a life of piracy that he has now condemned himself."

"If he is ever seen again," said Sean, sadly, "he will be captured and tried as a criminal."

"Maybe that will be a better life for him," said Jonathan. "His old life was done, his family name disgraced and his future dashed. I have no doubt he felt a new life, no matter how low, was better than his broken, old one. Maybe he can remake himself."

"Maybe, for that is what many do who immigrate to America," offered Delain.

The evening set in as HMS *Danielle* and her squadron approached Chatham. Mister Watt navigated easily into port, along with the *Trident* and the *Drake*, and Walker ordered the remaining ships to anchor nearby, off the coast. He meant to keep the prisoners onboard until he could make arrangements for their transfer ashore.

Unlike the last homecoming, no one knew they were arriving, no fanfare or greeting, just a slight bump as the ship nudged the wooden dock. And to Jonathan, who now longed to see his father and Miss Thompson, the silent and calm arrival was entirely agreeable.

"The sooner we are home, Sean, the better," he said.

"Agreed," Sean whispered.

"I assume that you will escort me to my auntie's home?" asked Delain.

"With pleasure, Miss Dowdeswell," said Jonathan. "And do not forget our appointment. It was iced cream, I believe?"

"It was, Mister Moore, how kind of you to remember."

Captain Walker sent a man from the dock to inform his wife of his successful return. Misses Walker immediately sent the carriage to collect her husband, then sent word to Nathaniel Moore that his son and his *other* son, were safe and at Chatham. Nathaniel quickly prepared his carriage and after stopping only to retrieve Miss Thompson, he rode as fast as was possible to meet the *Danielle*.

Upon seeing his son, Nathaniel flew across the docks and embraced him heartily.

"Jonathan! To see you again! It is the joy of a lifetime! William, thank you for delivering him to me safely! And Sean! It seems you have grown another three inches! And gained a bit of weight?"

"It could be," said Sean, smiling. "I have eaten a bit better on this trip, I can assure you!"

"And who is this lovely lady?" asked Nathaniel.

"This, Father, is the irrepressible Miss Delain Dowdeswell, adventurer!"

"How do you do?" Delain said sweetly, with a curtsy.

"It seems that once again, there is more to the mission than meets the eye," said Nathaniel. "William, why is Governor Dowdeswell's daughter aboard the *Dani*?"

"It is such a long story and I am so tired, it will have

to wait!" laughed Walker.

"How did the boys perform, William?" Miss Thompson asked as she finally had her turn at embracing the youngsters. "I heard the cruise was to be a simple tour of the warm and peaceful waters of the Caribbean. Looking at your... *collection*... of French ships anchored off shore, I assume you had your hands full?"

Walker laughed aloud, as did Harrison.

"We did attend to our duties in the Bahamas," said Walker.

"However," said Harrison, "Jonathan thought that capturing a pirate ship was more fun than just seeing sea turtles and one thing led to another."

Nathaniel looked at Jonathan quizzically, then frowned.

"It was HMS *Drake*, Father. I couldn't let it be handled by those ruffians!" he said, laughing.

"And if we didn't capture the pirate ship," added Delain, "Then we never would have made it to Africa and the Castle of Fire on Isla Sello!"

"Who would have known," said Sean, "that cannon that old could be made workable?"

"Oh dear," said Nathaniel to Miss Thompson. "I have a feeling I may not want to know all the details!"

"We will tell ya all the same, Captain, as we ride," said Steward. "I could use a bath."

"Agreed," said Harrison. "You could!"

Once again, the newspapers announced the successful exploits of Captain Sir William Walker and his daring crew. Walker could hardly walk into the entrance of the Admiralty to report for duty without being accosted by literally hundreds of well-wishers and fellow Navy men, all falling over themselves to congratulate him. *A bother,* he thought, *but it could be worse.*

Governor Dowdeswell's sister, Lady Bracknell, did indeed faint upon hearing the story of Delain's adventure and could not believe that she had survived through it all unscathed, even though the proof was there in the flesh. Penelope and Rebecca were delighted to see their sister and could not wait until the details of her African adventure were told.

As they had been away for quite some time, almost five months, all were pleased to learn from Jonathan's father that the King had indeed remedied the situation at the Admiralty. Barrow and Worthing, the two bloated Admirals that has caused such a fuss were reported to be in Australia and being eaten by hordes of mosquitoes.

"And I," said Nathaniel Moore, "Will hereby be known and addressed as *Admiral* Nathaniel Moore, *Adjunct to the King for Naval affairs.*"

Saturday, the twentieth of June finally arrived, as did a cool but sunny day, and Walker was finally released from the grips of the Admirals in Whitehall. He settled into his den with a modest fire and a glass of port, enjoying the solitude. Steward entered from time to time to poke at the flames that needed no poking and to add drink to the Captain's glass that actually did need refilling. This evening there was to be a small dinner and gathering, however, for most of the day, Walker snoozed and ate. He was napping again when his wife woke him to announce that his guests had begun to arrive and were waiting in his study.

The first to appear had been the family, more or less, of the Moores: Nathaniel and Jonathan, seemingly attached at the hip and happy to be together once again, along with Miss Thompson. She immediately excused herself to assist her sister, the Captain's wife, in the kitchen.

"Is Sean at his exams?" asked Walker.

"Yes, sir," said Jonathan. "He has been studying since we left Isla Sello. Gorman lent him a few books and spent all day yesterday with him, grilling and admonishing, mostly. Holtz had his hands full just getting Sean to his exams. I have never seen him so nervous! Though, he has gone to it. His desire to become a marine is truly inspiring."

"It is," said Walker. "And Barbara seems surprisingly happy, Nathaniel."

"Indeed and why not?" said Nathaniel, somewhat put out. "Who wouldn't be happy in her condition? A wonderful life and fantastic prospects. She's a cultured, enjoyable woman - "

"Who has a fancy for you, Father," added Jonathan, causing Walker to laugh.

"Yes, yes, and I her, Jonathan," admitted his father. "Are you agreeable to that? She is not your mother and never can be, however, we are all here and she loves us all so, even Sean Flagon."

"Hard to believe *that*," said Steward who happened by to fill a few glasses.

"I would be most happy if you continued on a straight and true course including Miss Thompson in your plans, Father," answered Jonathan. He of course missed his mother. And as it had been over six years now since he had seen her last and watched her slip from this life, he was now ready to move on. He wanted his father to be happy.

Steward re-entered the room and announced the Ladies Dowdeswell and Mister Harrison, along with Captain Langley. All joined Walker in his study for a few moments, then were called to dinner. The entire tale, now including detail from Delain, was told and retold for some. All were amazed and at times frightened, but that made Harrison, who somehow seemed to add details even to the parts of the story where he was not present, laugh and tease all the harder.

Nathaniel was alarmed, but not surprised at the news of Spears. He knew all along that the young man was disturbed and believed that it was best he was far away. His father would be beside himself and that would mean Nathaniel had to be extra careful dealing with him as he roamed the Admiralty. He had rightly suspected that Spears senior was behind his delay at being awarded admiral rank, but it mattered not to Nathaniel. He was feeling stronger each day and at times envied his friend William Walker, who would take to the sea within a few months at most.

As the evening happily went on and dinner was finished, all retired to the study for drinks and further tales. As they settled in, a messenger arrived in the form of Marine Captain Gorman. He accepted a warm drink of brandy and helped himself unabashedly to a bowl of sugared cherries that he swore went quite well with the drink.

"I have some news for you all and a delivery of a letter for Thomas Harrison, Lieutenant of the British Royal Navy, as it says so right here on this letter."

Harrison hurriedly opened the letter and read it to himself. His faced seemed to change from his usually rosy complexion to a sudden lighter shade of white.

"It is an invitation from His Majesty!"

"The King?" blurted Jonathan.

"None other!" said Harrison almost drunk with happiness. "It must be my assignment as a commander."

"The King remembered, Thomas!" said Jonathan. "He promised he would look into it for you and I bet he has. Has he, Gorman?"

"Why ask me?" Gorman said with a smirk on his face. "Do you think the King tells me all of his naval appointments and secret dealings? Just because I am a *covert military operative?*"

"Yes!" said the boys, and that sent the Ladies Dowdeswell into a fit of giggles.

"Well, even if he did, I would not tell you!" said Gorman, laughing as he downed a handful of the cherries. "These really are quite good," he added.

Finally a few moments before midnight, Sean arrived escorted by Holtz. They both seemed exhausted and defeated and were immediately placed on the soft couch and handed a drink and a sandwich from the leftover meat the rest had enjoyed for dinner.

"It is finished!" exclaimed Sean. "And good riddance!"

"Was it difficult? Have you just completed the exam?" asked Jonathan.

"We have been done for quite some time!" said Holtz. "However we were not dismissed. For some reason we were told to wait in an anteroom and after a few hours, a Captain Allan arrived and asked us to leave. He said the announcement of Sean's exams would be made tomorrow."

"It was the hardest thing I have ever done," said Sean. "And I have done some difficult things!"

"How well do you feel about your score?" asked Delain.

"Ah, I couldn't tell. By the end of the fifteenth hour, it was all a blur! Writing, speaking – well, I said so many 'yes sir's and 'no sir's, I think I have forgotten the difference!"

"It is all for naught, Sean," said Gorman matter-of-factly.

"How is that, Captain?" asked Walker.

"It is all political. Dolts like Hudson and Hicks, who can barely read and walk in the same *hour,* passed easily. I am sure you will make it, Sean," said Gorman, patting the boy on the shoulder.

"You know something, Captain Gorman," said Harrison.

"Indeed!" said Jonathan. "Just look at his face! All knowing and calm!"

The boys now rose from their chairs and surrounded Gorman quickly.

"Is there no escape?" Gorman called out, jokingly.

"Well? Do you know something, you old spy?" asked Harrison.

"As I just stated, I prefer the term *covert military operative,"* Gorman responded in an official tone as Harrison grabbed the Marine by the arm.

"It will all be announced tomorrow," Gorman said, laughing, as Jonathan and Sean also attached themselves to him. "I gave my word to the King and the Admiralty that I would not speak of any of it until then!"

"To the King?" said Nathaniel, pointing out Gorman's slip of tongue.

"So he does know about Harrison as well!" exclaimed Delain.

"And Sean!" added Jonathan.

"I am a clam, shut up tight until tomorrow, I gave my word!" offered Gorman in his defense.

"It will be tomorrow in less than three minutes!" announced Harrison. "Look at the clock!"

All eyes turned to the clock on Captain Walker's mantel. As the flames flickered, it was apparent that the time showed eleven fifty-seven.

Gorman tried to rise, but it was difficult with the boys holding him and soon impossible as Delain and her sisters joined in.

"I must be going!" he laughed as his captors brought him none too gently to the carpet. And held him down. "I beg assistance, Captain! Admiral? This is undignified!"

But Nathaniel Moore and William Walker were held tight by their ladies and could not, or would not, move to engage.

"I am sorry, dear man!" said Nathaniel. "You are alone at sea on this one!"

"Langley!" pleaded the marine. "Surely you can render some aid to an old friend!"

"These cherries *are* quite good!" Langley answered as he attacked the bowl, ignoring the request.

"And quite expensive!" added Walker, somewhat annoyed.

"Then that explains there exquisite taste!" Langley said, stuffing his mouth with a handful. "I will attend to these directly as you fight on, Captain Gorman!"

The youngsters playfully wrestled the Marine, holding him to the floor until the clock chimed midnight, then finally allowing him to stand.

"Well, Mister Harrison first, then!" said Gorman as he

straightened his jacket and re-adjusted his clothing. "The King remembered that he owed you a favor and he has assigned you a ship to command as a lieutenant. The only two available were the thirty-two gun *Alarm*, certainly too much to handle for a first-time command. The other ship is small and under gunned mostly, but has a teak deck and sails faster than the strongest wind."

"The *Echo*?" Harrison said, hoping that possibly it was not the case as he desired another. Yet even the *Echo* was a fine command and a famous and important ship. It had seen battle and sailed around the globe. Any lieutenant would be proud to command her.

"Guess again, Mister Harrison," said Gorman, smiling.

"The Periwinkle!" screamed Jonathan.

"None other, however the orders call her by her proper name, the eighteen gun fighting sloop HMS *Paladin*," answered Gorman.

Harrison was now overjoyed, and as the others stood and applauded, commencing back slapping and congratulations, Harrison was near tears.

"Heaven save us!" exclaimed Steward. "He will never live it down."

"And I believe," said Gorman, "that tradition demands you choose your officers and crew, Thomas."

"Does the *Paladin* require a midshipman?" asked Jonathan hopefully.

"Aye," said Steward.

"I volunteer!" Jonathan said quickly as all laughed.

"In addition, there is to be another lieutenant and also a few marines. Three I believe."

"Hudson and Hicks, I will demand it," said Harrison, proudly and confidently, as if he were standing upon the deck of the *Paladin*, giving orders and sailing away to adventure.

"And as you will need *one more*," said Gorman, "If I could suggest a name?"

"By all means, Captain Gorman," Harrison said.

Gorman waited for a moment, then continued as he looked about the room at all present.

"I know of a newly appointed marine, wet behind the ears as we say, but he promises to be quite the solider some day. I have sailed with him and spied as well. He is brave and cunning, and his test scores are just in; passed with flying colors; a certain *Marine Private* Sean Flagon!"

The room erupted in cheers and applause as Sean realized he had made his dream come true. Jonathan hugged him and Rebecca actually planed a kiss on his cheek.

"Bless us and save us!" Steward said jokingly with a smile showing his beaming pride at the success of the boys. "The mere idea o' these three scallywags sailing 'bout the world in such a swift craft, well, I can say that I'm glad I 'ad seen the *Paladin* previously in 'er best state. Sure we will never see 'er looking as smart again! Make all aware of o' my words!"

All laughed and cheered as Captain Walker brought out small glasses and poured everyone, even the boys and the ladies Dowdeswell, a taste of brandy.

It was Nathaniel who demanded to make the first toast, assured that there would be many more on this night and the precious evenings that followed before the next missions would take his son and friends away once again.

"Raise your glasses, my friends!" he said, and all followed orders to the letter. "To Mister Thomas Harrison, the new commander of HMS *Paladin*, hero of many battles, and I should point out, successful midshipman of mine for only a short time, but enough to make him presentable!"

The room laughed and toasted Thomas heartily, then Admiral Moore continued.

"To Marine Private Sean Flagon, my *other* son, as I like to say, a shining example of self-improvement and industry, but most of all, the power of friendship. A true hero by any standard."

"Hear! Hear!" all said in unison.

Then Nathaniel turned to his son, Jonathan, and spoke

slower and a bit more solemnly.

"And to Midshipman Jonathan Moore, the hero of the *Castle of Fire,* who always accomplishes astonishing and downright amazing feats as everyday occurrences. I could not have invented a more perfect son. I am blessed and proud. William, thank you for returning to me, my son, my very heart. To the victors and the newly promoted!"

All raised their glasses high and drank in salute of a job well done, and to those who accomplished the great mission.

With that, the lucky crew of HMS *Danielle* was sadly separated; however, the newest crew of His Majesty's Ship *Paladin,* also known as the Periwinkle, complete with purple stripe down her graceful sides, was now manned for adventure.

The End
of
Book Two

Coming Soon:

Book Three

The Adventures of Jonathan Moore

The Paladin Mission

Acknowledgements

During the creation of Jonathan Moore and his confidant, Sean Flagon, I thought of their friendship and how they conducted themselves, and wished that the book could continue so I could enjoy them further. Maybe a second volume? In a phone call with my sister, Barbara, shortly before *Skull Eye Island* was self-published, she gave me her review of the book and her thought that the Ladies Dowdeswell were an interesting bunch, and that *wouldn't it be fun if they became major characters in the second book?* I had thought that book two would be Jonathan and Sean joining Harrison on his first command, but why go so fast? Certainly Captain Walker, Harrison, Steward, and the others had another mission or two left in them. So off I went.

Then I realized in an effort to be at least mostly historical, it would be tough to get three young ladies aboard HMS *Danielle,* a man's world if there ever was one. But since I loved the idea so much, and since Jonathan was now technically a teen-ager, a female friend would certainly be in order.

This second book seemed to be easier to write in one sense, (because I knew that a few people besides me would possibly enjoy it) however, the absence of a few locations exactly where I needed them made things difficult, so I adjusted a small land mass from a point to an island and invented a castle as well.

Also, I tried to avoid extremely detailed descriptions of naval terminology, activities, ships and duties as well as ignoring the historically common *yet unsavory* elements of living on a ship in His Majesty's Navy with a bunch of grown men. It is a book for all ages. Even so, a few questioned my improper use of certain terms and situations. I now gratefully thank Captain Richard Bailey, Sailing School Ship *Oliver Hazard Perry,* for his guidance and kind corrections of this text and that of Skull Eye Island. Captain Bailey was long-time captain of 'HMS'

Rose, America's only Class A-size, ocean-going Sailing School Vessel, and has commanded over six tall ships since 1972. I am more than fortunate to have had access to his experience and precious time. Check out his work restoring the *Oliver Hazard Perry*: www.ohpri.org/

During the writing of Castle of Fire, there was a welcomed diversion: my great fortune at having *Skull Eye Island* selected as the winner of the 2012 Adventure Writer's Grandmaster Award sponsored by the Clive Cussler Collector's Society. It is a great honor and I must thank the panel members, especially Kerry Frey author of *Buried Lie* and Jeff Edwards author of *Seventh Angel* and *Sword of Shiva* (to name a few); and the other finalists for their hard work and fast friendship: Tim Fairchild, author of *Zero Point,* Scott Slater, author of *The Devil's Accomplice* and Patrick Parr, author of *English as a Second Life*. Meeting Clive and Dirk Cussler was mind-blowing, and having them say nice things about the book made for a great *distraction*.

Of course to my brilliant artist and illustrator, Michelle Graham, a thousand thanks and even more as I marvel at each illustration. They are all enchanting as inspiring. How many times can I open a file, look at your work and say out loud: *Oh my! Look at that!* About twenty-six times, I think!

Also, thanks to Rita Eder, star of the Hungarian National Fencing Team and most importantly and recently Lieutenant Brendan's fencing instructor, for the suggestions and terminology on everything 'swordish'.

Again I must thank my lovely wife, Pammy, for giving me the time to write and re-write, and for holding down the fort. It is a hard life with two working parents and two kids, let alone with one who spends his weekends in front of a computer, writing. The Viking Woman, as I call her, never missed a beat. She does it all and all well.

-Peter Greene, April 2014